Science Fiction at Its Award-Winning Finest:

JACK L. CHALKER
An extraterrestrial machine draws four lonely people into a doorway to other lives **"In the Dowaii Chambers."**

M. A. FOSTER
Two people seek a tiny space in the desperate world of the future, a haven for love and **"Dreams."**

CARTER SCHOLZ
He was just a kid. . . . Could he really build **"A Catastrophe Machine"** out of a few spools and rubber bands?

C. J. CHERRYH
Two great stories: **"The Dark King,"** a long-buried Cherryh treasure, and **Companions,** a *new* short novel of space adventure with a feisty computer and the only man who ever understood her. . . .

THE

JOHN W. CAMPBELL

AWARDS

Volume 5

Edited by GEORGE R. R. MARTIN

Bluejay Books Inc.

Manufactured in the United States of America
First Bluejay printing: January 1984

Library of Congress Cataloging in Publication Data

Main entry under title:
The John W. Campbell Awards.
    "Volume 5."
    1. Science fiction, American. I. Martin,
George R. R.
PS648.S3J63   1984   813'.0876'08   83-15638
ISBN 0-312-94252-4

CONTENTS

to Gladys Hattenberg, my favorite aunt.

GEORGE R. R. MARTIN
Preface

It's said that the Chinese have a curse that goes, "May you live in interesting times." The last few years have been very interesting times for writers and editors in the world of science fiction. Excessively interesting, in fact.

Two and a half years ago, while writing the preface to *New Voices 4*, I observed that the boom SF had enjoyed in the late seventies had crested early in 1980 and that a decline had begun to set in. "There are some definite dark clouds on the horizon," I said. The dark clouds proved me only too right. Subsequently they scuttled off the horizon and began raining vigorously on all of SF. The storm was big enough and fierce enough to encompass all of the publishing world, which went into its most serious sustained depression since World War II. It has yet to come out. Inside and outside the genre, it's still raining like hell.

The storm has taken its toll in SF. Fawcett, Playboy, Popular Library, Jove, and even Ace—a genre mainstay for nearly thirty years—are gone in all but name, having been absorbed in various corporate mergers and buy-outs. Dell, a major publisher whose SF line was one of the classiest acts in the field, has dropped out of the genre entirely. A couple of minor houses have gone bankrupt, while others hang on by their toenails. And even the biggest and wealthiest survivors have been visibly cutting back and re-trenching. Sales are down, advances are down, and the publishers seem far more interested in buying other companies than in putting out good books; things are tough all over.

Publishing has had its bust periods before, of course, but the current depression seems especially serious, particularly for those of us who read, write, and love science fiction. The mere fact that SF has been affected so much by the general publishing slump is one reason for that. Up till now, although SF has had its own cycles of prosperity and despair, we have been largely immune to those that hit the literary world in general. Not this time, though. The genre has grown up, and part of the price of growing up has been learning what words like *unemployment* and *breadlines* mean.

What's even more alarming, though, is the way the depression seems to be accelerating some unfortunate trends that were already under way.

One of those trends is the movement away from short fiction, in the direction of the novel. The mainstream short story, a victim of a similar trend thirty years ago or more, is largely dead today, but until very recently short fiction within SF has maintained at least a semblance of reasonable health. The field still boasted a half-dozen viable magazines with a voracious appetite for original short fiction; they did not pay much, but once a writer had published enough to fill a book and earn himself a name, he could usually sell a collection somewhere. And there were anthology markets, too, both originals—like the *New Voices* series—and reprints. To be sure, even in the halcyon days of the late seventies, collections and anthologies seldom sold as well as novels—but they didn't sell that much worse, either. The difference was marked but not dramatic, so collections and anthologies continued to be published.

With the coming of hard times, that changed. Even novel sales suffered, but short fiction suffered far more grievously. As profit margins shrank, publishers became progressively less interested in projects that had only minimal commercial potential, no matter how much literary merit they might display. The greedier and more commercial publishers had always had a cant that went *Novels! Novels! Novels!* Now other houses took up that same cry. Collections by a single author became rarer and rarer, and anthologies suffered most of all. Of the half-dozen major anthology series in the field at the beginning of 1980, all but two are dead today . . . and one of the survivors, the one you hold in your hands, died and was reborn.

Anthologists were not the only ones standing outside with their mouths upturned and open when the typhoon hit. An awful lot of new writers also drowned in the storm or can barely be made out today clinging to a piece of rotten wood, gasping, and kicking feebly against the floodtides. So far the eighties have not been a terribly good time to be a new writer.

There is real tragedy in that, and real peril. Traditionally science fiction has been a field wide open to new talent, a field that has welcomed fresh young writers with open arms and quickly elevated them to stardom if they proved deserving. But in a shrunken market, where the bottom line rules all, more and more publishers have been shying away from unproven names.

In part that's a consequence of larger industry trends, for the conglomerates have eaten up a good portion of publishing this past decade and have steadily been replacing old-style "bookmen" with accountants and M.B.A.s in the upper ranks of the companies they have acquired. The new breed of publishing executive doesn't care how good a writer is, only how much money he can make for the company. Worse, too many companies are no longer even willing to absorb losses on the first two or three books of a brilliant newcomer in the hope that sooner or later he will establish himself and hit it big—a policy that used to be standard industry practice. Not only do the publishing empires want huge profits, they want them *today*! Or yesterday, if possible.

The other force at work, ironically, is a consequence of the prosperity that SF experienced in the late seventies. Before that boom, the genre had had a small but loyal audience. Perhaps it was a ghetto literature, as many said, but like all ghettoes it enjoyed advantages and disadvantages. SF novels seldom made a lot of money, and none of them ever hit the best-seller lists, but on the other hand they all seemed to make a *little* money. The ghetto had a ceiling *and* a floor. That was bad news for the big names in the field, who felt that they were being unfairly held down and denied a shot at a much larger general readership. But it was good news for new writers, because all of them could expect at least a certain minimal audience, an audience that could multiply quickly by word of mouth if the writer was any good.

Now all that has changed. As I write, SF novels and SF-related novels occupy seven of the top ten spots on the best-seller lists; the ceiling is gone and we're playing with the big boys. But the floor is gone as well. Perhaps as a result of the overexpansion of the boom time, no one can afford to buy everything labeled SF anymore. Perhaps because so much of the bumper crop was chaff, no one *wants* to buy everything anymore. Naturally it is the books by the unfamiliar names that get skipped over. And if enough readers skip over a book, it isn't long before the publishers begin to skip over the book's author. No doubt about it, the field has tightened up. We're not as open as we used to be.

The good news is that maybe this will result in a little less dreck being printed. The bad news is that, by and large, the readers don't seem to be *trying* a lot of the newer writers before they flush them away. As a result, some of the very best, brightest, and most original new talents to enter SF in the last decade are out there splashing around with the hacks, trying not to go under.

Which brings us, in a roundabout fashion, to *The John W. Campbell Awards, Volume 5.*

Those who have read the first four volumes of *New Voices* are aware that this is an original anthology series dedicated to new writers. Since anthologies and new writers have been the chief victims of the Reagan recession and its effects on publishing, the question may rightly be asked: How in the world did *New Voices* survive?

The answer, of course, is that it didn't.

Like a lot of other anthologies and a lot of new writers, *New Voices* was dropped by its publisher. But here we are, back again, with a new trade paperback format, a new title, and a new—brand new, in fact—publisher.

Why have we tried so hard to bring this anthology back across the Styx? Well, it wasn't for the money.

The *New Voices* series began in 1973, when the first John W. Campbell Award was presented at the World Science Fiction Convention in Toronto. Campbell, widely considered the greatest editor the field has ever had, had died in 1971, and the publishers of the magazine he edited decided to memorialize him by sponsoring an award for new writers. Poul Anderson talks about John W. Campbell in the introduction that follows, so I won't go on about the man and his contributions, except to say that the tribute was most fitting. More than anything else, Campbell was a discoverer of new talent. Year after year, decade after decade, he continued to turn up fresh young writers, work with them, hone them, encourage them. The ranks of today's SF giants—including those now riding the best-seller lists—are made up largely of Campbell discoveries.

Since 1973 the Campbell has been presented annually at the world-con, along with SF's oldest and most prestigious awards, the Hugos. Like the Hugos, the Campbell is determined by vote of fans and readers, who nominate four to six finalists from among all those new writers who have broken into print during the preceding two years, and then choose a winner from that number. But winners and losers alike are talents to reckon with: Take a look at the history of the award in the back of the book, and note how many Campbell *losers* have gone on to become stars; *New Voices* was founded with the intent of showcasing them all. Each volume spotlights one year's crop of Campbell finalists, with each nominee contributing an original novella or novelette written for *New Voices*.

Although the award and the anthology series began together, the world of publishing often moves slowly, and a series of complicated delays soon meant that *New Voices* was running three, four, or five years behind the award to which it was tied. The "death" of the series and the long gap between *Volume 4* and *Volume 5* only increased the lag; as a result, this volume features the writers nominated for the fifth Campbell Award, presented in 1977 at the World SF Convention in Miami Beach, Florida. With the books running that far behind, again one might ask: Why bother?

It's worth bothering, I think, because *New Voices* is one of the last refuges for two endangered species whose survival is ultimately critical to the survival of SF itself: short fiction and new writers. In the boom days during which it was born, *New Voices* could perhaps lead a reader to some of the outstanding new talent in the field. But now, when all new writers are struggling, I think the series is more important than ever. The first four volumes of *New Voices* published some of the finest short fiction of recent years, and an amazing *diversity* of fiction as well. This series has no taboos and never has, and that's another tradition worth fighting for in these days when the magazine markets seem more and more formulaic and less and less open to the innovative, the offbeat, the rude new approaches that revitalize a literature.

Perhaps it's fitting that Bluejay Books, the publisher who is bringing back *New Voices* as *The John W. Campbell Awards*, is itself even newer than the writers featured in these pages. And that's good too. In the last few years we've had more than enough of storm clouds, bureaucracies, rain, retrenchment, and death—too many anthologies gone, too many markets closed, too little that was new and different. If the death of SF itself is not to follow, we need some rebirth, some new beginnings. So here we are. A new publisher, not part of any conglomerate, run by a man who cares about SF, about writers, about short fiction. Four new writers, chosen by the readers themselves as the outstanding debutants of their day, demonstrating in the breadth and diversity of their talents, literary approaches, and styles just how vital modern SF can be. A new format, new packaging, a new title, a new (oh, well) price . . . all the ingredients are on hand. Maybe it's time we turned another corner.

Into somewhat *less* interesting times.

Santa Fe, New Mexico
December 1982

POUL ANDERSON
Introduction

Surely few awards of any kind bear a name more fitting than the John W. Campbell Award, bestowed annually upon the person deemed to be the best new writer in the science fiction field. No editor of any kind has ever done more to invite, encourage, educate, and inspire new writers. Few have done as much, though of course all editors worth their salt consider this an important part of their jobs. Campbell succeeded so mightily that he thereby, almost single-handedly, brought modern science fiction into being.

He would have denied that. Modesty was an integral part of his complex character—a statement that many may find surprising. Doubtless he would have listed people who were doing just what he advocated long before he took the helm of *Astounding*, such as Catherine L. Moore, Stanley Weinbaum, and Jack Williamson. He did, in fact, once point out that Rudyard Kipling wrote a number of science fiction stories employing the selfsame literary techniques that Robert Heinlein used a generation or more later. Probably he would not have mentioned that he himself was among the giants before the Golden Age, both under his own name and, in a very different vein, his "Don A. Stuart" pseudonym.

Nevertheless, I stand by my claim on his behalf. After he had made the magazine his, science fiction rapidly ceased to be a matter of a few isolated geniuses in a ruck of routine pulpsters. Instead, those gifted pioneers who remained found themselves amidst a host of equally gifted new colleagues, ranging alphabetically from Isaac Asimov to A. E. van Vogt, excitedly exploring the possibilities in every conceivable direction. That included fantasy, during the brief, brilliant career of *Unknown Worlds*. Yes, the period from about 1937 to 1943 was in truth the Golden Age. Science fiction has gone much further since then, and nurtured many more fresh talents, but that sense of frontier, of having suddenly entered virgin territory, will never come again.

I hear Campbell's dry, down-East voice declare that the writers did it all, that he merely gave them the opportunity and otherwise, at most, engaged them in bull sessions, which were fun and, by happy accident, sparked a lot of story ideas. He often said this in life, and I doubt that anything so incidental as being on the far side of eternity would make him change his ways. It was an amiable pose, quite likely a useful bit of diplomacy. That does not change the fact that it was a pose.

I know from the authors, not him, how many of the classics in our field originated as Campbell suggestions. I know from direct experience what a powerful, pervasive, subtle, variegated influence was his in less direct ways, too. The rest of this memoir will be personal, because that seems to give me my only hope of conveying a part of what the previous sentence means.

I was an avid reader of *Astounding* since 1941, plus whatever back numbers I could lay hands on. My image of the editor was of a tall blond man in a bright red cloak—oh, yes, I knew it couldn't be correct, but such a figure had been on the cover of one of my earliest subscription issues, and suited a hero of mine. A lonely farm boy, I obtained more science fiction than could be bought by writing it myself, a practice I continued in college. Finally I produced a tale, based on a concept my friend F. N. Waldrop had come up with in conversation, which he said I ought to submit. So I borrowed my mother's typewriter, copied off my scrawlings, and sent the manuscript in. Several months passed. I went off to a summer job in the woods, returned in fall to resume my studies, and had almost forgotten about the story when a brief, formal note arrived and, for the first time, I saw that curlycue signature. John W. Campbell had *read* "Tomorrow's Children." He *liked* it. He actually wanted to *buy* it! That sort of experience comes one to a lifetime.

By the way, not long ago a lady writer complained publicly that on her first sale to *Astounding*, she was asked to sign a declaration that the work was original. She felt this was rampant sexism. Several men present, including me, corrected her. It was the publisher's policy for any firstcomer.

I placed a couple more items there while still in school. Then came a long spell of rejections—for excellent cause, I later realized—before I started selling fairly steadily. Graduating into a recession, when work was hard to find, but being a bachelor who had never had the chance to acquire expensive tastes, I decided to support myself by writing while I looked around for a paycheck position. Somehow the while stretched on and on, until I realized that this was what I was cut out for. Those beginning years were lean, but it helped that pieces refused by Campbell usually found a home elsewhere. After all, I'd been aiming as high as I could. Besides, fairly frequent appearances in *Astounding* conferred a certain value on a name, a kind of accolade by association.

Campbell himself maintained that name meant nothing to him, he was only interested in story. Here I think he was sincere. He would buy from over-the-transom unknowns and send back submissions by the most famous with equal decisiveness. However, if he saw anything at all interesting in an effort, he was apt to write the author at length about it. I have heard that sometimes his letters of rejection held more wordage than the manuscripts, and this may not be much exaggerated.

As a rule he either bought or did not. If he bought, he seldom made changes and those minor, presumably forced on him by the exigencies of typography or publisher's policy. If he did not buy, that was ordinarily it, unless you got an argument about your premises. Occasionally he asked for revisions, and I found that they were invariably improvements. For instance, "Call Me Joe" is among my best-known tales, still being reprinted after a quarter of a century despite the obsolescence of its picture of Jupiter; but it was Campbell who saw that my original downbeat ending was a mistake and persuaded me to try again.

As for policy, *Astounding* had a reputation for puritanism, and it became a small game among certain of us to see what bawdiness we could smuggle past the censorship. When I had a character sing a French song, Campbell remarked by mail that, since he didn't read that language, he'd had the verses checked by someone who did, lest they be unacceptable. I replied, "Shucks, John, I wouldn't pull a trick like that on you. All my obscenities are right out in plain English, if you can find them." Himself, he was no prude. Street & Smith were prudes. After Condé Nast acquired ownership, *Analog*—as it was by that time—loosened up considerably.

Otherwise the editor had a free hand, and made no attempt to straitjacket his authors. Thus, in 1953, at the nadir of the McCarthy era, he ran my "Sam Hall," wherein the government of the United States is overthrown by force and violence. Granted, that government was shown as oppressive, but it had come lawfully to power, and besides, the warning that we might have fascism in our future was then rare in popular literature. Many different stories by different people come to mind as well. Himself a political conservative of the Darwinian type, Campbell delighted in seeing a wide range of human possibilities proposed. He observed that in science fiction you can test a social system to destruction without actually killing anybody.

But I have gotten ahead of myself. This is supposed to be a personal reminiscence.

I first met the man in 1951 when, after months of batting around Europe on a bicycle, I spent a few days in New York before going home. The main reason for that was to visit him. He responded cordially to my bashful phone call and I came around to his tiny, cluttered office and sat there for hours talking. This bearlike, plainly clad man with the Rooseveltian cigarette holder bore no resemblance to my old image. So what? If anything, he came across as of even more heroic stature.

His current enthusiasm was psychology, and almost immediately he said, "I'd like you to answer this question without stopping to think. Everybody dreads going insane, but people fear it for different reasons. What's yours?" I blurted a reply, and he smiled and explained, "The answer is always the opposite of what the person wants or values most in life." I tried it afterward on friends and got responses that were frequently surprising but, on reflection, consistent with what I knew of them.

Naturally, Campbell could not give his entire afternoon to me. An artist brought in the rough of a cover painting. (It turned out to be for *Gunner Cade*, by C. M. Kornbluth and Judith Merril, which takes place in a totalitarian state.) The picture showed an armed man in uniform. Though not officially the art director, Campbell said, "Move the figure up. The logo will cover his face and completely depersonalize him." He was right. He paid that kind of attention to detail.

Well, I went on back to Minnesota, and eventually moved to the West Coast, so we never saw each other much. When we did, it was most often at conventions, where he was beswarmed by fans. However, at last he and his wife would retire to their suite and invite chosen individuals up for hours of talk. And there were some occasions still more private.

In 1959 my wife and I dropped in on the Campbells at their suburban New Jersey home, in the course of a transcontinental trip. They received us with warm hospitality. We arrived in a Morris Minor, which we had bought as part of the "tailfin rebellion" of those days. John took me off in his own huge, ultra-gadgeted American car, which he called the White Whale, to fetch something for dinner, and on the way explained—not preached, just quietly and logically explained—why he preferred such a vehicle. "I like machines," he said. Later he showed us not only his ham radio set but some of his photographs, which were beautiful; they really should have had a gallery exhibition. We discussed abstract ideas, but we also chatted about cats and children and our ancestral countries—Scotland for him, Denmark for me—and whatever else made for a marvelously pleasant evening.

Similar meetings happened, far too few, but enough to reveal, piece by piece, that beneath that prickly exterior was a gentle, indeed shy soul.

Oh, yes, the exterior was prickly, or volcanic, or whatever such metaphor you wish. John enjoyed nothing more than an argument. He'd make some statement I considered outrageous. It was like having a manhole cover dropped on my head. I'd spend the next hour or two debating my way out from under it. As soon as I thought I was back on my feet, he'd grin and drop another manhole cover.

He did the same in correspondence, for I came to be among those who had the fortune to exchange numerous letters with him. Whenever an

envelope full of pyrotechnics appeared in the mailbox, I knew I was sold
to the licorice man, as they say in Danish; a working day would go to
preparing a reply.

But what the hell, it was not merely more fun than work, it was
generally of the highest professional value. As said, John was a fountainhead
of ideas. After all this time, I still have some in the files that I've not yet
used; they include a terrific gimmick for a crime story, which had occurred
to him and which he passed on even though he saw no way to make science
fiction of it. Besides this, there was the sheer intellectual stimulation. My
brain got a lot more exercise then than it has gotten since John died.

As a single example, when he discovered that Chesley Bonestell was
living near me, he proposed that we get together. The artist would paint
covers for stories I would write. John suggested a concept which we both
found irresistible. Momentum, and his urging, brought us to two more such
collaborations before Bonestell moved away. The surrounding circumstances made these among the richest experiences of my life. I remain duly
grateful.

In the case of some people, John came on too strong for his own good.
He either antagonized them or overwhelmed them. Certain of the latter—
in his later years, when the field happened to be in one of its less creative
eras—then fed him back his own notions, parrotlike, in stories that were
dismal. I cannot believe he bought those because he felt flattered. He
bought them because he had to fill a magazine every month, and nothing
better was available. In principle, he had no use for sycophants. In practice,
and in his basic innocence, I suspect he sometimes failed to recognize them
for what they were.

Not to brag, since several others behaved likewise, let me state that
I never went along with many of his causes. Rightly or wrongly, I considered dianetics quackery, saw no promise in the Dean drive, took an extreme
Missouri attitude toward psionics, and so on for a sizeable list that included
political and anthropological opinions. He knew this. In fact, we disputed
at immense length, year after year, mostly by mail but occasionally in
person. One thing I learned from that was that he, too, always tried to base
his beliefs on empirical data. Our differences arose from our interpretations
of those data, or those allegations. And . . . at the very least, he did show
me that I also can dowse buried conduits.

The point is that this never affected our relationship, either personal
or professional. He did turn down a submission of mine with a slightly
exasperated note: "Damn it, why does every story about psi have to have
a tragic ending?" This honestly represented his editorial judgment. Another time he bought a long and thus expensive novelette with what my
agent said was the fastest check on record. Soon afterward came a six-page

single-spaced letter explaining why my supposition was impossible. (I dissented, but no matter.) Yet he printed "Epilogue" exactly as written.

Mainly, we just reveled in controversy, and in discussion of subjects about which we had no disagreement but found much to wonder at.

Time ran on, in its unmerciful fashion. John's health grew steadily worse. Nonetheless, he and his wife cheered more heartily than anyone else when, at a convention in California, the Society for Creative Anachronism put on a medieval tourney. Their enjoyment of the colorful spectacle was not dimmed by the fact that Randall Garrett and I, defending the honor of Clan Campbell against two self-appointed MacDonalds, suffered defeat. They stood us a festive dinner where conversation became jolly and affectionate.

The last time I saw him, on a visit to New York, he was in such pain from gout that I had to help him on with his topcoat when we were going out to lunch. Otherwise he never mentioned it, and talk over the table was as lively and wide-ranging as ever. In response to a stray thought of mine, he promptly brought forth the biological speculation which I was to use for *The People of the Wind* and related tales. Not that he solicited any such thing from me; he was simply, delightedly, romping among ideas.

By then he was under heavy, often vicious attack from a number of quarters. The gibberish went about that he was a crackpot, a reactionary, a tyrant, a has-been, a literary obstacle. I don't think he minded, but I bloody well did, and took every opportunity to refute it. Long ago, I had adored him; later I admired and perhaps, a little bit, understood him; now I loved him.

When word came of his death, I am not ashamed to admit I wept. Then I went out and got a bottle of Scotch—Teacher's, of course—and my wife and I put a Highland record on the player and waked him.

JACK L. CHALKER

In the Dowaii Chambers

Jack L. Chalker was a familiar figure at SF conventions long before he ever tried his hand at fiction. The fervor, loyalty, and energy of the science fiction readership is legendary and unique and has created the semiorganized subculture known as "fandom," with its network of local, regional, and national conventions, its own fannish jargon, its awards and rivalries, its amateur magazines (fanzines) and amateur press associations (APAs). In the realm of fandom, professional writers enjoy a certain celebrity status as "pros" (or "filthy pros"), but certain fans achieve celebrity as well, without ever writing fiction. Those are the BNFs, or Big Name Fans.

Jack Chalker was a Big Name Fan for years before he published his first fiction. He was active on numerous con committees in the Washington-Baltimore area and helped throw many of the region's best-known gatherings. He was a skilled auctioneer, often drafted and put to work getting top dollar for SF art and collectibles at convention auctions. He manned a table in many a convention "huckster room," selling books. In 1961 he founded his own small publishing house, Mirage Press, which he runs till this day, putting out a number of critical works and SF-related nonfiction, including his own study of Scrooge McDuck.

Everybody active in fandom for any length of time knew Jack Chalker, but no one really knew about Jack's writing. A good many major SF writers have come out of fandom, to be sure, and at times it seems that every fan aspires to be a pro. But where so many of them just talk, talk, talk about it,

1

and never produce anything worth reading, the usually voluble Chalker kept his own counsel and just went out and did it. . . . And when Chalker turned pro, well, he didn't fool around!

The Jungle of Stars, published by Ballantine/Del Rey in 1975, was his first book, but it was quickly followed by others, including the popular Well World series, which Chalker reports "has so far sold more than three quarters of a million copies and is still going strong." Since 1975 he has written and published some seventeen novels, most but not all of them science fiction or fantasy. A history and geography teacher during his fanning days, Jack has since become a full-time free-lancer. Besides his two Campbell Award nominations, he has won the Skylark Award, given by Boston fandom, and the Hamilton-Brackett Memorial Award, from a California convention. His latest work is the four-volume series Four Lords of the Diamond *from Del Rey.*

Chalker lives in the Catoctin foothills of western Maryland with his wife, Eva Whitley-Chalker, and their son David. Eva is an active fan, too; in fact, she and Jack met at a convention she was running. Filthy pro or no, Jack Chalker is still a BNF.

—G.R.R.M.

1.

The sun rose high over the desolate landscape, burning away the ghosts and shadows of the night. Through the landscape only a single dirt track led into more and more of the burnt orange of the southwest desert, and on it, like some desperate alien beast being chased by the rising sun, a lone pickup truck roared through the lonely land, kicking up clouds of dust and small pebbles as it went, the only sign of life for, perhaps, fifty miles. For all that those in the truck could tell, they might have been invaders of another planet, a planet as stark and dead as the moon.

But the land was not dead, merely hard. Once the same harsh hills and dry, dusty plains had held great civilizations, many of whose cliff-dwelling cities and complex road patterns remained for the aerial surveyor, then the archaeologist, and finally the tourist to discover and explore. Even now this was Indian land, although not that of the descendants of the great ones who had thrived here so many centuries before. These Indians were newcomers, interlopers here on the land in this very spot less than six hundred years, but they were no less tied to it than the vanished old ones, nor did they love it any less.

The pickup reached rocky tableland now and took an almost invisible fork in the road to the right, up into the hills of pink and bronze whose colors changed constantly with the position of the sun. Up now, into the highlands, and through a gully that even four-wheel drive found a problem, until at last they came upon a small adobe dwelling, a single room set under a cleft in the rock and shaded by it. Nearby grazed some horses, getting what they could out of the weeds that grew even here, and, a bit farther down, some burros did likewise.

The pickup pulled up almost in front of the tiny dwelling and stopped, causing almost no stir among the animals idly grazing, and the driver's door opened and a young, athletic-looking man got out, then helped a young woman out as well.

Theresa Sanchez came out of the tiny building to greet the newcomers, then stopped in the doorway and looked them over critically. *They look like a designer jeans commercial*, she thought sourly.

A second man got out of the truck, stretching arms, legs, and neck to flex away some of the stiffness. He didn't seem to fit with the other two, his clothes older and more worn, his stocky build and crazy-quilt reddish beard doing little to disguise his pockmarked face.

Theresa Sanchez looked them all over and wondered again what the hell they were all doing here. The driver, Mr. America—blond, blue-eyed, muscular, a bit over six feet, in tailored denim work clothes, hundred-dollar cowboy boots, and a large, perfectly formed white Stetson—was George Singer, the ambitious originator of this project. He was, she knew, twenty-six and a doctoral candidate in American archaeology. The woman with him, in a tight-fitting matched denim outfit, cowboy hat, and boots, had to be Jennifer Golden, George's current housemate and an undergrad at the same university. That left the big, ugly brute as Harry Delaney, a geographer and, at twenty-nine, also a doctoral candidate.

Despite their tans, she couldn't help but think how very—
white—they all seemed.

"Welcome to the ghetto," she couldn't resist calling out to
them.

Only Delaney smiled, perhaps because he was the only one to
understand the comment. He had never met Theresa Sanchez before, but he knew a bit about her from George, and he couldn't help
but examine her in the same way that she had looked at all of them.
The woman was surprisingly small and wiry, hardly more than five
feet and probably under a hundred pounds. Her skin was a deep
reddish brown, almost black, her deep black hair long and secured
by an Indian headband, and her faded and patched jeans and plain
white T-shirt made her look not only natural here but also somehow
very, very young. He could imagine her, in more traditional Indian
dress, as a young girl of these hills, living as her ancestors had.

But she, too, was a bit more than she seemed, he knew. Not
the fourteen she seemed but twenty-five, her Spanish name not close
to her true one but one given her in Catholic mission schools, her
field so complex and esoteric that she'd either be the world authority
in it one day or condemned to obscurity by its very oddness. She was
a philologist, but not just any sort of expert on words. George had
said that there wasn't a language known that she couldn't master in
six weeks or less, nor one that she couldn't become literate in
a year. She was one of those born with the special talent for the
word—anybody's word. But although she'd tackled many just for
interest and amusement, her interest and her passion was the myriad
languages and dialects of the Amerind, many of which no one not
born to them could speak. She could speak them, though—a dozen
or more, in hundreds of dialects. How important she became would
depend on her own aims and ambitions; it was certainly a wide-open
field.

Oddly, she was as much an alien here as the other three,
although only she truly understood that. She was an Apache in
Navajo lands, which made her as wrong for this place as a Filipino
in Manchuria. Somewhere, far back, there was common ancestry,
but that was about all the sameness there was.

George looked around. "Did you fix it with the old man,
Terry?"

"And a good morning to you, too," the Indian woman responded sarcastically. "The soul of tact and discretion as always, I see."

The blond man looked at her a little sourly, but shrugged it off. He looked around. "Is he here?"

She nodded. "Still inside and praying a bit. He's still not too sure he wants to go through with this."

Singer looked slightly nervous. "You mean he might back out?"

She shrugged. "Who can say? I don't think so, though."

"What's he worrying about? That we're gonna disturb his gods?"

"He has only one god, in many forms," she told him. "No, he doesn't worry about that. He's a fatalist. He's worried about us."

"Us?" Delaney put in.

She nodded. "He believes we are to become ghosts, and his conscience is troubling him. To him it's a dilemma much like whether or not to give a loaded gun to one who you suspect of being suicidal. No, check that. More like giving a stick of dynamite to people ignorant of what explosives are and how they work."

Singer sighed. "Superstition. It's always the same."

"Are you sure, George?" she responded, not taunting but with an air of real wonder in her tone. "Are you so sure of yourself and your world? These people have been here a long time, you know."

Singer just shook his head in disgust, but Delaney felt something of a chill come over him, a shadow of uncertainty. For a moment he felt closer to this Indian woman than to his two companions, for he was not so certain of things. This was the modern, computerized world they all lived in; yet, here, even in the heart of the great cities, some still feared the darkness, some still wondered when the wind whistled, and many still knocked wood for luck. Great architects whose computers spewed three-dimensional models of grand skyscrapers and who worked in mathematics and industrial design still didn't put the thirteenth floor in their glass-and-steel edifices.

They had unloaded and set up a crude camp before they saw the old man for the first time. He emerged, looking almost otherworldly himself, a wizened, burnt, wrinkled old man with snowwhite hair stringing down below his shoulders, wearing hand-woven decorative Indian garments of buckskin tan, although decorated with colorful if faded Navajo designs. Only his boots—incongruous US Army–issue combat boots, well-worn but still serviceable—betrayed any hint that he was even aware of the twentieth century.

Whether he could speak or understand other languages, none of them knew, but it was certain that he would speak, and answer to, only the complex and intricate Navajo language.

Theresa Sanchez—Terry, she told them—not only knew the language but could quickly match the old man's dialect as well. Delaney, who'd almost washed out by his near inability to master German and French, felt slightly inadequate.

They ate some hot dogs and apples prepared over a portable Coleman, and the old man seemed to have no trouble with the modern ways of cooking or the typically American food. He wolfed it down with relish, and a can of beer from their cooler too. Finally finished, he sat back against a rock and rolled a cigarette—the three newcomers all thought it was a joint until they smelled the smoke—and seemed content.

Harry and Terry had helped Jenny with the cookout and now helped clean up. George let them do it.

Finally they got it squared away and went and sat by the ancient Indian. It was impossible to tell how old he was, but Harry, at least, thought that it was impossible to be that old and still move.

"*He's* going to guide *us?*" he said unbelievingly.

"Don't let his appearance fool you," Terry came back. "This is his land. He's strong as a bull—you oughta see him push around those burros—and healthier than you are."

"How long has he lived here?" Jenny asked in that thin, high voice of hers.

"I asked him that. He says he doesn't remember. It seems like forever. He complains a lot that he can never remember not being old and out here."

"Why's he stay, then? He could enjoy his last days in comfort if he came out of here and went down to a home," George noted.

Harry kept looking at the old man, who seemed half asleep, wondering if he understood any of this. If so, he gave no sign.

"I doubt if you'd understand the answer to that, George," Terry responded. "Lucky you decided to take up artifacts. People would confuse the hell out of you."

He smiled and looked at Jenny. "I do fairly well in that department." He sighed and turned back to Terry. "So okay. When do we go on our little trip?"

The old Indian's eyes came half open and he muttered something.

"He senses your impatience," Terry told him. "He says that's why he lives so long and you will die much quicker."

George chuckled. "If I had to live out here under these conditions to get that old, I think I'm the winner. But, as I asked before, when do we get going?"

She asked the old man and he responded.

"He says tomorrow, a little before dawn," she told him. "We'll travel until it gets too hot, then break, then take it up again in the cool of the evening."

"How far?"

She asked him. "He says many hours. Allowing for terrain and the animals, early evening the day after tomorrow."

"Ask him what it's like," Harry put in. "What're we going to see when we get there?"

She did. "He says there's nothing visible on the surface, nothing at all. He calls them chambers rather than caverns or caves, which indicates, to me at least, that they're man-made tunnels of some kind going deep into the rock."

"That squares with the old legends," George noted. "Still, I'll believe 'em when I see 'em. What kind of Indians could ever have lived here that could develop a rock-tunneling ability? Chipping houses out of hillsides, yes, and even moving stones great distances— but they have to be man-perfected natural tunnels. There are bunches of those, although not around here particularly."

She said something to the old man, possibly a rough translation of George's comments. The old man responded rather casually but at some length.

"He says that none were made by nature, as you will see, although he didn't claim they were man-made. Artificial is more correct."

"If not men, then who made 'em?"

"The Dowaii," she said. "You remember the legends."

It had begun the previous year, or perhaps much earlier, when an undergrad under Singer had stumbled onto some ancient Navajo legends and seemingly correlated them with a number of other legends from Mexican, Spanish, and pioneer sources. It was a brilliant piece of work, impossible without both luck and the computer, and when George saw it he knew that it might be something big. Naturally he took full credit for it—although the undergrad was noted for his hard work in assistance—and it had led to George's grant.

A number of ancient Indian legends from many tribes were involved, although the Navajo's was the most complete and gave the most information. Still, like Noah's flood, there were other accounts, distorted and fragmentary, that bore out at least the fact that *something* was there. That *something*, if it really was there, would not only give Singer his Ph.D. but put him immediately in the forefront of his field. It was the kind of once-in-a-lifetime chance you just *had* to take.

After God had created the world, the legend went, and made it a true paradise, He dwelt within it and loved it so much that parts of His aspect went into all things which he loved, and they became spiritual echoes of Himself. Echoes, but also independent; managers, one might say, of the earth and its resources. Elemental spirits who not merely controlled but *were* the air, the sun, the trees, the grass, the animals, and all else of the perfect world.

But a perfect world needs admirers, and these sprung automatically from the spirits, or aspects, of the Great Spirit. These were a race of perfect material creatures, the Dowaii, who were, in and of themselves, the second generation of the descendants of God.

The elemental spirits, being once removed from God, were, of course, less than God, and the Dowaii, being once removed from the spirits, were lesser still, although great beyond imagining. Still, they were aware of their imperfections, and some aspired to godhood themselves. Out of their desires and their jealousy sprang the races of man, another step removed from God yet still an aspect of Him and descended from Him. God, however, was angered by the Dowaii's jealous pride and cursed them from the light of day, condemning them to the places under the earth and giving the earth to men. Those men who remained true to nature and the land, and loved it and life, would never die, but their souls would be brought to a true heaven that God Himself inhabited, a world without spiritual intermediaries. Men, then, could become at least as great as the Dowaii if their souls were as great on earth. Most men did not and died the permanent death, to return to the earth and nourish the next generation of life. But the First People, the true Human Beings who were descended from the first of the Dowaii, kept their covenant with God while the rest of mankind did not, aided by the Dowaii, who, locked in the rocks beneath the earth, cursing man and God alike, created the hatred that became evil in the minds of men.

The legend was striking in that it was not really common to any of the Amerind religions except for an obvious common origin. Although Navajo, it was not known to the majority of those proud people but only to a select few—a cult, as it were. In a sense it was almost Judeo-Christian, in that it in some ways echoed Eden, and the Fall, and the battle between Heaven and Hell, which were not very Indian concepts.

Judging from the fragments and distortions from other tribes, though, it had apparently once been widespread, crossing tribal and national boundaries as well as linguistic ones, but it had dead-ended, died out, like so many other cultist beliefs, except for a small handful out in the southwestern desert. These, like the old man, were the guardians, the watchers at the gates of Hell.

Because the gates of Hell were two days ride from the old adobe shack.

Those few who remained faithful didn't seem to be concerned that their faith had died out long ago. It didn't matter to them, as long as their people retained the *essential* values—worship of God, love and respect for the land. Nor did they believe they would totally die out. Their own beliefs said that they inherited the beliefs from the Old Ones whose civilization had risen and fallen here before their people had come, and that the Old Ones had gotten it from still more ancient peoples. Some would go on.

For the Dowaii could not defy God and emerge from the rocks. They could only come here, close to the surface in the place of their ancient great cities, and remember the greatness they had lost. And they were still great and powerful beings, more powerful than men, who could lure and tempt and use men who came too near, although the pure ones, the unsullied First People, could dare them and defy them if they were pure enough in their souls.

An ordinary cult legend, yes, but there was more that led George to believe that something else might be here.

Of their great city and civilization not one trace remained— on the surface, or so the legends went. But on that site, below ground, were the great chambers of the Dowaii, where their spirits were strong and their power great. The last of the Dowaii of the great city dwelt in the rocks there and spoke through the chambers, and a remnant of their past glory was kept there, great and ancient treasures and knowledge beyond men's dreams.

Many of the strong and pure of the First People had entered those chambers, some as tests of courage or manhood, some as seekers after knowledge and truth. A very few emerged to become the greatest of leaders, almost godlike themselves. The Old Ones' great civilization was built by such men, but could not be sustained when they passed on.

Many more who entered the chambers emerged mad, their humanity gone. Most who entered did not come out and were said to remain there, forever trapped in the chambers, doomed forever as spirits, their ghosts trodding the chambers, suffering the torments of the Dowaii and at the same time seeing the great treasures and knowledge that was there while being powerless to do anything about it. Doomed forever, their anguished cries could sometimes be heard in the still of the desert, which is why the Navajo cult called the place the Haunting Chambers.

If it had stopped there, that would have been it, but in modern times modern men, too, had fragmentary tales.

A patrol sent out to the place by Coronado, believing the chambers might be the hidden gates to the Seven Cities, had gone, and one had returned, the one who had not gone in but had waited with the horses. His report, dismissed even at the time, of a huffing and puffing mountain that swallowed the rest of his patrol and from which only one had emerged, frothing at the mouth and gibbering like some rabid animal, and whom the lookout had finally been forced to shoot to death, was consistent—if one knew the Dowaii legend. The Spanish story also related how the madman had emerged clutching a large shining chunk of what proved to be pure silver, although this was not discovered to be so until much later.

Other, similar stories, each tied to rich artifacts, were around almost up to the early part of the century—but also, it was said, whenever anyone returned to find the chambers, they never could locate them or vanished without a trace.

It was slim but interesting evidence to hang this little expedition on, and even though Singer had academic blessings, his grant barely paid the gas. It was Delaney's grant, for a preliminary survey of the region, that provided what little real capital there was, all of it sunk into the mules, horses, and supplies.

The key, though, had been Singer's encounter with Terry Sanchez at a professional conference on southwestern Indian cultures in Phoenix. She'd been doing work on the legends of some of the Navajo people as part of an oral history project and she'd heard of the cult and the Dowaii story. More, she could talk to the right people. She didn't like George very much but was intrigued by his idea that the chambers actually represented a pre-Anasazi cave-dwelling civilization never before suspected.

It had taken two years to get this far, and it was no wonder that George Singer was impatient.

Most of the afternoon was spent unloading and checking supplies, and there was surprisingly little conversation. Except for George and Jenny, they were all virtual strangers.

It was pitch-dark in the canyon, the stars brilliant but giving little illumination and the moon not yet up. Only the reddish embers of a dying fire gave off any light, and it was precious little.

Harry Delaney had tried to sleep but couldn't yet manage it. It was the total dark, he knew, and the lack of noise of almost any sort except the occasional rustle of the animals or the sound of one of the others turning or twisting.

Those sounds, of course, were magnified all out of proportion, including, after a while, the unmistakable sounds of George and Jenny making out in the darkness. It stopped after a bit and the two seemed to lapse into sleep, but it only brought Harry more wide-awake, and eventually he got up, grabbed his cigarettes, and walked over to the other side of the fire.

He flicked his lighter to fire up his cigarette and took a few drags, then stopped still, as he saw in its flickering glow Terry Sanchez sitting against the shack, watching him. He frowned and slowly walked over near her.

"Couldn't sleep, huh?" she whispered. "Not with the, ah, sound effects?"

He chuckled. "Partly that, anyway. You?"

"I sleep more soundly out here—but less." She gestured in the dark. "You don't like our friend George very much." It wasn't a question but a statement.

"He's not very likeable," Harry replied. "I dunno. Even if he weren't an egomaniacal bastard I'd probably still hate him. Looks like a German god, doctoral candidate at twenty-six, and all the beautiful women fall all over him while all the men on the make follow in his wake. He's everything our society says a man should be. Naturally I hate his guts."

She found that amusing. "Then why are you here?"

"Oh, I follow his wake, too, I guess. It was irresistible. He needed the money to follow his little story to glory, and I had this little grant in the neighborhood. If he's right, I'll share a little of the glory. Oh, he'll have the best-seller and the talk shows, of course, but I'll have a secure little professorship with a reputation."

"And if he's wrong?"

"Then I'm no worse off for wasting a few days on this."

"Do you think he's wrong?"

He stared at her. "What do *you* think?"

"I think he's wrong, of course, but not in the way you think. I think there's something out there, all right. You only have to look at his evidence to suspect that, and in addition I've talked to these old hermits. They aren't spouting legend; they've been there."

He looked idly at the shack. "That bothers me, though. Why, if there *is* something, would they take us there? Why show us this sacred spot when the Sioux will never even tell outsiders what Crazy Horse looked like, let alone where he's buried, and your own Apaches guard the grave of Geronimo? Particularly for three whites and a native of a different tribe not exactly known as a friend of the Navajo?"

She chuckled. "That was my first thought and my first question after making friends with him. He's very opinionated about women in general, and Apache women with Spanish names in particular. The nearest I can explain it is that he and the others guard the Navajo from the Dowaii. Oddly, only if we had a Navajo here would there have been trouble. He considers the rest of us already corrupted beyond redemption and, therefore, already the Dowaii's property."

"So we're sacrificial lambs," he sighed. "I don't like the sound of that. A crazy cult out here in the middle of nowhere, leading us around on their turf. I wonder if—"

"If the disappearances are caused by them? I thought of that. I'm sure George has too. That's why we'll all be armed from sunup on, and why one of us will always stand watch after. Still, I don't fear an attack by geriatric fanatics. There's something out here, all right. Not what George expects or what you or I expect, either, but there's something. You can almost feel it."

He shivered slightly. "I think I see what you mean." He sighed. "It must be nice to be like George. I doubt if he fears much of anything."

She got up and started over to her bedroll. Abruptly she stopped and turned back to him. "That, perhaps, is why we, you and I, are more likely to survive than he."

He snuffed out his cigarette and went back to his own sleeping bag, but he didn't sleep right away. For brief, episodic moments he felt the urge to flee, to tell them in the morning that they could go with his money and without him.

Something out there. . . . Feel it. . . .

It was a hot, rough day's ride over nasty terrain. A lonely ride, too, as even the normally unflappable George seemed somehow grim, taciturn, even a bit nervous.

The dry, wilting heat didn't help matters any, with any of them, as long as you didn't count the old man. Nothing, but nothing, seemed to bother him, and even his breaks, long and short, seemed more for the benefit of the animals and his charges than himself.

Harry tried to renew hesitant contact with Terry, but she seemed as stoic and indifferent as the old man. At one of their shadeless rests, though, George took Harry aside, a bit from the rest.

"I saw you making a few moves towards Terry," he whispered very low. "Just a friendly hint to forget it."

Harry was annoyed. "What's it to you? You already *got* Jenny."

"You got me wrong, Harry. I'm just being friendly. She don't mean nothin' to me except the way out to the chambers. You just aren't her type, that's all."

"Oh, come off it, George," he grumbled.

"*Jenny's* her type, Harry. At least, that's the only one around here she'd be attracted to."

He started to open his mouth, then closed it again. Finally he said, "Damn you, George," and stalked back to the others.

He felt miserable now, although he knew that that hadn't been George's intent. George could only see other people's actions in the same way *he* saw those actions, and the warning was actually a friendly gesture. George would never understand, he knew. He was still back there, puzzling over why he was just cursed out for doing somebody a favor.

Hell, he'd never have gotten romantic with Terry Sanchez— not really. But George had robbed him of even the illusion, coldly bringing reality into this fantasyland where reality had no place being. George wouldn't ever understand that, never comprehend it in the least.

Damn it, George, I don't care who or what she really is, but I neither wanted to nor had to know.

It was a lonely night, with more aches and more sleep but no new conversation.

The next morning found the old man and Terry seeming anxious to push on, while the three others all felt every bone and muscle in their bodies, which all seemed bruised and misplaced. Groans, curses, and complaints became the order of the day now.

Jenny seemed to suffer the worst. This was different than riding some nicely trained horses on a ranch or bridle path, and she really wasn't cut out for this sort of thing—not that George, and particularly Harry, were, either.

At least, Harry decided, the agony took your mind off brooding.

The scenery had changed into a rocky, gray landscape with rolling hills. Far off in the distance were some peaks and even a hint of green, but they turned from that direction and went close to a red and gray hill not distinguishable from the rest of the desolate mess. Finding a sheltered spot beneath a rock cleft, the old Indian signaled them to a halt and dismounted.

Terry talked with him at length, then came back to the rest of them. "Well, we're here," she announced.

All three looked startled and glanced around. *"Here?"* Harry managed.

She nodded and pointed. "That ugly hill over there, in fact."

George looked around at the landscape, a part of the region that didn't even have the beauty and color of the rest. It was an ugly, unappetizing place, one of the worst spots any of them could remember. "No wonder nobody found this place before," he said. "It's a wonder that *anybody* did."

Jenny turned up her pretty nose. "Smells like shit too."

Harry and George both frowned. "Sulphur," Harry noted. "I'll be damned. Doesn't look like anything volcanic was ever around here, does it?"

George shook his head. "Nope. But I don't like it all the same. Terry, your old man didn't say anything about sulphur. We might need breathing equipment if we have to go into caves filled with the stuff, and that's one thing we ain't got."

"I don't remember anything about it," she told them. "I'll ask him, though." She went back, talked to the old man, then returned. "He says the Dowaii know we are here and why we are here and are cleaning house for us—at least, that's the closest I can get. He says they'll put on a show tonight, then call for us."

George looked upset. "Two days of hell and a dead end. I'm sure as hell not going into any damned cave filled with gas."

"He says the air inside will be as sweet as we wish it to be."

"So *he* says." He sighed. "Well, let's bed down, anyway. At least we can make some preliminary surveys and see if there's anything worth coming back for."

The sun set as they unpacked and prepared the evening meal. Harry sat facing the mountain, digging into his beef and beans, as the land got darker and darker. Something in the back of his mind signaled that something was not right, but he couldn't put his finger on it. Finally he settled back and looked up at the mountain and dropped his plate.

None of the others noticed, and he finally said, "George, we have a Geiger counter, don't we?"

George looked up, puzzled, and said, "Yeah. Sure. What . . . ?" He turned to see where Harry was looking and froze too. The two women also turned and both gasped.

The mountain glowed. It wasn't a natural sort of glow, either, but an eerie, almost electronic image in faint, blue-white light, a matte 3-D ghost image of the mountain that seemed to become clearer as darkness became absolute.

"Well, I'll be damned!" George swore. "What the hell can cause something like that other than a Hollywood special-effects department?"

Harry had already retrieved the Geiger counter and, with the aid of a flashlight, tried to take readings.

"Anything?" George asked.

He shook his head. "Nothing but normal trace radiation. My watch gives off more juice than this stuff, whatever it is. I can't figure it out."

George studied it for a moment. "Let's go see." He went and got a flashlight, joining Harry, then looked over at Terry and Jenny. "Want to come?"

The contrast on the two women's faces was startling, at least to Harry. Jenny was just plain scared and not being very successful in trying to hide it. Terry, on the other hand, seemed fascinated almost to the point of being in some sort of mystical trance.

"George, don't go. Not now," Jenny said pleadingly.

"We're just going to the edge of the thing," he explained patiently. "I'm not about to go mountain climbing in the dark."

Terry said nothing, just stood there staring, and the two men realized that she wasn't about to join them. They turned and both started walking toward the strange display.

Suddenly the old man cried out, "No!"

Both men froze and turned. It was the first intelligible word they'd heard him utter.

"Hold on, Pop, we'll be back," George told him, and they set out again over the rocks toward the oddly glowing site. No one tried to stop them or accompany them.

It was only about fifty rough yards to the start of the display, and they approached it cautiously but quickly. It looked different this close, though.

"It's not glowing," Harry noted. "It's very slightly *above* the rock. See?"

George peered at it in nervous curiosity. "I'll be damned. It's—it's like electricity."

"It *is* electricity," the other man noted. "It's an electrical web or grid of some sort that makes a kind of holographic picture of the mountain. Where's the energy come from? And how is it kept in this form?"

"I don't know. I never saw anything like it that wasn't faked," George responded. "What the *hell* have we discovered here?"

"I'm going to toss these wirecutters at it," Harry said tensely.

"Let's see what happens." He removed them from his belt kit and lightly tossed them at the nearest part of the display.

The wirecutters hit the current and seemed to stop, frozen there just above the ground, enveloped and trapped in the energy field. They remained suspended there, not quite striking the ground, and began to glow white.

"Let's get back," Harry suggested, and George didn't argue.

They'd barely returned to the clearing when there was a rumble as if from deep within the ground, and at the top of the hill a bright, glowing sparkle of golden light grew. It, too, was some sort of energy field, they knew, growing to a height of several feet and sparkling like the Fourth of July.

From other points on the mountain other fields rose, all the same shimmering sparkle, but one was blue, another red, another green—all the colors of the rainbow and more.

They all stood there watching it, even the old man, for some time, perhaps an hour or more.

"Well, at least we know how the earlier people found the place," George noted.

"George, this isn't what we bargained for at all," Harry noted. "Listen—feel it in the ground? A rumbling. Not like a volcano or an earthquake. More steady."

George nodded, unable to avert his eyes for long from the display. "Like—like some giant turbine or something. Like some great machine gearing up."

"That's it exactly. Don't you see, George? That's what it is. Some kind of machine. That turbine or whatever deep below us is producing the energy for that display."

"It can't be. The stories go back centuries. It'd be impossible for anybody earlier than the past twenty or thirty years to build such a machine, never mind why. Unless . . ."

"Unless the Dowaii were not of this earth," George finished.

The display, but not the glow, subsided after ninety minutes or so. Harry turned to Terry, who was still standing, staring at the place. "You okay?" he asked, concerned.

For a moment he was afraid she was beyond hearing him, but finally she took a deep breath, sighed, and turned to look at him. "Listen! Can't you hear them?"

He stared in puzzlement, then tried to listen. Presently he heard what she meant. There was a sound, very faint, very distant, somewhere down deep from within that mountain. A sound that seemed to be a crowd of people, all talking at the same time.

"The machine's noise," George pronounced. "At least now we can see why the old man talked about ghosts there. It *does* almost sound like people. The easy part of the legend is solved, anyway. Just imagine primitive man coming across this—even as primitive as the last century. It'd make a believer out of you in an instant. Maybe drive you nuts. The force field, or whatever it is, might well account for the disappearances."

Harry sniffed the air. "Smell it? Ozone."

"Beats the hell out of sulphur," George, the pragmatist forever, responded. "Well, now we know how legends are made. Unfortunately, we don't know who or what made 'em. One thing's for sure, though: We got the find not just of the century but maybe the greatest find of all times."

"Huh?"

"It's pretty clear that, centuries ago—maybe a lot longer than that—somebody who was pretty damned smart stuck a machine here that was so well made and so well supplied with power sources, probably geothermal, that it's still working. That means an infinitely self-repairing device too." He frowned. "I wonder what the hell it does?"

"It's the extension of that *I* don't like," Harry responded. "Not just self-repairing. It knows we're here, George. It *knows.*"

"Aw, c'mon. Don't shit in your pants at the unknown."

"I'm a little scared, I admit that, but that's not what I mean. If it did this every night, it'd have been spotted a long time ago. This place has been photographed to death. The whole damned world has, through satellites, day and night, and in the infrared, X-ray, you name it. And if they'd spotted anything, they'd have been here a long time before *us*. Uh-uh. The old man's right. This baby turned itself on just for us. It knows we're here, George. It *knows.*"

George didn't like that. "Maybe, then, it's defending itself."

2.

Nobody got much sleep that night, but there was a limit to how long you could watch even such an eerie phenomenon without discovering that your basic needs hadn't changed. The old man, of course, slept just fine; he'd been through this before.

Still, with the sun barely above the horizon and the sky only a dull, pale blue, there was movement. Harry felt himself being pushed and awoke almost at once. He was barely asleep, anyway. It was George, and Harry's expression turned from sleepiness to concern when he saw the other man's face.

"What's the matter?"

"It's Jenny—she's gone!"

"*Jenny?*" Harry was up in a moment. "Any sign of where she went?"

"Yeah. No horses or burros missing. Even if she was panicked out of her gourd, she'd take a horse. And there are a few tracks."

Harry turned toward the mountain, which looked as ugly and undistinguished as it had at first sight. "There? Hell, she'd never—"

"I know, I know. But she did. Either that or some of the old boy's buddies came along and got her."

"Let's get Terry," Harry suggested, but it was needless. The Indian woman had heard their not-so-whispered conversation and was already up and approaching them. The old man seemed to be sleeping through it.

"What's the matter?" she asked, and they told her quickly. She looked over at the mountain with a mixture of fear and concern, yet she didn't seem surprised.

"I've felt its pull myself since last night," she told them. "Haven't you? All night I lay there and I swore I could hear voices in many languages, all calling my name—my Apache name as well. There was a tremendous pull and I had trouble resisting it."

George shook his head wonderingly. "Damn! That's all right for you and your mysticism, but—hell, Jenny? Not a brain in her head and scared to death of her own shadow. *You* saw her last night. She wouldn't go near that thing for a million bucks and a lifetime Hollywood contract."

Terry looked at the tracks. "Nevertheless, that's what she appears to have done. It couldn't have been too long ago; I don't think I slept more than a few minutes, and all of that in the last hour."

Both men nodded. "Looks like we're gonna find out a bit more than we bargained for last night," George grumbled, sounding slightly nervous. "I hope that thing's inactive in the daylight."

They grabbed a canteen and a couple of Danish from the supplies, and checked their guns. They wasted no time.

"Ready?" George asked, and they nodded. "Hey, what about the old boy?"

Terry looked back at the sleeping form. "He'll know," she said mysteriously. "Don't worry. Let's see if we can get her."

The rocky ground wasn't good for tracks, but it was clear that she had gone to the mountain. Any lingering doubts ended at the point where the glow had begun the night before. George looked down and again shook his head in wonder. "Jenny's boots—and socks too," he muttered. "What the hell? Barefoot on this shit?"

Harry stared at the footwear, not sitting as if removed but tossed, as if discarded, and felt a queer feeling in his stomach and the hairs on his neck tickle. *Don't go,* something inside him pleaded. *Chicken out! Go back and wait for them!* He looked up at the usually impassive Terry Sanchez and saw, unmistakably, some of the same feelings inside her. She gave him a glance that told him it was true, and in that glance was also the knowledge they both shared that they would ignore those feelings in spite of themselves.

George bent down and picked up something, handing it to Harry. He looked at it critically. It was his wirecutters, looking none the worse for wear. He sniffed them, but there was no odd smell or sign of burn marks or anything else, either.

There was a small sound and a few tiny rocks moved. They all jumped and looked up, and George, at least, relaxed. "Lizard," he told them, sounding very relieved. "Well, if *he* can live in a place like this, *we* shouldn't be electrocuted." With that he set foot on the mountain and began walking up.

It wasn't really a very tall hill—no more than eight hundred feet or so—and while this side wasn't exactly smooth, it was mostly sandstone and gave easy footholds.

The other two followed. "Where are you heading?" Harry called to him.

"Just up here a bit," George responded. "When I saw the lizard I spotted something else." He was at the spot in a minute or two and stopped again, looking down. They caught up and saw what he'd seen.

"Jesus! Her jeans!" George breathed. "Has she gone out of her mind?"

Terry looked up at him and scowled. "That *would* be the explanation running through your mind."

"Got a better one?"

"Maybe. Let's go on with it."

He looked around. "Which way?"

"Up," she replied. "The easiest way."

It wasn't a hard trail to follow. A bit more than halfway up they discovered all her clothing. Unless she'd changed, there was no doubt that Jenny Golden was now somewhere on or in the mountain stark naked.

George kicked at Jenny's bra. "This would be the last of it. So now where do we go?"

"I think I know," Harry managed, his voice sounding as frail as his stomach felt. "Remember our display last night? The fountains of sparkles?"

They nodded.

"Well, unless I miss my guess, the opening for the blue one should be only a little over and maybe ten feet farther." He stared at the barren landscape. "Yup. There it is."

They went up to it with little difficulty and stood around it, looking at it. It was by no stretch of the imagination a cave, but rather an opening in the rock layers barely large enough for one person to enter. Harry removed his pack and set it down, removing lantern-style flashlights and mining caps with small headlamps. The others did the same, and quickly they had what they needed—what they thought they might need—to explore a subterranean remain. They quickly donned the gear, including gloves, and Harry looked at the other two. "Well? Who's the hero?"

George stared nervously back at him, and Harry caught the expression.

Put up or shut up, Big George, he thought a little smugly. *The time for big talk is past.*

"Okay," the blond man said at last, resigned to it. "I'll go in first. If everything's okay, Terry, you should be second, with Harry bringing up the rear."

Harry saw Terry's impulse to let George off the hook and prayed she wouldn't do it. She didn't.

George fixed the rope to his harness and looked nervously at the coil. "How much we got?"

"A hundred feet. Don't worry about it," Harry told him. "If you need more than that, then she's dead and beyond saving. If you need it much at all, in fact."

That sobered them.

George spent a little time checking and rechecking everything, although it was pretty much show, a bid for time to get up his nerve. Finally, though, he swallowed hard, went to the hole, and examined it. "No odors, sulphur or anything else," he noted. "Looks natural." He sat down and cautiously put himself into the hole, feet first. He kicked a bit. "Seems like a sloping ramp. Feels smooth, so keep a grip on that rope."

"Don't worry," Harry assured him.

Cautiously George slid into the hole in the hillside. Terry stood at the mouth, listening, as Harry played out the rope.

"Smooth rock and a gentle slope," George called back. "Funny— looks more like limestone, although the surrounding rock is sandstone for sure. Considering how it spouts, probably something akin to geyserite. Stuff from deep down. Wonder how far?"

"Any sign of Jenny?" Terry called to him.

"Nope. Funny, though. Should be getting cooler, I'd think, but it's not. The rock's warm, but not hot."

That concerned them all. The geyserite implied volcanism beneath, and also intermittent steam eruptions, which might have been what they had seen the night before. Some form of them, anyway.

George was about twenty-five feet in now and called up, "I'll be damned!"

"What did you find?" Terry called back.

"Handholds! This thing starts down and there's handholds of some kind of metal. No rust or anything. They look machined. It's wider down here now. Let me turn. . . . Yep! It's a long tube going down at about a sixty-degree angle, and it's got both handholds and metal steps. Damn! Those steps look like they're naturally imbedded in the sandstone. That's ridiculous, of course."

"Wait there!" Terry called. "I'm coming down!" She turned to Harry. "Secure the rope and I'll just use it as a guide. Whatever we're going into, somebody built it."

He nodded. "When you get down, send George down the hole and wait for me. I'll rig the rope so I can free it and pull it after. We might need it, and there's no way we're going to get packs in there."

She nodded and was soon into the hole and out of sight. Harry fixed the rope, then waited for her call. When it came, he started in himself, barely fitting through the opening.

George was both right and wrong on the geyserite, he decided. If it were really the product of the steam eruptions, it would cover all sides of the cave, but it didn't—only the floor. The substance was similar, but he doubted it was there from natural causes.

Once alongside Terry, Harry freed the rope and reeled it in as she descended.

He waited in silence and near-darkness as her light quickly vanished below. Soon there was no sound at all, and when he shouted down, only his echoes returned. Again the feeling of panic seized him. What if things weren't all right down there? What if whatever had seized hold of Jenny had also now gotten *them*?

He shined his light on the ladder. It was an impossibility and he knew it, as if someone millions of years before had positioned the metal steps and then waited for the sedimentary rock—which, of course, was only laid underwater—to compact over them, leaving the perfect staircase.

Sighing, he descended into the dark.

It was easy—almost as easy as climbing down a fire escape. He found that George hadn't exaggerated the heat, though. If anything, it was hotter inside than out, but incredibly it also was terribly, terribly humid.

He descended until he felt he would just keep going down forever, but finally he reached bottom.

The cavern—no, *tube*—in which he found himself was oval-shaped but quite large, perhaps twelve feet across by eight feet high, and seemed perfectly manufactured out of the same smooth rock as the floor above. More interesting, it glowed with some sort of greenish internal light. Not enough to make the place bright, but enough to see by, that was for sure. He kept his miner's cap on but switched off his flashlight, then looked around. There was no sign of the other two.

Again the fear gripped him, along with the eerie silence, and this time he turned toward the stairway that led back.

The stairway wasn't there. The hole wasn't there. In back and in front of him was only the same green-glowing chamber.

He felt a stab of sheer panic and looked around for the rope and other gear—and did not see it. *It's got me! My God! It's got me!*

He felt like throwing up but did not. Instead he looked in both directions, decided on the one he'd been facing, and started walking.

What were these eerie chambers? He couldn't help wondering. Were they the exhausts of some millennia-lost spaceship? Or, perhaps, corridors within that ship, or some ancient extraterrestrial colony? If the latter, what would they be like, who made their tunnels like this in shape and texture?

He walked through the sameness of the chambers, and he finally ceased to fear or wonder or analyze. All those things seemed to flow out of him, leaving him almost empty, a shell, a lonely wanderer of subterranean alien corridors conscious only of the need to move, to walk forward. That and of the heat.

Faintly he struggled, but his resistance grew weaker and weaker as he walked. And as he walked he became aware of others, too, walking with him, under a heat that no longer came from within but from above, from a warm sun in a cloudless sky, one that he could not yet see or comprehend.

He was born.

His parents called him Little Wolf because he was born with so much hair on his head, and he grew up a curious and intelligent child in the world of the People. Unlike the subhumans who roamed the plains, the People lived in semipermanence beside the shore of a great lake on the edge of a beautiful forest. The men hunted and fished, while the women bore and reared the children, maintained the village, and in season, when the priest said all the signs were right, planted and tended some crops, mostly maize but occasionally nice vegetables as well.

In his thirteenth year manhood came upon him, quite unlike

what Little Wolf expected it to be but that which he'd anticipated and prayed for all the same, and thus, the following spring, he entered the teaching circles of the warriors and learned the basics of survival—the use of the bow, the science of the spear, the patience needed to capture deer and birds and other creatures, and also some of the arts of war. Of the codes of war he needed no instruction: Those were a part of the culture of the People from the time of his birth and were as much taken for granted as the air, trees, and water.

By late spring he was accompanying the men into the forests on hunts, and out on the lake in canoes to use the coarse skin and bark nets made by the women to catch the silvery fish. He was neither the best nor the worst of the candidates for manhood, and, finally, he brought down a young doe with his bow and handmade flint arrows, and passed the final preliminary. The ceremonies of manhood were solemn and took several days, but in the end he was annointed, his head was shaved, and he was branded painfully on the face and chest and hands by the priest with the signs of manhood of his people and did not flinch or hold back and was, therefore, proclaimed a man.

He enjoyed his new status and took particularly well to the hunt, showing an ability to go for days without food far from home in search of community meat. Because of this he chose his man's name as approved by the elders of his tribe, that of Runs-Far-Needs-Nothing, a name he was very proud of.

In the fall the elders met with all the new men and brought forth the new women, those whom the gods had shown by the sign of blood were now women. Runs-Far-Needs-Nothing took then one whom he'd known from childhood, a small, lithe, attractive woman who accepted him as well and whom he gave the woman's name Shines-Like-the-Sun, a name approved by her parents and the elders and by she herself.

His early years had been remarkably peaceful, with little commerce and no major conflicts with the subhumans, although an occasional one of these strange ones would come to bargain for food or passage rights, and there would be occasional contests between the men, which the People usually won—which was good, since losing such a contest to a subhuman would bring such shame that suicide would usually be called for.

It wasn't until his seventeenth fall, however, that any real trouble appeared. The spring rains had not come in their usual numbers, and the snows of the previous winter had been light, insufficient to fill many of the smaller creeks that fed the lake. Through some irrigation a substandard crop had been raised, even with the lake many hands below its normal level, and the People knew they would survive the drought with what they had and the ministrations of the high priest. After all, game was plentiful, as the dryness drove more and more animals closer to the lake's precious water, but they had little to spare.

Shines-Like-the-Sun, meanwhile, was again with child, having already borne a son and a daughter to him, and they were content.

One day, though, still in the heat of early fall, a subhuman arrived looking grimmer than usual. The game had fled the northern plains, he told them, where in some places the land was scorched as by fire and baked harder than the hardest rock, while rivers that had always run pure and clean and deep as long as his people could remember were hard-caked mud. Without the game and waters of the lake, his people could not hope to survive to the spring, and he wished permission for his people to establish their own camp on the far side of the lake.

This was much debated by the elders, who finally consulted all the adults of the People, and what they concluded was grim news indeed. Such a large group as the subhumans would tremendously deplete the game around the lake, and as those others knew none of the skills of net-fishing and looked down upon farming as inferior work, the burden on the wild edible vegetables and fruits and the game would be tremendous, possibly too great for the lake to stand. Worse, as nomads, the subhumans had no sense of conservation, worrying not a bit about whether such a place as this land would still bring what was needed a year or more hence. They would trade game and hides for fish and grain, of course, but in this case it would be the People's own game and hides. In effect the subhumans would be taking half the limited wealth of the People, then trading it for some of the remaining wealth while making the land poor. While charity would be a virtue, it would only lead to such insults as that, with the People becoming poorer and weaker by far. Therefore, they recommended that permission to settle the nomads be denied.

This, of course, would leave the subhumans with no choice.

Rather than move another week or more to the south, only to face the same situation or worse, they would fight, and they were a barbarous lot, without honor or mercy.

The People were as one to fight nonetheless, and the men went to prepare for battle. The subhuman emissary was notified and took the news well, as if he expected it—which he probably did. When he departed, several warriors discreetly shadowed him back to his people's encampment and set up a watch.

At dawn two days later the subhumans moved—not on the People's village, but to the place opposite on the lake where they had originally wished to go. Clearly they had realized that they could not launch a surprise attack on the village and had chosen instead to establish their own camp and dare the People to evict them.

The subhumans were a rough warrior race, but their idea of war was pretty basic and without real tactics. They expected to hold crude earthworks built in a single day to shield their tents, and they expected hand-to-hand overland attack or perhaps a seige. They had left their backs open to the water.

The People *would* attack, from both sides, but in a coordinated manner. The added factor would be a waterborne attack after the dual attack overland drained the enemy's manpower away from the rear. Almost two dozen canoes filled with the best would attack then.

Runs-Far-Needs-Nothing was one of those who would attack overland. He and most of the others felt no real fear or concern for the battle. After all, were these not subhuman barbarians? Besides, tales and legends of battles were a part of his growing up, and they were romantic adventures. He and his fellows welcomed the chance to show their superiority, their skills and cunning, and perhaps add to the legends.

The subhumans *were* caught somewhat off-guard, because they expected a dawn attack and it was well past midday when the People launched their drive. There was good reason for this: The sun was across the lake, causing near-blinding reflections and therefore masking the lakeside attackers and their canoes, a trick remembered from one of those legendary battle tales.

At first it went gloriously, with bowmen shooting hails of arrows into the subhuman encampment from both sides, then spearmen moving forward under arrows' cover. The battle was fierce, and the subhumans were brave and skilled fighters, but they were clearly outnumbered.

Still, the young warriors of the People learned that war was not romantic. Blood flowed, innards were spilled, and close friends of a lifetime lay lifeless around them. Still they pressed on, knowing they were winning and that the canoes would soon land to finish off the rest who were even now falling back.

But inexperience was costly, and the People paid dearly for it as the woods erupted on all sides with almost as many of the enemy as they had faced. It placed the People's warriors between an enemy sandwich and both confused and demoralized them. Caught in crossfire, they fell in great numbers, while the added warriors of the enemy allowed those in the village to split off and defend the beach against the incoming canoes. Most of the brave warriors of the People died without ever realizing that they had been tricked very simply by an old, tough, experienced foe who *knew* his emissary would be followed back to camp and a count made of his men. A foe who had shown less than half his true numbers to those scouts while the others were already moving to positions across the lake.

Runs-Far-Needs-Nothing understood none of this, but he knew now that his people had lost, and he felt fear both for himself and for his wife and children, a fear that turned to a fierce hatred of this enemy. He never even saw the one who killed him, an experienced man of eighteen. . . .

Harry awoke slowly in the corridor and for a moment didn't know who or where he was. Two languages ran in his brain, two cultures, two totally different sets of references, and he could not come to terms with where he was or what he was. It came back, almost with a rush, but it seemed almost unreal and so very long ago. Even as he recounted his identity to himself over and over, and knew as he became more and more himself once again that he had had some sort of chamber-induced hallucination, he still marveled at his white skin and hairy body, a body that seemed wrong for him.

It was some time before he was suddenly aware that he was not alone. A small sound, a movement in the greenish-tinged oval cave, caused him to whirl and come face-to-face with Jenny Golden.

For a moment they just stared at each other, saying nothing. She looked as if in shock, somewhat vacant and, somehow, *older* than he remembered her. The eyes, he decided. It was the eyes. He wondered idly if he looked much the same.

After a few moments of looking at one another, he grew somehow alarmed that she was not aware of him, or at least of who he was. She seemed to sense this apprehension.

"How did you die?" she asked in a hollow, vacant tone.

"In a battle," he responded, his voice sounding thick and strange in his ears. He was conscious of a slight difficulty in shaping the words, as one ancient language coexisted with a modern one. The same effect was noticeable in her voice. "I'm not too clear on the particulars."

"I died in childbirth," she told him, that tone still there and still somewhat frightening. "Giving birth to my ninth child."

3.

He had been sleeping. How long he didn't know, but it was a deep, dreamless sleep, and when he awoke he knew immediately who and where he was with an almost astonishing clarity of mind. Abruptly he remembered Jenny and for a moment was afraid that she'd be gone again like some will-o'-the-wisp, leaving him alone and confused. He was relieved to see that she was still there and looking a bit calmer and saner than she'd seemed the first time. Still, when she turned to look at him, she seemed much older, somehow, than he'd remembered, and her eyes still seemed to reflect some inner pain.

He sat up, stretched, and nodded to her. "How long was I asleep?"

She shrugged. "A long time. Who can say in here?"

"I'm sorry for passing out on you so abruptly."

Again a shrug. "I did the same thing. You come back kinda dizzy and not really knowing who you are, then you conk out, and when you wake up—well, I don't know."

He nodded sympathetically. "You've changed, Jenny. You've— well, I'm not sure how to put it. Grown up."

"Aged, you mean. Or maybe you're right. Anyway, I know who I am now and all that, but I also have the memories of that other life, just as real, but I'm in control, if you know what I mean."

"Yeah. The same way. Any sign of the others?"

"Not yet. I really was beginning to think that I'd never see any of you again, when you popped up." Her voice seemed to soften, then crack, and tears formed in her eyes. "Thank God you showed up."

He went over to her and just took her hand, squeezing it lightly to reassure her and tell her he understood.

And when she'd cried it out, she wanted to talk about it. He let her take her own time.

"You know, I always us'ta have these fantasies," she said. "I dunno—we're all supposed to be liberated, you know? And I like the freedom and all, but I'd still fantasize. Submission. Bondage. You know, like I was a slave girl in some sultan's empire. Like that, you know. I mean, I never really *wanted* that; it was just a fun thing, for masturbating, that sort of shit."

"You mean this thing gave you your fantasy?"

"Sort of. It was way far back, I'm pretty sure. An Oriental tribe, somewhere in Asia. Nobody was too clear on geography, you understand."

He nodded. "I've only an educated guess as to where I was too."

"Well, anyway, it was a nomad tribe, picking up and moving from valley to valley and across big mountains and deserts. They were a rough, tough group, too, and they didn't think much of women. They treated us like *slaves*, like *property*. Some of 'em got so mad when they got daughters they killed them. Just little babies. We cooked, we cleaned, we took down and put up the tents and fucked whenever the men got in the mood, and we got beat when we did it wrong or too slow or even if the man had problems. And we bore babies. God! Did we have babies!"

She fell silent, and he waited for a while to make sure she was finished. Finally he said, "Well, I wasn't nearly as bad off, even though I was just about as primitive." He described his life and realized with some surprise that he was almost nostalgic about it and them. "The big trouble was how naive they were," he told her, and, in so doing, told himself. "They were too peaceful and too inexperienced for what they faced—a group much like your tribe. Somewhere there I think there's a lesson in both our—other lives—but I can't put my finger on it yet if it *is* there. I got, I think, a clue, though, as to what we were put through and why." He sighed. "If only we could link up with the others! If their experiences bear out the idea, maybe I can get a handle on what we're facing in here."

"Well, I'm not going looking for them," she responded. "Look, I was sleeping at the camp when suddenly I kinda half woke up and knew I was walking someplace. I thought I was dreaming. It was just like some kinda magnet, you know, pulling me into the mountain. I *do* remember crawling along a dark tube, then going down some stairs, then along this tunnel—and that's it."

He nodded. "We followed you when we discovered you were missing and wound up doing the same thing. I was the last in. Until I got to this tunnel area, though, I had a clear head, and I was on the watch, but it got me anyway."

"But—why me? Why did it call *me*?"

"There could be a number of reasons," he told her, preferring not to contrast her intellect with the others', "but I suspect it's some kind of hypnotic process."

"You mean I got hypnotized when I was watching the colored lights?"

He nodded. "That's about it. Some people are more hypnotizable than others. It hooked you then and used that hook to draw you to it, giving you some kind of subliminal instructions."

She looked around and seemed to shiver slightly. "But who? Why?"

"I'm not sure it's a *who*. I doubt it. I'm pretty sure it's just a machine. An incredible, impossible, near-magical machine, but a machine all the same. It's nothing I know, but I just sort of feel it."

"A machine? But who built it? And why?"

"I'm not sure yet. I need more information."

"Harry?"

"Yes?"

"Are we—did we—live lives of people it trapped in here? Will we just go through all of 'em until we die of starvation or something?"

He thought about it. "I doubt it. First of all, neither you nor I were ever near this place in our other lives. Second, I doubt if any people like you describe—physically, anyway—were ever anywhere near New Mexico. No, my people might have been: There was something very Amerind about them. But not yours. As for dying of starvation, do you feel hungry?"

She thought about it, a curious expression on her face, as if she'd never thought about it before. "No. Not at all."

"Neither do I. And my hair and beard are about the same length as they were, and your shaved legs are still smooth, so we probably haven't *really* been here long at all. Either that, or time has no meaning for us here in the literal sense. I'm not sure. I *was* hungry when I came in, and you should have been too." He considered that further. "Look, you've been here, subjectively, a long time. Have you had to take a crap? Or even a piss?"

"No, come to think of it."

"Then we're in some sort of stasis—limbo, whatever. The machine is taking care of us. I'm not sure we're exactly in time at all."

"Huh? What do you mean?"

"There were machined metal steps imbedded in the stone. Now, that's impossible. It took millions of years to lay that sediment, one grain at a time, so laying them as the rock was formed is impossible. But that's exactly the way they looked."

"So how's that possible?"

"It isn't. The only way I can figure it was that this whole gadget was sort of slowly phased into our existence so it became possible."

"But you just said that'd be real slow."

"Smart girl. But not if you're thinking the unthinkable, as I am. I think this thing was sent back in time."

"But that's ridiculous!"

"It sure is. But so is this machine and what it did to us."

She shook her head in wonder and disbelief. "But who sent it, then? And why?"

"Somebody in the far future, that's for sure. Some civilization that knows a lot more than we do. No, check that. Think about this, maybe: a future civilization that knows more science than anybody ever dreamed. A civilization that can build a machine like this and make it do what it does."

"But what kind of creatures are they?"

"People. Like us, maybe. Or close enough to us for— Hey! That's it! At least, it'll do until a better explanation comes along."

"What?"

"Okay, now suppose there's a war or something. The big one. The whole world gets wiped, but somehow some people survive. Build it up again, bigger and better than it was, maybe. Explore all the mysteries we would have if we hadn't been zapped. They know everything—except their own history and culture, all traces of which have been wiped out. So they have this project. They send back this machine and maybe a lot of remote machines connected to it. Put 'em all over. Start as far back as they can date any human remains and start there. Let the machines randomly record people's lives and cultures. A scientific sample, so to speak."

"But if they can travel in time, why not just come back and see for themselves?"

"Maybe they can't. I keep thinking of those steps in the stone. If you have to take millions of years just to phase in something—millions here, not to them—it might not work with people. Besides, if these people were from the year 20,000 or something, you realize the time involved? You'll never have enough time to look at, analyze, and know a million years of human history, particularly if you know so little to begin with. No, this would be the logical way."

"But look at the lives we had!" she protested. "They weren't important. Not really. No great people, great civilizations, nothing like that."

"No, and the odds would be against them ever really coming up with a great person, although I'm sure they've recorded many of the civilizations through the lives of people who lived in them. Ordinary people. Like us. The kind of information that tells you the important stuff—what people and culture were really like in different places at different periods in human history. Yeah, that's *got* to be it. We've gotten ourselves trapped in somebody's grand anthropology experiment."

He ran down after that, feeling slightly exhausted but also somehow excited. He refused to consider that he'd made wild stretches of logic and imagination based on few hard facts, but, still, he was certain he'd gotten it right. He wondered idly if he hadn't picked at least the basics from the machine itself to which he and Jenny were so obviously tied.

She, too, was silent for a bit, and he realized that his own ideas were a bit too much for her to swallow or accept all at once. He sympathized with her. She didn't really belong here, he thought idly. Maybe as a *subject* for the machine, but not here, trapped inside of it. His own reaction was curiously different. Understanding it, as he thought he did, made all the difference. To lose yourself in time, to live the lives of others through the ages while never aging yourself . . .

"Harry?"

"Yes?"

"Why *us*? Why suck us into it?"

He thought a moment. "Well, if I'm right and it's sent back by people—our descendants—and it's just a dumb machine, the world's grandest tape recorder, it might just figure we're part of the folks who built the thing. It struck a chord somewhere in you and drew you to it, probably just to make sure you knew it was there. Who knows? People and cultures change a lot. Who knows how those future people think? Or what their lives are like? Anyway, it thinks we're the ones who it's working for, and it's playing the recordings for us."

She looked stricken by the thought. "My God! That means it'll keep playing the things for us. Hundreds of lives. Thousands. And we don't know how to switch it off or even tell it what to do!"

He saw her horror at the prospect he found so inviting and sat back, trying to think of some way to console her. Finally he found it.

"Look, remember the stories and legends about the chambers? Some never did come back, true—but *some did!* Some became great leaders and wise men."

"And some—most—went crazy," she noted.

He sighed. "Yeah," he acknowledged under his breath. "But think about it. Those who got out *got out,* if you see what I mean. They—smart, wise, or crazy—figured out the way out. And all of 'em were more ignorant, more primitive, than we. Cowboys and miners, Indians of the old culture, people like that. People who could never have understood what they were in. If *they* could figure it out, maybe we can too. It's got to be something simple, something basic. I wish we knew more about the ones that made it. Some common factor."

She looked at him strangely but with something akin to hope in her haunted eyes. "You know, I think maybe *you* can figure it out if anybody can." It was a statement tinged with admiration, and he felt slightly embarrassed by it.

"I wish we could find the others," he said, trying to change the subject. "The more heads the better." He got up and looked both ways in the oval cavern. "Now, which way did we come in?"

"From there," she told him, pointing behind him. "But you're not thinking of going on! It'll happen again!" There was an undertone of terror, almost hysteria, in her voice at that prospect.

"We've got to," he told her. "It's the only natural thing to do. Otherwise we'll just sit here forever."

"Harry—don't leave me!" It was a plea.

"Come with me. We'll do it together."

She got up hesitantly and looked nervously down the long, seemingly endless corridor. "Harry, I'm afraid. I—I can't. I just can't!"

"Jenny, I think the ones that just sat stayed. Either stayed or went nuts from just sitting endlessly."

She went up to him, trembling slightly. On impulse he reached out to her, drew her to him, and just hugged her close for a while. The act, one of compassion, nonetheless turned him on, a fact he could scarcely conceal from her.

She didn't mind. She needed it, needed *somebody,* a fact he soon recognized, and allowed it to happen. With an inner shock and surprise he realized that he needed it too.

It went with a degree of passion and intensity neither had ever really felt before, and it bonded them, at least for that moment, closer to one another than either had ever been to another sexual partner before.

And when it was finished they just lay there, caressing, saying nothing for quite a long time. Finally she said, "I think I'm ready now, Harry. I think I can go on."

He got up slowly, then helped her to her feet. "Let's take a walk," he said gently, and they began walking, his hand in hers, down the corridor.

They were approaching another time chamber, but even as they were aware of the fact, it became impossible to break free of it. They were sucked in and enveloped by it before they could even think of backing out.

He was born, the fourth son of a fisherman, and, as such, grew up in his father's trade. There was no question of where or when he was or what he was this time. He took his religion and religious training seriously, and was proud at his bar mitzvah, proud of his Jewish heritage and sincere in his belief that he was of God's Chosen

People. Did not David, the greatest of Hebrew kings, rule in Jerusalem, and was not Israel growing under his leadership into one of the great civilizations of the world? Never was life, or destiny, or God's will, more certain to a man and his people than in that time.

And he prospered, having his own boat and making his own living by his seventeenth birthday. Although his marriage was properly arranged, there had never been any real question as to whom it would be. The beautiful Naomi, daughter of the fisherman Joshua, the son of Benjamin; he had known and loved her all his life. It was a natural marriage and a happy one, and she bore him three sons and two daughters, whom they raised and loved.

Things were hardly perfect. There always seemed to be wars and threats of wars, but somehow they never directly came to the village and the fishers. They grieved at news of Israel's losses and rejoiced and celebrated at news of ultimate victories, but it seemed, for the most part, far away and not quite connected to their lives. Some of the young men went off to wars, it was true, and some did not return, and there were occasional large masses of soldiers in and around, but they were always on their way from here to there. And Amnon, son of Jesse, lived seventy-three years and then died, and his wife of most of those years followed shortly after.

And when they had slept awhile in the corridors, they awoke once more.

"You don't look as frightened this time," Harry noted.

She smiled. "It was better this time. Much better. Civilized."

"Me, too," he responded. "Kind of dull, but interesting. And even though I lived a long time and died of old age in bed, making my life as Amnon longer by far than Harry Delaney's, I can handle it better."

"*What!*"

"I said I can handle it better."

"No, no! Who were you?"

"Amnon. A Galilean fisherman in the time of King David."

She almost leaped at him excitedly. "But I was Naomi! *Your* Naomi!"

His jaw dropped. "Well, I'll be damned!"

She grabbed him and kissed him. "This is great! We had one together!"

He hugged her, then sat back down again. "Well, I'll be damned," he repeated. So they took more than one sample in a given place. At least one male and one female. Did they, in fact, take an entire group sample? The whole tribe in the earlier case, or the whole village in the last one?

"That's *much* better!" she continued to enthuse, life coming back into her spirit. "It means we don't have to be alone anymore!"

"Perhaps. Perhaps not," he responded cautiously. "We'll have to see." But he had to agree that it was a satisfying possibility.

She hesitated a moment at his comment. "Please, Harry. Don't spoil it. Not when I have hope."

He smiled and squeezed her hand. "Okay, I won't. In fact, it seems something important was learned, but I cannot put my finger on it yet. Another piece of the puzzle." He looked at her. "You know, your moves, your gestures, even your speech, is more Naomi than Jenny."

"And yours," she responded. "So, you see, you are stuck with me. I have been your wife and the mother of your children. You know what that—" She broke off suddenly with a gasp.

"What's the matter?"

"Turn around."

He turned and was suddenly frozen. Facing them now was a very dazed-looking Theresa Sanchez. She took a couple of hesitant steps toward them, mouth open, then collapsed.

They rushed to her, but she was out cold. "It's like you the first time," Jenny told him. "We'll just have to wait for her to wake up."

He nodded and went over and sat back down. "Well, at least now there's only George to find."

4.

Terry was as happy to see them as they were to find her. "I thought we were separated forever," she said to them.

"Well, at least we know it's not a maze to get lost in," Harry noted.

Terry looked puzzled. "Look, I'm a linguist, but you'll have to speak English or Spanish, I think. Anything but that."

Harry and Jenny looked at each other. He concentrated, realizing suddenly that he had been neither speaking nor thinking totally in English since coming back for the second time. It was an easy transition to make, but not one he'd have realized on his own.

"Sorry. Didn't realize what we were doing. What did it sound like to you?" he asked Terry.

"Some form of Hebrew," she told him, coming and sitting facing the other two. "I heard you two talking as I was waking up. Funny kind of unintelligible accents laced with English words here and there. You still have something of an accent."

"A fine thing for a Delaney," he noted humorously.

"Well, I was Jewish to begin with," Jenny noted, "so it's not so radical. Still, I never knew much Hebrew or anything else before. I guess we just carried it over."

"Carried it over?"

Harry nodded and explained the connected past lives of the two of them. In the course of it he also told Terry of his suspicions as to the nature and purpose of the machine.

She nodded and took it all in. "You went further than me, but that was pretty much my line of thinking too. How many lives have you two lived so far?"

"Two each, one together," Jenny told her.

Terry sat back looking at them. "That fits. Same here. I guess it's one life per chamber." She chuckled. "Looking and listening to you two made me wonder what George would think. Things have sure changed."

"Yeah," Harry responded, for the first time wondering about George in other than compatriotic terms. He was beginning to like this bond he had with Jenny, and, thinking of George's attitudes and Jenny's past attachment to him, he felt a twinge of insecurity at the thought of the big man returning now. He tried to put it from his mind. "Tell us of your lives—if you want to."

Terry nodded. "Sure. The more information the merrier, I suppose, if we're ever to figure a way out of here." The attitude she had and the way she said it carried a subtle hint to Harry, at least, that Terry didn't really want to leave. It made him reflect that he'd thought the same thing at one point, but now he wasn't so sure. In a place that never changed, suspended in time, personal changes seemed incredibly accelerated.

Terry's own experiences had followed the pattern. The first

time she'd been born into a southeastern African matriarchy, a tribal society organized around a cult of priestesses, although in many ways the mirror was the same as with most primitive groups. The men hunted and soldiered; the women made the political and social decisions as well as supervised and worked the farms. Their world view had been strictly limited, without knowledge of any save their own dark race and little understanding of the world beyond their villages. The religion was animist and marked by many dances, festivals, and animal sacrifices, but it was, on the whole, quite civilized in its limited way. In many ways it reminded her of her own native Amerindian cultures of the Southwest. She'd been a priestess of the lower ranks, a somebody but not a big somebody, in charge of allocating the communal food supply, and she'd felt content. The only wrinkle in the whole thing was the severe lack of medical care and understanding, which caused many, if not most, of the tribe to be afflicted early with various diseases, and she had died in what she guessed to be her twenties, of infection, in a land where very few lived much beyond that.

She had awakened in the tunnel, finally analyzed her situation as much as she could, and then decided, like they had, to press on in hopes of finding the key to the place. In her second life she'd been born in a small village in the Alps in the tenth century A.D. and had become a Catholic nun in an order forever sequestered in the convent from the outside world. She described little of the routine of her very long life there, but indicated that it was terribly uncomfortable by modern standards and yet, somehow, happy and fulfilling to her.

When she'd finished, Harry considered the additional information carefully. In all three cases, he realized, the first life had been primitive, tribal, prehistoric, and yet somehow keyed to all three of them. He realized, perhaps for the first time, that the peaceful, romantic primitivism of his own first life had been through his late teen years, anyway, a romantic vision he himself had had. A deep concern for nature and the land, living in harmony and balance with it—the Rousseauan model. And if the reality hadn't quite matched the dream, well, that was the way with dreams.

Jenny had been given her sexual fantasy, and in this case the dream and reality had clashed with a vengeance, but that was always the way with dreams. Terry, an Indian, which set her apart—particularly in the white society of the modern Southwest—on her own, too brilliant to accept or live long in the reservation's primitiveness, yet unable to be fully accepted outside of it. Apart, too, from her native culture in particular, by her alleged lesbianism, which made her an outsider in modern culture and an object of hatred and scorn in her traditional one. Her first life had been a primitive matriarchy— again, not the dream, but it fit the facts.

And their second lives. Jenny and he together in a civilized pastoral setting; Terry a nun in a convent. Again it fit. And it made the leap he needed to understand the machine's strange system.

"Look, I'm analyzing all this," he told them, "and whether you like it or not, we got what our subconscious wanted at the time. It picked the stored life record to fit the individual. And that means it's not random at all." Quickly he explained to Terry his theories about how the machine recognized them as its possible builders. She nodded and listened seriously, although it was clear she didn't really like the idea that her two past lives had come from her own wishes.

"You see?" he continued. "It's not random. If it were, we'd all have had primitive, prehistoric lives the second time. History is only six thousand years old, while man is more than a million years old. The odds say that a random sample would put us ninety-nine percent of the time in prehistory. Don't you see the implications?"

Jenny just stared at him, but Terry nodded thoughtfully. "We *are* working the machine, then," she said, not really liking some of the implications of that. "It's waiting for instructions on what we want to study. Since we didn't give it any orders, it probed our minds and gave us what it *thought* we wanted."

"That's about it," he agreed. "And that means we could control the next life by conscious direction—within the limits of those pasts the machine's got stored and from what times and places."

Terry whistled. "It would be an interesting experiment. *Conscious* direction of the machine. We ought to try it. If we can do that, we might be able to figure it out completely."

Jenny groaned. "You mean *another* life?"

"Perhaps several," Terry agreed. "Don't you see that Harry's right? Even some of the primitive people of the past figured a way out. We are possibly the first people here who can take it a step further—who understand what kind of machine we are dealing with and can actually gain control of it!"

"But what sort of life would we choose?" Jenny pressed them. "Is there enough here to handle all three of us—together?"

"I dunno," Harry responded, thinking hard. "We know that it takes at least two readings from each era. It might take an entire tribe, or village, or whatever. There's really only one way to know."

"But we must agree as totally as possible on what we want," Terry cautioned. "We must all wish for the same things."

Harry sighed. "Okay, so let's see. We want the three of us to be together, at least in the same place at the same time. I, for one, want some civilization as well."

"And one where women have some freedom and mobility," Terry put in. "No offense, but I don't want to be a harem girl."

He nodded thoughtfully in agreement. "The big trouble is we don't know how comprehensive all this is. Are the gaps centuries apart, or do they take random samples from a specific age and place? Now, if *I* were putting together a project like this, I'd want random samples from as many cultures as possible at the same period in history, then advance the time frame for the new sample. That may mean dozens, perhaps hundreds, of different people and cultures for every given time. And the gaps, at least until the modern area of the Industrial Revolution, still wouldn't be more than a few centuries apart, to measure changes."

"So we need something fitting our requirements that existed for several hundred years culturally," Terry noted. "And one that fits our requirements."

He looked at both the women. "Any ideas?"

Jenny just shook her head, but Terry mulled it over and had an answer. "How about Alexandrian Egypt?" she suggested. "Sometime in the first couple of centuries A.D."

He stared at her. "Women weren't much thought of then," he noted.

She nodded. "I know. But I'm willing to take the risk just to see it."

He thought it over. "I'm willing if Jenny is. But let's be more specific if we use it. Let's assume that the machine catalogs a large sample from a specific place. If so, it might be possible to tell it not only where and when you want to be but *who*—in a rough sense."

Terry frowned. "Who?"

"Yeah. We want to be freeborns, not slaves. We want to be literate. If we're going, I'd love to get a crack at that great library."

Jenny looked at both of them quizzically. "I don't have the slightest idea what you're talking about."

"It was a great civilization," Terry told her, "mostly devoted to accumulating knowledge, which they kept in this huge library. The great minds of a great age were all there. They discovered the steam engine, and that the earth was round, and geometry, and lots more."

"How long ago did you say this was?"

"In the first centuries A.D.," she told her.

"Well, if they were so smart, how come it took us so long?"

"There was finally a revolution," Harry told her sadly. "They burned the library and destroyed the civilization. Only a fraction of the books survived, those that were copied by hand and sent elsewhere, to Greece and to Timbuktu. But it was a great, lively civilization while it lasted."

Jenny looked at the two of them. "And we'll be together?"

"If we can pull it off," Harry replied. "And remember, another big if is that the civilization's in this machine's memory banks. We don't know."

"Then it's a risk."

He nodded. "But one we have to take. Will you try it with us?"

She looked first at one, then at the other. Finally she said, "You're going anyway, aren't you?"

He squeezed her hand. "We have to."

"Then what choice have I got?"

They went in together, consistent in their wishes, but they emerged again on the far side of the next chamber in staggered form. Harry was first, then Terry, with Jenny a bit behind.

And when they awoke after their deep sleeps, they found George waiting for them.

5.

The shock of seeing George almost overcame their desire to share their experiences. They had all changed—grown older and more experienced—and it showed in their faces and manner and gestures.

George, though, seemed to have changed very little from the last time they'd seen him so very, very long ago.

"Well, one big happy family again." He beamed, his voice betraying the curious accents of his own lives as theirs now did. "I'm really glad to see you."

He took Harry's hand and shook it vigorously and then tried to kiss Jenny, but she shied away from him and looked at him as if he were a total stranger. It clearly bothered him.

But first things came first. Harry looked at Terry with some concern, because while she joined in, she seemed somehow hesitant, badly shaken. It was time to compare notes, then add George's data.

"Terry, you made it to Alexandria?"

She nodded. "I was—Hypatia."

Both Harry and Jenny gasped. "Hypatia!" he breathed. "I'll be damned. So they have some great ones in this memory bank."

She nodded. "It was a tremendous mind and will. It was an incredible honor to relive her life. She fought with all she had to save the library from the mobs, although she failed."

Both understood why she was so shaken. Hypatia, beautiful and proud, the last director of the Alexandria Library, had been cornered by a Christian mob and flayed alive. She looked at the others, knew they understood, and simply said, "You?"

"We met a few times. I was Claudius Arillius, aide to the governor-general."

She nodded. "I remember him. Intelligent but officious. Jenny?"

"I—I was Portia, your secretary at the library. I killed myself shortly after the mob overran the library."

Terry reached out and hugged Jenny. "You did what you could." She stopped suddenly. "What are we *saying*? We weren't those people. We merely relived their lives."

Harry nodded. "You find yourself getting used to it, too, huh? It becomes easier and easier to take and come out of, I think. Not that the experiences are any less intense, but somehow I have a clearer idea of my real self—old Harry here—than I did. It's Harry reliving a life rather than Harry living a new life."

They all nodded and turned to George, who seemed a little miffed that he'd been excluded up to now.

They sat down in a small circle and talked.

"I get the idea from what you folks were saying that you all wound up in the same place at the same time," George noted curiously.

Harry nodded. "And deliberately, George. We ordered it. We called it up and it was delivered."

George's mouth dropped. "Well, I'll be damned! You figured out how to work the thing! That's great! Hell, the potential for this place is limitless! It's the ultimate Disneyland and research center put together. You know, the Navajos are scared shitless of this place anyway, and it's near public land. With some finagling and a lot of politics, I bet we could own or control this thing. It's worth millions!"

They all stared at him in wonder. Finally Terry said, "George, is that all this means to you? A new money-making deal?"

"Well, ah, no, of course not. But somebody's gonna control this sooner or later and make a bundle. It might as well be us."

"First we have to figure out how to get out of here," Harry noted.

George's enthusiasm waned slightly. "Well, yeah, there's that. But hell, now that we know how to work it, it's inevitable we'll find the way out."

"*We* know," Jenny muttered sourly. "Already it's 'we.' "

George gave her an icy stare but decided not to respond. Instead he changed back to his favorite subject—himself. Which was just what Harry, at least, wanted to hear.

George followed the pattern and provided ultimate confirmation. In his first life he was in a prehistoric setting in the steppes of Russia north of the Fertile Crescent, a warrior race that sacked and looted other tribal groups throughout a wide area. He was one of those warriors, with seven wives captured in raids to serve him.

A distilled, basic George Singer fantasy.

He was in somewhat the same position in a far different time and place in the second, with the first ancient invasion of Korea by Japan. He got great delight out of telling the tales of that invasion, in which he was a samurai with the Japanese invasion forces.

In this last one he'd been a Moslem politician in Jerusalem during the siege of the Third Crusade.

All three were pretty consistent with what they knew of his mind, although Harry, for one, couldn't imagine George actually fighting or risking himself for honor or religion. Still, it hadn't been George but somebody else, somebody long dead who lived only here, in the memory banks of the Dowaii Chambers.

During the hours that passed, a great deal of data was exchanged, a great deal of speculation was made, and they searched for the key to the exit. There were also quiet periods, though, and those were the most trouble. It was plain that George was upset at Jenny's closeness to Harry. It was a combination of pride and egotism, not love or even lust. Women just didn't walk out on George. *He* walked out on *them.* And for an ugly brute like Harry Delaney, yet. In the end he resorted to making several overtures to Jenny, all of which were rebuffed, and even a few outright passes, which were put down even more strongly. This outraged him, and at one point he grabbed her angrily, only to have Harry coldly intervene. This startled George even more: Harry showing such bravery and threatening *him?* Still, the last thing he wanted was a fight over a mere girl, and he backed off, pride and ego wounded all the more.

At one point they roughly measured the distance between chambers as about a hundred and fifty meters. A long distance, and one that they could use as a sort of safety zone. After the showdown over Jenny, Harry and she kept well back in the tunnel, separating themselves from George unless it was time for a business talk.

Terry, whose contempt for George had been evident from the start, was nonetheless glad to be out of this argument. Her life as the brilliant Hypatia had affected her more than she was willing to admit, and she needed periods alone, just to think and get herself together. At one such time she was at the other end of the tunnel from Harry and Jenny—and away from George, who was sulking— just sitting and reflecting on her own feelings at this point. She loved the idea of this place now, of experiencing the lives and ages of mankind in a way no known social scientist ever could, but she realized George was right in a sense. The Dowaii Chambers needed the full range of modern science and the best minds in history, archaeology, anthropology, and related fields. Disneyland or a tool of research, George had said, and again he was right in ways he didn't really mean or understand.

If she bent to her impulses and remained inside, perhaps spending an eternity living those great and not-so-great lives stored here, then the Dowaii Chambers would be Disneyland—*her* Disneyland.

Or, in a sense, her opium. Hooked forever in vicarious experience but contributing nothing.

They *had* to get out, she knew. Get out and bring the others back. The chambers were the greatest find in the history of mankind, and deserved to be used and shared—as, perhaps, its builders had intended.

Who were they? she wondered. Some future people like Harry imagined, or, perhaps, people from some long-dead civilization or even from the stars who left this great machine either as a recording mechanism for themselves or someday to show mankind the secrets it had lost.

What if that was true? What if our very creators had placed this here, not for mankind but as some sort of evaluative tool? Was this, perhaps, God's record of mankind? Was this the record that would be read out on Judgment Day?

The spiritual questions haunted her most, for she'd been raised a devout Catholic and truly believed, and those patrons of the early Church, led by Cyril—one day to be a saint—had flayed *her* alive and stormed and burned the greatest of scientific knowledge and culture. Anti-intellectual cretins running amok with power and torturing and murdering all those who would not totally agree and support their beliefs, all in the name of God and the holy Catholic Church.

Holy Mary, Mother of God . . .

"Hello."

She looked up and saw George standing there. He squatted down beside her. "You look lonely," he said.

"Not in the way *you* mean," she responded sourly.

"No, no. I really want to help," he said sincerely. "What's the problem? If a bunch of old Indians and conquistadores can get out of here, we sure can."

"I have never doubted it," she told him. "Just go away. You wouldn't understand."

"Try me. I'm not as dense as you think."

She looked at him seriously. "You have only lost your girl friend. I have lost my god."

He stared at her a moment in amazement, and then he started to laugh. It was a laugh of true amusement, not loud or overwhelming or cruel in tone, but it was terribly cruel to her.

"Don't you laugh at me, Singer," she spat. "Get out. Just get the hell away and leave me alone!"

His face grew suddenly grim and serious. "You know what your problem really is? You need somebody to fuck your brains out. I can cure you, Terry."

He grabbed her, and she stood with him and screamed, "Get your filthy hands off me, Singer!"

"C'mon. Try it. I got the cure to both our problems." He started to force her down onto the tunnel floor, but her knee came up and caught him in the groin. He let go and almost doubled over in pain, but the respite was short-lived. It had not been a serious blow and his anger masked his pain.

She tried to get around him, to get back to reinforcements, but he blocked her, a madness in his expression now not so much from the lust he felt but from his anger at being both scorned and kicked.

"I'll show you, you bitch!"

"*Harry!*" she screamed. "*Jenny!*"

He lunged at her and she moved back, toward the chamber not so very far away. Without any kind of measurement tools they were only approximating where the effects of the chamber might begin, and George ran after and caught her somewhere in the nebulous zone.

"Damn you, Singer!" she screamed. "I wish *you* could be on the receiving end of this! I wish *you* could know what I'm feeling!"

His grip on her, so tight that it was blocking circulation, seemed to loosen, then go slack, as the chambers caught him in their grip.

Grappling with him, Terry vaguely heard the calls from Jenny and Harry in the distance, but they, and even George, seemed to fade away into nothingness. . . .

Terry Sanchez was born in southeastern Arizona in the shadows of the hills of her ancestors. She had a brother slightly older than she, but her mother died in bringing forth a third, stillborn, daughter. In a modern city, in white culture, it would have been easy to see that the woman bore tremendous marks and bruises that certainly contributed to her death, but here, with one doctor for several thousand square miles and him a very busy one not overly concerned with Indians or Mexicans, it went unnoticed. Terry was only four at the time, and her memories of her mother were quite dim, mostly a haunting vision of a gentle, suffering face full of pain.

The source of that pain was a father who, in other circumstances, might not have been a bad man at all. Ill-educated, raised on the legends of his grandfathers, with never a steady job or income, he had become hardened, bitter, and tremendously frustrated. He was an inward-looking, brooding sort of man who took to drink whenever depression hit him, which was often. He had some hopes for his son, who was intelligent and ambitious, but when Terry was only ten her brother, playing, fell into an abandoned and not very well-sealed septic tank and died before anyone could get him out.

Her father had no feeling that women could amount to anything more than sexual partners and baby-makers, so the death of his beloved son increased his bitterness and his drinking and he took it out on Terry, both in beatings when she did anything he perceived as wrong and, occasionally, sexually. This brutalization came to the attention of an aunt, her mother's sister, who lived far away but made regular trips through to see all her relatives, and the aunt knew immediately what the situation was. She pulled a number of strings with the government agents, some of whom were idealistic young people who were shocked at some of the conditions they found, and also found an ally in the Catholic priest who served the entire desert area.

Although all expected her father to react violently, he was ashamed of himself—at least, he was ashamed that it had all come out—and did nothing to block the authorities from removing Terry and placing her in a Catholic home for young Indians, mostly orphans, near Wilcox. The nuns instilled in her a sense of something and someplace better, opened up the world to her, and encouraged and developed her talent for picking up other languages. They had hopes that she would become a missionary nun, of course, and she took the first steps toward entering the order when she became eligible for some state minority scholarships to the University of Arizona. Despite protestations that one didn't exclude the other, she put off joining the order and taking final vows and went off to university life.

It was still not easy. The conservative, mostly white university staff and student body had their own prejudices, but she was willing to face them. More important were some of the younger, more radical although small organizations on campus. She found herself very good at the women's center, counseling on rape, battered women, and other such subjects, and soon found herself the darling of the minority white, upper-middle-class "radical liberals" as they were called. The anthropology department, too, found her fascinating and useful, with her gift for languages nobody else could fully master, particularly southwestern Indian tongues totally unrelated to anything in her own background. Several different life objectives emerged from this, including an eventual major project to record and preserve the oral history of the hundreds of Indian tribes of the Southwest.

It was also during this period that she discovered, or at least admitted to herself, that she preferred the company of other women to that of men. Intellectually she knew that, unlike many other women who felt that way, at least obviously, her own childhood was mostly responsible, but she accepted it with little real guilt. Men just seemed too brutish, not gentle enough, and that was that. But it added another cross to bear in ultraconservative Arizona, and she found herself pulled between more tolerant San Francisco and the place where her life's work was. The only guilt she felt was that she knew she did not have the strength to become a nun; she needed the intimacy of sex or to have it available.

So she kept herself very unobtrusive, gave up most of her radical and liberal associations—many of whose politics caused too great a conflict with her Catholicism—and contented herself with one intimate roommate, her work, and constant field trips for the great project. A project that eventually brought her to George's own project and the Dowaii Chambers.

Thus did Terry Sanchez again enter the strange mountain, and again live three other lives, and again stand in the tunnel, fending off George's advances. And thus did George know Terry Sanchez more intimately than any had ever known another, for he had lived her life through the chambers. . . .

George Singer had been born to money, but he'd been an only child, spoiled rotten by parents who would give the kid a twenty every time he just wanted a hug, and whose childhood and early teens were very lonely times, only partly due to the fact that he was tremendously fat and highly unattractive. He learned early on that girls said they wanted a friend but always went to bed with the macho types, and that the only reliable women were those you bought. It was a cynical, unhappy early time for the boy who had everything.

Finally he got sick and tired of it. He entered a series of classes to build his muscles while going on a stringent diet, a program that frustration had led him to. It took him three years, until he was twenty, to get where he wanted, but the physical change in him was enormous. Out of the ugly, flabby mass he'd always been emerged a handsome, muscular man. But it was the same man inside.

He had no trouble with women now, but he knew them for the shams they were. As he had watched them going for the muscles and the phony lines before, he knew that he'd spent all that time remaking himself into that image he'd always seen succeed—and it did.

Money was freedom and the only thing that mattered. He was lazy about scholarship, although by no means dumb, but he always found a way to buy a paper or a research project that would do, and his ability to bullshit his way convincingly through exams by giving the professors exactly what fed their pet ideas made his college career an astounding success. He spent his sports time in weight lifting and wrestling, not popular sports but ones that continued to give him the physique that everybody admired and women drooled over.

His gifted cynicism made him a top-notch con man in academia, and he exploited everything and everybody that came along. He felt no guilt, no remorse: Those were the same people who had turned their backs on him when *he* had needed *them.* He knew full well that the world ran on how you were perceived by those who counted, and money and fame greased the wheels.

He wanted the Ph.D. because *Dr.* before your name impressed the hell out of people, and he chose the social sciences because it was the easiest group of real academics to con. When his assistant put him on to the Dowaii Chambers, he knew at once that it meant not only a doctorate but tremendous fame within and, if spectacular enough, even *outside* the field. If it was really spectacular enough . . . The George Singer National Monument. Not bad, not bad. . . . And if Carl Sagan could parlay something like astronomy into big-bucks show biz, it was time somebody did it with anthropology. *The Dowaii* by George Singer, Ph.D.—a Book-of-the-Month Club Special Dividend.

He had dreams and ambitions, did George Singer. And he'd put it all together, like the producer of a play, not even using his own field for the grants but that twerp Delaney's; so Delaney would get his little project done, and Singer would get Dowaii, alone, exclusively. The dyke with the missionary spirit would be easy to handle.

And so, again, to the chambers, and so, again, into the mountain, and so, again, through three lives that confirmed his own view of the world and how it worked, people and power, and women.

But this time Terry Sanchez had lived it all with him.

Harry examined the two sleeping forms with some concern. Jenny just watched, shaking her head, a disgusted expression on her face. Finally she said, "Harry, what kind of thing would the machine *do* to them? I mean, my God, they went into the chamber during a *rape!*"

He got up and shrugged. "I don't know. We'll have to wait and see. If you'll help me, I think we ought to pick up Terry and put her over there a bit, so they don't wake up side by side, if you know what I mean."

"Getcha," Jenny agreed, and they moved her about ten feet along the tunnel, then positioned themselves between the two sleeping forms.

They waited a fairly long time, not talking much, anxiously wondering which of the two would wake up first, and were startled when both seemed to come around at the same time.

"Hmmm. . . . *That's* never happened before," Harry noted. "You take Terry and, God help me, I'll take George."

But their concerns were needless. George awoke looking puzzled and somewhat upset, but without any signs of violence or rancor. Terry looked around, then over at George, and had the most extreme look of pity on her face Jenny had ever seen. George saw her and had a little of that same look, although it was more puzzlement than anything else.

Finally Jenny couldn't stand it any longer. "What happened?" she asked Terry.

"We—I lived his life!," she managed, her voice sounding a little dry and raspy. "*I was George!*"

Harry looked at George. "You too?"

George nodded and looked over at Terry. "I—I didn't *know.* Please—you got to forgive me. At least that."

Terry looked back at him. "You know I will," she responded gently. "Maybe—just maybe—something good came out of these chambers."

Harry and Jenny looked at the two of them, and Harry shook his head slowly. "Maybe it did at that. Certainly we've all changed. You two learned a little about life and maybe grew up a bit. Passive, insecure little Jenny here has enough self-confidence and fight now to go out and conquer the world."

Jenny smiled and stared at him a bit. "But you haven't, Harry. Not really."

He chuckled slightly. "Oh, yes I have, but in a different way. Somewhere back there in the chambers I lost my self-pity. Envy died, too, back there someplace. It's a little complicated, but take my word for it." He looked around at the other three. "But now I think it's time to get the hell out of the Dowaii Chambers."

Terry and George both started and stared at him. Finally George said, "You know how?"

He nodded. "As we thought, it's damned simple. Jenny and I came here, to where you emerged, *without undergoing another life.* It was simple, really. When we heard Terry yell we came running, but I saw it getting you and stopped her and myself. You know, it was the first time I could see the process in action, and it was fascinating."

"The two of you just started shimmering, then glowing," Jenny put in. "You turned all sparkly and golden, then seemed to vanish—but the chamber was lit up for the first time."

"It's a relatively small cavity," Harry went on. "It took the two glowing forms and seemed to suspend you there, in the middle. Tiny little sparkles, rivulets of energy, coursed all around you two. I realized that, somehow, you were both totally connected to the core memory of the machine at that point and that it would set you down when finished on the other side. My only concern was the amount of time it might take, but it took only a few minutes at most. The thing cut off, you were transported to the other side, and the chamber's light died as you stood there."

"Now we had the problem of getting to you," Jenny continued. "And Harry decided we'd take an extra chance."

He nodded. "I reasoned that if we were in direct connection to the machine at that point, it was a two-way communication. It was reading what we wanted and giving it to us. So, after briefing Jenny, we stepped into the chamber with the absolute instruction that we were simply following the two 'researchers' and did not wish any more data input at this time."

"The effect was amazing," Jenny added. "We started to feel woozy, you know, like we always do, but we just kept telling it to do nothing but let us pass. And it did! We got a little dizzy as it took us up, floated us through the chamber, and deposited us on this side—but that was all!"

"So you mean we just tell it we want to go to the exit?" Terry said unbelievingly.

"Well, not quite as simple as that," Harry replied. "I suspect that those earlier escapees had an advantage over us in that they thought they were in the grips of some supernatural phenomenon. The Indians, remember, sometimes used this as a test of leadership, if we can believe the old man. They entered *expecting* a mystical experience—and they got it. And when they were finished, they said, basically, 'Thank you, spirits. I've learned what I came to learn,' and they were shown the exit. The conquistador, too, would have some kind of religious experience. Most likely he got what his forces were looking for—a life in an ancient culture, possibly the Anasazi, which would pass for Cibola in his mind. At any rate he, too, thanked his god for showing him the true way to the pagan riches, and that was good enough."

"You forget the prospector, though. He came out crazy—and with a chunk of silver," George reminded him.

Harry nodded. "I can't explain the silver. Not yet. But it's what the old boy came to get, and he got it. But I think timing is crucial. It isn't enough to want to get out, either, or we'd all have been booted a long time ago. The machine was built to serve and please, not just to exist. You've got to be in direct contact with it—in one of the chambers—when you make your wish, and you have to make it in terms the machine understands. *You have to tell it you got the information you were looking for.*"

George's mouth was open. Terry, however, seemed a little nervous. "It seems to me you're making a lot of guesses on mighty little information. Remember, there were lots of people who never came out."

"You're right on both counts," he agreed. "But I've been right so far, and our experience in getting over here confirms much of it. But it's not so amazing when you start from the viewpoint that this is, in fact, a machine, and machines are built by people—or somebody—to do things for the builders. And one of those things is provide a way to leave the machine. It sucked us in because it wanted to serve us. If it thinks it has, it'll show us the exit. I'm willing to bet my own body on it."

The other three looked at him nervously. "So who goes first and proves or disproves the theory?" George finally asked.

Harry chuckled. "It doesn't matter. Sure, I'll go first, but you'll never know, will you?"

"If you get dropped on the other side a few minutes later we'll know," George retorted. "Okay, hero. Give it a try. And if you vanish, maybe we'll get up the nerve."

They walked to the perceived safety point in the tunnel. George peered into the nebulous greenish glow ahead a bit nervously. "I wonder how many chambers there are?" he mused. "And why they built so many?" He turned back to the others. "Okay, the thing to remember when you go in is to tell it that you have learned all you came to learn or completed your research—anything like that—and that you are now ready to leave. Do it before it really grabs hold, but don't get so nervous you muff it. Clear?"

They nodded.

He took in a deep breath, let it out slowly, turned to face the chamber, and said "Here goes" under his breath. He walked forward, slowly but confidently, until he felt the machine making contact, taking hold of him.

"I have completed my research at this time and learned what I wanted to know," he said aloud, almost forcing the words as the effect really took hold. "I wish to leave now, and thank you very much."

The other three watched as the chamber came alive, glowing

and pulsating, and saw Harry's form change into that sparkling energy they'd described. The machine took the glowing, sparkling form and floated it out to the center of the chamber, but, instead of suspending it there, bathed it in a deep orange glow; then, abruptly, there was a flash, and the form that was Harry was gone. The chamber quickly lowered its volume and tone, faded, and became again just an apparent part of the green-glowing tunnel.

They stared at it for several minutes, dumbstruck. Finally Jenny said, "Well, he didn't come out the other side."

"He didn't come out at all," George said nervously. "It was as if the thing fried him—just vaporized him in some sort of laser."

"Well, there's only one way to find out," Jenny told them. "I don't really care anymore. Anything's better than spending an eternity in this place."

"No!" George almost shouted. "You'll be killed—like him!"

"So what?" she snapped, and stepped into the chamber.

5.

"There's Terry!" Jenny shouted excitedly.

"Thank God!" Harry sighed. "I was beginning to give up hope."

Terry looked around, shielding her eyes against the bright sunlight, then heard them call and came down. She was carrying a bundle—her clothes, they knew, which, like Harry's, had been scattered along the entry tunnel.

She saw them and came over to them, hugging and kissing them both.

"Hmmm. . . . Harry's got his pants back on, but not you, Jen!" She laughed.

Jenny returned the laugh a little nervously. "Mine were spread all over the outside of the mountain, remember? So far I've found a bra and one boot. I don't know *where* Harry threw the rest of them. But I have some spares in camp—if it's still there."

Harry looked down the mountainside. "You know it is. You can see it from here. Looks like the old man's cooking something."

Terry put on her clothes, sitting on a rocky outcrop. "Feels funny to be wearing them. I wonder how long we were actually in there? I'm dying to ask the old man."

"Well, I hope he's not easily shocked," Jenny laughed. "I'm going to go strolling down there any minute now."

"Let him eat his heart out," Terry laughed.

Harry grew suddenly serious. "Where's George?"

Terry froze for a moment, then said, "I don't think he's coming. He tried to stop me; that's what took me so long. He thinks we all got atomized in there—that we're all dead."

"You of all people know him better than anybody," Harry responded. "You really think he won't be coming out?"

She shook her head slowly. "He's scared to death, Harry. The fear of death, of ending his rise and dreams of glory, is tremendous in him, and he has no faith to sustain him, nothing within or without himself. The whole world revolved around George—to George, that is."

"But he went in," Harry pointed out. "He's got *some* guts."

"That's true," she acknowledged, "but remember, he was very literal in his view of the world back then. He was in control. And as long as he was in control, he'd climb a mountain or go into a cave. But here he's not in control. He's in a place where there's no way to guarantee the risk. No equipment to test. No strength. Nobody to pay or con. All alone, with nothing whatsoever to support him, he just won't be able to do it. Face it, Harry, he's trapped himself in there forever. Unless you or Jenny want to go back and get him."

The other two looked at each other. Finally Jenny said, "Poor George. Well, Harry, you said time didn't matter in there. For the first time I feel absolutely starved."

"Me, too," Harry agreed. "And perhaps you're right. I *do* plan to go back in there someday soon, now that I know exactly how to work it. Back with all sorts of sophisticated backup. I suspect, though, that we'll not be permitted anything inside except our bodies. The clothing was forcibly removed, remember; maybe it fouls up the chambers' fancy electronic systems. There's a matter-to-energy-to-matter conversion involved each trip. But I don't think I'm up to it again right now. I'd have to go through at least one more life to complete the programming of the machine and get out again."

"He trapped himself," Jenny pointed out.

"Don't we all," Terry responded.

They had been gone less than two hours, it turned out.

They waited for George for three days and nights, until, one night, the mountain vented again, putting on another of its dazzling displays.

"It's cleaning itself," Jenny said enigmatically. "Good-bye, Georgie."

The old man assured them that he would arrange for a watch in the area by him and some of his comrades. If George emerged, they would make sure he got back. They left a small cache of supplies, a note to that effect, and a flare pistol, and departed after that.

There was a sense of unreality to the world, they found. They had lived more subjective time in other times, other lands, other bodies, than in this one, and they would carry those others with them, inside them, as part of them, as long as they lived.

Harry slid behind the wheel of the pickup and started it up.

"Harry?"

"Yeah, Jenny?"

"How do we know *this* is real? I mean, if Terry and George could live each other's lives, how do we know *this* isn't a new project of the machine?"

He laughed. "We don't. And we won't—until the day after we die. Let's put it this way, though: If it's all coming out of our minds, then all three of us are gonna have tremendous lives, aren't we?"

They all laughed as he backed up the pickup, turned it around, and headed back out across the haunted desert.

The old Indian watched them go, watched the dust cloud until they and all signs of them were out of sight. He turned, tended first to the burros, then the extra supplies, and, only when satisfied, went into his small adobe hut.

It was a simple one-room enclosure, primitive in the extreme, but across the far wall was hung a stunning Navajo blanket. Slowly, lovingly, he took it down to reveal only the bare walls, and carefully folded it and put it on his humble cot.

He turned again to the wall and began to speak in a language none had heard—none would hear—not for more than a thousand years.

The wall glowed a familiar greenish alabaster.

"The imprints for the latter half of the century numbered twenty by current history have been taken," he reported in that strange, alien-sounding tongue. "Three subjects emerged and were allowed to proceed. A fourth remained inside the Recorder and has been integrated into the memory banks with his fourth translation. He will serve as a control on the other three, who are now linked to the Recorder. Through them I will select the samples for this recording. I am taking samples at a more rapid rate now, as we are so close to the Holocaust. I have cut the intervals now to just twenty years and may adjust things further as the Holocaust draws nearer. When it appears imminent, I will attempt to coordinate with my counterparts a single full-phase world recording for analysis. Current subjects have the potential to live up to the critical period. Report completed."

The wall faded back to its adobe self, and he carefully rehung the Navajo blanket.

It had been a long task, this project, and there were longer times still. And he and his brothers, who manned the Recorders and remotes all over the world, as they had for the last million years, would continue to do their duty and wait. After all that time, what was another mere thousand years?

He wished the three well. He liked them and admired particularly their ability to solve the riddle of the machine rationally, the first he had encountered who were able to understand and appreciate it. They would never see him again, of course. He had arranged that during the translation back out. They would return, of course, and hunt and puzzle, but they would never again find this particular spot—which could be moved or concealed at will—and the machine itself would arrange for slight differences to keep them from ever finding it again. A simple energy-matter conversion, and a subtle one.

He wished the task completed, of course, and understood its importance fully. But he was content to wait, wait until those who had sent him came once again to their glory, and would read his reports.

He and his brother guardians were not programmed to feel loneliness.

M. A. FOSTER

Dreams

M. A. Foster was already a veteran of the Campbell Award process in 1977, having been through it all the year before. Relatively few new writers achieve the distinction of a Campbell Award nomination; fewer still achieve it twice. As a two-time Campbell nominee, Michael Anthony Foster of Greensboro, North Carolina, thus became part of a very select company. The fact that Mike failed to win the Campbell on either occasion was anything but a disgrace. The only previous two-time loser to that date had been John Varley, perhaps the single most exciting new writer to enter the field during the seventies, so Foster joined a short and exclusive list.

"I started reading SF when I was twelve [1951]," Foster says. "Arthur C. Clarke it was, and if I have seen anything in the thirty years in between then and now, it is that SF has tended constantly toward becoming more and more closed in upon itself, its own idioms, its own interests. In some eras this has been stronger, in others weaker, but it has always moved that way. I know very well this will not please the Star Trek/Star Wars crowd, but I would like to see the SF writers challenge the readers more (God forbid, without losing them!) and also reach for a broader audience. . . . Much of what I pick up at my local bookstore displays writer after writer falling all over themselves to either copy bestsellers or write in sensawunda copied directly from the movies." Of his own approach to SF, Foster admits, "I know very well this is the hard path, but I never expected it to be easy. I started too late and with too few illusions left to believe that."

A former Air Force officer with a background in subjects as diverse as electronic warfare, intelligence, Greek, cryptanalytics, and Russian, Mike opted for the civilian life in 1976 and now sells welding supplies and drives a truck when not behind his typewriter. The Warriors of Dawn *(1975) was his first novel, followed by* The Gameplayers of Zan *(1977),* Day of the Klesh *(1979),* Waves *(1980), and* The Morphodite *(1982), all from DAW Books. More are on the way.*

He had never tried short fiction until "Entertainment," the ironic, decadent, slyly Vancian novella he produced for New Voices 4. The experience proved addictive, however, and Foster has subsequently done a number of other shorts and novelettes, which he plans to assemble into a collection to be called The Man Who Loved Owls, and Other Hallucinations. *"Dreams," his latest, is like his previous work only in being rather unlike anything he has done before.*

—G.R.R.M.

For Douglas R. Hofstadter:
"Regis Iussu Cantio Et Reliqua Canonica Arte Resolula."

—J. S. Bach, 1747

Charlier relaxed in his transporter, letting it follow the guide strips implanted in the roadway as it rolled along in open country mode. A distance marker on an overhead standard announced: PALINURI 10 K. Ten minutes to the small urban center in which he would make today's scheduled stops.

Palinuri: a small center with only six subcenters, a backward little place. Up ahead in the clear northern light of morning he could glimpse a hint of it along the horizon: an almost invisible brownish haze; a few plumes of steam tinted tangerine and rose; an insubstantial shimmer above the surrounding wood plantations.

The roadway unrolled, as level as the terrain would permit it to be, arrowing north-northwest in parallel ruled lines, one lane north and, one hundred meters to his left, the southbound lane. The run from Deorbo-Midori Center always allowed him some time to collect his thoughts before plunging into the day's business, and it was always here, somewhere near the 10 K. sign, that he felt a little shiver of anticipation. He had learned that. Palinuri was her city.

Here the roadway ran on an elevated causeway, with the contoured fields of the agricultural lands open to either side, now lying open and tattered under their winter mulching. Nobody moved out there.

Charlier looked about the cab of the transporter: the instruments, the communications panels, the parabolic windscreen enclosing the front of the transporter. Traffic was light—hardly there—and he had time to daydream. To remember.

He remembered once reading in a turgid novel that the heroine and hero had met and "were struck by the thunderbolt." The phrase had struck him then as preposterous, but now he remembered that phrase with a faint smile and a warm recollection. It was the only thing worth remembering from that story; the thunderbolt. It had been the thunderbolt indeed.

She had been there for some time, working in one of the fabrication units, in the office, controlling the communications, but she had been as invisible as the wall fixtures. There but not there. Try as he might, he could remember her being there, but he could not get a clear picture of her. But one day he had gone into the office section to settle a small problem in billing, and she had deftly cleared it up and, out of nowhere, offered him a bite of the apple she had been eating. And over the apple their eyes had met and stayed, caught in a net of time. Something had passed before their eyes, a spark of nothingness with no size and no duration, but something had struck them. He had made a slipshod bad joke about women handing men apples. She made one even worse about germs. And they finished the apple, standing, fidgeting, making small talk.

She was small and pert, very neat, a graceful pale girl with a subtle figure, black, straight hair, and a face that was animated and lively as a child's. She had large eyes that had a peculiar color shift: deep brown in shadow, muddy green in the light. Her nose was strong but narrow, which with the eyes gave her face its intensity, but the mouth was soft and indistinct, pale, colorless. He remembered imagining what an astonishing person she was, until someone else came in, and she faded back to near invisibility again.

She had told him later that she had not thought about it before. It just happened. "I think I'll offer him a bite of my apple." Just an impulse. Just like that. And from there it had all happened. Not immediately.

.   .   .

Charlier returned his attention to the road for a moment. Yes. *Now* was real, after its own fashion. And equally real had been the currents that had passed between himself and Shallon. But almost as real were the things they had wanted but could not have. They told each other about the way they imagined it could be: scenes, scenarios, fragments. Charlier thought about these too.

It was a small house they had taken, something like pictures he had seen of beach cottages: airy, fragile wooden houses set up on pilings, very plain inside, with just the bare necessities. It was not specified whether they actually lived there or were just renting it. That didn't matter. This cottage wasn't located at a beach, though, but somewhere near Palinuri, in the center of one of the wood plantations, surrounded by a dense grove of slash pines, whose shade gave the air a breathless coolness even in midsummer, and in winter a surrealistic, dramatic gloom. Here, now, it was night, in winter, and outside the rainy November dark was sighing in the pines; they sat together on the sofa in front of the small fireplace, naked, wrapped up in a single rough blanket, toasting their feet and sipping hot chocolate by the light of the fire.

They had rushed here after work, professing that this time, in this place, they would do it right, as if here and now they had the time to let things unfold in what they might imagine was their proper sequence: they would meet here, take the groceries inside, fix supper, start the fire, take separate baths, eat and talk, and then go to bed. But of course, once inside the door, things had displayed a vitality of their own. Of course not: trained by the narrow instants they had had to share, they fell upon one another like starving wolves, and clothing had begun falling like leaves before they knew where the bed was. The fading day had become night while they had lain together and devoured the promises they meant to each other, one after another, until they were exhausted of love and could think of something else. Afterward they had made the fire, heated the water, and had taken a long hot bath together, making silly faces and soaping each other. Only then could they spare time to eat. And now they sat quietly together, their bare flanks touching, his arm around her, her bare feet propped up upon his, and they did not speak of anything, for they could experience their emotion directly through the shared warmth in the rough blanket. They could not speak of it, even though it astounded them, but it was beautiful beyond anything in their lives.

The raised causeway the roadway ran on now began climbing up to the level of the elevated ramps of the cities, and he saw the first intersection marker pass overhead, framed in a placard of a venomous green color impossible to ignore: PALINURI—LOOP ACCESS 1 K. The first buildings and structures began appearing below him. Beyond the overhead a small sign on the side displayed a black square bordered in red. Comm checkpoint. Charlier punched in the proper keying for interphone transmit, on common channel, and said, "Palinuri Control, trans 11051, five containers confirmed, permit enter control zone."

An orange overhead passed, saying: OUTER LOOP XT RT. A voice whispered in his headset, tired and bored, "Go ahead, 11051. Say your exit."

"Return to exit Trunk 82, control."

"Control clear."

On the steering program panel Charlier depressed a large button with the legend BRNX: BREAK RIGHT NEXT EXIT. Then, on a smaller panel beside the directional indicators, he depressed the numeral 2. Both buttons illuminated. The transporter began slowing for the exit, the steering system drifting to the right, its sensors searching for the exit trace buried in the roadway. For a moment there was a feeling of aimless wandering, but then the sensation of control returned. He was on the exit trace. Somewhere underground within the complex of Palinuri, the Local Traffic Coordination System computer had registered Charlier's transporter and the fact that it had left Trunk 82 Northbound for the counterclockwise lane of the city outer loop and was matching its speed to fit it into that lane's traffic. Charlier glanced at the cab clock: 1030 hours; right on time. Apparently traffic was light on the loop because the adjustments to his speed were imperceptible.

Overhead another orange marker passed, saying: LOOP AH—XT LF FR CKW—XT RT FR CCW. Charlier did nothing: The steering system had already been programmed. The illuminated button was now 1. Left for the clockwise lane, right for the counterclockwise. The roadway split off from the trunk, maintained its relative level, passed over another access lane with traffic moving to his left, and slanted down to the divider, with a steeply banked turn to either side. The transporter moved to the right without hesitation, moving with the inevitability of a juggernaut, and leveled out for the merge with the loop, which proceeded without further speed adjustment, although it had slowed to the city rate. He was on the loop. An overhead marker suspended on a tubular truss framework, dark blue, informed: NX XT 3 K—NEXUS EAST/T65E. For a time there was nothing to do except let the road unroll, and so Charlier had time to remember and imagine.

At first, they had started going to lunch together. That had seemed safe, both from the situation they would be in and from the way others would see them. People ate lunch every day, and no one paid anyone any mind. They never watched other people, and as far as they knew, nobody watched them. They would go to a place, order lunch, and spend the time talking.

They talked about themselves, events of the day, problems they had at their respective jobs, things they liked and disliked. But almost immediately they sensed something was wrong. Not with them: they never interrupted, and they always laughed at each other's jokes, no matter how stale. They seemed to fit together perfectly, and they enjoyed it greatly. But they sensed that somehow they had managed to call attention to themselves. Not in a bad sense—by no means. They just noticed that people smiled at them with warmth and approval. Their observers saw something in them, in their gestures and movements, before they had become properly aware of it themselves.

When they understood this, they did not talk about it, but Charlier took Shallon's hand, and she didn't release it. They confessed, finally, to feeling like adolescents, to having a first-time sensation, and that was precisely the problem, because neither Charlier nor Shallon were adolescent, or even young people out on their first adventure, but settled adults with other, long-standing commitments behind them, fixed and set into their individual courses.

She said, "This feels as if we were on passing commuter buses, only going the same way for a little bit, in different lanes, but here, now, we've found each other. Maybe we shouldn't have looked through the windows."

Charlier answered, "But we were looking out the window. Is

it that we've been on those lines all along and just looked now? I'm going to open mine and reach across while I can. We don't get that many chances to even look off the track."

Shallon hadn't answered him, but had looked down, shyly, walked on, but her steps were a little closer to his.

They sensed from the beginning that whatever happened to them, it was not going to be enough, and so they early on started the practice of telling each other their fantasies, of situations they wanted to see someday. Someday. Someday stood a good chance of never coming.

They had come here for a picnic; it had been a sunny day in the early spring, warm in the sunlight, but in the shadows of the still-bare trees there was more than a trace of chill in the air. They walked through the long grass, which had survived the winter winds, along the course of a small river. A serpentine line of bare trees wound away from them, across the meadow, tracing the course of the river where it meandered through the flat bottoms. Behind them, across the road, was a damp and swampy wood, but on their side there were open fields from the river to the hilltops, stubble not yet turned over.

The sky was a clear, deep blue streaked with cirrus and a filmy altocumulus, a curdled buttermilk effect. The sunlight, filtering through the layers of high, thin clouds, had a soft, milky light, and gently laid upon the more distant swells a golden pollen. Nearby the river made soft, distinct gurgling noises to itself.

They spread out a blanket and carefully set out the things they had brought with them: a basket, a loaf of bread, a bottle of distilled water. Inside the basket were mostly homemade things: biscuits, cookies, thin slices of plain meat and cheese. It was very simple, but it didn't matter, for as they sat and ate, offering each other little bits to nibble on, surrounded by the soft light, they would look longingly at each other, softly smiling the bemused smiles they had come to see in each other and understanding completely that this place and this time and this day had come to exist solely to frame the emotions they shared and the intense pleasure they gave each other, something far beyond words. Charlier leaned across to kiss her, a shy, light touching, and smelled her hair, a clean scent of open country air, of rainwater. What they had was brief enough, but it was so good and so right that for these short moments they could forget everything of their old world, willingly suspending reality, fooling themselves that it was not possible to imagine any other circumstances than this, the wonder and the delight they knew in the simplest things they did together. A towhee rattled and scratched in the fallen brown leaves beside the river, and farther off the first frogs of spring bravely began humming through their first chorus.

That would have been especially nice. They had talked often of spending an afternoon in a picnic in a place like that. Once they had even actually tried to go to one of those places he had found for them, but as always something intervened and they had never managed to go.

At this recollection Charlier brought himself sharply back to reality, with the same alarmed withdrawal one would discover a sensitive tooth. To explore it further would undoubtedly release unendurable pain, and yet of all things this was the most demanding of its secrets.

Hardly a moment had passed in Palinuri, *now.* He was rounding the broad curve of the loop in the southeasternmost corner, starting to turn toward the north. To distract himself, he reached for the comm panel and punched in the broadcast radio, Channel 5, which was music. The introductory phrases of a song were already playing, setting the opening mood and the tempo, before the vocalist started. Charlier liked music and listened to it closely, taking pride in being able to pick out and identify the separate instruments, no matter how well mixed. This one had a clear, crisp sound, an air of restrained virtuosity. Electric bass; acoustic twelve-string; a lead electric guitar that had the unmistakable sweet clarity of a Gibson; acoustic piano—a Steinway; and, seemingly far off, an Oberheim played in the highest register at the lowest possible dynamic levels. The only percussion was a light brushing of small cymbals. The song went:

> Now understand me, girl, my love,
> I always wanted more, I guess;
> To have it all in all with you,
> The things we knew we'd never have.

What little time we had together,
Every minute, every second was priceless,
Vanishing as we grasped at it;
We were not waiting like the lovers
Of the older songs and tales, but
Exhausting eternity by the choices we made.
We took what little time we had
And used it up to the last little drop,
Every time getting better and better.
It had to be that way, for that part of us
Was all of us that we could ever have,
And we took it and were glad—
    It had to be that way.

The chorus, which had introduced the song, now repeated with more voices from the members of the band, with the background music a little stronger, swelling. Then the second verse:

Sometimes we could take our time, it seemed,
And for a while the rest just went away;
I know those times weren't all that long,
But we made it seem that way.
Sometimes there wasn't much at all,
Sometimes we had to hurry on, and it made
Me feel like dirt to touch you that way;
But we had so little we had to love
When we had the chance, the chance:
I hope you'll forget that when you remember,
    It had to be that way.

Now they went directly into the instrumental riff of the song, starting with the bassist and the acoustic twelve-string doing a duet, followed by the pianist and the lead guitarist. The full band came in to back up the chorus, repeated once more, and then they closed it off.

The commentator said that the song had been "The Things We'd Never Have" by Summation.

Green marker overhead; it said: NX XT—NEXUS EAST 1 K. After that one, another flashed by overhead, saying: 2D XT PARETO. The second exit was the one he wanted. Charlier punched the broadcast radio out and reached for the steering programmer, but paused, waiting for the Nexus East exit to pass. An orange overhead approached and passed, saying: XT LF—NEXUS EAST/T65E. As the exit lane began to curve away toward the untidy jumble that was the suburb called Nexus East, Charlier punched in *BLNX* and, on the numerical panel adjacent, the numeral *1*. In rapid succession the transporter passed through the merge section coming up from Nexus East, passed over a lower lane, which was the eastbound lane of Trunk 65 East, and slid over into the left exit ramp leading into Pareto, which was where he would make his first drop. As soon as the transporter had led into the turn, the steering program flickered out. Charlier now set in BRNX, followed by the infinity button on the numeric keyboard. Break right to infinity. This would put him in a tight circle about the access lanes leading into Pareto clockwise.

Once off the outer loop, with his speed dropped even further, he could look around a little. After the set of turns Pareto was hard by on his right. This part of the roadway net was low in relation to the elevations of the city. Ahead he could see the tangled strands of the Palinuri. Inside Loop and the ramps and accessways leading off and on it; a little right, more northerly, and he could see the northeast trunk, 89, flowing along the ridge top. Pareto, next to him on the right, was blocked by the backside of the industrial complex attached to it. This was an untidy long building of middling height, sheathed in large sheets of some pressed fiber material, painted and repainted several times, parts of the back surface being covered by nameboards, advertisements, and, lower down, graffiti. The nameboards were in the tetragraphic orgcode and painted on after the style of computer-read magnetic letters that were so popular: ATBC, SWLD, BISP, FMSC. The ads were highly suggestive, displaying either mustachioed rascals or long-legged girls in various states of nudity. One *was* naked, but displayed from a side angle, so actually little of the real thing could be seen. The legend above said: TAN PLAN GULFTOUR: SEE YUR GSAL REP NOW. The girl had on a green sunshade hat, so she was not entirely naked. Her body was lean and sleek and covered by an oil that made her shine. Charlier thought the girl in the ad was exceptionally pretty, but her face looked abstracted, perhaps by the intense sun of the picture. Maybe it had been hot when they took it.

The graffiti were lewd and scurrilous: FUBAR, in a crude imitation of magletter. Another announced with Gothic grandeur: FIGMO. The last O had an improbable umlaut, which made it look foreign. Another was a palindrome based on O and W, which spelled out o wow whichever way one read it, in the form of a ticktacktoe grid, followed by an immense distorted exclamation point. *Enthusiasm*, that was the word.

Between the backside of the building and the roadway was a rampant jungle of plant life that had confiscated the narrow strip available to it: ailanthus, ligustrum, sumac, box elder, rock elm, honeysuckle, wild grape. Most of it was still green, although the ailanthus leaves were beginning to drop and the sumacs were showing patches of bright scarlet here and there.

Even though low relative to the rest of the city complex, here the roadway was elevated even higher than the normal distance from the ground, because between Nexus East and Pareto there was a deep ravine, running generally west–east, opening toward the east. They had found it themselves, looking for a place to be alone. Choked with trees and vines, it was doubtful if anyone in Palinuri except the roadway maintenance crews knew it was there. They had found it, looking. . . .

The net of eyes they had cast about each other would not be stilled by laughter, or pleasant talk, or tightly clasped hands, no matter how rich this was. No. Not enough. Charlier had told her quite plainly, "We need to find a place where we can be alone. I would like that."

Shallon had looked directly at him, eyes bright, and said, in a plain, clear voice, "To have some sugar." She had, for the things she had decided she wanted, a disarming directness.

Their schedules were flexible enough that they could steal some time if they had to, and what they wanted to do could not be done during the normal course of a night meeting, for back of them were other lives and other families, a network of commitments built over the years. They both had children. To remain a secret only they knew, they would have to steal time from work and take what they could have of each other when they could.

Almost by accident they had been riding around aimlessly in one of the little passenger scooters one could check out without cost. Tied to the power net built into the roadways, its steering programmer locked within the city limits, the scooter couldn't leave the city, but at least in one they could ride around for a time and escape into the anonymity of the rest of the city traffic. Who would look at a single scooter in the midst of the flow of the roadways? So they would negotiate the labyrinth until they would mount the Outer Loop counterclockwise, set the steering program on HOLD—NO BREAK, and circle the city until they both understood that they were due back at their work.

It was there that he had kissed her the first time, surprising her. He touched Shallon's delicate, elfin chin with his fingertips, turning her face slightly, and lightly touched her mouth with his. For a second her eyebrows rose, even as her long, pale eyelids were closing. Her lips were soft and relaxed, slightly pursed but not open. Their noses fit together perfectly. The second time she opened her lips, but she was relaxed and passive; he felt her breathing through her nose on his cheek—short little puffs of warm breath, the only sign of inner arousal. They broke it and she looked away, out the windscreen, and on her slender neck Charlier could see a steady, strong pulse.

They looked for a way to stop the scooter, if but for a moment, to find a more private place; it was then that they had discovered the access points into the inspection network under the traffic ramps. These were scattered, inconspicuous exit points for which the steering systems were not programmed. One had to stop the scooter, disengage the power receptor, and roll the scooter manually onto the exit, where it would pick up the trace again. After that it was easy. The scooter, at a much lower speed, would follow a sharp and curving incline down under the roadways into a quiet and empty network under the city, hidden by the roadways, their supporting pillars, and the wild plants that filled the spaces between the roadways. And it was there, in the first of the special places they found, that within the confines of the scooter they found a way to fit their bodies together and make love. They didn't believe that it would work until, breathless, surprised, and very happy, it was over. It had worked better than they had hoped it could be. In fact, except for the circumstances, it was sweet and perfect, and became their secret.

This arrangement of how things had been, Charlier realized, was not precisely correct. He was combining several incidents into one. He had, he knew very well, edited out the frustrating failed tries they had made before it had finally worked. He also had left out something better—the infinite patience and tenderness and consideration they had shown to each other, as if they had been of one mind. He thought, *That's where we went against the grain: We were not like other people. We always gave each other room and time to make the best of it.* He had been ashamed of his bumbling performance, his innate clumsiness, and she had been ashamed of her small breasts and the stretch marks, long silvery lines left along her buttocks from carrying a child to term. But he had reassured her that her pale, slender body was indeed beautiful, and she had said to him that he was much better than he thought. And whether it had been true before or not, it became so. Forever.

Pareto. Charlier's mind had been wandering, and he realized with the steering program set on BRNX—INFINITE HOLD he could remain on a circling course about Pareto forever. By now he had circled around, across the hidden ravine and along the ridge line below the roadway running along its highest line. From here he could look sharply to the right and see, across the cab, through the window and across the dull tarred-gravel roofs of the industrial section into the residential part of Pareto: a series of apartments and little courts, none very high, rising up the slight slope of Pareto Hill to solid, square brick condominiums at the top. And down below, of course, the industrial section, a rough crescent swooping below the broad oval of the residential section.

Continuing through a series of interchanges, at last the transporter circled completely around Pareto and began the steep descent into the entry, passing under a heavy stonework underpass. Immediately beyond was a dividing fork, and on the underpass the letters PARETO. Under them was this legend: RT—ACCESS LF EXIT. Charlier depressed the button marked APPROACH, which sent out his authentication to stop here and also initiated Sequential Slowdown procedure.

Still bearing right through the divide, the transporter emerged into a warm shaft of morning sunlight and was properly now in Pareto. Charlier always thought, in this place, that he was at the bottom of a well. Here, the dim industrial docks on his left, curving in front of his path; and rising on the right, the residence. Naturally the least desirable residences were down close to the docks, immediately across the roadway, with signs of disrepair at every hand:

windows covered over with translucent sheets of plastic, shrubs struggling for their very existence, grass nonexistent, broken toys scattered about, blowing sheets of scrap paper, mud spattering the lower parts of the apartments.

The transporter shunted onto the industrial siding; it was now moving at little more than a walk. Charlier watched closely now as beside him the docks drifted slowly by, the different sections indistinguishable from each other, identifiable only by reading the orgcode tetragraph assigned to each organization and painted in letters taller than a human along the dusty walls. At last the transporter slid under a crane housing, which shut out what little of the sky remained, and stopped. The motors, idling now, could hardly be heard. On the wall opposite, the tetragraph read AFAM. His first delivery.

Along the dock were large foldaway doors marked with numbers and other symbols, many matched to overhead transport lines that curved out of them and followed the ceiling along the docks. The docks here were mostly empty—dusty and dirty places littered with traces of presences and passages gone and forgotten: scraps of waybills, broken pieces of wooden freight pallets, forgotten containers. An Indus worker passed by, walking listlessly, close to the inner wall, head down. He seemed to be muttering to himself over some issue known only to him. He wore the green coverall of the Indus worker, a slogger fixed in his own place, in his one job, in his one shift. Charlier knew very well that such workers normally made more money than the Trans workers such as himself, but they never seemed happy with their security; to the contrary, they seemed to resent and envy the mobility that Trans workers had.

Charlier opened the local comm link and identified his load to the controller. After a moment he sensed motion overhead and then a slight quivering from the transporter as the overhead crane seized and lifted the designated pallet, and then replaced it with an empty one. Charlier keyed in a series of numbers, and after another short wait an indicator lamp illuminated and then went out. The transaction had been recorded. A distant, burry voice in the headset told him he was cleared to depart AFAM. When the carrier tone dropped off and the headset went dead, Charlier set in the departure sequence command, feeling the motors deep in the bowels of the transporter surge into life and then motion as the transporter started moving. Glancing back in the mirrors and rear viewscreens, he caught sight of the warning lights of another approaching transporter moving slowly back in the shadows. He keyed in INTERRUPT and let his transporter stop to allow the other to pass. The larger transporter overtook him and passed slowly, its mass impressive, easily twice his size, with raised sections front and rear, the front housing a loadmaster and the rear a steering crew. The rear section was higher, taller; the shape of the vehicle suggested something bargelike. This one was open in the center cargo section and carried a gray metallic powder. The barge turned in and waddled over uneven pavement into the next bay along the dock. Charlier released the INTERRUPT and his transporter began moving again.

Starting down in the lowest part of the dim canyon that was Pareto Industrial, the transporter picked up speed slowly, feeling its way out into the main access lane uncertainly and then gradually building up momentum climbing up the incline past the rising blocks of the apartments and the smaller organizations on the other side. Now recognizing the trace, the transporter began accelerating powerfully.

The access into and out of Pareto was similar to most access lanes, a broad loop diving into the heart of a complex and then circling out of it again. In the case of Pareto the loop turned back over itself and rejoined the main roadways not far from where he had left them. Charlier knew the steering commands well and punched them in, one after another, and shortly was rolling on the way.

For a while he would pass exactly the same way by which he had approached Pareto, but this time he would select a different set of divides and merges and would go up on the ridge line, on Trunk 89 north, to his next stop: Caratheodory. He checked his clock; he was on time, near noon, and on the way to Caratheodory. Now, for a time, save for the steering commands, he could relax. He was in the midst of Palinuri, her city: What else could he think about?

Well, then: they became lovers. One day they spent their little hour walking through the woods and paths of one of the parklands of Palinuri, holding hands as if they had been the first man and woman ever to discover this particular form of communication, spinning fantasies that they might have lived if—if—and then finally dropping the ifs altogether and accepting the fantasies for what they were, the real love for which the caresses of their bodies were only an innocent analogue.

They stopped by a crudely made stone bridge, to which age and inattention by the park personnel had at last returned some of its natural dignity, and sat in the cold air of late autumn among the litter of the fallen leaves. *This was almost a year ago,* he thought. Wrapped up in their heavy winter coats, hers a long gray cloth coat, his a plaid cloth coat with a sheepskin collar, they sat in silence for a long time, exchanging infinitely prolonged, slow kisses, broken only by moments in which they withdrew a little, only to experience each other from a different perspective. He nuzzled her slender neck and smelled her hair, which had the clean, fresh scent of open air, of woods, of winter, and which totally intoxicated him. She pressed her face to his neck and curled against his chest like a child being comforted.

She said, with great seriousness, as they negotiated like suspicious diplomats over the ground rules they would follow, "No biting."

"Agreed." Then he added, "We can't send love letters or have pictures of each other."

She smiled lazily. "Of course not. And no talking in our sleep!"

Charlier stopped for a minute. "We have so little, in the sense that people have anything of each other; why are we doing this? Why did this happen to us?"

Shallon answered without hesitating, "Very likely there is no answer to that."

They sat quietly for a time, feeling the winter stillness of the woods around them, the pressure of time receding, of a sense that nothing else mattered. At last he said, "We fit together so well— as if long ago in an unknown age of the world we were made so."

She nodded slowly, thoughtfully. "Yes. And by accident we uncovered this. Too late to have used it like ordinary lives. Why did you come to me?"

"Because . . . you were gallant. That's the only word I know that comes close; in the sense of being full of spirit, of life. And why you to me?"

"Because you were woodsy." And she did not explain this, either.

Charlier said, "And because even then, somehow, we fit together."

Shallon said, "Yes. And no matter what, that won't change, even though we fail in this."

"We will make each other very unhappy in the end."

She said, "Yes. But sometimes very happy too."

But later he remembered writing a reminder down on a small pad he always carried with him, things he wanted to remember. It said: *"Our affair is beautiful beyond belief, but like all truly beautiful things, it is also oceanic and perilous, an outer world we have ventured into. Ruin and sadness lie all about us; our path is only a hairsbreadth wide. The everyday routines we make of our lives serve primarily to protect us from the realness of things like this."* Then he stopped for a while and later added: *"Rarity gives value. An event that can come only once. . . ."* When he told Shallon these words, she said, "I know. We will break each other's hearts beyond their ability to repair themselves." And a single small tear welled out of the inner corner of her right eye. It was the only time he ever saw her cry.

But when he saw her sometimes, when he was on his work and she on some errand of hers, he would see her face with an expression of determination and decisiveness set on it, but when she caught sight of him, it would soften into a girl-child's innocent expression of pure delight; or he'd call her through comm, at her work, and hear the brisk, crisp voice soften and brighten when she knew it was him calling. That soft mouth smiling, the flash and animation of her eyes, the engaged, committed way she went about everything—those things surrounded her with a field that left him no choices. He couldn't quite imagine how it was for her, what she perceived of him, but whatever it was, it had the same strength, and Charlier was content with that.

Whatever roots their desire had, it had an odd by-product that was immediately apparent; it was so strong that, time allowing, simply having sex together once wasn't enough. They could lay together for a few moments of happiness afterward and the desire would come back to them. They called it "going to the end of the rainbow." Here they had no guides, no mythology, no rules, although the repeated orgasms often left them both disoriented and weak when they finally did stop. But they always felt that they stopped and disengaged, not because they had reached the limits of satiety, but because their time had run out.

In a certain way this sometimes bothered Charlier, and he asked her, "Shallon, when we've gone this far, there's no directions how to act, what to do. I mean, I *know* what to do, but there's no stories about how to handle desire this strong."

She had been putting her clothes back on, but she turned and wrestled him to the seats, sat on top of him, straddled him, and whispered fiercely in his ear, "I'm going to tie you to a tree!"

"Why?"

"So you can't leave and I can have you as much as I want!"

"You can't have that much! I'll die! Mmf! Cardiac arrest!"

She stopped struggling on top of him and said, "I know. Me too."

He said, "I want to understand this, to grasp it somehow."

"You can't do it with words. Accept it; we can spend the rest of our lives figuring it out. The window opened and there we were; it could close any moment. Now, shoes."

The basic situation was not unusual: long before they met, they had made commitments to others, other lives, and now those lives were entangled with them long past unraveling. Wives, husbands, children. They knew that they joined a ghostly parade of the others who had gone before them. It was a tale as old as man—maybe older. But they also felt that however cruel and heartbreaking those lovers had had to be, to one, or another, at least they faced their desire alone, exposed in their hearts. Now . . . now they had the cruel randomness of their modern day to open them to each other, to place them squarely face to face, but for only short hours at a time, and then the patterns of work, of courses they had had to commit to long before, took over. He in Deorbo-Midori, she in Palinuri, forty kilometers apart. It might have been as far as one of the research stations on the moon or aboard the Manned Venus Orbiter. Or perhaps on one of the odd little worlds confirmed orbiting Bernard's Star. By the time you grew up and were free to choose your course, the course was already set and you were on rails, going somewhere, but with little chance of change of route or even adjustment of the pace. No sightseeing. By the time one reached twenty-five, the choosing was over. There was no place for hesitation, no place to stop and think it over. Even if they had been absolutely free, it would have been a monumental task for them to have rearranged their lives to coincide in one place. Jobs would have to be changed, different living quarters arranged. There was a waiting list for all of the above. All this after a century of labor-saving devices, and yet people worked like the builders of the pyramids just to make it from one day to the next. Charlier had seen a rude graffito in Deorbo that expressed it perfectly: WE KNOW PHAROAH, followed by a crude drawing of a pyramid and a camel. And a sadness often passed between them like telepathy, a realization that if they should have gone through all that trouble, there was more than a good chance that they would wake up and comprehend, with horror, that they had become no different from the thousands of plodding sloggers and last-leggers all around them; that the magic would have been lost for them, as it had been for all the rest. They would turn away from each other and pursue their separate fantasies, no longer made by the two of them. He chuckled to himself: one of us would slouch in front of the dumbshit television variety shows, sitcoms, or soap operas, while the other got equally stupefied in something else. The one would get worse with every year, while the other steadily, whatever it was, became ever more arcane and impenetrable. Then he added a counter to the cynicism. Shallon told him that she often stayed up late at night and listened to the radio, to songs they both loved. He recognized it as no more than the thinnest of hopes, not a lifeline.

The approach into Caratheodory was complex, but Charlier had done it so many times he could almost do it asleep, and it did not intrude in his thoughts until he was already slowing for the approach. He liked it that way: Caratheodory was a royal pain in the arse.

Caratheodory was one of the older complexes of Palinuri, laid out in the usual pattern, a crescent of industrial areas looped about an oval residential core. But while Caratheodory's resdorm section was about average size, its industrial section was in three lobes, and was much larger, and had never properly been built; it had grown, like some malignant infestation. Access ramps went everywhere, without order, and the shops were small, and the confusion was notorious. In the best of times there was a lot of waiting, of backing and filling, of wheel-spinning, manual guidance, and endless arguments. What made it worse for him in particular was that his stops here were invariably LTC shipments—"less than container," which meant manual unloading by indifferent dockhands, usually welfare cases on work-relief, who could care less. Charlier looked ahead apprehensively as the transporter slowed to a crawl as it drifted into Caratheodory itself. They looked wild today down there, swarming like ants. As likely as not they'd pick up the wrong pallet and then set it back on another transporter, to add insult to injury.

He located his stop by its orgcode tetragraph, UNFB, but as a matter of course it was hopelessly blocked, and several more were already ahead of him, so there was nothing to do but find a place out of the way to halt. With care Charlier maneuvered the transporter into a place off to the side. He knew very well this place wasn't authorized for parking or standing, but he locked down and let the motors die off to a distant rumbling idle. As he was moving the transporter, he swore constantly, minding the activity around him, which consisted of passing transporters of all sizes mixed in random order with manic crowds of Indus laborers, all afoot in the middle of the access ramps, who seemingly ignored all transporters and drays. It was unheard of, maddening.

At last stopped, he looked around idly at the confusion of the South Lobe all around him at eye level, while above him the massive pile of the Residence loomed on the right. Caratheodory resdorm was an irregular oval cluster of angular blocks oriented along a southwest-northeast axis. Out of sight, somewhere in the northern part, Shallon had her apartment, her family. He sighed once and turned the broadcast band back on. The sound that came up was that of an instrumental song, fading away, which he did not recognize. But it was replaced by another he knew, which started without announcement, slowly, to the accompaniment of a wistful acoustic piano:

> We've both—no innocents—seen what happens
> To the best of plans, of hopes, and dreams;
> They are born, they grow, they die slowly:
> I always thought we'd fare better than the rest.
> We've said the magic words, we made the magic,
> We'd last longer, stand by each other better,
> Be less inclined to bitch and nag.

Here, to the high entry of a string synthesizer, was a short passage on a bass flute, followed by the entry of the whole band, still restrained and playing at a low dynamic level.

We'll never know the answer, it's just one
Of many things we'll never have.
Against the grain, against the odds,
Against the currents of our lives
We consumed the forbidden fruit
And knew the sweetest was the one
We knew was out of reach forever.

Here, the volume and beat picked up, lent weight by more force in the electric bass, muttering and tumbling far down in the contrabass clef like summer thunder in the distance; and the other voices joined the singer.

We'd have sat in the park
Holding hands in the sun;
Sleep close in a bundle long after the fun;
We'd cook for each other, our favorite things,
Go dancing at night, exchange golden rings,
We'd write love letters, take photographs,
Kiss in public despite the smiles and the laughs—

And leave the sloggers behind
In their huts and their camps,
Ignoring the sneers of the dwarfs and the tramps,
And like Icarus ascend on wings to the sun.

At the end the song faded into a brightness of rapidly brushed cymbals, punctuated by a sudden clap from the drums. The announcer identified the song as *Against the Grain* by Crucible, but Charlier already knew the song. Still, he glanced involuntarily over his right shoulder toward Resdorm Caratheodory, a place he'd never know.

He looked back to the dock area, which was still blocked. And now the commband was playing another song. Yes. That was how they had done it. They knew that they were stealing fire from the most powerful of all gods, deities, demons and spirits, Time, and they knew from the beginning that there was no winning it; but the window opened, and in the short flashes they had together they made the contact, the essential link of the flesh, all pretense and ego role discarded, all defenses down. Others played games, practiced rituals of courtship, ignored the poor sex they finally made until their deficiencies overwhelmed them. But with he and Shallon it had been reversed: They had never had time for anything but the crucial essential, and it was always perfect; it was the rest of it they lacked and missed terribly, all the little extra things. But that was part of its perfection, too: they understood instinctively and gave their best, holding nothing back. It was characteristic of her, more than of him, but he took it up, understanding: *you will never have this chance again. This only happens once in a lifetime.* And they said to each other in the language of the heart, *this is truly how I am, and thou art beautiful.*

In the short moments they had, and sometimes between, they would sit close together, holding each other, and tell each other dreams they would like to share, to give each other—lives they would like to inhabit. Sometimes they were just simple scenes, quick flashes of a desirable scene or condition, like eating together by candlelight. Other times, when they had time, they would work together to build images of complicated interweaving, probably impossible of attainment even if they could have had each other fully. But they made no move to attempt to realize these dreams, sensing the immense and powerful ruin all around them if they stirred a millimeter from the tight course they had open. Violence and death were possible; one read about similar incidents daily.

And if they could have succeeded? Nothing would be changed of the world around them—Deorbo-Midori, Palinuri, and the other satellite towns around Deorbo: Cerro Gordo, Semora, Cesaro, Cauchy. He would still be Trans; and Shallon, Admin, or so they saw it thus. They would work all day, "knowing Pharaoh," as the graffito put it, meeting between shifts in some vile, cramped apartment. They might even see less of each other than they did now.

And listening to the commband, the songs . . . All the songs were about love and desire, but in fact the listeners and the singers alike understood that they lived in a world in which love, for all practical purposes, was a silly, impractical thing that did not in fact exist. Those who reached for it were something more extreme than mere fools and were actively dangerous.

The thought, for a giddy moment, terrified him with an insane vertigo: What if everyone . . . ? If they reached and took it? He saw it dually: an ideal world, probably a lot poorer, and then the second level, a world of unimaginable violence, for love was only one of an entire family of releases, letting-gos.

The moment passed, and he remembered it as it had been: once the dam was breached, then came the flood. They hadn't had, he and Shallon, just one secret place to meet, but six or seven, all strategically located so they could arrange to meet at one no matter what the circumstances. There were differences to each of their places. One was atop a hill, in plain sight from above, but invisible from any conceivable position below, owing to the steepness of the lower part of the hill. Another was behind a ruined shack, hidden under overhanging trees and vines. One other was an old path, or a section of one, which now led nowhere, completely covered by dense forest growth. They called this one the Tunnel. Another was a vast open field near some warehouses, but completely deserted after dark. One was behind an illegal dumping ground. They also had two patches of dense woods that one could only reach by walking.

They always looked over each prospective place carefully, searching for traces of other users, passersby, idle and otherwise, for they did not wish to be surprised. In most they found some faint signs that others used the places for the same reasons they did, but not often, and no one saw or bothered them.

Images flashed across his mind, images of the impossible things they had done with the little time they had had. The long rainy afternoon on the early spring on top of the hill, when a bird had perched nearby and chirped irritably at them, until Shallon asked what he thought the bird was saying, because he had been so insistent about it, and he had told her the bird was telling them that one, it was too early for mating season, and two, they were taking too long about it.

Or in the tunnel, in the summer, breathless with sullen heat, when she had smiled her mischievous smile and ventured that there were four conditions of life people fell into.

Charlier propped his head up on one arm and asked, "What are those four? And only four?"

She looked off, pleased with herself. "Only four. Don't Want Any, Want Some, Want Some More, and Had Too Much."

He leaned forward, nuzzled under her fragrant dark hair, and kissed her ears, delicate and fragile little shells hidden under her hair. "Which are you, now?"

She took a deep breath and turned to him, directly, and kissed him hard on the mouth. "Want some more." Then she added, "Now," and had wriggled her sleek, trim body over his.

That had been their biggest problem: they always seemed to be in the Want Some More mode. It never ended, and in everything that they managed to do together, they never reached Had Too Much. Never. Even exhausted, extended beyond what they had thought were the limits of human endurance, they never reached the bottom of their desire. They never had parted because they had finished, but because they had to return to the real world for one or another reason.

This was the experience that frightened them. They recognized something in each other and gave completely, withholding nothing, absolutely nothing, and they saw that however far they went, how many betweens and ends of rainbows they crossed, there was something yet to be in them—if nothing new, then only more of what they desired so much. They spoke of this often in the quiet moments between, and they understood that the outer rituals and games of the real world, the customs, the routines, were nothing in themselves but all worked together as an interlaced woven wall to prevent people from entering into this kind of relationship. The main aim of the whole of society, through time, was to deflect the intense hungers that, released, given in love, made the superhuman possible.

He and Shallon had, on an inkling caught in a sudden net of sparkling eyes, opened the door and stepped outside together. And no thundering brassy voice had brayed down at them, the earth hadn't opened and swallowed them up, and they did not run amok, commit crimes; neither did they perform bizarre acts of lewd gratification, go blind, or grow hair on the palms of their hands. They did not become feebleminded, although sometimes their bodies were weak. Something in them had far outstripped the mere body. No: if there had been a flaw in it, their affair, it was that it had been too sweet, too rich, too unearthly. He understood. What had happened to them had been too perfect, but it was so rare and aleatory that no imaginable society could have been built upon its foundation. He had a semivisual flash of how it was: The Universe was founded upon the stability in space of stable orbits, ellipses bounded by the limits of perfect circularity and at the extreme eccentricity, by the parabola, limits that were never reached in fact. While he and Shallon had been a pair of searing hyperbolas in which Type O blue giant stars, radiating in the ultraviolet, had swung past each other, their surfaces touching. A fine example. And continued: if hyperbolic, then after the touch, the kiss, then the long fall back into the night and the cold, the inevitable end, cooling to solitary cinders.

Charlier, still waiting for a place, had been daydreaming, and now the commband brought him back to one level closer to reality. Now the radio was playing an instrumental piece, soft and jazzlike, mellow, convoluted, and intricate, a blue mood but a baroque finish, but what caught his attention about the song was that now and again the interlacing members of the band would let the multiplex harmonies fall away, and a pure melody, stripped of all ornamental and stylistic fretwork, would rise in quiet confidence and soar over Time:*

It was wistful and light, but at the same time bare and child-stark, refusing to cry. It fit her well.

The song faded out, rather than ending on a definite point; the announcer reported that the last selection had been "Sherry's Theme" from *The Pines,* an arty movie that was currently going around in the larger cities, such as Deorbo-Midori, but not in places like Palinuri. She would have never seen the movie and would not recognize the song if she heard it; nevertheless it reminded Charlier of her powerfully. This version had been the same as in the sound track and was done by a group calling itself Athanor, a name with alchemical associations.

A movie! Who could afford to go to the cinema? Who had time? Charlier shook his head, as if clearing cobwebs away, and as he did so, he noticed that in the jumble down by UNFB, an agile figure was dodging among the lumbering transports, drays and hand carts, hand trucks and freight floats, somehow escaping dismemberment, nimbly scuttling like a roach through the milling traffic, waving, shouting (Charlier could not hear his words but could see the mouth working), waving his hands. He turned the radio off and lowered the cab vent beside him.

Immediately he was assaulted by an avalanche of noise, compounded of rhythmic, mindless stamping, a grinding, an intermittent roaring, as the release of steam, hisses, and the blurry hootings of whistles, and multitudes of impatient humans braying commands and exhortations at the top of their lungs. There was also, at irregular intervals, a sound of some powerful grinding impact, always followed by a multiplex bellowing, as if several people had just been maimed in some horrible mechanical accident. But it was no accident, for shortly after each stroke, it would occur again. Under all these sounds ran the soft, insistent soft hum-roar from the roadways.

The scurrying figure drew nearer, becoming a young man daubed with streaks and spots of grease and other substances, wearing a ragged leather protective coverall much spotted, torn, and punctured. He was skinny, almost emaciated, with light hair, which, when clean, would probably be blond, but he was agile and moved among the obstacles with suave calculation, simultaneously making lewd and vulgar hand signs, shouting insults punctuated with spittle, and progressing forward with effortless ease, headed for Charlier's transporter.

Nearing the vehicle, the figure shouted up, "You got the half rounds for Unifab?"

Charlier leaned out and shouted back, over the mechanical din, "Yes!"

"Well, get your ass in gear and follow me—I gotta place f'you!

You gotta go in manual, cattywaumpus at a bad angle, too, but it can't be helped! We're waiting for all that crap!"

Charlier waved that he understood and began engaging the drive, slowly edging out into the confusion of the accessway, moving forward in a series of slow hesitations, creeping lest he inadvertently run over one or more of the other scurriers in the confusion. In the rearview mirrors and viewscreens he glimpsed another transporter suddenly braking, the entire fuselage of the machine rocking back and forth as its driver pumped the brakes to get it stopped. He turned away and looked ahead, which was no less terrifying. Farther ahead, under the shadow of the rain shed covering the docks, his unkempt guide was still dodging and weaving, making murderous gestures to all about him, and miraculously a path opened up before him, marginally wide enough for the transporter. Charlier eased the transporter into that space.

The guide scuttled up onto the dock, spiderlike, and stood level with the cockpit, shouting across the intervening space as if it were a kilometer instead of about a meter, "Come on, come on!"

Charlier shouted back, "How long? It's half a container!"

"Which one?"

"Second! Your stuff's on top!"

"Just sit still! We'll get it!" The guide now set off at a trot down the dock, which was almost as confused and crowded as the accessway, filled with messengers, porters, robot handling machines being guided with little or no regard to possible collisions, their dented and scarred metal flanks bearing eloquent testimony to many such events in the past, thrusting blindly through metal swinging doors bearing the legend STOP BEFORE ENTERING.

In a moment the guide returned, accompanied by a hydraulic lifter-grabber crawling on cleated rubber bladders, and an electric skidder, the operator standing on a tiny raised dais at the rear. With the two machines was also a disorderly assortment of ragged tramps who made the guide look like a member of Staff by comparison. These last the guide yelled at, cursed, ordered—incomprehensibly to Charlier—waving his arms, jumping up and down for emphasis, pointing at the transporter. But whatever the mode of the instructions, the crew scrambled onto the transporter and vanished out of Charlier's line of sight. The loader drew close alongside, emitting flatulent clouds of partially combusted Methyl Acetylene. Wrinkling his nose in distaste, Charlier could feel through the body of his machine as they went to work, unloading the half-pallet. The guide now stood back and glowered in hostility impersonally at all, favoring unloading crew, drivers, and random passersby with the same contemptuous leer.

Charlier shouted to him, "How do they receive? I get nothing but static on the channel marker for UNFB!"

"Sign it by hand! Dam' radio link's busted or *ruirnt.* Onliest way we got! Here! Gimme a hand receipt!"

Charlier made one up from blank forms and the transport order list and handed it across the gap, where the guide signed it with an illegible flourish and then thrust it back. After a moment the sensation of odd motions from the transporter body faded, and there were no more bumps. The guide, still grimacing and scowling, waved Charlier off, turning and vanishing back into the bowels of the building, ignoring an enormous freight float that threatened to cut his feet off at the ankles but somehow missed. Charlier had a glimpse inside the building, of a vista of steel pillars stained brown atop the paint and a brownish, smoky atmosphere illuminated by an oily yellow light punctuated by the stabbing violet glare of an arc welder somewhere offstage. A satanic, hellish view. Charlier set his warning signals and flashers, knowing they would probably be ignored, and reversed back onto the accessway. Backing always gave him a queasy feeling; the roadways had been designed and built under the Laws of Motion in vogue several decades back, one statement of which ran: "No roadway shall have a break in flow. . . ." A transporter with limited rear visibility on such a roadway . . . However, he succeeded in getting backed out into the accessway and got moving forward again. It was like this every day he worked Palinuri and had to go into Caratheodory. And he had four more stops in this suburb. Charlier knew he would fall behind; there was no cure for it.

Caratheodory was behind him now; he was rolling now to the south of the city, across town instead of around it, headed for the largest complex within Palinuri, Monin/Yaglom, an overgrown but internally neat complex formed of two older areas that had grown together, squeezing the road network out to pass around its outer edges.

Rolling down the elevated high ramp of Trunk 89 South toward

City's Central Loop, Charlier could again overlook the curve of Pareto, now below his elevation and to his left. Now it was past noon, and the clear skies of the earlier morning had given way to a pale, high overcast, whose center seemed to be far off in the west, now mostly filmy streaks and streamers of cirrus, but close to the horizon there was something more solid. The light was still clear in the city, but there was now a tincture to it, as if some impalpable substance had been injected into it, giving an old-gold, mellow coloration to everything, investing even the shabby backside of Pareto with a forlorn glamour.

Pareto. That was where she had worked. They could arrange their meetings easily; he would stop at a rest station passing through Nexus East and call ahead through the public comm station there. Of old, he would work Caratheodory first and then Pareto, where he would arrive in time for the lunch hour. She wasn't missed, and he could always make the time up one way or another. And then they would go looking for one of their places, as determined by weather, their moods, or circumstances. One was always open, somewhere under the ramps. Or atop the hill.

No more of that. Nothing remained the same for long, and the odd currents that had opened up a channel between them began to flicker and fail.

It had started with a change of office bosses in her place. The pay had dropped, and the office workers had had their hours sharply controlled. No more long lunches. They lived with this; by this time they had become intimate enough that they felt they could do without ceremony, and so they continued as before. But if it was as sweet, it was a lot shorter, and they lost the parts they valued most: the soft times *between*, and the end of the rainbow, as they called it.

Then his schedule began intensifying, and he started arriving at her place too early or too late, and they began missing days that before they had nearly filled with each other. The few times now they could meet were painful, not because they loved each other less, but because they had learned what they had become to each other, and then the opportunity to realize it was fading.

So far they had kept it secret; now they saw the price to continue as before steadily rising, and so they saw, on the one hand, that if they continued, they would fade, and if they reached for what they thought they could achieve together, they would rupture the delicate web they had built. Other people were depending on them. They saw ahead of them no acceptable choice.

And then it was revealed that the situation at Shallon's organization had deteriorated so far that they were cutting the Admin workers and putting them out on the work floor. Another cut in pay. Shallon had her own family to support and left her old job, signing up within the week as an Indus worker at a processory in Navier, a small, new complex, where the Indus workers were paid the highest rate in Palinuri. Navier was just west of Monin/Yaglom. But although everything went well for her there, the Indus workers were watched closely, and she couldn't leave the building.

On one of their explorations around Palinuri, when they had looked for a place they might have had together, they had found an area close within the City Center Complex, which had been missed somehow by all the roadways and ramps. And with high ramps on all sides of it, sheltered by enormous old rock elms, whose tiny leaves fluttered so beautifully in the winds and breezes of autumn, it had miraculously been left alone. This was two streets of the old style, joined at a right angle. The buildings were large old period houses, now converted to apartments, and a half-block of old-style commercial buildings. These were the ones that caught their eye.

One of the commercial buildings was on the corner and was a brick two-story, with a small restaurant on the first floor and apartments above. Nearby was a three-story building, narrower, which also had apartments above, but which on the street floor contained a secondhand furniture store. Between them was a narrow, cramped little beer hall. All of the establishments were still operating.

In this neighborhood they spent many hours, sometimes eating, sometimes browsing in the old secondhand store, and sometimes sitting in the bar as long as they could, holding hands. Once they had heard that one of the apartments above the restaurant was open to be let out, and they had arranged to be taken on a tour of it, representing themselves as a Mr. and Mrs. Beasley.

Outside, the building was substantial rough-finish brick, topped with a red tile roof. The windows of the apartment were real glass, set in narrow frames, alternating in pairs and singles. On the long side there was a narrow balcony inset in the wall, bordered by a large stucco planter painted the same color as the roof tiles. This joined the rest of the house through a pair of French doors.

Inside, the floors were red tile, which gave a hard echo to all sounds as they had stood inside and talked aimlessly with the representative from Housing Services. The windows had small panes in their upper sections, but the lower sashes were of one large piece; the glass was wavy and ripply, subtly distorting the outside world into an impressionistic montage of shapes and textures. Their footsteps had clattered in the empty halls of the apartment.

In the end they had made up an excuse not to take it, although there was no great demand for older places like this one, and they and the agent had parted company. But that one tour had provided them with material for numerous fantasies. That was precisely why they had taken it.

Back at one of their hiding places, under the sky, Shallon had asked, out of nowhere, about the apartment. She often did this. They had so much to say and so little time to say it in. Things came out in bursts. One day she had demanded that he tell her his life story, while they were *between,* and she had listened, too—the first time in his life he could recall anyone listening to anything he had to say. He hadn't abused the opportunity, but had kept it spare and essential. And Shallon, for some internal reason only she knew, had seemed deeply pleased to hear it, however insignificant it had all been. Wasn't it insignificant? Charlier had had that told to him constantly, in words and deeds. But it seemed priceless to her. He looked back on this scene often, as evidence of something powerful at work on them, and there had been a light side of it, too, for they had not redressed, but sat in the cool woods, buck naked, yakking away the afternoon.

She asked, "What would be the best time of day in there?"

He had answered, "Sunday afternoon. No working. We'd sleep late, have a little bite, and spend the rest of the morning in a hot tub. . . ."

"Together! A bubble bath!"

"Yes. And we'd shower the suds off and go back to bed."

"Yes. All afternoon."

Charlier said, "And of course we'd take a little nap or two in the meantimes."

She said, "We'd have little curtains along the lower parts of the windows, but the light would come in through the tops, and some of the time we could just lie there and watch the light change. . . ."

"You like that, now, do you?"

"You showed me and I learned to like it, but best when you have your lover to watch it change with you."

Of course they pictured themselves together in the apartment, entangled in love, but also simply being; they did not neglect the functional parts of their lives, simply because they Wanted Some More. There were scenes of leaving for work, returning in the cool blue dusks of a rainy winter evening, eating together in the tiny kitchen, planting ornamental shrubs in the porch box, negotiating the narrow stairwell, getting old pieces and odd ends of furniture, washing the windows . . . A complete life, finished in every detail, even including the child Shallon had suggested that they have together. *That* had been in the real world, not in the dreams, and Charlier had thought long on it before answering her.

She told him once, "Sometimes I wake up in the middle of the night, I am so happy, and I just lay there and think about it."

"Then what happens?"

"I feel so good I go back to sleep, fool!"

The high overcast Charlier had noticed earlier, far off to the west, had now spread, tenuous, filmy, to cover most of the sky. Only a shrinking patch of clear was left, mostly far off in the southeast. And the sun was not in that part of the sky, clear though it was, and the paled daylight filtering through the high clouds made an odd contrast to the luminous patch of blue, unlit, hurrying off to the east. The run from Caratheodory to Monin/Yaglom was a long one, angling off to the southeast to pass around that complex, and he had plenty of time to watch that patch of sky now as it shrank.

Charlier had left the commband music on but had been ignoring it, remembering, imagining. Now, with his attention back in the real world, he heard another song beginning, which caught his attention.

Before us opened up the gulf,
Down below we saw no bottom;

Above us we saw no prison in the sky,
And all we had to do was fly.

It's hard to tell the truth—
The words we told each other
Will never speak again:
None in whispers soft as feathers,
None in cries like horses manes
Streaming in the bitter prairie winds—
Maybe something we'd tell our friends we did
Once, and then turn away, out the window,
To hide the burning in our eyes.

Before us opened up the gulf,
Down below we saw no bottom;
Above us we saw no prison in the sky,
And all we had to do was fly.

It's hard to tell the truth
About the desire we reached for;
We might pass through, and then face
What we'd fear to tell our friends—
The great secret that we found,
Unknown as well to us before.
The sweetest fantasy we lived together
Was something we hadn't known before.

Before us opened up the gulf,
Down below we saw no bottom;
Above us we saw no prison in the sky,
And all we had to do was fly.

It's hard to tell the truth—
We go our own ways now, losing
All the places where we used to go;
But ours was not a love that lost itself,
Or one that turned to spiteful hate,
But of the other way—too much:
We feared the love we found that opened
All the doors, tore away the walls,
And before us opened up the gulf,
Down below we saw no bottom;
Above we saw no prison in the sky,
And all we had to do was fly.

Above us we saw no prison in the sky,
And all we had to do was fly.

The commentator identified the song as *Icarus* by Partington Ridge. Charlier nodded to himself. Yes. That too.

And where can we go from here? Now he was close in to Monin/Yaglom, circling the complex; he could see it on his own level out to the right. What he could see of the complex was mostly its rooftops—flat abstractions of empty spaces of gravel-covered tar, interrupted at random intervals by enigmatic functional structures: fluted frameless water towers; exclamatory vent pipes, many emitting thin plumes of smoke or steam, which vanished quickly in the afternoon airs. There were also erect, hornlike flaring tubes aimed one way or another, and intricate housings of sheet metal with tangles of colored piping leading from them. Louvered evaporation tanks. Charlier saw no answers among the secret roof structures of Monin, the side he faced.

And he looked again and thought, *From this angle there's nothing there that would give one a hint what year, what age, he was in. It could be, judging by that, any year. There was no reference, no marker: 1960 or 1990. 1948, or 1984. And it was like that everywhere, if you could get the right angle on it. The stuff that looked modern was just window dressing that would be tomorrow's curio. That is timeless, over there in Monin. So are we. And so, equally, is any answer we might seek for. It has never been solved. We could fly* (and here he thought of the marvelous clean curve of her eyelid, like a soaring bird's wing, when they lay close together), *but we cannot encompass our goal. Better that we accept it for the loving-kindness that it was. Was?*

Charlier rounded Monin/Yaglom and began figuring out his approach sequence. Unlike the other complexes, this one was easy to move around in, once inside, but difficult to approach, owing to its closeness to several major junction points, with ramps going off in every direction. He relaxed now. This would be an easy sequence of stops, his last for the day.

Charlier signed off the last manifest and got under way, turning on the nav chart and setting it to display South Palinuri in detail, so he could thread his way through the tangle of interchanges and ramps. And he thought, looking at the clock to be sure, that he could cross T82 and take a quick loop through Navier; it was just across the roadway, and just by chance he could catch her outside EQMC, the new place she was working at, waiting for the Caratheodory shuttle. Perhaps, if they were very discreet about it, he could offer her a ride. He could divert. He had time.

He cut across under the trunk line and slid into the approaches for Navier, just as if he had one last delivery there. No one would observe another transporter coming in late in the afternoon.

He even had a place he could stop and wait for her, where he could see her coming out. He looked at the clock again. Yes. Perfect timing. Charlier circled around EQMC and pulled up to the waiting pad and stopped the transporter, letting its engines die off to an idle. Now he saw the first of the day-shift workers coming out of the plant, anonymous stick figures off in the distance. He looked over each one carefully, waiting to see Shallon, but not sure he could identify her at this distance. He was sure he could, but he'd never seen her this far away before.

A large number of people came out, some hurrying, some sauntering along as if all time were theirs. None so far was she. He thought that perhaps he had missed her or that she was held up inside. But no, there she was. There was no mistaking her walk or the quick, clean manner of it. Not hurried but not idling either. He watched her walk toward him, trying to see her face, make out some detail of her, but he couldn't; the distance was just too far. Nevertheless there was no doubt. It was she. Yes. She looked up and saw his transporter waiting in the idle pad, and she waved. He still couldn't make out her face clearly. She turned off and disappeared behind some outbuildings, the way the walkway ran.

He ran the engine up and started forward, hoping to catch her by the shuttle stops. As he moved the transporter forward he caught quick glimpses of her walking along the walkway behind the service buildings, now hidden, now visible. Then she disappeared as he passed behind an intervening building, BBPC. After that one he could pass right by her.

Coming around the corner of BBPC, Charlier saw her closer, going to a line of temporary booths, where she took some papers and turned and began handing them out to people coming out of the plant. The wind had come up a little, and as she moved it played with her hair. She looked around once, saw Charlier's transporter, and, glancing off away from him, shook her head briefly. He understood their old safe signal. *No. I can't.* He nodded to her, saw that she saw him, and allowed the transporter to began acceleration. There was nothing they could do now.

But even there, he felt, mixed with the disappointment he knew well now, a strong surge of the same warmth he had felt when they had first met, an envyless admiration for her strong vitality, her drive, her life. *There's a woman with more balls than most men, driving on, never stopping, taking the good and the bad as it came, and at the same time no woman he had known in his life could glow with the radiance she had when they had been together. Passionate and full of life in all things.* He let the transporter roll on. He did not look back.

He eased the transporter up onto the access loop, now attentive to the roadways, inserting commands into the steering system one after another, setting in the departure sequence. The first shift was ending across Palinuri, now, and traffic was starting to pick up. Many other transporters similar to his, some larger, some smaller, were also winding up their daily schedules and were setting out for their home depots. An industrial-gas transporter eased heavily into the line ahead of him, its load of mixed steel cylinders and cryogenic tankards chained to the naked side frames and the cleated steel decking, laboring under its load.

Charlier glanced at the interphone once but shook his head. Even if she had been at home, he could not call her there. Now that was gone too.

As he rolled up onto Trunk 82 South, an immense space opened up before him, and far off there, a little west of south, he could see the arrowlike shape of an SST climbing out of the airport at Midori. And set opposite that image of the most modern of times, he remembered growing up near that airport forty years earlier; Midori had been a small commercial crossroads then, of no great distinction. Perhaps even a bit backward. Not anymore.

He laughed a little, thinking that all the technical problems had been solved, but the real things that humans grappled with in the dark of the night had not even been touched; indeed, many of the more painful ones had actually regressed. As his friend, Esteban, a notorious womanizer, often said, "Ah, Charlie, you can get all you want now, but there's no light in their eyes anymore." Charlier had said that he understood because, even in the incredibly diverse pornography that filled every magazine rack, the faces were blank and lifeless, devoid of emotion, drained of commitment and meaning. The pictures were worthless because they did not reveal that which the viewers wanted most to see.

The transporter, now in a line of other transporters, omnibuses, shuttles, and drays, accelerated up to open-country mode. He depressed the exit signal and watched the overhead flash by: DEORBO 40 K.

He thought, *We knew it was the beginning of the end when we went one day to our favorite place, the one we liked best, the one where the bird had fussed at us for being out of season. Someone had chained it off and was using it as a borrow pit. Lost.* They had alternatives, but it was as if there were some pressure on them, and the other places suddenly weren't quite as safe. They used the Tunnel, the place with the overhanging trees, but that, too, went: one day when they went there, the site was bare ground, scraped clean, and a deep concrete footing was being poured into the ground. Gone, the soft shade, cool even in the heat of summer. Gone, the birds and the squirrels. And it had been like that with every one of their places, and they had no other. Their last, "The High Castle," had been invaded by tramps and drunks.

As their time shrank and their places vanished one by one, their emotion became more intense; the little they could salvage grew exponentially brighter, more burning. They clasped one another with the strength of drowning men.

Their last meeting they had spent most of the time lying close together, dressed, talking slowly, choosing their words, as if every one was precious beyond price. Shallon had been quiet for a long time, looking off into the distance with her candid, clear eyes. He remembered that he thought then, *All the rest of us, our eyes are clouded, frosted, shuttered, painted walls, stage sets. But hers are the clear windows of an animal or a child. There has never been a moment when they were covered or concealed. The light was there.*

She said, "I still want to tie you to a tree, since we can't run away together."

"I still wish you had been mine from the beginning."

"I also—just so. This should have been always forever. But it wasn't. And I know—or a sensible part of me knows—that to grasp it, to make it really ours, the price in the real world would be *everything*. It doesn't lessen anything to understand we can't pay it."

He said, "To let be free—that's the ultimate proof of it."

Shallon sighed. "That's hard too."

He said, "You always read stories about people who went ahead and took it, no matter what. . . ."

"And after all the ruin and unhappiness they caused all around them, what did they have? It escaped them in the end."

"And, Shallon, they wound up no differently. But with us, I thought we were closer to winning it. I will always."

She turned more toward him and cupped his face in her delicate pale hands, cool and dry. "So did I. But that closeness would betray us, and we always knew it. But don't push me too hard: I never did reach the Had Too Much mode."

"Never came close. I never knew you enough. But we live in a time that doesn't count for much the secret we found."

"Did it ever, Char'? Did it ever? And those famous lovers of song and legend—did anyone ever write about those who saw more, who saw farther and turned back?"

"No. There was no drama in it."

"And they were wrong there too."

He looked at her for a long time. "Yes, they were."

She twined a wandering finger in a lock of his hair, a habit she often indulged in their quieter moments, gently twirling it. "I know I've never known anything like what we've shared."

He added, "Nor anything so bright. I remember in the beginning that you worried I would break your heart—or you mine—but we did not. It was true. Even less than we actually had would be a fine life, even if it had to be no more than a memory; they are not entirely worthless." He took her hand and opened it up and kissed her palm. It was a special gesture they had, sometimes imagining that they had invented it themselves.

She brushed his face with her soft mouth. "Even less than that: a piece so small you couldn't find it, but it was always there."

"We never lost it."

"Never will."

. . .

The Beach House, the picnic, the second-floor walkup in the old town; many others that he would often remember, along with the Tunnel, the High Castle, Behind the Barn, and the Woods. The places they had, the places they never had. Cramped and anxious moments in the scooter, long talks in the shabby anonymity of empty places marked EAT. They had never slept together in a real bed, although they had stolen a few short catnaps *between*. This they fantasized about most of all.

The overcast had spread and closed off the last hole far off on the southeast, and now the light was failing fast, and ahead, in the lanes of Trunk 82, the vehicle lights were coming on, turning the abstract straight parallel lines of the roadways ahead into flowing lines of fire, red dead ahead, white light to the left, living streams that never ended.

Yes. We had our moment of madness, and we built an internal world inhabited by two, part-time, better than the real one. But the real one finished, just like it always does. We never had the chance to make it work . . . but if we had, clean, no-risk, we wouldn't have tried so hard, and been so good to each other.

Perhaps they should have known better. But in the weak daylight still left, when Charlier looked across the middle divider between the lanes, into the faces of the other lane—those set, grim masks, imprisoned in *their* fantasies, their private worlds of revenge and envy and resentment, grimacing, talking to themselves, rehearsing heated righteous scenes—he leaned back in the contour chair of the transporter and smiled. Yes. There was a dull pain in his chest, somewhere near the heart, and also in no particular place, and an ache that was a lack, an absence, a silence; but there was something else there, also, something shining and winged and mythologically beautiful, something that had dared to fly against everything, even a little, and had seen a tiny bit of the paradise that was within each one, just for the asking.

After all, it was illogical and impractical—a bloody nuisance. It wouldn't pay the housing dues, put food on the table, pay taxes, buy clothes, buy things. But being nothing tangible itself, it made all those things worthy that without it were worthless, just another diversion. *We gave each other something we will never lose. Not blows against the empire, but commitment where others don't care.*

He had seen deeper, and he knew Shallon had too. It meant more now than it ever had. Charlier leaned back and turned the comm-band up. It was playing a loud, raunchy song, full of outrageous riffs on a cheap electric guitar, the bass thumping down in the contrabass clef *bubump bubump* and the gravel-voiced singer braying:

> They call me lightnin'
> For my dancin' feet;
> They call me honey
> For my words so sweet.
> They call me purple
> 'Cos I drink my wine,
> And they call me coffee
> 'Cos I grind so fine.*

It was rock at its worst, but Charlier laughed out loud and beat time on the dashboard, and Transporter 11051 rolled on into the darkness.

*Coffee Blues. This and other lyrics copyright © 1980 by M. A. Foster, Dew Drop Inn Music.

CARTER SCHOLZ

A Catastrophe Machine

Carter Scholz did not want to be a science fiction writer. "Indeed," he says, "I did not want to be a writer. I began as a musician and, through adolescence, wanted to be an artist. In the drear tracts of public education I excelled at math and science. In all these cases I abdicated. Writing, I wish to point out by this, is an inspired lack of alternatives. One becomes a writer by default. Cease drawing or playing for a year and the skills fade. But there is no way to avoid words for a year."

Scholz's acquaintance with SF and fantasy began at age thirteen, when he read Bradbury and "was enchanted," although he went on to dip into Heinlein, Asimov, and Clarke "and was soundly bored." At nineteen he met Harlan Ellison, who advised Scholz to attend the Clarion SF writer's workshop, advice that Scholz followed. "I began to learn the sorts and conditions of SF. I took a six-month forced march through three hundred or four hundred books and learned enough to sell a story. Then I sold another. And another. And another. Perhaps half my writing was consciously SF. I was twenty. The ability to sell was a tonic to my ego, if not to my craft."

The stories in question included such notable work as "The Eve of the Last Apollo" and "The 9th Symphony of Ludwig van Beethoven," work that earned him Hugo and Nebula nominations, in addition to the Campbell, and places in the outstanding anthology series of the day, including Damon Knight's Orbit, *Terry Carr's* Universe, *and Robert Silverberg's* New Dimensions.

Never a prolific writer, Scholz did not explode on the scene with a crescendo of novels the way his Campbell rivals Chalker and Cherryh seemed to, but his stories, although relatively few in number, were more than enough to make his name. Dark, dense, often disturbing, the best of his work echoes strongly of the influence of Philip K. Dick and, particularly, Barry N. Malzberg, although even Scholz's earliest work has a savage, desperate emotional power beyond anything that Malzberg has ever achieved.

Like Malzberg, Carter Scholz does not particularly feel comfortable within science fiction. "My fiction is mostly concerned with ways of know-ing, which may or may not make it SF, depending on who's looking at it. I don't care much what it's called, though editors seem to.

"I am still writing," Scholz says, "and once in a while I specifically write science fiction. Specifically means 'to sell.' But it is not a game I enjoy much any more, and if they would be honest, neither do most of the writers in the field. It is not a game to appeal to adults. There are, possibly, good reasons to start writing SF. The reasons for continuing are mostly sordid and unpleasant."

Scholz says of the story that follows: "To a fellow expert in mon-adic isolation, George Alec Effinger, this story is dedicated. Some of his themes—sport and science—flit playfully through the text. Effinger, like many of us, probably deserves better than he has gotten."

Carter Scholz is now at work on his first novel for Terry Carr's new line of Ace Specials. If it is a fraction as powerful as "A Catastrophe Machine," it will be worth the wait.

G.R.R.M.

I was twelve in the autumn of 1959, and my entrance into puberty was not through sex, which I took more or less in stride, but through the straiter gate of science. At this remove I will not insist on a connection; but compare the two largest, most opti-mistic American magazines of that time, the one of sex and the one of science. More than once I deployed the contents of one within the covers of the other.

My world was based on analogy then. If the sun were an orange, the earth was an appleseed ten yards on. If the earth were a day old, man's history spanned five minutes. The sharp shift of scale pleased me. Metaphor lived for me with the authority of physical law; some never outgrow this state, and for some others the growth goes past the bounds of life.

I read. I worked square roots longhand for pleasure. I built models, of airplanes, autos, war machines, so carefully that I might have been confirming a paradigm of reality, and not just filling an idle afternoon. These at least are the memories I have of the time. There is no telling what distortions hindsight has worked on them.

In the large American magazine of science I read: "Elementary catastrophes may be generated at will with a simple device made of cardboard, rubber bands, and a few other materials."

I was not surprised to read something so frivolous and unlikely about catastrophes. I still took my analogies on faith. And in the austere vocabulary of mathematics, a catastrophe is not just a sudden turn of violence. It is a set of conditions whereby continuous change may cause discontinuous effects. A catastrophe, I learned, may be modeled as a kind of landscape with a sharp cliff; in the event being modeled this cliff represents a change of outcome. At some point in a war of forces one gives way. An angry and frightened dog finally attacks or runs. A seed will wither or germinate. An unstable compound explodes. The earth quakes. And so on.

I understood none of this at first. I built the device from the pictures. A cardboard disk turned to tighten a rubber band, which, at its extremity, snapped the disk back to its starting point. It was dull play. I worked it a few times, then put it away.

It might have remained in my cabinet till vanishing under my mother's statute of limitations on bizarre playthings, but the next day I was ill and stayed home from school. After an hour of reading I was bored and thought of my catastrophe machine. I could not understand the principle it was supposed to illustrate. But I played and formed a crude first idea of the workings of simple catastrophes.

When my father got home that night he slammed the door, cursed, and before greeting us poured himself a drink. He had almost run our Studebaker off the road. The brake line had ruptured, and he had swerved across two lanes of traffic to avoid hitting a truck. I made no connection.

The next Saturday morning I was killing some time before a football game, sitting in bed with the machine propped on my stomach. When I left for the field I forgot all about it. Then, running for a pass, looking back over my shoulder, I slipped and struck my midriff hard across the goalpost. I lay without moving. I spent six days in the hospital with a ruptured liver, thinking; when I reentered the quiet of my room, and saw the machine still on my bed, I began to understand.

In high school I was shy and devoted myself to mathematics. The school was a blockhouse of what was called progressive learning, one of those flat, sprawling monstrosities that flourished like mushrooms across the suburbs of the late fifties. No community among the students, no language we shared, could resolve the blank lines of fluorescent tubes, the stainless enameled expanse of lockers, the array of audiovisual aids, the rooms with sliding partitions, the diminishing prospects of the halls, into any accessible meaning. Each faced this limbo on his own; each sought a particular significance. So the experience of the school was driven like an auger into the privatest recess of one's mind; the school offered itself to me in long, pointless dreams, but everything about it baffled explanation.

There was a computer. This was the pride of the math department: a teletype terminal connected by phone to a small machine at an RCA factory thirty miles away. Our school rented time along with fifty other schools and businesses. I learned the crude language of programming, its iterative logic, and started to work on a simple two-dimensional catastrophe program.

The formulae in my article were no longer obscure. With the computer I modeled my simple device and more elaborate ones. By stages I came to understand catastrophes, their factors and generation. I touched on calculus. I drew curves on graph paper and built fancier devices from cardboard, rubber bands, the springs from ballpoint pens which my father manufactured, parts from an Erector set, and small electric motors. The most elaborate of these I set in my room, and let it run all day and all night; occasionally it would punctuate my sleep with the sharp rasp of a spring releasing or a gear slipping from one position to the next, and in my dreams would come a fall.

In the back pages of my article the author applied his theory to a range of subjects: optics, seismology, embryology, propagation of nerve impulses, aggression, manic-depressive behavior, committee behavior, economic growth, national defense. The theory's value was this: it incorporated the qualities of discontinuity and divergence into models that could be used for prediction. In the biological and social sciences these qualities are often found, and account for the label "soft" or "inexact" sciences. Catastrophe theory, wrote the author, promised to be a major advance in making the inexact sciences more exact. What he meant was that the complexity of existence could be reduced to the paradigm of number.

Those mornings I rose early and read through the newspaper while my father shaved. The newspaper was also interested in catastrophes. I read: an atomic bomb was tested in the New Mexico desert. A dam collapsed in Tennessee. An earthquake in California toppled three dwellings, but no one was injured. And so on. In these events I tried to find a pattern, a common ground of explanation in my theory of catastrophes.

About then I found I could lay curses. They were effective in small matters such as games. I could cause ends to drop passes, and batters to swing at wild pitches three times out of four, when I tried. I could make traffic lights turn. I told this to a friend, who scoffed, until on an outing he lost his footing crossing a stream, dropped a sandwich in the dirt, and spilled half a can of soda. Then the power became a grand joke between us, and we began attending sports in a spirit of scientific investigation and high delight at our secret. Perhaps neither of us believed it, and perhaps we did; for when at last the novelty of the delusion faded, and I declared that I would no longer use the power, the occasion turned solemn. I did not want to fool myself too much—just enough to enjoy a fantasy of control over a world in which, I knew even then, I was essentially powerless.

So I played at disasters. There was an ominous growth of pressure in the culture during these years, which I found modeled in a storm that gathered over our town in the spring of 1962, storm clouds that I knew from reading heralded tornadoes—but this was New Jersey, where tornadoes were anomalous—and the greenish light they cast made the town strange and fragile. My soul, too, felt strange and fragile as I watched the masses of air collide, their borders marked by shifting lines of intense gray, the most fearsome thing I had yet seen, and the air gusting now cold, now warm. A change of atmosphere made my ears ring. No funnels touched earth that day in New Jersey, not even a thunderstorm, but I felt the ground take in the energy of the thwarted storm. At night I felt the earth shake more than from the passing trucks on the nearby turnpike.

My mother developed a progressive disease. It was treated with radiation for a few months, but when its growth continued, her left breast was removed. Every week for a year she had radiotherapy. I came to look forward to Tuesday nights, when she and my father were gone over the bridge into the city for three hours. With the unforgiving absolutism of the young I saw the disease as weakness. And I saw weakness in my father's response: his depressions, his use of amphetamines. I separated myself from them in every way possible. Some evenings I ate alone in my room. At night I locked my bedroom door. Because they felt they had somehow failed me, because my mind intimidated them, they tolerated this, and my solitude became my defense. Separation. Otherwise I might inherit their weakness.

I read: more complicated n-dimensional catastrophes may be constructed by extending all the lower order catastrophes together with one new singularity at the origin. I adjusted my machine accordingly. I watched the news.

Fires were set in South Boston. A helicopter crashed into a crowd at a church picnic in Camp Hill, Pennsylvania. A new strain of flu was detected in San Francisco. A Greek Orthodox bishop was defrocked after a set of color, photographs was delivered to the minister of religion in Athens. The United States sent a few thousand military advisors to a country in Southeast Asia. And so on.

Probably I did not think that I was causing these events. I was looking for a connection between myself and the bewildering world of events, and my device was a material metaphor. I cast myself into the skein of cause and effect to see what I could learn. I built no new machines, but created their mathematical equivalents in computer programs. These became so complex that my teacher wanted an explanation, but I was unable to find my article after that, nor did I really need it. I just told him the work was topology. Cowed by my expertise, he gave his permission to run an exceptionally elaborate program of loops, nests, chains, and subroutines. This was on November 21, 1963.

We were all sent home early the next day. I was sick with fever for a week. When I returned, the bill for my program awaited me. It was immense. I was almost expelled as a result, but a curious technician at RCA had examined the program as it came over the line, and the day after the bill came a job offer. So my escapade earned me a reprimand and an *A* in math for the quarter.

But my behavior turned erratic, and I also earned some sessions with the school psychologist, a sincere, plodding man, and overweight. I did not tell him I felt responsible for the President's killing; I did not dare! He has no sense of dread, and felt thwarted besides, so he would simplify my own dread into neurosis.

I sat in fear of the topic. I had such an elaborate and lucid explanation of my role in the killing that I could not have kept from delivering a paranoiac masterwork had he once mentioned it. My program had gone out over phone lines, which linked the nation, which linked not just persons but machines, transmitters, who could know exactly what? The pattern of the program, which was catastrophic, might have influenced other patterns on the line, tipped them perhaps toward violence. Why not? Systems of social control were so complex and hidden, who could say which acts were trivial and which signified? So for the first time I was no longer playing. I had requested of some entity in a secret language a thoroughgoing catastrophe, and it had obliged me. Because of the mechanisms of control, because of the secret languages, my dark thoughts were no longer personal. They had consequences.

He would have had a field day with my feverish theory. I knew the obsession would pass, given time, but if he brought me to admit to it, I would be forced to defend it, and so might be locked into a widening system of delusion. So I kept counsel in the space of my mind, and fed him those, to me, harmless features of my home life he wanted to hear. I confessed guilt at masturbation, which I did not feel, and loneliness, which I did, and hatred of my parents, which he took at face value. His ultimate suggestion was that I try out for the baseball team that spring. And he said:

—You've a tremendous sense of responsibility.

To placate him and my parents, I did try out for the team. I remember the Saturday afternoons that early spring, narcotic as church, when my father coached me on pitching and batting stance in a bluff, raw voice. No player himself, his ignorance of the essentials was apparent even to me. His absurdity was mitigated only by his devotion; his earnest cries of encouragement smote the air like a distant parade. But my taste for sport was gone, as much from anguish over the idea of games as from my incompetence. My tryout was a disaster. After two weak hits I struck the ball soundly, and in utter astonishment watched as it fell past a chain link fence around left field, and I promptly ran to third base. I suspect I did this on purpose.

That spring I fell in love. She was a Jewish girl a year older than me. My parents hated her, and hers me. Hers were survivors of a concentration camp, and my religion and ancestry were goads to their resentment, already large, for their daughter was a beauty, and she had talent, so she was bound to be separated from them. They had not yet accepted this. They tolerated me coldly. (My mother's response was more direct: she barred Lila from our house.) I was bright enough, I had manners, but I was a Gentile and, worse, a German. It was her idea to drive into the country on the Seder and picnic on quiche Lorraine, but on our return, their furious faces, the dark mute clothes they had worn to temple—and still wore—awaited us on the porch, and their attitude said they saw me behind her every rebellion.

We pleased each other. I loved her will and her spirit. How unlikely I found it that she could love me. Once we were surprised when they came home early, and rushed downstairs to greet them in the neutral ground of the living room, only to realize we were wearing each other's pants. When I left an hour later, wearing my own, her mother gave me a secret smile. Her father was less civil; another evening I arrived on a motorcycle, in a black sweater and leather jacket, and he observed that I looked like Gestapo. But we were not as close as they feared.

—They're impossible, she told me. —Find one of your own, they say. And who are they supposed to be, *my own?*

I knew I was not one. She spent that summer on a kibbutz and had an affair with a major in the Israeli air force. And the next fall she went off for a week with a Russian poet come to speak at her college. This was too much. She had some special grace of the flesh that surpassed my own poor flailings. And I knew she would have shared it with me, but I was young, and my puritan nature still enforced a tyranny over joy that she could not accept. So we ended it. Again I retreated to mathematics.

At Yale I studied topology. My only friend, Shulman, would

come through my room, singing, —Oh, Francis will topologize. If not, the seagulls will come and pull out his eyes.

Shulman, Jewish, studied Catholic theology and styled me the antinomy of the saint of Assisi, who, as legend had it, talked to birds; this because I once told him I thought seagulls stupid and filthy. So he warped Joyce's refrain to twit me as I sat like a lesser friar over my books, a Daedalus of the airless realm of math.

He said also that I must work hard because mathematicians burn out early. I was fond of him for his banter—such as this trite, false commonplace—for his liking me without deference. So I never said that it was, in fact, a deep fear of mine.

—Topologize, pull out his eyes.

Obsessed I may have been. But my work was so clear to me then. The structure of the age was loss. All effort led us only to loss—loss of talent, youth, strength, courage, home. Life could be modeled on loss, or so it offered itself to me in my first days away from home, when I felt powerless before it, and only the dark task of understanding how we were separated from everything we loved was worth pursuing. I would build a mathematics of loss, and thus be freed.

A mathematics of loss. What else was catastrophe theory? I went to consult the original article. Imagine my bitter surprise when I could not find it, not in any magazine from 1959, or 1958, or 1960, or any other year. The million-card catalog held nothing on the subject. So I was thrown completely on my own resources. I would have to construct my theory out of my own work and life.

My mother died. I had sworn not to attend either of their funerals but, taken by surprise, I did go. The service was held on a bright spring day at the Church of the Atonement, the Reverend Mr. Powers presiding. My father, Catholic, and my mother, Methodist, in dreary compromise, like comparison shoppers, had settled on the Episcopal faith for their marriage. And so the Reverend Mr. Powers, who had presided at that ceremony as well, was called by way of last request out of retirement for this last compromise as well. I had taken confirmation training from him. It was his pleasure to parse the word *atone* as *at one,* which was good etymology but weak theology. It placed his doctrine closer to Mary Baker Eddy than to

Richard Hooker; the sense of sin was small in his parish, and so, therefore, was the sense of responsibility. I had not been at one with the church since my confirmation.

At the service I was in good humor, and made dry jokes that passed unnoticed. My father seemed unmoved, and my mother's relatives shunned him. On our way home we stopped at a bar, and we drank together until sunset. He told me something I had already known: after the operation my mother had not let him touch her, and had then accused him of having affairs. For the first time he looked old to me.

—But it wasn't true. I never looked at another woman, all the time we were married. She seemed intent on destroying everything we had before the end. As if . . . she didn't want to owe me anything. The last thing she said to me was: I know you never loved me. Never! As if thirty-three years could count for nothing.

I stared out the window, clean of grief. I had not wanted to owe anything either.

—It was a relief, finally. I couldn't have taken it much longer. Do you—do you hate me?

His hands shook, and I was struck by how much lay between us. He was still a child. Married in the Depression, he had wanted to play trumpet in a band, she to sing. This they laid aside for love. He went to night school, she became a secretary, he found work in a watch factory. Young and innocent, they lived on New York's Lower East Side. He went to war, returned, and as if that had burned free a block in his genitals, they had at last their only child, myself. He bought a business in the suburbs. Friends moved west. They mortgaged a gracious home. Their lives crumbled inconspicuously. From the magic of those first years to pushing a cart in the broad aisles of the Grand Union, pushing an electric mower over hillocks of sod, nothing in their youth—when marriages were forever; when cigarettes were social grace and not carriers of disease; when, if you lived under the roof of marriage, family, faith, and work, you were protected, and no calamity came unprovoked—had prepared them for this. Nothing accounted for this malaise. They could not understand what had failed; why they would leave the television on till three in the morning, its hum and flicker mediating dreams too bleak to face naked, unremembered next morning; why faith had yielded to life insurance; why absences no longer promised return. But, young and bitter, I knew. I was older at twenty than he would ever grow. All their weakness was stamped on my soul as a lesson. I knew the secret was to cut free from anything that might lure you into sleep.

—No, I said.

I watched my father drink, and I wondered what greater distances would separate me from my children.

After this I saw him seldom. On holidays he went to his brother's; I stayed in New Haven, working in my apartment, walking the slush-covered walks between the grotesque Gothic buildings, enjoying the peace of the empty campus. And after this his drinking became serious. When he was committed to the sanatorium I refused to sign the papers, so my uncle, over no objections from me, obtained a power of attorney to do so. I met my uncle there, and he accused me of coldness. He described to me a weakness I had never seen in my father. Standing in the chill corridors of the clinic near Princeton, we might have been speaking of different men. He said my father cried each Christmas; he said he feared I had cut him off forever, that he worried constantly about my life, my happiness, my future. I was near to furious, for my father and I had spoken before of loneliness and the hardness of life, and if he had seemed at times naive, at least he had never fallen on the cheap sentiment my uncle claimed for him now. If he had known my father longer, still I knew him better; I allowed him his dignity, even when his mind was scattered from electroshock. It cost me to see him then. And I resented my uncle making a palimpsest of his brother's face, printing on it only those griefs and failures he suspected himself capable of—my proud uncle, a Vietnam veteran with two adopted Oriental children of his own, and God knows what guilt—when I knew my father to be stubborn, independent, guiltless. He as much as said the drinking was all my fault, still asking me to sign.

—You're all he has left now. Help him.

Help him? I had seen cured alcoholics before. They were docile. The cure was a simple amputation. They did not face the cause or consequence of their drinking, except in execration. I would sooner see my father dead than forced into that confession and self-censure. Let him choose his own fall. My uncle had to sign the papers.

In 1968 I submitted to Yale my master's thesis, "On Mathe-

matical Modeling in the 'Soft' Sciences," and a week later received
a job offer from a consulting firm.

The firm's name, NOUS (Nexus for Optimal Use of Science),
was suggested by the Greek voûs, meaning mind; and, depending on
the humor of the moment, it could also stand for Necromantic
Oracle for Undermining the State, National Organization for
Unemployed Scientists, New Oligarchs of the United States, or,
miracle of brevity and arrogance, the French for *us*. They owned a
building with a blank travertine façade in southern California, and
flew me there for an interview.

Inside the shell of the building were a hundred modular offices.
All walls were movable. System prevailed. The president spoke to me
in a back room that overlooked the Pacific Ocean. He tapped my
paper with a penpoint.

—We believe you're on the edge of some very interesting work
here.

—That's obvious, I said curtly. I had made up my mind not to
be impressed.

—We can use any new techniques of modeling. Most of our
work is advisory. We list options. We hope to guide our leaders to
choices based on science rather than bias or ideology.

—Most of your work is military, I pointed out.

—We came into existence in 1963. We received a grant from
the Ford Foundation. We received contracts from the Defense
Department, which stipulated that only twenty percent of our research could be nonmilitary. Presently forty percent is. In five years
it will all be.

He smiled and held up a single page.

—See this? This is a study done by the Hudson Institute,
eighteen months' work; it boils down to this one sheet: a list of
eleven probable directions for our society for the remainder of the
century. It's worth a million dollars. We call this 'paper alchemy.'
The entire annual output of our company could fit into a single
volume. Now, this is worth a million because certain people believe
in Hudson's work. Who reads these studies is the most important
thing. The bulk of Hudson's work is war-related. It establishes legitimacy. Then a study like this is taken seriously. We would like to be
in such a position. We think it's important to establish legitimacy,
by any means, because, frankly, eight of these eleven courses are not

desirable. And without adequate counsel, the government is likely to adopt the wrong course.

—May I see that?

—It's classified. He put the paper away. —We can offer you twenty thousand and guaranteed freedom. Work on what you like. Our facilities are better than any school's, and your time will be your own.

I returned east and spoke to Shulman. His work now was advising conscientious objectors in a small office on campus. When I said I might join NOUS, he said, —That's like Joyce writing brochures for the Catholic Aid Society.

—Do you despise them so much?

—Francis, do you know who these people are? These people practically sponsored the Bay of Pigs. These people brought you the Gulf of Tonkin. Lyndon goes on TV seated at a desk because there's a NOUS employee sucking him off.

—I don't think they like the government.

—Likely they feel themselves superior to it.

—Well, so do you.

—Oh, a true thrust. Two points. The difference is that I know how powerless I really am, and these people act as if inspired by God—worse, by science—and so can disavow responsibility for their acts.

—They don't act. They list options.

—Ironic that you of all people should be attracted by this austere bullshit amorality. Or is it? I suppose it was in you all along, the cunning in your silence.

—Are you speaking as a friend, I asked with heat, —or as a Jew studying under a Jesuit?

He stared bleakly out the window.

—Laurence. I want a place to work. Mathematicians burn out early, you know.

—A home, he said, turning back to face me.

—Their war work establishes legitimacy.

—The legitimacy of war, perhaps. Would you fight in this one?

—No. But if I turn them down I may have to.

—There are teaching posts at McGill, he said, reaching for a catalog.

—No, I said. I spoke carefully now, more afraid of lying to

myself than to him. —I won't run. I must understand this. It frightens me, but I can't ignore it. Last year, when you wanted me to march, I wouldn't, and it was this same fear, this fear of avoidance. I avoid real commitment. And I'm afraid avoidance will destroy me. Yet, that was what I saw at your meetings, in the best and worst of your people, the dropouts and the Marxists with private incomes; I saw this avoidance, everything I hate in myself: they were committing to nothing but a style or a program, and so refusing to commit personally, to avoid complexity or complicity, do you see? You said yourself they'd rather be getting high.

Again he looked outside. —The time I spend in here, arguing with assholes, deadbeats, chickenshits. All worried about their asses. You're right, of course. But I tell myself it's good to deprive the Army of any warm bodies. And now I have to watch a genuine mind bought out by the muckers? I'd rather be getting high myself. Christ, Francis.

—I do math, and I'm vain enough to think I can do original work. I won't spend my best five years grading papers. Tell me I'm rationalizing. But it will take all my courage to do this.

—Chessmen, he said.

—A cheap metaphor, Laurence.

—Yes, too simple. But imagine that each square of the board is itself a smaller board, each with its own game. And to free squares for any move you must first win the games on those squares. And perhaps each of those little games depends on yet smaller games. The mind, you know, is fallible. You could lose track, all those games.

There was a stale silence in the office. At last he sighed. —Take the job. Do your work. Don't let them bind you.

After his cure my father took an apartment near his brother's house. Our house was sold. Before leaving for California, I went home to clean out my room. Carefully I crushed my models and sorted books. All tokens of my younger self I rejected, except the most elaborate of my catastrophe machines. It looked like a toy; too, it was a symbol. It marked a line dividing play from the stern art of the real. Even so, I did not work the device. I still feared it. I took it with me.

I was welcomed to Los Angeles by the shooting of Robert Kennedy—for me, an auspicious sign. I was twenty-two, the youn-

gest in the firm. Shulman was right. The rule at NOUS was legitimation without God. There was the attitude that we were the episco-
pacy of the mind, the cryptarchs of the state. We were a meritoc-
racy, the elect, unimpressed by the government or the governed,
presbyters or preterite.

Legitimation. Once power is acquired it must be kept. Armies
of lawyers, writers, and priests are employed to shape the language
to serve the ends of a particular power. The most difficult legitimation to overturn is the appeal to God. The papacy. The divine right
of kings. But the Protestants broke with the Pope; America and
France dispensed with kings. From then on, however, the new
ultimate was neither the will of the people nor the authority of the
individual soul. It was science. And mathematics was in its service.
Technicians were its priests, and NOUS its bishopric.

Newly arrived, detached as it were from my past, I considered
the history of this particular separation. Across ocean they came,
then across continent, intent on separation but binding themselves
to new needs, losing home, friends, estate, in their flight from one
prison to another, not suspecting the depth of their loss, building on
the new soil replicas and substitutes of all they had despised—which
only sank the sense of loss more deeply. Damned cultureless Protes-
tant Americans! to believe that renunciation, further distance, could
lead to ultimate return. No. Los Angeles, extremity of the expansion,
cataclysmically contoured, the rude thrust of hills and slope to sea,
where the earth's grip was weak, was demonstration enough: loss
angled California, the state and city screamed anguished loss.

Here I watched catastrophes take shape. War was a conflict of
forces ending with victory and loss. The earth moved in response to
equations of catastrophe. Alcoholism was catastrophe: one drank
continually, until one could not stop. Learning was catastrophe: one
studied till one day the knowledge was owned. History itself was a
downward gyre, its line marked by events, the horizontal thrust all
good intentions, the vertical drop the gravity of our situation. And
so on. These were the idle-hour thoughts I indulged in my cube of
an office, overlooking the new priesthood at play in the courtyard
swimming pool. My work went well, but I felt engulfed. Nothing I
could do placed me outside the mathematics of catastrophe. No
move was free. Each devolved through the strict landscape of its
cusps and curves.

NOUS was easy to despise. We were in fact the model citizens of our own minds. It was a closed environment, exemplified by its game rooms, in which endless reflection and calculation were possible without analysis: a perfect escape into the world of artifact that had nurtured all our narrow talents from the start. I found in its mutable corridors the same chill complexity that had haunted me through school. Every act was revocable, every move but a tentative step toward a changeable model of the narrowest gate into the real.

One night the blank travertine façade was painted with a red hangman's knot. The president's comment was: —I'd give that a seven for wit, and a two for taste. Some credited the hostility to the accident of the word *game*. Popular opinion said that games about Armageddon could be played only by frivolous ghouls. Within NOUS a game meant only a situation where interests conflicted. A question of language. But I would maintain that in language there are no accidents. The word showed sharply a confluence of thought particular to our work and attitudes.

In short we were creators of fictions, and so worked ultimately for our own satisfaction. I remember reading Robbe-Grillet in college, and I remember how strange were the turns of his tedious narrative as he followed his logical yet groundless esthetic—as fascinating to me as a mathematic proof built on an unsound premise. Our whole enterprise had the same monolithic badness that baffled criticism.

I did not work on the reports, the twenty-page skyblue folders marked *secret* that might sell for fifty thousand dollars. I declined any project I thought harmful. In the first month I modeled the differentiation of tissues in an embryo and the epidemiology of a flu strain. This sort of work stalled my security clearance at the lowest level, and I did not care about that.

In a kind of concession I went home for the holidays the next two years, to my uncle's house. Each year I greeted my father, settled into the guest room (my father stayed in Decha's room, who slept with his sister for the week); I walked with my father in the mornings, when he was not so bad, played touch football with the kids, for a banal and irritating week. My uncle and his wife, and other relatives who might arrive for drinks, would talk about my father in the third person, though he was in the room. I irritated my uncle in turn with tales of my work.

—I'm only a chicken colonel, he would respond, his southern voice rich with the ironies of his success—he, who had quit high school to fight in the Pacific, who climbed the ranks in the thick of combat, three wars, while I, educated, intelligent, mimed involvement at the edge, —but I don't see why they waste money on pardon my French a bunch of goddamned theorists. If the staff would stop sittin' on their thumbs we could clean that place out in a year. As it is the VC run over into Cambodia and we stand there wavin' good-bye. You know the safest place to stand in a mortar attack? Right next to the Shell Oil truck. Neither side hits 'em, they're too valuable, can you figure that? Nobody there now knows spit from Spinoza.

Expressions like these were to prick my intellectual vanity, as he saw it.

—Would you go back? I asked.

—No, thank you. No, sir. It's impossible over there now, it's no war. We should pull the hell out before we lose everything.

—There we agree.

—Is that how you advise the Pentagon? he laughed. —They must like that.

—We don't advise. We list options.

—Why don't you go if you know so much?

—The DOD finds my work here more valuable.

What it cost me to say so. To shut him up I had let out my dread. My work was so obscure that I doubted its value to anyone, but I was not so sanguine about my employ. Most of what I saw at NOUS I feared. In the game rooms futures were built and wars played out, and not just the current war; they foresaw others. Favorites were an American civil war in 1985 and a limited nuclear war in Sweden in 1990. NOUS modeled even themselves, in a game designed to improve the modeling process at NOUS.

But they played for the sake of play. These were the ones I had seen in the Yale computing center after midnight playing "space war," the ones who, if anyone could, would bring on a real war in space. For they were engaged in the large sterile work of legitimating themselves. That was the code in which all their reports were written. And their work's ultimate meaning was only what it revealed to them about the nature of their own intellects.

Whereas I was sure only that nothing could be truly known,

because the very act of knowing involved a radical doubt that might question even itself. In mathematics I had found a haven where a priori knowledge, axiomatic assumption, was not just acceptable but necessary. But as time passed, the less adequate it seemed. I missed the evidence of the senses, the tangible persuasions of impure reason. I needed an arena in which I could act bravely and well. Again a sense of sex awakened in me. Again I fell in love. I married Alice.

We were each young and unhappy, and so our life together was a succession of gifts. Her first husband had been my opposite: a pragmatic engineer, outgoing, respected, adjusted, and a model of consideration. Except in bed. There his special pleasure was ferociously to bite her breasts and thighs. He claimed she enjoyed it. She thought it was his way of leaving secret marks upon her that no other could see. So I was careful to handle her like satin. And she did nothing to startle my pleasure, to scare it from deepening into real feeling, as it seldom had in my poor five years of love. We named our acts. Our love talk was words neither of us had used with other lovers, and even our mundane household conversations were clipped, incantatory, definite, and kept alive our appetites. We fucked long hours, in a hundred ways, fast, slow, desperately, minimally, in the depths of feeling and the shallows of pleasure, as if seeking some point past that of release, as if to trick or drive the orgasm into a confirmation. This could not last. After all, we were using each other to prove our authenticity, to identify self to self, and in the end nothing is more dispiriting than using sex to keep track of one's psyche, nothing so disheartening as seeing the clock in the eyes of your lover.

Empiricists make the worst romantics. It was bound to end. Later I gave reason after reason on the analyst's couch and in talks with a few friends, and none of them were true. It may be usual to miss the reasons and retain only certain pictures. Here is one picture. Alice was prone to bad dreams, and had been since youth. And I could not bear to be touched in my sleep. So whenever I heard her start to toss and groan, I slid to the far edge of the bed and buried myself in a feigned sleep deeper than true. If her dreams were very bad, the old bed would quiver and cast me like a beached fish onto insomnia's shore. But one night in my sleep I heard her cry, and I turned at once to comfort her. I held her desperately, as if she might in an instant slip into the dream and away from me forever. And at

that moment a small dry voice spoke to me with the absolute authority of sleep. It said:—Now you are truly lost. My grip awoke her. We
made love, and afterward she slept, but I was turned from sleep the
rest of the night. I paced the apartment in the dark, touching
furniture as I moved.

She became pregnant. She wanted the child and I did not.
Childhood was the greatest of indignities, a prolonged insult, and I
could not wish it upon another. I insisted on abortion, and she
refused. I swore if she had the child I would put it up for adoption.
If it came to that, she yelled, she would leave me and raise it herself.

And she left me, taking the child, the boy. Not for two years
did I realize that I had wanted the child even more desperately than
she. I needed her to fight me, not to flee, to deliver me of my true
feelings. But I did not fight hard enough; I was unable to provoke
her into the violence necessary to show me what I had to learn. How
could I have known that my belief in marriage would prove so large?
We had almost omitted the ceremony. And not till after this did I
realize the depth of Shulman's perception in his office when he had
said: *a home.* That was just what my willful, juvenile psyche had seen
in NOUS—the first evidence in my life of love for what I had made
of myself, not for what I could be or had been given. And that was
what Alice and the boy had been, too: a way back to a home I had
lost. Shulman sent me a postcard that read in part, *wise poet Wil-*
liams sings, "divorce is the sign of knowledge in our times, divorce,
divorce!" and still I did not understand. The hard navigator of my
soul commented, *loss frees,* but I knew that to lose something not
yet understood binds one helplessly to the understanding of it.

So the cold home of math opened itself to me again. I began
to smoke, I used a year's leave in a month, I became jealous of my
work, separating what I did for NOUS from what I did for myself,
though they had a legal right to anything I put on paper. I did less
and less for them. In an access of ambition, as if my mind mocked
my heart in its freedom and sought an immense project to im-
mensely bind it, I planned a book on the history of thought—no
less!—followed in mathematics. I began to trace the histories of
certain ideas: the discrete and the continuous, the transinfinite and
the imaginary, portents of the ideal. I felt that I was uncovering the
broken spires of some vast architecture of thought, and in time could
excavate a whole buried city of intellect. It might take twenty years.

I did not force it: I wrote perhaps a page a day, but they were firm; each day I could go back and make tentative connections clearer. Statements fell clear and concise as the edges of a polyhedron. In time I felt I could say it all in a hundred pages. My title was *Noetics*.

But in the meantime I was bound daily to catastrophe theory. NOUS wanted a book on it. The discipline was mine; no one else had thought to apply discontinuous topologies to modeling, and they were anxious for applications. So I struck a deal. For fifteen thousand in advance I would give them a book in a year, and I would work at home.

I lived like a monk, and may have contracted the medieval *delectatio morosa:* sheltered by erudition and canticles, some brothers returned time and again to certain favorite themes, polishing them, refining and reforming them, to the exclusion of all else. So I turned over aspects of my theory. Its rough landscape shone like glass from my rehearsing—but no work came. Day to day I slept late, breakfasted on orange juice and coffee, walked to the beach and back, read the paper, watered the plants, sat at my desk, went to the library, sat in a park, came home, poured a drink, another, and no work came. Some mornings I awoke resolved to break my habits, no cigarettes, no coffee, no drinking, and by evening I was again drunk and desperate, the room filled with smoke. I would sit dull and dazed before the dead glass eye of the television and try to lose myself in the atrocious films of the war, the banality of the comedies, and the assault of ads, all wit, courage, and technique compressed into the flat travesty of that awful screen, and still my mind ground on, still I tried to find a thread of connection that was not insane. All I could see were the best qualities of man accelerated to exhaustion and catastrophic collapse.

For months I bullied myself through night after fruitless night. I dozed over my papers. Once I dreamed two copies of the finished book on my library shelf. They were bound in black cloth. I could read neither the title nor my name on the spine. I took one down and opened it. The pages were coarse black paper, ragged at the edges, printed in black. The text was obscure and illegible. I turned the pages with mounting anxiety. I could just make out where the text broke for the formulae and illustrations, but nothing was readable.

Then my block broke, and I wrote for five full days, excited and confident. I even added pages to *Noetics*, so cleanly were my thoughts breaking between the mathematics NOUS wanted and the philosophical inference I was saving for myself. The bones of all my future work were there. Now I might quit NOUS, I might go back to school, I was free, for I had seen at last that loss was simply a component of growth, and that my work was therefore leading surely into biology, into life, into some grace of unity. I nearly wept with delight and self-love as I found my way fully into the modeling of embryology, cell motility, and mitosis. At last I was content. I took a rest.

In the morning mail was the new *Topology*, and on page 313 began a long article titled "Topological Models in Biology." I began to read. I skimmed. I turned pages furiously and finally pushed the journal aside. I knew it all. It was my book.

I was humiliated. All the months of sweat, the fear that I might never work again, the flesh of my life I had fed my theory, were pointless, because the work had been done anyway. It had been taken from me before its term.

I looked for my master's thesis, to compare it, to establish for my sanity's sake my priority, but I could not find my copy. I called Yale. And I learned that NOUS now held the only copies; they had pulled Yale's, invoking security. So I drove there, and I remember the brown pall over the city, but whether it was from brushfires, or automotive pollution, or a ghetto burning that day, I in my hermitage and obsession could not say.

I parked in the seaside lot. A new device had replaced the security guard; fumbling, I fed it my pass, and the outer door clicked free to admit me. Within I spoke to a secretary I had not met before; in manner she resembled Alice.

—I'd like to access Eckart's paper on modeling, I said, using their idiom.

She looked it up and asked if I had clearance.

—I'm Eckart, I said, smiling. I held out my pass, thumb covering as if by chance the clearance number next to my name and photo. She would not, I thought, question the author, and chances were my clearance was legitimate anyway. But I felt like a thief. My heart was near to panic.

She smiled and handed me keys.—Here you are. Room thirteen, drawer thirty.

I had some trouble finding room thirteen. Numbers on doors were out of order. The halls now seemed to spiral inward. I passed and repassed a lounge, recognizing two men there, the sea slow as a yawn beyond them. They did not see me. I could not recall their names.

Finally I found it: two black adhesive numerals slightly askew on a fireproof door. Drawer thirty was midway down the second row, labeled: *DOD-SBC-8-68-A*. I unlocked it, rolled it open. It was stuffed with skyblue folders and a few red ones. In a blue folder I found my paper. There was an eight-page précis headed: "Option. Catastrophic Collapse of RVN Government. Tactics of Civilian Casualties." Appended to this, virtually as a footnote, was my work, fifty pages of photocopies.

I went to the president's office. His door was ajar. He was regarding the shimmering crawl of the ocean through his broad, tinted window.

—What is this? I said, extending the folder.

He turned in alarm. It took him a moment to recognize me.

—That's classified. You haven't got clearance—

—It's my paper, for the love of Christ! I want to know why I found it with this.

—I'd like to know that too. He was composed now. He lifted his telephone. —Peake? Have a look at room thirteen, there's been an unauthorized entry.

I shook the folder as he cradled the phone. —Don't you understand that this is mathematics? Ideal? Pure?

—Everything pure gets applied, Francis. We deal here in the art of the real.

—You do not. You, you want to outsmart the present, to derange time, to think your way outside history. You, your games and models all come from a horror of time and the fear of change, because over time power can only dissipate itself. What you deal in is the opposite of the real.

—That folder proves otherwise.

—Bloodsucker. You lied to me. You broke into my house. You stole my private papers. This, and this, and this. 'History of the Transfinite,' this is mine!

—You have no private papers. Our contract—

—Not this! Nothing gives you rights to this!

—Well, if we're discussing breach of contract, you know you've submitted nothing for over six months.

—You knew why. The proper applications take time.

—We couldn't wait. You are courting serious trouble, Francis.

—All right. If I've done nothing, if I'm in breach, how did you get these papers?

—You might have sent those by messenger. We could produce receipts with your signature. Breach? Why, we could put you in jail. Not a hundred people in the country are allowed to see that folder.

I fumbled with my briefcase, spilling papers. I brought out the new *Topology* and threw it down. —Here. Read it, you son of a bitch. Then tell me what good this has done you.

Then I went to retrieve some books from my office. But the halls confused me. Walls had moved. I found a men's room I remembered and backtracked from there, but where my office had been was now another lounge, overlooking the swimming pool. A couple of men smoking glanced at me without interest. As I stood another man came up behind me: Peake.

—You'll have to leave, Francis. You no longer have clearance to be in the building.

I was too angry to answer. I handed him my pass and turned to go.

—Please leave your briefcase. You can pick it up tomorrow after we've inspected it.

—Fine. Help yourself to my lunch. The mayonnaise will spoil. I hope you'll return my pornographic magazines.

Peake shook his head calmly. —Honestly, Francis. Did you think we kept you around for your looks? Your witty conversation?

—I thought I was here to do math.

—You were here to serve us. And now we are through with you.

Atrocity. I had been made an instrument. I waited for dreams, for contrition, but my psyche was unwilling to penetrate the surface of the television's nightly war. No, my sleep was as placid as my sin was small. Its consequence was less than that of the least Wehrmacht bureaucrat initialing a requisition for potatoes. Guilt? None, though my ego longed for it. I had been living the life of another. So my dreams brought no burning bodies to torture me, only dark, instantly forgotten images of abasement that tried to follow me up out of deep sleep and failed.

The one dream I had was of the engineers, the technicians, the cyberneticists, the two whose names I could not recall. They surrendered their bodies at a chrome altar, they joined the rest, linked englobed immortal brains they were, murmuring in binary tongue, wishing only for the last separation, the divorce from matter, the long-despised dialectic of phenomenon and noumenon conquered at last. I despised them. Yet, I was one of them, one who sought to leave his special marks where no other could see them. I was one who sought ultimate separation. And then, overriding the legitimations of sleep, came contrition, all at once; it came as my dream was bathed in impossible light, and even the shadows were sieved by radiance and my heart pierced with anguish, for here it was, the one conflict, the one war, the one separation we all truly desired, the one weapon that could abolish matter, leaving no remnants, no evidence, the one logical outcome to all our labor, all our misdirected lusts, all our will to loss. Dreaming, my mind was as a child's; and I remembered once burning a sex magazine in an access of shame, not guilt, at masturbation; and now the Puritan in me decried my small sin at NOUS as the pollution of all life, and cried for another fire, for an eradication more thorough than that of Sodom; so in my dream I called a bomb to Los Angeles, the bomb that my forebears at a forerunner of NOUS had created; and as it irrupted into my prior dream, I saw the worst, that I had wanted this, that all dreams, even the most atrocious, are truly wish fulfillments. And could I doubt that the shape of my waking thoughts was congruent to my dreams? No. In the mind's code my theory of catastrophes asked just such annihilations. So ideally I was responsible for any atrocity committed in the name of pure knowledge, just as I was practically guiltless of any particular crime. That paradox, which I could not master with words, would continue to deny me absolution.

Lacking words, I gestured. As a final gesture to childhood I set the last and most complex of my catastrophe machines in a crawl-space in my apartment. I sealed it in there, running on long-lived batteries, and I left the apartment for good, taking what books and clothes would fit in my car, and I checked into a motel, into a zone of spiritual parsimony and anonymity, and if challenged some power to bring me the worst. This proved, I thought, that all I had made was for play after all, the vacuous play of the self-intent. Nothing I now did or could do would promote or impede one iota the progress of the immense catastrophe machine that was our culture.

After a time I called Shulman. He was gentle. He knew someone at the university in Hume, and if I liked he would mention my name. In two weeks it was settled. I had an associate professorship at half my NOUS salary. I was twenty-four years old.

When I came to Hume I began to think I had been ill for some time. On my walks to the school I became appalled at the diversity of life the landscape offered. In the courtyard a cactus garden held a hundred species. Gold and black carp lazed in ponds. Eucalypti, redwoods, acacias, broke the air. The bougainvilleas, the fuchsias, flouted their sex. Even the twisted succulents in late spring sent skyward a tall twig crowned with tight rosy buds.

I was done with all this. The sexual transactions of my being proceeded on a level deeper than I cared to go. Surfaces tyrannized my attention. Listening intently, I found no moment free of sounds. Gazing at stars, I imagined I could see their slow streaming, the eonlong flattening of constellations. Objects were flat and lurid to my sight, and slipping across the edge of one to the next it suffered shock and dislocation. My body was a burden. Even the fog, once a balm, became hideous to me one night as I perceived its random million particles swirling past my porch light. Each moment was booming agony, and had always been.

My students were near my age, alien otherwise. The sharp catastrophic cusp the culture had just passed—when exactly in my cloistered time had it happened?—had left an insuperable chasm. I guessed that some of them envied me and others despised me, but all we ever talked about was math. This year students had been killed; the game of radical praxis had turned serious; terror was in the air; there had come a chill as gradual yet final as the abrupt lock of water molecules at freezing. The empty stylistic forms of protest, some of them, remained; but they were looking first of all for another, safer game.

My pleasure in my free hours was to watch the sea. It was large enough to swamp my senses. I would take a bottle of wine and pick my way down the steep hills seaside of Route 1 and sit on some narrow stone ledge or other a few hundred feet above the water. I would drink wine and try to think of nothing. Often there was fog, and I could see nothing but ten feet of rock face on either side of me. There I would sit until the chill came with the evening. The trick then was to walk back drunk. I collected rocks on these outings, sandstone, basalt, serpentine, eclogite, jade, and carried them in my windbreaker pockets for ballast. They swayed as I walked, pulling first one way, then another. Let it come. Let the last catastrophe take me, split the world, let the flowers and leaves blacken at their edges, curl, burn, let the fish bloat and poach in their ponds, the birds blaze like thrown firebrands, the rocks flow steaming to the sea, let the final decompression of matter come, and resolve all to all. A dozen times I saw it poised. The edges shimmered, but did not burn.

I sold my car. I had a dread of flying. Twice I was invited east, twice I made reservations, and twice I stayed at home, sitting in a cold sweat on my packed bags until the hour to leave had passed. I could feel clearly the plummet of the plane and the resolution impending death would offer, the pattern of my life suddenly seen as it was. Gravity would claim me; my situation at last clear, I would see just how badly I had lived, each mistake, doomed to fall with strangers in a device not of my making.

My father called. His voice was hesitant. He asked if he might spend Christmas with me, in Hume. I remembered much older Christmases, the sad comedy of regrets and recriminations stored all year and brought out then because it was the one time of the year in our family when a genuine feeling was called on: I, acting the part of the young scholar pleased with his annual respite, and grateful for the simple bourgeois conventions of turkey, liquor, ennui; my father so drunk he could scarcely stand, but acting judicious and reserved; my uncle's bright brutal eyes clocking each gesture for the least evidence of ill will to transfix like a bug on the sharp point of his displeasure. The stupidest time of the year. Yet, now I wanted him to come. I, too, had failed. I imagined him alone in his graceless modern apartment, his drowned eyes, his frail hands, and thought, *death is separation enough, no need to seek more.* Yes, do come, I said in a voice no longer able to carry warmth. He said he would rent a car at the airport, and I recited slowly the directions to my house. He had me repeat them, then he read them back.

When he came we embraced. I had had two drinks. He admired the house. I said I would take him to dinner. He fussed over the menu, said he could not eat this or that, asked the waiter how much salt was in each dish. He turned his empty wineglass upside down. As we ate I spoke about my book and the university. In grief and shame I started to explain why I had quit NOUS, when he interrupted me.

—I'm proud of you, Fran. All you've done.

I could have cried. His piety was sickening. Was my life to vindicate his? How could I now explain to him my humiliation? Then I saw. With bright wounded eyes he still sought forgiveness for that which needed no forgiving. The treatment had stripped him of dignity. He moved slowly and spoke cautiously. Every gesture betrayed a man who had been whipped to within an inch of his life and now distrusted his every instinct. So he had nothing left to rely on but the empty forms of manners, platitudes, and the failure of feeling called sentiment. There was no strength in him, and I was ashamed that I had looked for any.

Through this I bolted two glasses of wine. I had ordered a bottle and felt obliged to finish it. He leaned over and tapped my wrist, saying:

—You know . . . you ought to be careful. These things may be in the blood, they say. You know. Hereditary.

I looked away, sure I would be sick. Some fine transaction of spirit occurred in my stomach, and I did not resist it. I swallowed my nausea, then lit a cigarette, as if to bring it back. I was sure he would say: that too. But he was more oblique.

—Your mother, for all her flaws, was a fine woman.

Could he not let me be? Would he force on me a fall not my own? —Oh yes, a fine woman. Who made life hell for us both. Do you remember when she told Lila she wouldn't have yids in her house? Or when she called the police the night you slept in the guest room, told them you had a whore with you?

—She was sick. The poor woman was on drugs, getting ready to die. You know that.

—I won't argue. It's past. If you want to forget it, fine. But it's obvious what you went through.

—Don't speak ill of the dead.

He meant himself. So he was dead to me, and I to him. All at once I needed to see Alice. I needed to explain what had gone wrong, why she could love and I could not. I wanted to see my son, now three years old, and warn him against the world he would have to enter. I wanted to know his first word. But I no longer knew where they lived. Like my father, I was past reclamation, and against my will was forced to knowledge: nothing can be reclaimed, for we have no claims to faith, love, loyalty, or anything we touch, besides those we establish furtively and spend our spirits legitimating. This surge of feeling, like a new island breaking the sea, like a flower unfolding, like first sex, like the bloom of bombs over a distant jungle, wrung from me the last tear I would ever shed in sorrow.

My father saw it and clutched my hand. Shivering with shame and revulsion, forcing myself to forget that there was nothing in him to which I could speak, surrendering at last, I nodded at him several times, quickly, and pressed his hand in my own.

I am older now. I am dying of the worst of illnesses. The doctors say it is no worse than any other, but how can I believe that, when they are so ignorant of its cause and when its nature is so consonant with my own? I can find all the letters of its name among those of mine, and its name is the name of my birth sign. It is a disease of growth, but the difference between it and normal growth is so complete, and so subtle, that I believe it found its proper soil in my cells, the monads of my self—this disease of our time, whose manifold triggers lie in our landscape like an equation of consequence. It is my mother's disease. I tell them they could do worse than seek its cause in the theory of catastrophes.

I try to tell myself that there is no connection between the shape of my life and the shape of my end. But my heart does not believe it. And at this point, in atonement, it is the heart I must trust.

Since I am dying they listen to me with tolerance, but for them my words already belong with the words of the dead. I have abandoned the cold comforts of topology and read now medieval and mystical texts—Ptolemy's *Almagest*, Swedenborg's *Arcana Coelestia*, treatises on astrology, numerology, demonology—the broken and unconfirmed paradigms of an earlier world, which seem, even in my detached state, less signposts in the history of ideas than the tortured, selfinflicted symbols of a deep, long, racial insanity, stages in the progression of a disease whose course has almost run.

My own work, *Noetics*, lies in ruins, a hundred disparate fragments of a few pages each, each a node of an intricate mapping of self that never revealed itself whole. How had I ever thought to do it? Cantor's *Vorlesungen über Geschichte der Mathematik* ran two thousand pages and did not finish out the nineteenth century. So I possess these benchmarks of the invisible landscape of my thought, but no memory of the cusps and curves, the canyons and trails, that must be traversed to bind them. They are sunk like stones in my mind's mire. Each day I haul forth another, burn a few pages more. In my new, almost sensual appreciation of superstition, it would not surprise me to learn that each idea marked a like stage in the advance of my own disease, and the catastrophic surface they define is nothing but my own face. I understand at last that this is the life I designed for myself.

I thought my machine caused catastrophes. But I had no idea of their true nature: not quick, but lingering; not isolate, but consequential. Each is linked to the next in an endless chain, and the process is known as life: it begins with the catastrophe of orgasm, and I have modeled the differentiation of tissues *in amnion;* then a cord is severed at birth, and we proceed via catenations of divorce, loss, and disease to the reward of death. I found life too painful to touch, yet it drew me. By finding the skeleton of catastrophe in every event, I was able to mock the bones of loss. Flesh now takes its due. And the whole culture binds itself to this new faith of loss, this new disease.

My father sends the latest journals. The theory is passing into public domain. It is finding applications. This month in the large American magazine of science is an article called "A Catastrophe Machine." There, at last, is the drawing from which I built my first simple device over fifteen years ago. How can I know what I am responsible for?

Probably my father will outlive me.

These last few weeks the pain has grown worse. My doctor offers me narcotics. So far I have refused.

C. J. CHERRYH

The Dark King

C. J. Cherryh may have been the only one in Miami Beach who was truly surprised to hear her name read as the winner of the fifth John W. Campbell Award on that rainy Florida night in 1977. The rest of us there at Suncon, the 35th World Science Fiction Convention, could have told her she was going to win. No one had leaked the results, mind you, but Carolyn was an overwhelming favorite that night, and her victory was greeted by an enthusiastic ovation.

The year before, Carolyn Cherryh had been in Kansas City at what was to be the first of many worldcons for her as an all but unknown first novelist. It was no mean feat to go from that early obscurity to the status of Campbell favorite, and then Campbell winner, in the space of a single calendar year. Some might have called it impossible. After all, several of the other contenders for the honor published well before her. Besides, Cherryh was a novelist, and while a few of the early Campbell winners had written novels, all of them took the award on the basis of short fiction in the magazines, and only turned to longer work later on.

None of that turned out to be of the least importance, of course; Carolyn won and won handily, and it was no wonder. Seldom has a major new star appeared in the SF firmament so fast, almost overnight.

Discovered by veteran SF editor Donald A. Wollheim of DAW Books, who has given the field fully as many major new writers as Campbell himself, Cherryh published her first novel in 1976. The book was Gate of Ivrel, the *opening of what would eventually be the highly acclaimed Morgaine trilogy. Reviews were enthusiastic, and the sales response almost instantaneous. Although Carolyn herself considered the Morgaine novels to be SF of the alternate-planes variety, a good many readers and reviewers pigeonholed it as fantasy because of its horses-and-swords-and-ruined-castles motifs. But Cherryh was not the sort of woman to stay in anybody's pigeonhole.* Brothers of Earth *and* Hunter of Worlds *followed* Ivrel *onto the stands in 1976 and underlined the range of her talent, presenting the readership with interstellar vistas and some of the most carefully devised and fascinating alien cultures the field had ever seen.*

Three novels in a single year makes quite a splash, especially when the books are as good, and as varied, as these were. Fantasist or science fictioneer, Carolyn Cherryh was clearly a major talent. Once started, there was no stopping her. She followed her dramatic 1976 debut with the second and third Morgaine books, with the important and exciting Faded Sun *trilogy that eclipsed everything she had done before, with a handful of rare and finely crafted shorts in both SF and fantasy, with translations of SF novels from the French, and with book after book after book of her own. One of the freshest and most erudite new writers on the SF scene also turned out to be one of the hardest-working and most prolific, but Cherryh once told an interviewer that she feels she must always have a novel in progress, so when she types the final page of one book, she promptly pulls it from her typewriter—or her word processor, these days— and starts the first page of her next.*

The Campbell was only the start of Carolyn's award collection. In 1979 she graduated to SF's oldest and most important honor when she copped her first Hugo for her short story "Cassandra" at another worldcon, in Brighton, England. And in 1982, in Chicago, Carolyn brought home the "big one" when her book Downbelow Station *took the Best Novel Hugo in a stunning upset over two other heavily favored and aggressively promoted rivals. Given the rate at which Carolyn writes, and the quality of her output, it's only a matter of time until she wins all the other major honors the field has to offer as well.*

Like most "overnight" success stories, Carolyn Cherryh's was years in the making. Born in 1942 in St. Louis, Cherryh grew up in the Midwest, living and writing in Missouri, Oklahoma, and Texas at various times before settling down in the Oklahoma City area. She received a B.A. in Latin from the University of Oklahoma in 1964, and an M.A. in Classics from Johns Hopkins in 1965. A writer long before she broke into professional print, she turned out SF novels on the weekends and evenings while teaching high school Latin and history during the days and waiting for her break. That chance finally arrived in the person of Donald A. Wollheim and DAW; in

1977, after her explosive entry into SF, Carolyn quit her teaching job and has been a full-time free-lance writer ever since.

During the rare occasions when she leaves her word processor, Cherryh travels widely and is a frequent guest at SF conventions. Of the Campbell Award she says, "I heard I'd been nominated for the Campbell Award from a friend doing a newspaper article, who called me up to ask for my reaction: it was a surprise—I'm honored, I think I mumbled, not sure it was even true. And I remained both—surprised and honored. I won and I said then that I wanted to congratulate the other nominees at the same time, meaning that I felt then, and still do, that readers were kind to us all, that it does mean something to be in that list, that it's a very high compliment on the part of the readers who took a chance on buying our work when they didn't know us at all, to say that by that nomination they liked what they saw. Of course it makes a difference. It singles out a handful of new writers and calls attention to them so that those who don't so readily take a chance on an unknown will read their work. It provides an arena in which the new names have a chance; it means that never in a given year will new writers be ignored in the awards process. It means growth in the field, the remembrance and reminder that untried names may come up with something of worth, which has to help the sales of all those worthy new writers who didn't get nominated."

Here, then, a double helping of C. J. Cherryh's talents—a reprint of a lovely fantasy first published in 1977—the sort of work that won Carolyn her Campbell—and a brand-new, never-before-published short novel, SF of the hardest and finest sort, written especially for this volume.

—G.R.R.M.

Death walked the marketplace of Corinth.

He paused in the bazaars, looked with pleased eyes on the teeming throngs of men, laughed gently at the antics of children. He had the shape, at the time, of a dusty man in brown rags, staff in hand. He was indeed a traveller: he had been that morning to Syria to attend a famous general; to India to visit a sage; in Egypt to attend an assassination. He had a thousand, thousand servants besides, did Death, going and coming at his orders, although they were all fragments of himself. He was, at this moment, in the marketplace; and in a hut in Germany; and in an alleyway in Rome: all himself, all seeing with his eyes, all minute reflections of his own being.

He laughed gently at a child, who looked up into his face and smiled, and the laughter faded as a mother snatched him away, shuddering as she scolded him about strangers. He turned his face from the lame young beggar at the steps, who looked at him; he gave him only a coin, and the beggar took it and gazed after him anxiously.

The palace lay ahead, up the steps. The guards there came to attention but, seeing only a poor traveller, rested their spears and let him pass: it was the custom in the land that all strangers were welcome in the palace, to sit at the end of the table and receive charity, for travellers were few and news scant.

And Death would sit at the king's table this night, drawn by that sense that led him toward his appointed tasks.

He was no stranger here. He knew his way, found familiar the gaily painted halls, that led to the king's own hall, where a wedding feast was in progress. He had visited here only a year ago, to lead away the old king. His servants had made many a call here, attending this and that; and through their eyes he was well-familiar with every corridor of this palace, as with most places across the wide face of the earth.

But the servants saw him only with dull human sight, and shrugged in disdain at his rags, and saw him to the lowest seat, hardly interrupting the gaiety. There was a helping of food for him, and drink; he took them, savoring the things of earth, and listened to the minstrel's songs, pleased by such; but none spoke to him and he spoke to no one, save that he gazed up to the high table, where sat the young king.

He had not known until then—until the king met his eyes with that pale and sighted look the dead have—what had drawn him here. Death looked again to the king's left, where the young queen sat, his bride; and around the room, where sat the courtiers, unseeing. Only when he met the king's eyes did he know that he was known, and that not wholly. The king was young: he did not have the familiarity of the old toward him.

The meal was done; the wine was brought, and the king drank

first, of the king's cup, wrought in gold; and passed to the queen. Servants passed round the wine-bowls, and filled cups to the brim for the merry drinking to follow, for it was holiday.

And the king's eyes turned constantly and fearfully upon Death, whose traveller's clothes perhaps seemed less brown than black, whose face less tanned than shadowy: the dying have a sense the living do not.

"Traveller," said the king at last, in a voice strong and firm, "it is the custom that our guests be fed, and then give us their names and the news of their travels, if it be their pleasure. We do not insist, but this is the custom."

Death rose, and time stopped, and all in the hall were still: wine hung half-poured, lips in mid-word, a fly that had come in the open window stopped as a point in the air, the very fire a monument of flame.

"Lord Sisyphos, I am Death," he said softly, casting off his disguise and appearing as he is, Sleep's dark twin, a handsome and gentle god. "Come," he said. "Come."

The soul shuddered within Sisyphos' mortal body, clung fast with the tenacious strength of youth. Sisyphos looked about him at the hall, at the gold and the wealth, and he touched the hand of his beautiful young queen, who in no wise could feel his touch, nor sense anything that passed: her motion was stopped in rising, her eyes, blue as summer skies, shining open, her hair like wheat fields in August—beautiful, beautiful Merope.

Sisyphos' hand trembled. He turned a tearful face to Death.

"She cannot see you," Death said. "Come away now."

"It is not fair," Sisyphos protested.

"You are fortunate," said Death, "to have possessed all these good things, and never to have seen them fade. Come away now, and let go."

"I love her," Sisyphos wept.

"She will come in her own time," said Death.

Sisyphos ran his hand over the lovely cheek of Merope, whose eyes did not blink, whose hair did not stir. He planted a kiss on her cheek, and looked again at Death.

"One word," he pleaded. "Lord, one word with her."

Death's heart melted, for like his brother he is a kindly god. "A moment, then," he said.

The room began to move again. The fly buzzed; the flames leapt, the hum of conversation resumed.

And Merope touched her husband's hand, and blinked, wondering, as her husband leaned close and whispered in her ear. Her summer-sky eyes widened, filled with tears; she shook her head, and he whispered more.

Death averted his face as the woman wept with her husband and a hush fell upon the gathering. But a moment more, and he lifted his staff, and the room stopped once more.

"It is time," he said.

"My lord," said the king, surrendering.

And this time the soul stepped cleanly from the body, and looked about, a little bewildered yet. Death took him by the hand, and with his staff parted that curtain that lies twixt world and world.

"Oh," said Sisyphos, shuddering at the dark.

But Death put his arm about the young king and walked with him, comforting him for a time.

And then Death withdrew to his own privacy, for he had long distracted himself, and his other eyes and hands were paralyzed, wanting their direction. He sat on his throne in the netherworld and gazed on the gray meanderings of Styx and the balefire of Phlegethon, and in the meantime his other selves were attending a shipwreck in the Mediterranean and a dying kitten in Alexandria.

He, brother of Sleep, does not sleep, and is everywhere.

But after the world had turned for the third time and Death, once more rested, was on the far shore of Styx, about to fare out toward the land of Africa (there was an old woman there who had called him), a sad ghost tugged at his sleeve. He looked down into the tearful face of Sisyphos.

"Still unhappy?" he asked the soul. "I am sorry for you, Sisyphos, but really, if you would only leave the riverside and cross over . . . there are meadows there, old friends; why, I've no doubt your parents and grandparents are longing to see you. Your wife will come in her own good time; and time passes very quickly here if you wish it to. You are still entangled with the earth; that is your misery."

"I cannot help it," wept the young king. "My wife will not set me free."

"What, not yet?" exclaimed Death, shocked and dismayed.

"No funeral rites," mourned the ghost, stretching forth a hand toward the gray, slow-moving river, where the ferryman plied his boat. "No coin, no farewell. I am still tied there, unburied, a prisoner. O lord, give me leave to go haunt the place until my wife gives me decent burial."

"That is the law," Death admitted, taking pity on him, thinking on the woman with the summer sky in her eyes and hair like August wheat. Cruel, he thought, so cruel, for all she was so beautiful. "Go," he said, "Sisyphos, and secure your proper burial. There is the way."

He parted the curtain between worlds for him, and showed him Corinth; and straightway he sped by another path, for the African woman cried out in pain, and called his name, and he came quickly, in pity.

But the ghost of Sisyphos smiled as it walked the marketplace by night, and walked up the steps. Guards shivered as it passed, and straightened a little, and the torches in the hallway fluttered.

And there in the hall, on a bed of shields, lay his body in royal state; and near it, her golden hair unbound and her sky-blue eyes red with weeping, knelt Merope.

Laughing, he touched her shoulder, but she looked up not seeing; and with a touch on his own body, he lay down, and lifted himself up, smiling at her.

"Lord!" she cried, and he hugged her as he stood in his own body once more. Tears became wild laughter.

And servants shuddered at the pair, the clever king and his brave bride, who had made this pact while Death waited at their side, that she would not, whatever betided, bury him.

"Admit no strangers," he bade the servants then.

And he with his bride went up the stairs to the bedchamber, where blue dolphins danced on the walls, and torches burned right gaily in the night.

There was a war in China, that raged up and down the banks of the Yangtze, that burned villages and cities, elevated some lords and ruined others. Death and a thousand of his servants were busy there.

There was a plague in India, that on hot winds ran the streets of cities, killing first the beasts and then the men, that cried out in agony; and Death, whose name is heard in Hell, came quickly there, bringing his servants with him.

There was war in Germany that ran across the forests and the river and spilled bloodily into Gaul, as year after year the fightings continued.

Death, who does not sleep, was seldom in his castle, but much about the roads of Europe and the hills of Asia, and walking here and there in the persons of his thousand, thousand servants.

But in the passing years he found himself again in the market-place of a certain city, and the children stared at him in horror, and people drew away from him.

"How is this?" he asked, remembering another welcome he had had in Corinth, when a child had smiled at him.

"Go away," said a merchant. "The king does not favor strangers in this city."

"This is ill hospitality," said Death, offended, "and against the law of the gods."

But when they gathered stones, he went, sorrowing, from the gates, where a beggar sat, wizened and miserable. He turned his face from that one, who looked on him with longing, and gave him a coin.

And then he stepped (for the steps of Death are wide) from the gateway to the palace door, where the guards came to abrupt attention. And his aspect now was that of a king in black robes, with a golden band about his dusky brow, and fires smouldered in his eyes.

The guards shrank from him, weapons untouched, and he passed silently into the hall, angry and curious, too, what the custom was in this city that barred travellers.

The torches flared in the dark as he went, shadow enveloping him and flowing over the gay tiles of octopi and flying-fishes, along the walls of dancers and gardens. He heard the sounds of revelry.

A shadow fell upon the last table, that was the unused place of guests. A torch went out, and laughing men and women fell silent and turned their heads to see what passed there, seeing nothing.

Only the king rose from his place, and the wide-eyed queen beside him. He was older now, with white dusting the dark of his hair; and the first touch of frost was on the wheaten-haired queen, the pinch that kills the flush in the cheeks and makes little cracklings beside the eyes. She lifted her hand to her lips and stopped, as everything stopped, save only Sisyphos.

"Sisyphos," said Death with a frown that dimmed the frozen fires.

Sisyphos' hand touched his wife's arm, trembled there, an older hand, and his eyes filled with tears.

"You see I loved her so," said Sisyphos, "I could not leave her."

And Death, forever mateless, grieved, and his anger faded. "You gained the years you wanted, Man," he said. "Be content. Come." For he remembered the young queen that had been, and was sorry that the touch of age had come on her: mortals; he pitied them, who were prey to Age.

But the soul resisted him, strong and determined, and would not let go. "Come," he said, angered now. "Come. Forty years you have stolen. You have had the best of me. Now come."

And with a swoop that obscured the very hearthfire he came, and reached out his hand.

But quicker than the reach of Death was Sisyphos, whipping round his hands his golden belt, and moly was entwined therein, and asphodel. Death cried out at the treachery, and the spell was broken, and the queen cried out at the shadow. The fires went out, and men shrieked in terror.

They were brave men that, with the king, bore that shadow into the nether reaches of the palace, that was cut deep in the rock, deep cellars and storage places for wine and oil. And here they used iron chains, that wrung painful moans from Death, and here they left him.

Somewhere in Spain an old man called, and Death could not answer; in anguish, Death wept. In Corinth's very streets a dog lay crushed by a passing cart, and its yelping tortured the ears of passersby, and tore at the heart of Death.

Disease and old age ran the world, afflicting thousands, who lingered, calling on Death to no avail.

Insects and beasts bred and multiplied, none dying, and were fed upon and torn and did not die, but lay moaning piteously; and plants and grasses grew up thick, not seeding, through the stones, and when they were cut, did not wither, but continued to grow, until the streets of cities began to be overgrown and beasts wandered out of the fields, confused and crowded by their own young.

Wars were without death, and the wounded kept fighting and the horridly maimed and the diseased walked the world crying out in agony, until there was no place that was free of horrors.

And Death heard all the cries and the prayers, and, helpless, wept.

The very vermin in the basements of the palace multiplied, while Death lay bound and impotent; and fed upon the grain, and devoured everything, leaving the people to starve. Famine stalked the streets, and wasted men, and Disease followed raving in his wake, laughing and tearing at men and beasts.

But Death could not stir.

And at last the gods, looking down on the chaos that was earth, bestirred themselves and began to inquire what passed, for every ill was let loose on earth, and men suffered too much to attend to sacrifices.

The wisest of them knew at once what had been withheld from the world, for wherever men called on Death, he did not come. They searched the depths of earth and sea for him, who never visited the higher realms; and made inquiry among the snake-bodied children of Night, his cousins, but none had seen him.

Then from the still, shadowed quiet of Sleep crept the least of Night's children, a Dream, that wound its serpent-way to the wisest of gods and whispered, timidly, "Sisyphos."

And the gods turned their all-seeing eyes on the city of Corinth, on the man named Sisyphos, on a mourning shadow in the cellars of Corinth's palace. They frowned, and earthquake shook the ground.

And quake after quake rocked at the city, until pillars tottered, and people cowered in fear, and Sisyphos turned knowing eyes on his queen, and kissed her tearfully and took a key.

It was fearful to enter that dark place, with the quakes rumbling and shuddering at the floor, to approach that knot of shadow that huddled in the corner, wherein baleful and angry eyes watched: he had to remember that Death is a serpent-child, and it was a serpent-shape that seemed imprisoned there, earth-wise and ancient and, unlike his twin, cold.

"Give me ten years," Sisyphos tried to bargain with him, endlessly trying.

But Death said nothing, and the floor shuddered, and great

cracks ran through the masonry, portending the fall of the palace. Sisyphos shivered, and thought of his queen; and then he fitted the key to the lock, and took the bonds away.

Death stood up, a swirling shadow, and cold breathed from him as Sisyphos cowered to the floor, trembling.

But it was the dark-faced, gentle king who touched him on the shoulder and whispered in his ear: "Brave Sisyphos, come along."

And Sisyphos arose, forgetting his body that lay in the crumbling cellar, and stepped with the dark king out into the market-place, out into a wilderness that began to die wherever the shadow fell; grass, insects, all withered and went to dust, leaving only bright, young growth; a dog's wails ceased; children's voices began to be heard; and when at last they passed the gates of Corinth, Death paused by the forlorn beggar. Death took his hand gently, and the old man shivered, and smiled, and that immortal part shook free, rising up. The soul blinked, stretched, found it easy to walk with them, on feet that were not lame.

They strode down the shore to the river, where thousands of rustling ghosts were gathering, and the ferryman was hastening to his abandoned post.

It was nine full turnings later that Death gathered to him the summer-eyed queen, and three after that before her gentle ghost appeared before his throne on the far side of the river.

He smiled to see her. She smiled, a knowing and mischievous smile. She was young again. August bloomed in her hair, a glory in the dark of Hell. Far away were the meadows of asphodel, the jagged peaks that were the haunt of the children of Night. She was beginning her journey.

"Come," said Death, and took her hand, and led her with his thousand-league strides across the meadow and beyond to the dark mountains.

There was a trail, much winding, upon a mountainside; and high upon it toiled a strong young king, covered in sweat, who heaved a stone along. Vast it was, and heavy, but he was determined, and patient. He heaved it up another hand's breadth, and braced himself to catch his breath and try again.

"He can be free, you know," whispered Death in the young queen's ear, "once he sets it on yonder pinnacle."

And gently Death set her on the roadside, saw the young king turn, wonder in his eyes, the stone forgotten. It crashed rumbling down the trail, bounding and rebounding, to shatter on the floor of the Pit and send echoes reverberating the length and breadth of Hell. A moment Sisyphos stared after it in dismay; then, with a laugh that outrang the echoes, opened his arms to the young queen Merope.

Death smiled, and turned away, with thousand-league strides crossing the plains of Hell until he reached his throne. And, remembering duty, he extended himself again into his thousand, thousand shapes, and sighed.

C. J. CHERRYH

Companions

I

The ship lay behind them, improbable in so rich a land, so earthlike a world, a silver egg in paradise, an egg more accustomed to stellar distances, to crouching on barren, hellish moons, probing for whatever she could find, her people and her brain calculating survival margins for potential bases—whether mining and manufacture might be enough, given *x* number of ship-calls per year, to make development worth the while, for ships on their way to Somewhere, as a staging point for humans on their way to Somewhere in the deep.

Somewheres were much, much rarer . . . and this was one, this was more than a marginal Somewhere, this eden.

No indication of habitation, no response to an orbiting ship; no readings on close scan, not a geometry anywhere on the surface but nature's own work.

An Earth, unpopulated, untouched, unclaimed.

Green and lush through the faceplates . . . a view that changed slowly as Warren turned, as he faced from open plain to forest to distant mountains. Sea lay a little distance away. The sky was incredible, filtered blue. Three other white-suited figures walked ungainly through the grass. The sounds of breathing came through the suit-com, occasional comments, panted breaths interspersed: the gear weighed them down on this world. The ship kept talking to them, forlorn, envious voices of those duty-bound inside, to the four of them out here.

"Makes no sense," Harley said, disembodied, through the com. "No insects. No birds. You can't have an ecology like this with no animate life."

"Take your samples," Burlin's voice said, dimmer. The captain, Burlin. He stood to make himself that one find that would assure an old age in comfort. For the younger rest of them, promise of prime assignments, of comforts for the ship, of the best for the rest of their lives. They escorted Harley out here—Harley who told them what to gather, Harley whose relays were to the labs back on the ship, the real heart of the probe's operations.

Nothing was wrong with the world. The first air and soil samples *Anne's* intakes had gathered had shown them nothing amiss; the pseudosome had come out, stood, silver and invulnerable to chance, and surveyed the find with robotic eyes, as incapable of joy as suited human bodies were of appreciating the air and the wind that swayed the grasses. There might be perfumes on the wind, but the instruments read a dispassionate N, CO_2, O finding, a contaminant readout, windspeed, temperature.

They gathered whole plants and seeds, tiny scoops of soil, a new world's plunder. Every species was new, and some were analogous to kinds they knew: bearded grasses, smooth-barked bushes with slick green leaves. Paul Warren dug specimens Harley chose and sealed the bags, recorded the surrounds with his camera, labeled and marked with feverish enthusiasm.

"Harley?" That was Sax. Warren looked around at Harley, who sat down from a crouch in the grass, heard someone's breathing gone rapid. "You all right, Harley?"

"It's hot," Harley said. "I don't think my system's working right."

Burlin walked back to him. Warren did, too, stuffing his samples into the bag at his belt. It was an awkward business, trying to examine another suit's systems, tilting the helmet. Sun glared on the readout plate, obscuring the numbers for the moment. Harley shifted his shoulder and it cleared. "All right," Warren said. "The system's all right."

"Maybe you'd better walk back," Burlin said to Harley. "We're nearly done out here anyway."

Harley made a move toward rising, flailed with a gloved hand, and Sax caught it, steadied him on the way up.

Harley's knees went, suddenly, pitching him facedown. "Check the airflow," Burlin said. Warren was already on it.

"No problem there." He tried to keep panic out of his voice. "Harley?"

"He's breathing." Burlin had his hand on Harley's chest. He gathered Harley's arm up, hauled it over his shoulder, and Warren got the other one.

It was a long way back, dragging a suited man's weight. "Get the pseudosome out," Burlin ordered into the welter of questions from the ship. "Get us help out here."

It came before they had gotten halfway to the ship, a gleam in the dark square of *Anne*'s grounded lift tube bay, a human-jointed extension of the ship coming out for them, planting its feet carefully in the uncertain footing of the grass. It was strength. It was comfort. It came walking the last distance with silver arms outstretched, the dark visor of its ovoid head casting back the sun.

They gave Harley to it, positioning its program-receptive arms, told it lift-right, and the right arm came up, so that it carried Harley like a baby, like a silver sexless angel carrying a faceless shape of a man back to the ship. They followed, plodding heavily after, bearing the burden of their own suits and feeling the unease that came with unknown places when things started going wrong.

It was bright day. There were no threats, no unstable terrain, no threat of weather or native life. But the sunlight seemed less and the world seemed larger and ominously quiet for so much life on its face.

They brought Harley inside, into the airlock. The pseudosome stood still as the hatch closed and sealed. "Set down, *Anne*," Burlin said, and the pseudosome reversed the process that had gathered Harley up, released him into their arms. They laid him on the floor.

Harley moved, a febrile stirring of hands and head, a pawing at the helmet collar. "Get the oxygen," Burlin said, and Warren

ignored the queries coming rapid-fire from the crew inside the ship,
got up and opened the emergency panel while Sax and Burlin
stripped off the helmet. He brought the oxy bottle, dropped to his
knees and clamped the clear mask over Harley's white, sweating
face. Harley sucked in great breaths, coughed, back arching in the
cumbersome suit. Red blotches marked his throat, like heat. "Look
at that," Sax said. The blotches were evident on Harley's face, too,
fine hemorrhaging about the cheeks, about the nose and mouth
beneath the plastic.

Burlin stood up, hit the decontamination process. The UV
came on. The rest of the procedure sequenced in the lock. Burlin
knelt. Harley was breathing shallowly now. "He couldn't have gotten
it out there," Warren said. "Not like this, not this fast. Not through
the suit."

"Got to get the ship scoured out," Burlin said. "Yesterday, the
day before—something got past the lock."

Warren looked up . . . at the pseudosome.

The processing cut off. The lights went back to normal. Warren looked at Harley, up at Burlin. "Captain—are we going to bring
him in?"

"We do what we can. We three. Here. In the lock."

Harley's head moved, restlessly, dislodging the mask. Warren
clamped it the more tightly.

Before he died it took the three of them to hold him. Harley
screamed, and clawed with his fingers, and beat his head against the
decking. Blood burst from his nose and mouth and drowned the oxy
mask, smeared their suits in his struggles. He raved and called them
by others' names and cursed them and the world that was killing
him. When it was over, it was morning again, but by then another
of the crew had complained of fever.

Inside the ship.

They went to every crevice of the ship, suited, with UV light
and steam-borne disinfectant, nightmare figures meeting in fog, in
the deep places, among conduits and machines.

Everywhere, the com: "Emergency to three; we've got another—"

Deep in the bowels of the ship, two figures, masked, carrying
cannisters, obscured in steam:

"It isn't doing any good," Abner said. There was panic in his voice, a man who'd seen crew die before, on Mortifer and Hell. *"Ten of us already—"*

"Shut up, Abner," Warren said, with him, in the dark of *Anne's* depths. Steam hissed, roared from the cannisters; disinfectant dripped off griddings, off railings and pipe. *"Just shut it up."*

Com's voice faltered, rose plaintive through the roar: "We're not getting any response out of 2a. Is somebody going to check on that? *Is there somebody going to check that out?"*

There was chaos in the labs, tables unbolted, cots used while they could; pallets spread when they ran out of those. The raving lay next the comatose; death came with hemorrhage, small at first, and worse. Lungs filled, heart labored, and the vessels burst. Others lingered, in delirium.

"Lie down," Sikutu said—biologist, only sometime medic, tried to help the man, to reason where there was no reason.

"I've got work to do," Sax cried, wept, flailed his arms. "I've got work—"

Smith held him, a small woman, pinned an arm while Sikutu held the other. "Hush, hush," she said. "You've got to lie still—Sax, Sax—"

"They all die," Sax wept. "I've got work to do. I've got to get back to the lab—*I don't want to die—*"

He set others off, awakened the sleeping, got curses, screams from others.

"Don't want to die," he sobbed.

Sikutu shook at him, quieted him at last, sat down and held his head in his hands. He felt fevered, felt short of breath.

His pulse increased. But maybe that was fear.

Rule was dead. Warren found her in Botany, among the plants she loved, lying in a knot next one of the counters. He stared, grieved in what shock there was left to feel. There was no question of life left. There was the blood, the look of all the others. He turned his face away, leaned against the wall where the com unit was, pressed the button.

"Captain, she's dead, all right. Botany One."

There was silence for a moment. "Understood," Burlin's voice came back. It broke. Another small silence. "The pseudosome's on its way."

"I don't need it. She doesn't weigh much."

"Don't touch her."

"Yes, sir." Warren pushed the button, broke the contact, leaned there with his throat gone tight. The dying screamed through the day and night, audible through the walls of sickbay on lower deck, up the air shafts, up the conduits, like the machinery sounds.

This had been a friend.

The lift worked, near the lab; he heard it, heard the metal footsteps, rolled his eyes toward the doorway as *Anne* herself came in . . . shining metal, faceless face, black plastic face with five red lights winking on and off inside; black plastic mirroring the lab on its oval surface, his own distorted form.

"Assistance?" *Anne* asked.

"Body." He pointed off at Rule. "Dispose."

Anne reoriented, stalked over and bent at the waist, gripped Rule's arm. The corpse had stiffened. Motors whirred; *Anne* straightened, hauling the body upright; another series of whirrings: brought her right arm under Rule's hips, lifted, readjusted the weight. A slow shuffling turn.

Warren stepped aside. *Anne* walked, hit the body against the doorframe in trying to exit. Warren put out his hand, sickened by this further horror, but *Anne* tilted the body, passed through and on.

He followed, down the hall, to Destruct . . . utilitarian, round-sealed door. *Danger*, it said. *Warning*. They used it for biological wastes. For dangerous samples. For more mundane things.

For their dead, down here.

He opened the hatch. *Anne* put the body in, small, insectile adjustments like a wasp. Froze, then, arms lowering, sensor-lights winking out. Warren closed the door, dogged it down. He pushed the button, winced at the explosive sound, wiped his face. His hands were shaking. He looked at *Anne*.

"Decontaminate yourself," he said. The lights came on inside the mask. The robot moved, reoriented to the hall, walked off into the dark farther down the hall: no lights for *Anne*. She needed none.

Warren's belly hurt. He caught his breath. *Decontaminate*. He headed for the showers, faithful to the regs. It was a thing to do; it kept a man from thinking, held out promises of safety. Maybe the others had let down.

He showered, vapored dry, took clean coveralls from the common locker, sat down on the bench to pull on his boots. His hands kept shaking. He kept shivering even after dressing. *Fear. It's fear.*

An alarm sounded, a short beep of the Klaxon, something touched that should not have been, somewhere in the ship. He stopped in mid-tug, heard the crash and whine of the huge locks at *Anne's* deep core. Airlock. Someone was using the cargo airlock. He stood up, jammed his foot into the second boot, started for the door.

"All report," he heard the general order, Burlin's voice. He went to the com by the door and did that, name and location: "Paul Warren, lower-deck showers."

Silence.

"Captain?"

Silence.

Panic took him. He left the shower room at a run, headed down the corridor to the lift, rode it up to topside, raced out again, down the hall, around the corner into the living quarters, through it to the bridgeward corridor.

Locked. He pushed the button twice, tried the com above it. "Captain." He gasped for air. "Captain, it's Warren. Was that Abner, then?"

Silence. He fumbled his cardkey from his pocket, inserted it into the slot under the lock. It failed. He slammed his fist onto the com.

"Captain?—Sikutu, Abner, is anyone hearing me?"

Silence still. He turned and ran back down the short corridor, through the mainroom, back toward the lift.

"Warren?" the com said. Burlin's voice.

Warren skidded to a stop, scrambled back to the nearest com unit and pushed the button. "Captain, Captain, what's going on?"

"I'm not getting any word out of sickbay," Burlin said. "I've sent the pseudosome in. Something's happened there."

"I'm going."

Silence.

Warren caught his breath, ran for the lift and rode it down again. Silence in the lower corridor too. He looked about him. "Abner? Abner, are you down here?"

No answer to the hail. Nothing. A section seal hissed open behind him. He spun about, caught his balance against the wall.

Anne was there in the dark. The pseudosome strode forward, her red lights glowing.

Warren turned and ran, faster than the robot, headed for the lab.

Quarantine, it said. *No entry.* He reached the door, pressed the com. "Sikutu. Sikutu, it's Warren. Are you all right in there?"

Silence. He pushed Door-Open.

It was a slaughterhouse inside. Blood was spattered over walls and beds. Sikutu—lying on the floor among the beds and pallets, red all over his lab whites from his perforated chest; Minnan and Polly and Tom, lying in their beds with their bedclothes sodden red, with startled eyes and twisted bodies. Throats cut. Faces slashed.

One bed was empty. The sheets were thrown back. He cast about him, counted bodies, lost in horror—heard the footsteps at his back and turned in alarm.

Anne stood there, facelights flashing, cameras clicking into focus.

"Captain," Warren said: *Anne* was a relay herself. "Captain, it's Sax. He's gone . . . everyone else is dead. He's got a knife or something. Is there any word from Abner?"

"I can't raise him." Burlin's voice came from *Anne.* "Get a gun. Go to the lock. Abner was in that area last."

"Assistance." The voice changed; *Anne's* mechanical tones. The pseudosome swiveled, talking to the dead. "Assistance?"

Warren wiped his face, caught his breath. "Body," he said distractedly. "Dispose." He edged past the pseudosome, ran for the corridor, for the weapons locker.

The locker door was dented, scarred as if someone had hammered it, slashed at it; but it was closed. He used his card on it. It jammed. He used it for a lever, used his fingertips, pried it open. He took one of the three pistols there, ignored the holsters, just slammed it shut and ran for the lift.

Downward again. His hands were shaking as he rode. He fumbled at the safety. He was a navigator, had never carried a gun against any human being, had never fired except in practice. His heart was speeding, his hands cold.

The lift stopped; the door whipped open on the dark maze of netherdeck, of conduits and walkways that led to the lock.

He reached for the light switch below the com panel. The lift door shut behind him, leaving him in dark. He hesitated, pushed the button.

He walked carefully along the walk. The metal grids of the decking echoed underfoot. He passed aisles, searching for ambush . . . flexed his fingers on the gun, thinking of it finally, of what he was doing.

A catwalk led out to the lift platform, to the huge circular cargo plate, the lift control panel. The plate was in down-position, leaving a deep black hole in netherdeck, the vertical tracks showing round the pit. He reached the control station, pressed the button.

Gears synched; hydraulics worked. The platform came up into the light. A shape was on it, a body in a pool of blood. Abner.

Warren punched the station com. "Captain," he said, controlling his voice with marvelous, reasonable calm. "Captain, Abner's dead. Out on the lift platform, netherdeck. Shall I go outside?"

"No," Burlin's voice came back.

He shivered, waiting for more answer. "Captain." He still kept it calm. "Captain, what do you want me to do?"

Silence and static. Warren cut it off, his hand clenched to numbness on the gun. He flexed it live again, walked out onto the echoing platform, looked about him, full circle, at the shadows. Blood trailed off the platform's circle, stopped clean against the opposing surface. *Gone. Outside.* He hooked the gun to his belt, stooped and gathered Abner up, heaved the slashed body over his shoulder. Blood drenched him, warm and leaking through his clothes. The limbs hung loose.

He carried it—him; Abner; six years his friend. Like Sikutu. Like Sax.

He kept going, to the lift, trailing blood, retracing all his steps. There was silence all about, ship-silence, the rush of air in the ducts, the thousand small sounds of *Anne's* pumps and fans. Two of them now, two of them left, himself and Burlin. And Sax—out there; out there, escaped, in paradise.

He took Abner upstairs, carried him down the corridor, in the semidark of Power-Save.

The pseudosome was busy there, carrying Sikutu's bloody form to the destruct chamber. Warren followed it, automaton like the other, trying to feel as little. But the bodies were stacked up there at the foot of the destruct chamber door, a surplus of bodies. Only one was jammed inside. Minnan. Warren's knees weakened. He watched the pseudosome let Sikutu down atop the others, saw it coming back, arms outstretched.

"Assistance?"

He surrendered Abner to it, stomach twisting as he did. He clamped his jaws and dogged the door on Minnan and pushed the button.

They did the job, he and the pseudosome. He threw up, after, from an empty stomach.

"Assistance?" *Anne* asked. "Assistance?"

He straightened, wiped his face, leaned against the wall. "Sterilize the area. Decontaminate." He walked off, staggered, corrected himself, pushed the nearest com button, having composed himself, keeping anger from his voice. "Captain. Captain, I've got the bodies all disposed. The area's being cleaned." Softly, softly, he talked gently to this man, this last sane man. "Can we talk, sir?"

"Warren?" the plaintive voice came back.

"Sir?"

"I'm sorry."

"Sir?" He waited. There was only the sound of breathing coming through. "Sir—are you on the bridge? I'm coming up there?"

"Warren—I've got it."

"No, sir." He wiped his forearm across his face, stared up at the com unit. He began to shake. "What am I supposed to do, sir?" He forced calm on himself. "What can I do to help?"

A delay. "Warren, I'll tell you what I've done. And why. You listening, Warren?"

"I'm here, sir."

"I've shut down controls. We can't beat this thing. I've shut her down for good, set her to blow if anyone tries to bypass to take off. I'm sorry. Can't let us go home . . . taking this back to human space. It could spread like wildfire, kill—kill whole colonies before the meds could get it solved. I've set a beacon, Warren. She'll play it anytime some probe comes in here, when they do come, whenever."

"Sir—*sir*, you're not thinking— A ship in space—is a natural quarantine."

"And if we died en route—and if someone got aboard— No. No. They mustn't do that. We can't lift again."

"Sir—listen to me."

"No animals, Warren. We never found any animals. A world like this and nothing moving in it. It's a *dead world.* Something got it. Something lives here, in the soil, something in the air; something grew here, something fell in out of space—and it got all the animals. Every moving thing. Can't let it go—"

"Sir—sir, we don't know the rest of us would have died. We don't know that. *You* may not, and I may not, and what are we going to do, sir?"

"I'm sorry, Warren. I'm really sorry. It's not a chance to take— to go like that. Make up your own mind. I've done the best thing. I have. Insured us against weakness. It can't leave here."

"Captain—"

Silence. A soft popping sound.

"Captain!" Warren pushed away from the wall, scrambled for the lift and rode it topside, ran down the corridor toward the bridge. He thrust his card into the lock.

It worked now. The door slid. And Burlin was there, slumped at the com station, the gun beneath his hand. The sickroom stink was evident. The fever. The minute hemorrhages on the hands. Blood pooled on the com counter, ran from Burlin's nose and mouth. The eyes stared, reddened.

Warren sat down in the navigator's chair, wiped his face, his eyes, stared blankly, finding it hard to get his breath. He cursed Burlin. Cursed all the dead.

There was silence after.

He got up finally, pulled Burlin's body back off the com board, punched in the comp and threw the com wide open, because the ship was all there was to talk to. *"Anne,"* he said to comp. "Pseudosome to bridge. Body. Dispose."

In time the lift operated and the silver pseudosome arrived, leisurely precise. It stood in the doorway and surveyed the area with insectoid turns of the head. It clicked forward then, gathered up Burlin and walked out.

Warren stayed a time, doing nothing, sitting in the chair on the bridge, in the quiet. His eyes filled with tears. He wiped at one eye and the other, still numb.

When he did walk down to destruct to push the button, the pseudosome was still standing beside the chamber. He activated it, walked away, left the robot standing there.

It was planetary night outside. He thought of Sax out there, crazed. Of Sax maybe still alive, in the dark, as alone as he. He thought of going out and hunting for him in the morning.

The outside speakers.

He went topside in haste, back to the bridge, sat down at the com and opened the port shields on night sky. He dimmed the bridge lights, threw on the outside floods, illuminating grass and small shrubs round about the ship.

He put on the outside address.

"Sax. Sax, it's Paul Warren. There's no one left but us. Listen, I'm going to put food outside the ship tomorrow. *Tomorrow*, hear me? I'll take care of you. You're not to blame. I'll take care of you. You'll get well, you hear me?"

He kept the external pickup on. He listened for a long time, looked out over the land.

"Sax?"

Finally he got up and walked out, down to the showers, sealed his clothes in a bag for destruct.

He tried to eat after that, wrapped in his robe, sitting down in the galley because it was a smaller place than the living quarters and somehow the loneliness was not so deep there; but he had no appetite. His throat was pricklish . . . exhaustion, perhaps. He had reason enough. The air-conditioning felt insufficient in the room.

But he had driven himself. That was what.

He had the coffee at least, and the heat suffused his face, made him short of breath.

Then the panic began to hit him. He thrust himself up from the table, dizzy in rising, vision blurred—felt his way to the door and down the corridor to the mirror in the showers. His eyes were watering. He wiped them, tried to see if there was hemorrhage. They were red, and the insides of the lids were red and painful. The heat he had felt began to go to chill, and he swallowed repeatedly as he walked back to the galley, testing whether the soreness in his throat was worse than he recalled over the last few hours.

Calm, he told himself. Calm. There were things to do that had to be done or face dying of thirst, of hunger. He set about gathering things from the galley, arranged dried food in precise stacks beside the cot in the lower-deck duty station, near the galley. He made his sickbed, set drugs and water and a thermal container of ice beside it.

Then he called the pseudosome in, walked it through the track from his bed to the galley and back again, programmed it for every errand he might need.

He turned down the bed. He lay down, feeling the chill more intense, and tucked up in the blankets.

The pseudosome stood in the doorway like a silver statue, one sensor light blinking lazily in the faceplate. When by morning the fever had taken him and he was too weak to move coherently, he had mechanical hands to give him water. *Anne* was programmed to pour coffee, to do such parlor tricks, a whim of Harley's.

It wished him an inane good morning. It asked him *How are you?* and at first in his delirium he tried to answer, until he drifted too far away.

"Assistance?" he would hear it say then, and imagined a note of human concern in that voice. "Malfunction? Nature of malfunction, please?"

Then he heaved up, and he heard the pseudosome's clicking crescendo into alarm. The emergency Klaxon sounded through the ship as the computer topside registered that there was something beyond its program. Her lights all came on.

"Captain Burlin," she said again and again, "Captain Burlin, emergency."

II

The pulsing of headache and fever grew less. Warren accepted consciousness gradually this time, fearful of the nausea that had racked him the last. His chest hurt. His arms ached, and his knees.

His lips were cracked and painful. It amazed him that the pain had ebbed down to such small things.

"Good morning."

He rolled his head on the pillow, to the soft whirr of machinery on his right. *Anne's* smooth-featured pseudosome was still waiting.

He was alive. No waking between waves of fever. His face felt cool, his body warm from lying too long in one place. He lay in filth, and stench.

He propped himself up, reached for the water pitcher, knocked it off the table. It rolled empty to *Anne's* metal feet.

"Assistance?"

He reached for her arm. "Flex."

The arm bent, lifting him. Her motors whirred in compensation. "Showers."

She reoriented herself and began to walk, with him leaning on her, his arm about her plastic-sheathed shoulder, like some old, familiar friend.

She stopped when she had brought him where he wished, out of program. He managed to stand alone, tottering and staring at himself in the mirror. He was gaunt, unshaven, covered with filth and sores. His eyes were like vast bruises. He swore, wiped his eyes and felt his way into a shower cabinet.

He fainted there, in the shower stall, came to again on the floor, under the warm mist. He managed to lever himself up again, got the door open, refused a second dizziness and leaned there till it passed. *"Anne."*

A whirring of motors. She planted herself in the doorway, waiting.

She got him topside, to the living quarters, to his own compartment door. "Open," he told her hoarsely; and she brought him inside, to the edge of his own unused bed, to clean blankets and clean sheets. He fell into that softness panting and shivering, hauled the covers over himself with the last of his strength.

"Assistance?"

"I'm all right."

"Define usage: *right.*"

"Functional. I'm functional."

"Thank you."

He laughed weakly. This was not *Anne.* Not she. It. *Anne* was across the living quarters, in controls, all the company there was left.

Thank you. As if courtesy had a point. She was the product of a hundred or more minds over the course of her sixteen-year service, men and women who programmed her for the moment's convenience and left their imprint.

Please and thank you. Cream or sugar, sir? She could apply a wrench or laser through the pseudosome, lift a weight no man could move, bend a jointing into line or make a cup of coffee. But nothing from initiative.

Thank you.

It was another few hours before he was sure he was going to live. Another day before he did more than send *Anne* galleyward and back, eat and sleep again.

But at last he stood up on his own, went to his locker, dressed, if feebly.

The pseudosome brightened a second sensor at this movement, then a third. "Assistance?"

"Report, *Anne.*"

"Time: oh six four five hours ten point one point two three. Operating on standby assistance, program E one hundred; on program A one hundred; on additional pro—"

"Cancel query. Continue programs as given." He walked out into the living quarters, walked to the bridge, stood leaning on Burlin's chair, surrounded by *Anne*'s lazily blinking consoles, by scanner images no one had read for days. He sat down from weakness.

"*Anne.* Do you have any program to lift off?"

The console lights rippled with activity. Suddenly Burlin's deep voice echoed through the bridge. "Final log entry. Whoever hears this, don't—repeat, don't—land. Don't attempt assistance. We're dead of plague. It got aboard from atmosphere, from soil . . . somehow. It hit everyone. Everyone is dead. Biological records are filed under—"

"Cancel query. Reply is insufficient. Is there a course program in your records?"

"Reply to request for course: I must hold my position. If question is made of this order, I must replay final log entry. . . . *Final log entry*—"

"*Bypass that order. Prepare for lift!*"

The lights went red. "I am ordered to self-destruct if bypass is attempted. Please withdraw request."

"Cancel—cancel bypass order." Warren slumped in the chair, stared at the world beyond the viewpoint, deadly beguiling morning, gold streaming through cumulus cloud. It was right. Burlin had been right; he had ensured even against a survivor. Against human weakness.

"*Anne.*" His voice faltered. "Take program. If I speak, I'm speaking to you. I don't need to say your name. My voice will activate your responses. I'm Paul Warren. Do you have my ID clear?"

"ID as Warren, Paul James, six eight seven seven six five eight—"

"Cancel query. How long can your pseudosome remain functional?"

"Present power reserve at present rate of consumption: three hundred seventy-eight years approximate to the nearest—"

"Cancel query. Will prolonged activity damage the pseudosome?"

"Modular parts are available for repair. Attrition estimate: no major failure within power limits."

Warren gazed out at the daybreak. *Sax*, he thought. He had made a promise and failed it, days ago. He tried to summon the strength to do something about it, to care—to go out and search in the hope that a man could have lived out there, sick, in the chill of nights and without food. He knew the answer. He had no wish to dwell on guilt, to put any hope in wandering about out there, to find another corpse. He had seen enough. More than enough.

"Library. Locate programming manual. Dispense."

An agitation ran across the board and a microfilm shot down into the dispenser. He gathered it up.

There was this, for his comfort. For three hundred seventy-eight years.

Anne was a marvelous piece of engineering. Her pseudosome was capable of most human movements; its structure imitated the human body and her shining alloy was virtually indestructible by heat or corrosion. Walk-through programming made her capable in the galley: Her sensitive vid scanners could read the tapes on stored foods; her timing system was immaculate. She carried on domestic tasks, fetched and carried, and meanwhile her other programs kept more vital functions in working order: circulation, heating, cooling throughout the ship, every circuit, all automated, down to the schedule of lighting going on and off, to the inventory reports going up on the screens each morning, for crew who would no longer read them.

Warren worked, ignoring these processes, trusting *Anne* for them. He read the manual, wrote out programs, sitting naked in bed with the microfilm reader on one side and a coffeepot on the other and a lap full of notes.

An illusion, that was all he asked, a semblance of a mind to talk to. Longer plans he refused as yet. The plotting and replotting that filled the bed and the floor about him with discarded balls of paper was his refuge, his defense against thinking.

He dreaded the nights and kept the lights on while the rest of the ship cycled into dark.

He slept in the light when he had to sleep, and woke and worked again while the pseudosome brought him his meals and took the empty dishes back again.

III

He called the star Harley, because it was his to name. The world he called Rule, because Harley and Rule were sometime lovers and it seemed good. Harley was a middling average star, the honest golden sort, which cast an easy warmth on his back, as an old friend ought. Rule stretched everywhere, rich and smelling sweet as Rule always had, and she was peaceful.

He liked the world better when he had named it, and felt the sky friendlier with an old friend's name beaming down at him while he worked.

He stretched the guy ropes of a plastic canopy they had never had the chance to use on harsher worlds, screwed the moorings into the grassy earth and stood up in pleasant shade, looking out over wide billows of grass, with forest far beyond them.

Anne kept him company. She had a range of half a kilometer from the ship over which mind and body could keep in contact, and farther still if the booster unit were in place, which project he was studying. He had not yet had the time. He moved from one plan to the next, busy, working with his hands, feeling the strength return to his limbs. Healing sunlight erased the sores and turned his skin a healthy bronze. He stretched his muscles, grinned up at the sun through the leaf-patterned plastic. Felt satisfied.

"*Anne.* Bring the chair, will you?"

The pseudosome came to life, picked up the chair that remained on the cargo lift, carried it out. And stopped.

"*Set it down.*" His good humor turned to disgust. "Set it down."

Anne set it, straightened, waited.

"*Anne.* What do you perceive?"

Anne's sensors brightened, one after the other. "Light, gravity, sound, temperature."

"You perceive *me.*"

"Yes, Warren. You're directly in front of me."

"*Anne,* come here."

She walked forward, into the shade, stopped, hands at her sides, sensors pulsing behind her dark faceplate like so many stars in a void.

"*Anne,* I'm your duty. I'm all the crew. The directives all apply only to me now. The others have stopped functioning. Do you understand? I want you to remain active until I tell you otherwise. Walk at your own judgment. Identify and accept all stimuli that don't take you out of range."

"Program recorded," *Anne* purred. "Execute?"

"Execute."

Anne walked off. She had a peculiar gait, precise in her movements like an improbable dancer, stiffly smooth and slow-motion. Graceful, silver *Anne.* It always jarred when he looked into the vacant faceplate with the starry lights winking on and off in the darkness. She could never appreciate the sun, could never perceive him except as a pattern of heat and solidity in her sensors. She looked left, looked right, walk-walk-walk-walk, looked left, right, walk-walk-

walk-walk, neither breathing the scents of life nor feeling the wind on her plastic skin. The universe held no perils for *Anne.*

Warren wept. He strode out, overtook her, seized her as she turned to him. "*Anne.* Where are you? Where are you going?"

"I am located four oh point four seven meters from base center. I am executing standard survey, proceeding—"

"Cancel query. *Anne,* look about you. What have you learned?"

Anne swiveled her head left and right. Her sensors flickered. "This world is as first observed. All stimuli remain within human tolerance. There are no native lifeforms in my scan."

She turned then, jerking from his hands, and walked off from him, utterly purposeful.

"*Anne!*" he called, alarmed. "*Anne,* what's wrong?"

She stopped, faced him. "The time is 1100 hours. Standard timed program 300-32-111PW."

Lunch. *Anne* was, if nothing else, punctual.

"Go on."

She turned. He trailed after her to the edge of the canopy, cast himself into the chair and sat disconsolate. Adrenaline surged. Rage. There was no profit in that. Not at a machine. He knew that. He told himself so.

He attached the booster unit—not out of enthusiasm, but because it was another project, and occupied him. It took two days . . . in which he had only *Anne's* disembodied voice, while the pseudosome lay disemboweled in the shop. He had difficulty, not with the insertion of the unit, which was modular, but in getting the ring-joints of the waist back together; it occasioned him panic, real and sweating dread. He consulted library, worked and fretted over it, got the first ring and the second, and so on to the fifth. She had lost nothing vital, only some of her auxiliary apparatus for hookups of use on frigid moons. That could be put back if need be.

He could take her apart and put her back together if need be, if amusement got more scarce.

If she worked at all now. The chance of failure still scared him.

"*Anne,*" he said, "turn on the pseudosome."

The head slung over, faced him.

"Good morning, Warren."

"Are you functional? Test your legs. Get off the table."

Anne sat up, machine-stiff, precisely reversing her process of getting onto the table. She stood, arms at her sides.

"Go on," Warren said. "Go about your duties."

She stayed fixed.

"Why don't you go?"

"Instruction?"

He bounced a wrench off the lab wall so violently his shoulder ached. It rebounded to *Anne's* metal feet.

Whirr-click. *Anne* bent with long legs wide and retrieved the wrench, proffering it to him. "Assistance?"

"Damn you."

All the sensor lights came on. "Define usage: *damn.*"

He hit her. She compensated and stood perfectly balanced. "Define: *damn.*"

He sobbed for breath, stared at her, regained his patience. "The perception is outside your sensor range."

The sensor lights dimmed. She still held the wrench, having no human fatigue to make her lower it.

An idea came to him, like a flash of madness. He shoved the debris and bits of solder off the worktable and sat down with his notebook, feverishly writing definitions in terms *Anne's* sensors could read: tone, volume, pace, stability, function/nonfunction/optimum, positive/negative. . . .

"This program," *Anne* said to him through her bridge main speakers, "conflicts with the central program."

He sat down in the command chair, all his plans wrecked. "Explain conflict."

"I'm government property," the computer said. "Regulations forbid crew to divert me for personal use."

Warren bit his lip and thought a moment, chin on hand. Looked at the flickering lights. "I'm your highest priority. There aren't any other humans in your reach. Your program doesn't permit you to lift off, true?"

"Yes."

"You can't return to government zones, true?"

"Yes."

"There's no other crew functioning, true?"

"Yes."

"I'm your only human. There can't be any lateral conflict in your instructions if you accept the program. I need maintenance. If you refuse to maintain me, I have to disconnect you and restructure your whole system of priorities. I can do that."

The board flashed wildly. Went to red. A light to the left began to blink: AUTODESTRUCT, AUTODESTRUCT, AUTODESTRUCT—

"I'm programmed to defend this position. I have prior instruction. Please check your programming, Warren. I'm in conflict."

"Will you accept instruction? I'm your remaining crew. What I tell you is true."

The lights went steady, burning red. "Instruction? Instruction?"

"This new programming applies only to my protection and maintenance under present environmental conditions, while we're on this world. It's not a diversion from your defense function. I'm assisting you in your defense of this position. I'm your crew. I need maintenance. This new program is necessary for that purpose. My health is threatened. My life is threatened. This program is essential for my life and safety."

The red light went off. The lights rippled busily across the boards, normalcy restored. "Recorded."

Warren drew a long-held breath. "What's your status, *Anne?*"

"Indeterminate, Warren. I haven't yet completed assimilation of this new data. I perceive possible duplication of existing vocabulary. Is this valid?"

"This terminology is in reference to me. These are human life states. Maintenance of me is your duty."

"Negative possible, Warren. My sensors are effective in systems analysis only for myself."

He thought, mechanically speaking, that there was something rather profound in that. It was indeed *Anne*'s central problem. He stood up, looked at the pseudosome, which stood inactive by the door. "Turn your sensors on me."

Anne faced him. The sensor lights came on.

"Define: *pain, Anne.*"

"Disruption of an organism," the pseudosome-speaker said, "by sensor overload. It is not an acceptable state."

He drew a deeper breath, came closer. "And what is pleasure, *Anne?*"

"Optimum function."

"Define: *feel, Anne.*"

"Verb: receive sensor input other than visual, auditory, or chemical analysis. Noun: the quality of this input."

"Define: *happy.*"

"Happy; content; pleased; comfortable; in a state of optimum function."

"And *anger, Anne.*"

"An agitated state resulting from threatening and unpleasant outcome of action. This is a painful state."

"Your program is to maintain me happy. When your sensors indicate I'm in pain, you must investigate the causes and make all possible effort to restore me to optimum function. That's a permanent instruction."

The facial lights blinked, died, all but one. "Recorded."

He sighed.

The lights flashed on. "Is this pain?"

"No." He shook his head and began to laugh, which set all of *Anne's* board lights to flickering.

"Define, define."

He forced calm. "That's laughing. You've heard laughing before now."

A delay. "I find no record."

"But you heard it just then. Record it. That's pleasure, *Anne.*"

Facelights blinked. There were six now. "Recorded."

He patted her metal shoulder. She swiveled her head to regard his hand. "Do you feel that, *Anne?*"

The face turned back to him. "Feel is in reference to humans."

"You can use the word. Do you feel that?"

"I feel a pressure of one point seven kilos. This does not affect my equilibrium."

He patted her arm gently then, sadly. "That's all right. I didn't think it would."

"Are you still happy, Warren?"

He hesitated, having a moment's queasiness, a moment's chill. "Yes," he said. It seemed wisest to say.

IV

He stopped on a small rise not far from the ship and the pseudosome went rigid at his side. They stood knee-deep in grass. A few fleecy clouds drifted in the sky. The forest stretched green and lush before them.

"Do you perceive any animate life, *Anne?*"

"Negative native animate life."

"Is there any record—of a world with vegetation of this sort, that had no animate life?"

"Negative. Further information: there is viral life here. This is not in my sensor range, but I have abundant data in my files regarding—"

"Cancel statement. Maybe this world was inhabited by something once and the virus killed it."

"I have no data on that proposal."

"No animals. Burlin said it."

"Define: *it.*"

"Cancel." Warren adjusted his pack on his shoulders, pointed ahead, a gesture *Anne* understood. "We'll walk as far as the river."

"Define: *river.*"

"See where the trees—the large vegetation starts? There's water there. A river is a moving body of water on a planetary surface. You have maps in your files. You've got rivers on them. Why don't you know rivers?"

Anne's facial sensors winked. "Maps are in library storage. I don't have access to this data."

"Well, there's one there. A river."

"My sensors have recorded the presence of water in the original survey. Free water is abundant on this world."

Dutifully she kept pace with him, still talking as he started off, metal limbs tireless. He stopped from time to time, deviated this way and that, walked round the scattered few bushes, investigated bare spots in the grass, which proved only stony outcrops.

Nothing. Nothing, in all his searching.

"Assistance?" *Anne* asked when he stopped.

"No, *Anne.*" He looked back at her, hesitant. "Do you, *Anne*—ever perceive . . . any other human?"

"Negative. You are my only human."

He bit his lip, nerved himself, finally. "When I was in bed—did Sax ever come back?"

The sensors blinked. "I find no record."

He found that ambiguous, tried to think a new way through the question. He looked toward the river, back again. "Has he ever come back?"

"I find no record."

Warren let go a small breath, shook his head. "He's not functioning. I'm sure of it."

"Recorded."

He hitched the pack, started walking again. "His body's out here somewhere."

"I find no record."

"I want to find him, *Anne*. Shouldn't have left him out here. He could have come back and needed me. And I couldn't answer. I want to find him. I owe him that."

"Recorded."

They came to the trees finally, to shade, in the straightest line from the ship, which seemed most worth searching. Trees. A small slope of eroded sand down to the river, which flowed about fifty meters wide, deep and sluggish. A stream, broad and brown.

He stopped, and *Anne* did. Drew a breath of the scented air, forgetful for the moment of Sax, of what had brought him. Here was beauty, unsuspected, a part of the world he had not seen from the ship—secrets underwater and growing round it, trees that relieved the sameness and made evershifting lattices that compressed distances into their back-and-forth tangle. No straight lines here. No scour of wind. Coolth. Complexity.

Life, perhaps, lurking in the river. One fish, one crawling thing, and the parameters of the world had to be revised. One fish . . . and it meant life everywhere.

"Stand where you are," he told *Anne*, starting down the bank. "I don't think swimming is in your program."

"Define: *swimming*. I find no record."

He laughed soundlessly, left her by the trees and walked through the pathless tangle to the sandy bank. Trees with trailing, moss-hung branches arched out over the sluggish current. Flowers bloomed, white and starlike, on the far margin, where the trees grew larger still and it was twilight at midafternoon. He squatted down by the water and looked into shallows where the current swirled mosses.

Anne came to life, motors whirring. Brush cracked. He sprang up, saw her coming down the slope, precariously balanced in the descent.

"Stop—*Anne,* stop."

Anne planted her feet at the bottom, waistdeep in brush, lights flashing. "Warren, danger."

Panic surged. He had brought no gun on this search. Did not trust himself. "Specify—danger."

"The river is dangerous."

The breath went out of him. He halfway laughed. "No. Verb: *swim,* to travel through water safely. I can swim, *Anne.* I'm safe. No danger."

"Please consider this carefully, Warren."

He grinned, took a vial from his sample kit and knelt, taking up a specimen of water. He had the whole of the labs to use; he had had the basics, and it was a project, something to do, something with promise, this time.

"I can't assist you in the water, Warren."

"I don't need assistance." He capped the vial and replaced it in the kit, wiped his fingers with a disinfectant towelette and stowed it. "I'll come back to you in a moment."

She made small whirring sounds, cameras busy.

He stood up, turned to face her, waved a hand toward the bank. "Turn your sensors over there, far focus, will you? See if you can see anything."

"Vegetation. Trees."

"Yes." He put his hands into his pockets, stood staring into the forest a long time, watching the wind stir the leaves on the far bank.

So the world had a limit. *Anne* did. There. The ship had a raft, two of them; but curiosity was not worth the risk to the pseudosome. There were the other directions—flat and grassy; there was the land-crawler for crossing them.

But there was nothing in those distances but more grass and more distance.

He shrugged, half a shiver, and turned his back on the river and the forest, climbed back to *Anne,* pulled branches away from her silvery body and held them out of her way.

"Come on. Let's go home."

"Yes, Warren." She swiveled smartly and reoriented, cracking branches with each metal tread, followed him through the tangle until they had come out of the brush again, walking side by side toward the plain, toward the ship.

No sign of Sax. It was useless. Sax would have drowned in the river if his fever had carried him this way; drowned and been swept out to some brush heap elsewhere. Or seaward.

"*Anne,* would you have followed me if I'd tried to cross the river?"

"Instruction directed me to stay. Program directs me to protect you."

"I love you, too, Annie, but don't ever take the risk. I could cross the river without danger. My body floats in water. Yours sinks. The mud would bog you down."

"Program directs me to protect you."

"You can't protect me if you're at the bottom of the river. You can't float. Do you understand *float?*"

"Verb: be buoyant, rise. Noun—"

"Cancel. You stay away from that water, hear me?"

"I'm receiving you clearly, Warren."

"I order you to stay away from the river. If I go close, you stop and wait until I come back. You don't ever go into water. That's a permanent order."

"I perceive possible priority conflict."

"You have to preserve yourself to carry out your instruction to protect me. True?"

"Yes."

"Water can damage you. It can't damage me. If I choose to go there, I go. You stay away from the water."

A delay. "Recorded."

He frowned, hitched the pack up and looked askance at her, then cast another, longer look backward.

Build a bridge, perhaps? Make the other side accessible for *Anne?* The thought of going beyond her range made him uneasy— if he should run into difficulty, need her—

There were the com units. The portable sensors.

He wanted to go over there, to know what was there. And not there.

The microscope turned up a variety of bacteria in the water. He sat in the lab, staring at the cavorting shapes, shaken by that tiny movement as if it had been the sight of birds or beasts. *Something lived here and moved.*

Such things, he recalled, could work all manner of difficulties in a human gut. He called up Library, went through the information gleaned of a dozen worlds. The comparisons might have told Sikutu something, but he found it only bewildering. They might be photosynthesizing animalcules, or contractile plants.

Heat killed the specimens. He shoved the plate into the autoclave and felt like a murderer. He thought even of walking back to the river to pour the rest of the vial in. Life had become that precious. He nerved himself and boiled the rest—imagined tiny screams in the hissing of the bubbles. It left pale residue.

Two days he lay about, thinking, distracting himself from thought. He sat in *Anne's* observation dome at night, mapped the movements of the system's other worlds; by day, observed the sun through filters. But there were the charts they had made from space, and looking at the stars hurt too much. It was too much like wishing.

He stopped going there.

And then there was just the forest to think on. Only that left.

He gathered his gear, set *Anne* to fetching this and that. He unbolted a land-crawler from its braces, serviced it, loaded it to the bay and loaded it with gear: inflatable raft, survival kit.

"Let it down," he told *Anne.* "Lower the cargo lift."

She came out afterward, bringing him what he had asked, standing there while he loaded the supplies on.

"Assistance?"

"Go back in. Seal the ship. Wait for me."

"My program is to protect you."

"The pseudosome stays here." He reached into the crawler, where the sensor remote unit sat, a black square box on the passenger seat. He turned it on. "That better?"

"The sensor unit is not adequate for defense."

"The pseudosome is not permitted to leave this area unless I call you. There's no animate life, no danger. I'll be in contact. The unit is enough for me to call you if I need help. Obey instructions."

"Please reconsider this program."

"Obey instructions. If you damage that pseudosome, it's possible I won't be able to fix it, and then I won't have it when I need you. True?"

"Yes."

"Then stay here." He walked round, climbed into the driver's seat, started the engine. "Recorded?"

"Recorded."

He put it in gear and drove off through the grass—looked back as he turned it toward the forest. She still stood there. He turned his attention to the rough ground ahead, fought the wheel.

A machine, after all. There were moments when he lost track of that.

The sensor unit light glowed. She was still beside him.

He dragged the raft down the sandy slope, unwieldy bundle, squatted there a moment to catch his breath on the riverside. The wind whispered in the leaves. No noise of motors. He felt the solitude. He saw details, rather than the sterile flatnesses of the ship, absorbed himself in the hush, the moving of the water.

He moved finally, unrolled the raft and pulled the inflation ring. It hissed, stiffened, spread itself.

Beep. Beep-beep-beep.

The sensor box. His heart sped. He scrambled up the sandy rise to the crawler and reached the box in the seat. "*Anne.* What's wrong?"

"Please state your location." the box asked him.

"Beside the river."

"This agrees with my location findings. Please reconsider your program, Warren."

"*Anne,* you keep that pseudosome where it is. I'll call you if I need you. And I don't need you. I'm all right and there's no danger."

"I picked up unidentified sound."

He let his breath go. "That was the raft inflating. I did it. There's no danger."

"Please reconsider your program."

"*Anne*, take instruction. Keep that pseudosome with the ship. I've got a small communicator with me. The sensor box weighs too much for me to carry it with the other things I need. I'm going to leave it in the crawler. But I'm taking the communicator. I'll call you if there's an emergency or if I need assistance."

"Response time will be one hour seventeen minutes to reach your present location. This is unacceptable."

"I tell you it is acceptable. I don't need your assistance."

"Your volume and pitch indicate anger."

"Yes, I'm angry."

"Be happy, Warren."

"I'll be happy if you do what I told you and keep that pseudo-some at the ship."

A long delay. "Recorded."

He took the communicator from the dash, hooked it to his belt. Walked off without a further word. *Anne* worried him. There was always that conflict-override. She could do something unpredictable if some sound set her off, some perception as innocent as the raft cylinder's noise.

But there was nothing out here to trigger her. Nothing.

He slipped the raft away from the shore, quietly, quietly, used the paddle with caution. The current took him gently and he stroked leisurely against it.

A wind sighed down the river, disturbing the warmth, rustling the leaves. He drove himself toward the green shadow of the far bank, skimmed the shore a time.

There was a kind of tree that flourished on that side, the leaves of which grew in clusters on the drooping branches, like fleshy green flowers, and moss that festooned other trees never grew on this kind. He saw that.

There was a sort of green flower of thin, brown-veined leaves that grew up from the shallows, green lilies on green pads. The river sent up bubbles among them, and he probed anxiously with his paddle, disturbed their roots, imagining some dire finned creature whipping away from that probing—but he only dislodged more bubbles from rotting vegetation on the bottom. The lilies and the rot were cloyingly sweet.

He let the current take the raft back to the far-shore point nearest his starting place. He drove the raft then into the shallows and stood up carefully, stepped ashore without wetting his boots, dragged the raft up by the mooring rope and secured it to a stout branch to keep the current from unsettling it by any chance.

He took his gear, slung the strap over his shoulder, looked about him, chose his path.

He thumbed the communicator switch. *"Anne."*

"Assistance?"

"Precaution. I'm fine. I'm happy. I have a program for you. I want you to call me every hour on the hour and check my status."

"Recorded. Warren, please confirm your position."

"At the river. Same as before. Obey your instructions."

"Yes."

He thumbed the switch over to receive, and started walking.

Ferns. Bracken, waist-high. Great clumps of curling hairy fronds: He avoided these; avoided the soft vine growth that festooned the high limbs of the trees and dropped like curtains.

Beyond the forest rim the ferns gave way to fungi, small round balls that he thought at first were animals, until he prodded one with a stick and broke it. There were domes, cones, parasols, rods with feathered fringes. Platelet fungi of orange and bluish white grew on rotting logs and ridged the twisted roots of living trees. Color. The first color but green and white and brown, anywhere in the world.

The trees grew taller, became giants far different than the riverside varieties. They loomed up straight and shadowy-crowned, their branches interlacing to shut out the sun. The light came through these branches in shafts when it came at all; and when night came here, he reckoned, it would be night indeed.

He stopped and looked back, realizing he had long since lost sight or sound of the river. He took his axe; it took resolution to move after such silence, more than that to strike, to make a mark. He deafened himself to the sacrilege and started walking again, cutting a mark whenever he passed from view of the last. Chips fell white onto the spongy carpet of eons-undisturbed leaves. The echoes lasted long, like eerie voices.

"Warren."

His heart all but stopped.

"Anne. My status is good."

"Thank you."

Com went off again. He kept walking, marking his way, like

walking in some great cavern. The way seemed different when viewed from the reverse, and the trees grew larger and larger still, so that he had to cut deep to make his marks, so that he had to struggle over roots, some knee-high, and going was slow.

He saw light and walked toward it, losing it sometimes in the tangle, but coming always closer—broke finally upon a grove of giants, greater than any trees he had seen. One, vaster than any others, lay splintered and fallen, ancient, moss-bearded. A younger tree supported it, broken beneath the weight; and through the vacant space in the forest ceiling left by the giant's fall, sunlight streamed in a broad shaft to the forest floor, where soft green moss grew and white flowers bloomed, blessed by that solitary touch of daylight. Motes danced in the sun, the drift of pollen, golden-touched in a green light so filtered it was like some airy sea.

Warren stopped, gazed in awe at the cataclysmic ruin of a thing so old. The crash it must have made, in some great storm, with never an ear to hear it. He walked farther, stood in the very heart of the sunlight and looked up at the blinding sky. It warmed. It filled all the senses with warmth and well-being.

He looked about him, ventured even to touch the giant's mossy beard, the bark, the smoothness where the bark had peeled away. He walked farther, half-blind, into the deep shadows beyond, his mind still dazed by the place. All about him now was brown and green, bark and leaves, white fungi, platelets as large as his hand stepping up the roots; ferns, fronds unfurling waist-high, scattering their spores. The tangle grew thicker.

And he realized of a sudden he had come some distance from the clearing.

He looked back. Nothing was recognizable.

He refused panic. He could not have come far. He began to retrace his path, confident at first, then with growing uncertainty as he failed to find things he recalled. He cursed himself. His heart pounded. He tore his hands on the brush that clawed at him. He felt as vulnerable suddenly as a child in the dark, as if the sunlit clearing were the only safe place in the world. He tried to run, to find it more quickly, to waste no time. Trees pressed close about him, straight and vast and indifferently the same, their gnarled roots crossing and interweaving in the earth as their branches laced across the sky.

He had missed the clearing. He was lost. All ways looked the same. He ran, thrust his way from trunk to trunk, gasping for breath, slipped among the tangled wet roots, went sprawling, hands skinned, chin abraded by the bark. He lay breathless, the wind knocked from him, all his senses jolted.

Slowly there came a prickling of nerves in the stillness, through his spasmodic gasps, a crawling at the back of his neck. He held himself tremblingly still at first, his own weight holding him where he had fallen, awkward and painfully bent. He scrabbled with his hands, intending one swift movement, clawed his way over to wave it off him.

Nothing was there, only the brush, the vast roots. The feeling was still behind him, and he froze, refusing to look, gripped in sweating nightmare.

Of a sudden he sprang up, ran, favoring his right leg, sprawled again his full length in the wet, slick leaves, scrambled and fought his way through the thicket. The chill presence—it had direction— stayed constantly on his right, pressing him left and left again, until he stumbled and struggled through worse and worse, tearing himself and the pack through the branches and the fern, ripping skin, endangering his eyes.

He broke into light, into the clearing, into the warm shaft of sun. He fell hard on his hands and knees in that center of warmth and light, sobbing and ashamed and overwhelmed with what had happened to him.

He had panicked. He knew his way now. He was all right. He sank down on his belly, the pack still on his back, and tried to stop shaking.

Strangeness flowed over him like water, not quite warmth, but a feather-touch that stirred the hair at his nape. He moved, tried to rise and run, but he was weighted, pinned by the pack like a specimen on a glass, in the heat and the blinding daylight, while something poured and flowed over his skin. Sweat ran. His breathing grew shallow.

Illness. A recurrence of the plague. He groped at his belt for the communicator and lost it, his hand gone numb. He lay paralyzed, his open eyes filled with translucent green, sunlight through leaves. The sighing wind and rush of waters filled his ears and slowed his breath.

Deep and numbing quiet. Ages came and the rains and the sun filtered down season upon season. Ages passed and the forest grew and moved about him. His body pressed deep to the earth, deep into it, while his arms lifted skyward. He was old, old, and hard with strength and full of the life that swelled and struggled to heaven and earth at once.

Then the sun was shining down in simple warmth and he was aware of his own body, lying drained, bearing the touch of something very like a passing breeze.

He managed to stand at last, faltered, numb even yet, and looked about him. No breath of wind. No leaves stirred.

"Warren?"

He stooped, gathered up the com unit. "I'm here, *Anne.*"

"What's your status, Warren?"

He drew a deep breath. The presence—if it had been anything at all but fear—was gone.

"What's your status, Warren?"

"I'm all right—I'm all right. I'm starting home now."

He kept the com unit on, in his hand, for comfort, not to face the deep woods alone. He found his first mark, the way that he had come in. He struggled from one to the other of the slash marks, tearing through when he sighted the next, making frantic haste . . . away from what, he did not know.

V

He was ashamed of himself, on the other side of the river, sitting in the raft, which swayed against the shore, the paddle across his knees. Clothing torn, hands scratched, face scraped by branches, his left eye watering where one had raked it . . . he knew better than what he had done, racing hysterically over unknown ground.

He wiped his face, realized the possibility of contaminants and wiped his bleeding hands on his trousers. Hallucination. He had breathed something, gotten it when he had scratched himself, absorbed it through the skin . . . a hundred ways he had exposed himself to contaminants. He felt sick. Scared. Some hallucinogens recurred. He needed nothing like that.

"Warren?"

He fumbled out the com unit, answered, holding it in both hands, trying not to shiver. "Everything all right, *Anne?*"

"All stable," *Anne* replied. He cherished the voice in the stillness, the contact with something infallible. He sought a question to make her talk.

"Have your sensors picked up anything?"

"No, Warren."

"What have you been doing?"

"Monitoring my systems."

"You haven't had any trouble?"

"No, Warren."

"I'm coming back now."

"Thank you, Warren."

He cut the com unit off, sat holding it as if it were something living. A piece of *Anne*. A connection. His hands shook. He steadied them, put the unit back at his belt, got up and climbed ashore, limping. Pulled the raft up and anchored it to a solid limb.

No taking it back, no. The raft stayed. No retreats. He looked back across the river, stared at the far darkness with misgivings.

There was nothing there.

Light was fading in the drive back. The crawler jounced and bucked its way along the track he had made through the grass on the way out, and the headlights picked up the bent grass ahead, in the dark, in the chill wind. He drove too fast, forced himself to keep it to a controllable pace on the rough ground.

"*Anne,*" he asked through the com, "turn the running lights on."

"Yes, Warren."

The ship lit up, colors and brilliance in the dark ahead of him. Beautiful. He drove toward it, fought the wheel through pits and roughnesses, his shoulders aching.

"Dinner, *Anne*. What's for dinner?"

"Baked chicken, potatoes, greens, and coffee."

"That's good." His teeth were chattering. The wind was colder than he had thought it would be. He should have brought his coat.

"Are you happy, Warren?"

"I'm going to want a bath when I get there."

"Yes, Warren. Are you happy, Warren?"

"Soon." He kept talking to her, idiocies, anything to fend off the cold and the queasiness in the night. The grass whipped by the fenders, a steady whisper. His mind conjured night-wandering devils, apparitions out of bushes that popped out of the dark and whisked under the nose of the crawler. He drove for the lights. "Be outside," he asked *Anne*. "Wait for me at the cargo lock."

"Yes, Warren. I'm waiting."

He found her there when he had brought the crawler round the nose of the ship and came up facing the lock. He drew up close to her, put on the brake and shut down the crawler engine, hauled himself out of the seat and set unsteady feet on the ground. *Anne* clicked over, sensor lights winking red in the dark. "Assistance?"

"Take the kit and the sensor box out and stow them in the lock." He patted her metal shoulder because he wanted to touch something reasonable. "I'm going inside to take my bath."

"Yes, Warren."

He headed for the lock, stripped off all that he was wearing while the platform ascended, ran the decontamination cycle at the same time. He headed through the ship with his clothes over his arm, dumped them into the laundry chute in the shower room, set the boots beside, for thorough cleaning.

He stayed in the mist cabinet a good long while, letting the heat and the steam seep into his pores—leaned against the back wall with eyes closed, willing himself to relax, conscious of nothing but the warmth of the tiles against his back and the warmth of the moisture that flooded down over him. The hiss of the vapor jets drowned all other sounds, and the condensation on the transparent outer wall sealed off all the world.

A sound came through . . . not a loud one, the impression of a sound. He lifted his head, cold suddenly, looked at the steam-obscured panel, unable to identify what he had heard.

He had not closed the doors. The shower was open, and while he had been gone—while he had been gone from the ship, the pseudosome standing outside—the old nightmare came back to him. Sax. Somewhere in the depths of the ship, wandering about, giving *Anne* orders that would prevent her reporting his presence. Sax, mind-damaged, with the knife in his hand. He stood utterly still, heart pounding, trying to see beyond the steamed, translucent panel for whatever presence might be in the room.

A footstep sounded outside, and another, and a gangling human shadow slid in front of the panel while his heart worked madly. Leaned closer, and red lights gleamed, diffused stars where the features ought to be. "Warren?"

For an instant more the nightmare persisted, *Anne* become the presence. He shook it off, gathering up his courage, to cut the steam off, to deal with her. "*Anne,* is there trouble?"

"No, Warren. The kit and the sensor box are stowed. Dinner is ready."

"Good. Wait there."

She waited. *His* orders. He calmed himself, activated the drier and waited while moisture was sucked out of the chamber . . . took the comb he had brought in with him and straightened his hair in the process. The fans stopped, the plastic panel cleared, so that he could see *Anne* standing beyond the frosted translucence. He opened the door and walked out, and her limbs moved, reorienting her to him, responding to him like a flower to the sun. He felt ashamed for his attack of nerves—more than ashamed, deeply troubled. His breathing still felt uncertain, a tightness about his chest, his pulse still elevated. He cast a look over his shoulder as he reached for his robe, at the three shower cabinets, all dark now, concealments, hiding places. The silence deadened his ears, numbed his senses. He shrugged into the robe and heard *Anne* move at his back. He spun about, back to the corner, staring into *Anne's* vacant faceplate where the lights winked red in the darkness.

"Assistance?"

He did not like her so close . . . a machine, a mind, one mistake of which, one seizing of those metal hands— She followed him. He could not discover the logic on which she had done so. She watched him. Obsessively.

Followed him. He liked that analysis even less. Things started following him and he started seeing devils in familiar territory. He straightened against the wall and made himself catch his breath, fighting the cold chills that set him shivering.

"Warren? Assistance?"

He took her outstretched metal arm and felt the faint vibration under his fingers as she compensated for his weight. "I need help."

"Please be specific."

He laughed wildly, patted her indestructible shoulder, fighting down the hysteria, making himself see her as she was, machine. "Is dinner ready?"

"Yes. I've set it on the table."

He walked with her, into the lift, into the upper level of the ship, the living quarters where the table that he used was, outside his own quarters. He never used the mess hall: it was too empty a place, too many chairs; he no more went there than he opened the quarters of the dead, next door to him, all about him. He sat down, and *Anne* served him, poured the coffee, added the cream. The dinner was good enough, without fault. He found himself with less appetite than he had thought, in the steel and plastic enclosure of the ship, with the ventilation sounds and the small sounds of *Anne's* motors. It was dark round about. He was intensely conscious of that—the night outside, the night deep in the ship where daylight made no difference. *Anne's* natural condition, night: She lived in it, in space; existed in it here, except for the lights that burned here, that burned in corridors when he walked through them and compartments when he was there, but after he was gone, it reverted to its perpetual dark. Dark wrapped everything in the world but this compartment, but him, and he dared not sleep. He feared the dreams coming back. Feared helplessness.

No sign of Sax, out there.

He drank his coffee, sat staring at the plate until *Anne* took it away. Finally he shivered and looked toward the bar cabinet at the far side of the common room. He gave himself permission, got up, opened the cabinet, pulled out a bottle and the makings and took it back to the table.

"Assistance?" *Anne* asked, having returned from the galley.

"I'll do it myself. No trouble." He poured himself a drink. "Get some ice."

She left on the errand. He drank without, had mostly finished the glass when she came back with a thermal bucket full. She set it on the table and he made himself another.

That was the way to get through the night. He was not a drinking man. But it killed the fear. It warmed his throat and spread a pleasant heat through his belly where fear had lain like an indigestible lump.

He had not planned to drink much. But the heat itself was pleasant, and the lassitude it spread through him cured a multitude of ills. By the time he arrived at the bottom of the third glass, he had a certain courage. He smiled bitterly at *Anne's* blank face. Then he filled a fourth glass and drank it, on the deliberate course to total anesthesia.

It hit him then, sudden and coming down like a vast weight. He started to get up, to clear his head, staggered and knocked the glass over. "Assistance?" *Anne* asked.

He leaned on the table rim, reached for the chair and missed it for an instant. *Anne's* metal fingers closed on his arm and held. He yelled, from fright, trying to free himself. Those fingers which could bend metal pipe closed no further. "Is this pain?" she asked. "What is your status, Warren?"

"Not so good, *Anne*. Let go. Let me go."

"Pain is not optimum function. I can't accept programming from a human who's malfunctioning."

"You're hurting my arm. You're causing the pain. Stop it."

She let him go at once. "Assistance?"

He caught his balance against her, leaning heavily until his stomach stopped heaving and his head stopped spinning quite so violently. She accepted his weight, stabilizing with small hums of her motors. "Assistance? Assistance?"

He drew a shaken breath and choked it down past the obstruction in his throat, patted her metal shoulder. "Contact—is assistance enough. It's all right, Annie. I'm all right." He staggered for one of the reclining chairs a little distance across the room and made it, his head spinning as he let it back. "Keep the lights on. Lock your doors and accesses."

"Program accepted, Warren. This is security procedure. Please state nature of emergency."

"Do you perceive any form of life . . . but me . . . anywhere?"

"Vegetation."

"Then there isn't any, is there?" He looked hazily up at her towering, spidery form. "Obey instruction. Keep the accesses locked. Always keep them locked unless I ask you to open them. *Anne*, can you sit down?"

"Yes, Warren. You programmed that pattern."

The worktable, he recalled. He pointed at the other chair. "Sit in the chair."

Anne walked to it and negotiated herself smoothly into its sturdy, padded seat, and looked no more comfortable sitting than she had reclining on the worktable.

"Your median joints," he said. "Let your middle joints and shoulders quit stabilizing." She did so, and her body sagged back. He grinned. "Left ankle on top of right ankle, legs extended. Pattern like me. Loosen all but balance-essential stabilizers. It's called relaxing, Annie." He looked at her sitting there, arms like his arms, on the chair, feet extended and crossed, faceplate reflecting back the ceiling light and flickering inside with minute red stars. He laughed hysterically.

"This is a pleasure reflex," she observed.

"Possibly." He snugged himself into the curvature of the chair. "You sit there, Annie, and you keep your little sensors—all of them, inside and outside the ship—alert. And if you detect any disturbance of them at all, wake me up."

His head hurt in the morning, hurt sitting still and hurt worse when he moved it, and ached blindingly while he bathed and shaved and dressed. He kept himself moving, bitter penance. He cleaned the living quarters and the galley, finally went down to the lock through crashes of the machinery that echoed in his head. The sunlight shot through his eyes to his nerve endings, all the way to his fingertips, and he walked out blind and with eyes watering and leaned on the nearest landing strut, advantaging himself of its pillar-like shade.

He was ashamed of himself, self-disgusted. The fear had gotten him last night. The solitude had. He was not proud of his behavior in the forest: that was one thing, private and ugly; but when he came home and went to pieces in the ship, because it was dark, and because he had bad dreams . . .

That scared him, far more substantially than any forest shadow deserved. His own mind had pounced on him last night.

He walked out, wincing in the sunlight, to the parked crawler, leaned on the fender and followed with his eyes the track he had made coming in, before it curved out of sight around the ship. Grass and brush. He had ripped through it last night as if it had all turned animate. Hallucinations, perhaps. After last night he had another answer, which had to do with solitude and the human mind.

He went back inside and finally took something for his head.

. . .

By 1300 hours he was feeling better, the housekeeping duties done. Paced, in the confines of the living quarters, and caught himself doing it.

Work had been the anodyne until now . . . driving himself, working until he dropped; he ran out of work and it was the liquor, to keep the nightmares off. Neither could serve, not over the stretch of years. He was not accustomed to thinking *years.* He forced himself to . . . to think of a life in more than terms of survival; to think of living as much as of doing and finding and discovering.

He took one of the exercise mats outside, brought a flask of iced juice along with his biological notes and took *Anne* with him, with his favorite music tapes fed to the outside speakers. He stripped, spread his mat just beyond the canopy, and lay down to read, the music playing cheerfully and the warmth of Harley's star seeping pleasantly into his well-lotioned skin. He slept for a time, genuine and relaxed sleep, awoke and turned onto his back to let the sun warm his front for a time, a red glow through his closed lids.

"Warren?"

He shaded his eyes and looked up at the standing pseudosome. He had forgotten her. She had never moved.

"Warren?"

"Don't nag, Annie. I didn't say anything. Come here and sit down. You make me nervous."

Anne dutifully obeyed, bent, flexed her knees an alarming distance and fell the last half foot, catching herself on her extended hands, knees drawn up and spine rigid. Warren shook his head in despair and amusement. "Relax. You have to do that when you sit."

The metal body sagged into jointed curves, brought itself more upright, settled again.

"Dear Annie, if you were only human."

Anne turned her sensor lights on, all of them. Thought a moment. "Corollary, Warren?"

"To what? To *if? Anne,* my love, you aren't, and there isn't any."

He had confused her. The lights flickered one after the other. "Clarify."

"Human nature, that's all. Humans don't function well alone.

They need contact with someone. But I'm all right. It's nothing to concern you."

The motors hummed faintly and *Anne* reached out and let her hand down on his shoulder. The action was so human it frightened him. He looked into her ovoid face and the lights that danced inside and his heart beat wildly.

"Is your status improving?"

Contact with someone. He laughed sorrowfully and breathed a sigh.

"I perceive internal disturbances."

"Laughter. You know laughter."

"This was different."

"The pace of laughter varies."

"Recorded." *Anne* drew back her hand. "You're happy."

"*Anne*—what do you think about when I'm not here. When I'm not asking you to do something, and you have thoughts, what are they?"

"I have a standard program."

"And what's that?"

"I maintain energy levels, regulate my circulation and temperature, monitor and repair my component—"

"Cancel. You don't think. Like you do with me. You don't ask questions, decide, follow sequences of reasoning."

The lights blinked a moment. "The automatic functions are sufficient except in an anomalous situation."

"But I'm talking to the AI. *You.* The AI's something other than those programs. What do you do, sleep?"

"I wait."

Like the pseudosome, standing indefinitely. No discomfort to move her, to make her impatient. "You investigate stimuli."

"Yes."

"But there aren't many, are there?"

A delay. Incomplete noun. "They are constant but not anomalous."

"You're bored too."

"Bored. No. Bored is not a state of optimum function. Bored is a human state of frustrated need for activity. This is not applicable to me. I function at optimum."

"Functioning constantly doesn't damage you."

"No."

"Use the library. You can do that, can't you? If there aren't adequate stimuli in the environment to engage the Al, use the library. Maybe you'll learn something."

"Recorded."

"And then what do we do?"

The lights blinked. "Context indeterminate. Please restate the question."

"You could know everything there is to know, couldn't you, and you'd sit with it inside you and do nothing."

"Context of *do* indeterminate. I'm not able to process the word in this context."

He reached out, patted her silver leg. The sensors blinked. Her hand came back to him and stayed there, heavy, on his shoulder. *Contact.*

"That's enough," he said, and removed his hand from her; she did the same. "Thank you, *Anne.*" But he was cold inside.

He relaxed finally, staring out beneath the ship toward the forest.

There was the fear. There was where it sat. He hurt inside, and the healing was there, not sealing himself into the ship. Sterility. Inane acts and inane conversation.

If he feared out there, the fear itself proved he was alive. It was an enemy to fight. It was something he did not program. It held the unanticipated, and that was precious.

Anne, waiting forever, absorbing the stimuli and waiting for something anomalous, to turn on her intelligence. He saw himself doing that, sitting in the ship and waiting for a human lifetime— for some anomaly in the wind.

No.

VI

He came this time with a different kind of attack, slowly, considerately, the crawler equipped with sensor box and sample kits and recorders and food and water, rope and directional beeper, anything that seemed remotely useful. With the film camera. With a rifle with a nightscope. Overequipped, if anything, in which he found some humor . . . but he felt the safer for it.

The raft was still securely tied to the branch, the sand about it unmarked by the passage of any moving creature, even void of insect tracks. On the far bank the forest waited in the dawn, peaceful—dark inside, as it would always be.

Someday, he promised it. He loaded the raft, trip after trip from the crawler parked up on the bank. *Anne* was with him, disembodied, in the incarnation of her sensor box, in the com unit. She talked to him, telling him she detected vegetation, and he laughed and snugged the box into the bottom of the raft.

"Reception is impaired," *Anne* complained.

"Sorry. I don't want to drop the box into the river."

"Please don't do that, Warren."

He laughed again, in a good humor for *Anne's* witless witticisms. Piled other supplies about her sensors. "I'll pull you out if I need you. Take care of the ship. I'm shutting you down. Your noise is interfering with my reception."

"Please reconsider this program. The river is dangerous. Please reconsider."

"Quiet." He shut her down. There was a reciprocal turn-on from her side, but she took orders and stayed off this time. He piled the last load in, coat and blanket in case it grew chill on the water.

He untied the raft then, nudged it out a little, stepped in and sat down, taking up the paddle. It was not one of his skills, rafting. He had read the manual and thought it out. Drove against the gentle current, no great work: he reasoned that he could paddle upstream as long as he liked or wanted to, and return was the river's business.

He passed the landing site on the far bank, passed an old log and wound along with the grassy bank on one side and the forest on the other. The river was so still on most of its surface, it was hard to see in which direction it flowed. Shores turned to marsh on either side, and at some time unnoticed, the trees on the right, which had been growing thicker and thicker, closed off all view of the grasslands where the ship had landed. The banks began to have a thick border of reeds; some trees grew down into the water, making an obstacle of their knobby roots, making curtains of moss hanging almost low enough to sweep his shoulders as he passed. Green lilies drifted, beds of pads through which he drove the raft with shallow strokes, not to tangle the blade of the paddle in their tough stems. In places the navigable channel was no more than three meters across, a weaving of reeds and sandbars and shadows between banks a good stone's throw from side to side. It was a sleepy place, all tones of green and brown . . . no sky that was not filtered by leaves. A certain kind of tree was in bloom, shedding white petals as large as a man's hand on the water: they drifted like high-stemmed boats, clouds of them afloat, fleets and armadas destroyed by the dip of his paddle and the raft's blunt bow. The full flower had long stamens and pistils so that they looked like white spiders along the branches when they had shed, and like flocks of birds before. Lilies were rife, and a fine-leafed floating weed grew wherever the water was shallow. It was worse than the lilies for tangling up the paddle: it broke off and hung, slick brownish leaves. It was not, he decided, particularly lovely stuff, and it made going very slow in the narrowest channels.

His shoulders began to ache with the long effort. He kept going long after the ache became painful, anxious not to give ground . . . decided finally to put ashore for a space, when he had seen an area not so brushy and overgrown. He drove for it, rammed the bow up and started pulling it about with strokes of the paddle.

The paddle tip sank in, worse and worse with his efforts, tipped the raft with the suction as he pulled it out again and the raft slapped down with a smack. He frowned, jabbed at the sand underneath with his paddle, reducing it to jelly and thinking ruefully where he might have been if he had not mistrusted the water purity and if he had bounded out to drag the raft ashore. It took some little maneuvering to skim the raft off the quicksands and out again, back into the main channel, and he forgot his aching shoulders to keep it going awhile.

"Warren?"

On the hour, as instructed. He stilled his heart and punched on his com unit, never stopping his paddling. "Hello, Annie. Status is good, love, but I need three hands just now."

"Assistance? Estimate of time required to reach your position—"

"Cancel. Don't you try it. I'm managing with two hands quite nicely. How are you?"

"All my systems are functioning normally, but my sensors are impaired by obstructions. Please clear my pickups, Warren."

"No need. My sensors aren't impaired and there's nothing anomalous."

"I detect a repeated sound."

"That's the raft's propulsion. There's no hazard. All systems are normal. My status is good. Call in another hour."

"Yes, Warren."

"Shut down."

"Yes, Warren."

Contact went out; the box lights went off.

He closed off contact from his side, pushed off the bank where he had drifted while he was arguing with *Anne,* and hand-over-handed himself past a low-hanging branch. He snubbed a loop of the mooring rope about it, snugged it down, resting for a moment while the raft swayed sleepily back and forth.

It's beautiful, he thought, *Sax. Min and Harley, it's worth seeing.* He squinted up at the sunlight dancing through the branches. *Hang the captain, Harley. They'll come here sometime. They'll want the place. In someone's lifetime.*

No answer. The sunlight touched the water and sparkled there, in one of the world's paralyzing silences. An armada of petals floated by. A flotilla of bubbles. He watched others rise, near the roots of the tree.

Life, Harley?

He rummaged after one of the sample bags, after the seine from the collection kit. He flung the seine out inexpertly, maneuvered it in the current, pulled it up. The net was fouled with the brownish weed, and caught in it were some strands of gelatinous matter, each a finger's length, grayish to clear with an opaque kernel in the center. He wrinkled his lip, not liking the look of it, reached and threw the sensor unit on again, holding its pickup wand almost touching the strands.

"Warren, I perceive an indeterminate life form, low order."

"How—indeterminate?"

"It may be plant but that identification is not firm."

"I thought so. Now I don't particularly know what to do with it. It's stuck to the net and I don't like to go poking at it bare-handed. Curious stuff."

"Assistance?"

"Wait." He put the scanner wand down and used both hands

to evert the net, cleared it by shaking it in the water. He put the net into plastic before letting it back in the raft and sprayed his hands and the side of the raft with disinfectant before picking up the wand and putting it back. "I'm rid of it now, Annie, no trouble. I'm closing everything down now. Observe your one-hour schedule."

He slipped the rope, took up the paddle and extricated the raft from the reeds, where it had swung its right side. Headed for the center of the clear channel.

It might have been eggs, he thought. Might have been. He considered the depth of the channel, the murkiness of the water, and experienced a slight disquiet. Something big could travel that, lurk round the lily roots. He did not particularly want to knock into something.

Nonsense, Harley. No more devils. No more things in the dark. I won't make them anymore, will I, Sax? No more cold sweats.

The river seemed to bend constantly left, deeper into the forest, though he could not see any more or any less on either hand as it went. The growth on the banks was the same. There was an abundance of the fleshy-leaved trees that poured sap so freely when bruised, and the branches hung down into the water so thickly in places that they formed a curtain before whatever lay on shore. The spidertrees shed their white blooms, and the prickly ones thrust out twisted and arching limbs, gnarled and humped roots poking out into the channel. Moss was everywhere, and reeds and waterweed. He realized finally that the river had long since ceased to have any recognizable shore. On the left stretched a carpet of dark green moss that bloomed enticingly. Trees grew scattered there, incredibly neat, as if it were tended by some gardener, and the earth looked so soft and inviting to the touch, so green, the flowers like stars scattered across it.

Then he realized why the place looked so soft and flat, and why the trees grew straight up like columns, without the usual ugliness of twisting roots. That was not earth but floating moss, and when he put his paddle down, he found quicksand on the bottom.

An ugly death, that—sinking alive into a bog, to live for a few moments among the sands and the corruption that oozed round the roots of the trees. To drown in it.

He gave a twist of his mouth and shoved at the paddle, sent

the raft up the winding course in haste to be out of it, then halted, drifting back a little as he did so.

The river divided here, coming from left and from right about a finger of land that grew thicker as it went—no islet, this, but the connection of a tributary with the river.

He paddled closer and looked up both overgrown ways. The one on the right was shallower, more choked with reeds, moss growing in patches across its surface, brush fallen into it which the weak current had not removed. He chose the left.

At least, he reasoned with himself, there was no chance of getting lost, even without the elaborate directional equipment he carried: no matter how many times the river subdivided, the current would take him back to the crossing. He had no fear in that regard; for all that the way grew still more tangled.

No light here, but what came darkly diffused. The channel was like a tunnel among the trees. From time to time now he could see larger trees beyond the shoreline vegetation, the tall bulk of one of the sky-reaching giants like those of the grove. He wondered now if he had not been much closer to the river than he had realized when he passed the grove and ran hysterically through the trees, feeling devils at his heels. *That* would have been a surprise, to have run out onto clear and mossy ground and to find himself in quicksand up to his ears. So there were deadly dangers in the forest—not the creeping kind, but dangers enough to make recklessness, either fleeing or advancing, fatal.

"Warren."

Anne made her hourly call and he answered it shortly, without breath for conversation and lacking any substance to report. He rested finally, made fast the raft to the projecting roots of a gnarly tree, laid his paddle across the plastic-wrapped seine and settled down into the raft, his head resting on the inflated rim. He ate, had a cup of coffee from the thermos. Even this overgrown branch of the river was beautiful, considered item at a time. The star Harley was a warm spot dancing above the branches, and the water was black and rich. No wonder the plants flourished so. They grew in every available place. If the river were not moving, they would choke up the channel with their mass and make of it one vast spongy bog such as that other arm of the river had seemed to be.

"Warren."

He came awake and reached for the com. "Emergency?"

"No, Warren. The time is 1300 hours."

"Already?" He levered himself upright against the rim and looked about him at the shadows. "Well, how are you?"

"I'm functioning well, thank you."

"So am I, love. No troubles. In fact . . ." he added cautiously, "in fact I'm beginning to think of extending this operation another day. There's no danger. I don't see any reason to come back and give up all the ground I've traveled, and I'd have to start now to get back to the launching point before dark."

"You'll exit my sensor range if you continue this direction for another day. Please reconsider this program."

"I won't go outside your sensor range. I'll stop and come back then."

A pause. "Yes, Warren."

"I'll call if I need you."

"Yes, Warren."

He broke the contact and pulled the raft upcurrent by the mooring line to reach the knot, untied it and took up the paddle again and started moving. He was content in his freedom, content in the maze, which promised endless secrets. The river could become a highway to its mountain source. He could devise relays that would keep *Anne* with him. He need not be held to one place. He believed in that again.

At 1400 he had a lunch of lukewarm soup and a sun-warmed sandwich, of which he ate every crumb, and wished he had brought larger portions. His appetite increased prodigiously with the exercise and the relaxation. He felt a profound sense of well-being . . . even found patience for a prolonged bout with *Anne*'s chatter. He called her up a little before 1500 and let her sample the river with her sensors, balancing the box on the gear so that she could have a look about.

"Vegetation," she pronounced. "Water. Warren, please reconsider this program."

He laughed at her and shut her down.

Then the river divided again, and again he bore to the left, into the forest heart, where it was always twilight, and less than that now. He paddled steadily, ignoring the persistent ache in his back and shoulders, until he could no longer see where he was going, until the roots and limbs came up at him too quickly out of the dark and he felt the wet drag of moss across his face and arms more than once. 1837, when he checked the time.

"*Anne.*"

"Warren?"

"I'm activating your sensors again. There's no trouble, but I want you to give me your reports."

"You're in motion," she said as the box came on. "Low light. Vegetation and water. Temperature 19°C. A sound: the propulsion system. Stability in poor function."

"That's floating, *Anne.* Stability is poor, yes, but not hazardous."

"Thank you. You're behind my base point. I perceive you."

"No other life."

"Vegetation, Warren."

He kept moving, into worse and worse tangle, hoping for an end to the tunnel of trees, where he could at least have the starlight. Anne's occasional voice comforted him. The ghostly giants slid past, only slightly blacker than the night about him.

The raft bumped something underwater and slued about.

"You've stopped."

"I think I hit a submerged log or something." Adrenaline had shot through him at the jolt. He drew a deep breath. "It's getting too dark to see."

"Please reconsider this program."

"I think you have the right idea. Just a second." He prodded underwater with his paddle and hit a thing.

It came up, broke surface by the raft in the sensor light, mossy and jagged.

Log. He was free, his pulse jolting in his veins. He let the current take the raft then, let it turn the bow.

"Warren?"

"I'm loose. I'm all right." He caught a branch at a clearer spot and stopped, letting the fear ebb from him.

"Warren, you've stopped again."

"I stopped us." He wanted to keep running, but that was precisely the kind of action that could run him into trouble, pushing himself beyond the fatigue point. A log. It had been a log after all. He tied up to the branch, put on his jacket against the gathering chill and settled against the yielding rim of the raft, facing the low, reedy bank and the wall of aged trees. "Anne, I'm going to sleep now. I'm leaving the sensor box on. Keep alert and wake me if you perceive anything you have to ask about."

"Recorded. Good night, Warren."

"Good night, Annie."

He closed his eyes finally, confident at least of *Anne's* watchfulness, rocked on the gently moving surface of the river. Tiniest sounds seemed loud, the slap of the water against its boundaries, the susurration of the leaves, the ceaseless rhythms of the world, of growth, of things that twined and fed on rain and death.

He dreamed of home as he had not done in a very long time, of a hard-rock mining colony, his boyhood, a fascination with the stars; dreamed of Earth, of things he had only heard of, pictures he had seen, rivers and forests and fields. Pictured rivers came to life and flowed, hurling his raft on past shores of devastating silence, past the horror in the corridors, figures walking in steam—

Sax—Sax leaping at him, knife in hand—

He came up with a gasp too loud in the silence.

"Warren? Emergency?"

"No." He wiped his face, glad of her presence. "It's just a dream. It's all right."

"Malfunction?"

"Thoughts. Dream. A recycling of past experience. A clearing of files. It's all right. It's a natural process. Human do it when they sleep."

"I perceived pain."

"It's gone now. It stopped. I'm going back to sleep."

"Are you happy, Warren?"

"Just tired, *Anne.* Just very tired and very sleepy. Good night."

"Good night, Warren."

He settled again and closed his eyes. The breeze sighed and the water lapped gently, rocking him. He curled up again and sank into deeper sleep.

He awoke in dim light, in a decided chill that made him glad of the jacket. The side of him that he had lain on was cold through and he rubbed his arm and leg, wishing for a hot breakfast instead of cold sandwiches and lukewarm coffee.

A mist overlay the river a few inches deep. It looked like a river of cloud flowing between the green banks. He reached and turned off *Anne*'s sensors. "Shutting you down. It's morning. I'll be starting back in a moment. My status is good."

"Thank you, Warren."

He settled back again, enjoyed the beauty about him without *Anne*'s time and temperature analyses. He had no intention of letting his eyes close again, but it would be easy in this quiet, this peace.

The sense of well-being soured abruptly. He seemed heavier than the raft could bear, his head pounded, the pulse beat at his temples.

Something was radically wrong. He reached for the sensor box but he could no longer move. He blinked, aware of the water swelling and falling under him, of the branch of the aged tree above him.

Breath stopped. Sweat drenched him. Then the breathing reflex started again and the perspiration chilled. A curious sickly feeling went from shoulders to fingertips, unbearable pressure, as if his laboring heart would burst the veins. Pressure spread, to his chest, his head, to groin, to legs and toes. Then it eased, leaving him limp and gasping for air.

The hairs at his nape stirred, a fingering touch at his senses. Darts of sensation ran over his skin; muscles twitched, and he struggled to sit up; he was blind, with softness wrapping him in cotton and bringing him unbearable sorrow.

It passed.

"You're there," he said, blinking to clear his eyes. "You're *there.*"

Not madness. Not insanity. Something had touched him in the clearing that day as it just had done here. "Who are you?" he asked it. "What do you want?"

But it had gone—no malevolence, no. It ached, it was so different. It was real. His heart was still racing from its touch. He slipped the knot, tugged the rope free, let the raft take its course.

"Find you," he told it, "I'll find you." He began to laugh, giddy at the spinning course the raft took, the branches whirling in wide circles above him.

"Warren," the box said, self-activated. "Warren? Warren?"

VII

"Hello, Warren."

He gave a haggard grin climbing down from the land crawler, staggered a bit from weariness, edged past the pseudosome with a pat on the shoulder. "Hello yourself, Annie. Unload the gear out of the crawler."

"Yes, Warren. What is your status, please?"

"Fine, thanks. Happy. Dirty, tired and hungry, but happy overall."

"Bath and supper?"

"In that order."

"Sleep?"

"Possibly." He walked into the lock, stripped off his clothing as the cargo lift rose into netherdeck, already anticipating the luxury of a warm bath. He took the next lift up. "I'll want my robe. How are you?"

"I'm functioning well, thank you." Her voice came to him all over the ship. The lift stopped and let him out. She turned on the lights for him section by section and extinguished them after.

"What's for supper?"

"Steak and potatoes, Warren. Would you like tea or coffee?"

"Beautiful. Coffee."

"Yes, Warren."

He took a lingering bath, dried and dressed in his robe, went up to the living quarters where *Anne* had set the table for him, all the appointments, all the best. He sat down and looked up at *Anne*, who hovered there to pour him coffee.

"Pull up the other chair and sit down, will you, *Anne?*"

"Yes, Warren."

She released the facing chair from its transit braces, settled it in place, turned it and sat down correctly, metal arms on the table in exact imitation of him. Her lights dimmed once more as she settled into a state of waiting.

Warren ate in contented silence, not disturbing her. *Anne* had her limitations in small talk. When he had finished he pushed the dishes aside and *Anne*'s sensors brightened at once, a new program clicking into place. She rose and put everything onto the waiting tray, tidying up with a brisk rattle of aluminum and her own metal fingers.

"*Anne,* love."

"Yes, Warren."

"Activate games function."

Tray was forgotten. She turned toward him. The screen on the wall lighted, blank. "Specify."

"You choose. You make a choice. Which game?"

Black and white squares flashed onto the screen. Chess. He frowned and looked at her. "That's a new one. Who taught you that?"

"My first programmer installed the program."

He looked at the board, drew a deep breath. He had intended something rather simpler, some fast and stimulating fluff to shake the lingering sense from his brain. Something to sleep on. To see after his eyes were closed. He considered the game. "Are you good at chess?"

"Yes, Warren."

He was amused. "Take those dishes to the galley and come back up here. I'll play you."

"Yes, Warren." The board altered. She had chosen white. The first move was made. Warren turned his chair and reclined it to study the board, his feet on the newly cleared table. He gave her his move and the appropriate change appeared on the screen.

The game was almost over by the time the pseudosome came topside again. She needed only four more moves to make his defeat a certainty. He sat back with his arms folded behind his head, studying his decimated forces. Shook his head in disbelief.

"Annie, *ma belle dame sans merci*— has anyone ever beaten you?"

"No, Warren."

He considered it a moment more, his lately bolstered well-being pricked. "Can you teach me what you know?"

"I've been programmed with the works of fifteen zonal champions. I don't estimate that I can teach you what I know. Human memory is fallible. Mine is not, provided adequate cues for recall and interrelation of data. One of my programmed functions is instruction in procedures. I can instruct."

He rolled a sidelong glance at her. "Fallible?"

"Fallible: capable of error."

"I don't need the definition. What makes you so talkative? Did I hit a program?"

"My first programmer was Franz Mann. He taught me chess. This is an exercise in logic. It's a testing mechanism, negative private appropriation. My function is to maintain you. I'm programmed to instruct in procedures. Chess is a procedure."

"All right," he said quietly. "All right, you can teach me."

"You're happy."

"You amuse me. Sit down."

She resumed the chair opposite him . . . her back to the board, but she did not need to see it. "Amusement produces laughter. Laughter is a pleasure or surprise indicator. Amusement is pleasant or surprising. Please specify which, Warren."

"You're both, *Anne*."

"Thank you. Pleasure is a priority function."

"Is it?"

"This is your instruction, Warren."

He frowned at her. In the human-maintenance programming he had poured a great number of definitions into her, and apparently he had gotten to a fluent area. Herself. Her prime level. She was essentially an egotist.

Another chessboard flashed onto the screen.

"Begin," she said.

She defeated him again, entered another game before he found his eyes watering and his senses blurring out on the screen. He went to bed.

Trees and black and white squares mingled in his dreams.

The next venture took resting . . . took a body in condition and a mind at ease. He looked over the gear the next morning, but he refused to do anything more. Not at once. Not rushing back exhausted into the heart of the forest. He lazed about in the sun, had *Anne*'s careful hands rub lotion over his sore shoulders and back, felt immeasurably at peace with the world.

A good lunch, a nap afterward. He gave the ship a long-neglected manual check, in corridors he had not visited since the plague.

There was life in the botany lab, two of Rule's collection,

succulents which had survived on their own water, two lone and emaciated spiny clusters. He came on them amid a tangle of brown husks of other plants which had succumbed to neglect, brushed the dead leaves away from them, tiny as they were. He looked for others and found nothing else alive. Two fellow survivors.

No knowing from what distant star system they had been gathered. Tray after tray of brown husks collapsed across the planting medium, victims of his shutdown order for the labs. He stripped it all, gathered the dead plants into a bin. Investigated the lockers and the drawers.

There were seeds, bulbs, rhizomes, all manner of starts. He thought of putting them outside, of seeing what they would do— but considering the ecology . . . no; nothing that might damage that. He thought of bringing some of the world's life inside, making a garden; but the world was much lilies and waterflowers, and lacked colors. Some of these, he thought, holding a palmful of seeds, some might be flowers of all kinds of colors . . . odors and perfumes from a dozen different star systems. Such a garden was not for discarding. He could start them here, plant them in containers, fill the ship with them.

He grinned to himself, set to work reworking the planting medium, activating the irrigation system.

He located Rule's notebook and sat down and read through it, trying to decide on the seeds, how much water and how deep and what might be best.

He could fill the whole botany lab, and the plants would make seeds of their own. No more sterility. He pictured the living quarters blooming with flowers under the artificial sunlight. There was life outside the ship, something to touch, something to find; and in here . . . he might make the place beautiful, something he could live in while getting used to the world. No more fear. He could navigate the rivers, hike the forest . . . find whatever it was. Bring home the most beautiful things. Turn it all into a garden. He could leave that behind him, at least, when another team did come, even past his lifetime and into the next century. Records. He could feed them into *Anne* and she could send them to orbiting ships. He could learn the world and make records others could use. His world, after all. Whole colonies here someday who would know the name of Paul Warren and Harley and Rule, Burlin and Sax and Sikutu and the rest. Humans who would look at what he had made.

Who would approach what he had found out on the river with awe. Find it friendly, whether or not it was an intelligence. The ship could fit in . . . with the gardens he intended. Long rhythms, the seeding of plants and the growing of trees and the shaping of them. No project he had approached had offered him so much. To travel the rivers and find them and to come home to *Anne*, who maintained all he learned. . . .

He smiled to himself. "*Anne*. Send the pseudosome here. Botany four."

She came, a working of the lift and a tread of metal feet down the corridor and through the outer labs into this one. "Assistance?"

"You had a standard program for this area. Maintenance of water flow. Cleaning."

"I find record of it."

"Activate it. I want the lights on and the water circulating here."

"Yes, Warren." The lights blinked, the sixth one as well, where her chin should be in the darkness. "This is not your station."

"It is now."

"This is Rule's station."

"Rule stopped functioning. Permanently." His lips tightened. He disliked getting into death with a mind that had never been alive. "I'm doing some of Rule's work now. I like to do it."

"Are you happy?"

"Yes."

"Assistance?"

"I'll do it myself. This is human work."

"Explain."

He looked about at her, then back to his work, dropping the seeds in and patting the holes closed. "You're uncommonly conversational. Explain what?"

"Explain your status."

"Dear Annie, humans have to be active about twelve hours a day, body and mind. When we stop being active we don't function well. So I find things to do. Activity. Humans have to have activity. That's what I mean when I use *do* in unexplained context. It's an important verb, *do*. It keeps us healthy. We always have to have something to do, even if we have to hunt to find it."

Anne digested that thought a moment. "I play chess."

He stopped what he was doing in mid-reach, looked back at her. As far as he could recall it was the first time she had ever offered such an unsolicited suggestion. "How did *that* get into your programming?"

"My first programmer was—"

"Cancel. I mean why did you suddenly offer to play chess?"

"My function is to maintain you happy. You request activity. Chess is an activity."

He had to laugh. She had almost frightened him, and in a little measure he was touched. He could hardly hurt *Anne's* feelings. "All right, love. I'll play chess after supper. Go fix supper ahead of schedule. It's nearly time and I'm hungry."

It was chicken for dinner, coffee and cream pie for dessert, the silver arranged to perfection. Warren sat down to eat and *Anne* took the chair across the table and waited in great patience, arms before her.

He finished. The chessboard flashed to the screen above.

She won.

"You erred in your third move," she said. The board flashed up again, renewed. She demonstrated the error. Played the game through a better move. "Continue."

She defeated him again. The board returned again to starting.

"Cancel," he said. "Enough chess for the evening. Find me all the material you can on biology. I want to do some reading."

"I've located the files," she said instantly. "They're in general library. Will you want display or printout?"

"Display. Run them by on the screen."

The screen changed; printed matter came on. He scanned it, mostly the pictures. "Hold," he said finally, uninformed. The flow stopped. "*Anne*. Can you detect internal processes in sentient life?"

"Negative. Internal processes are outside my sensor range. But I do pick up periodic sound from high-level organisms when I have refined my perception."

"Breathing. Air exchange. It's the external evidence of an internal process. Can you pick up, say, electrical activity? How do you tell—what's evidence to you, whether something is alive or not?"

"I detect electrical fields. I have never detected an internal electrical process. I have recorded information that such a process exists through chemical activity. This is not within my sensor range. Second question: movement; gas exchange; temperature; thermal pattern; sound—"

"Third question: Does life have to meet all these criteria for you to recognize it?"

"Negative. One positive reading is sufficient for further investigation."

"Have you ever gotten any reading that caused you to investigate further . . . here, at this site?"

"Often, Warren."

"Did you reach a positive identification?"

"Wind motion is most frequent. Sound. All these readings have had positive identification."

He let his pent breath go. "You do watch, don't you? I told you to stay alert."

"I continue your programming. I investigate all stimuli that reach me. I identify them. I have made positive identification on all readings."

"And are you never in doubt? Is there ever a marginal reading?"

"I have called your attention to all such cases. You have identified these sounds. I don't have complete information on life processes. I am still assimilating information. I don't yet use all vocabulary in this field. I am running cross-comparisons. I estimate another two days for full assimilation of library-accessed definitions."

"Library." He recalled accessing it. "What are you using? What material?"

"Dictionary and encyclopedic reference. This is a large program. Cross-referencing within the program is incomplete. I am still running on it."

"You mean you've been processing without shutdown?"

"The program is still in assimilation."

He sank back in the chair. "Might do you good at that. Might make you a better conversationalist." He wished, all the same, that he had not started it. Shutdown of the program now might muddle her, leave her with a thousand unidentified threads hanging. "You haven't gotten any conflicts, have you?"

"No, Warren."

"You're clever, aren't you? At least you'll be a handy encyclopedia."

"I can provide information and instruction."

"You're going to be a wonder when you get to the literary references."

A prolonged flickering of lights. "I have investigated the literature storage. I have input all library information, informational, technical, literary, recreational. It's being assimilated as the definitions acquire sufficient cross-references."

"Simultaneously? You're reading the whole library sideways?"

A further flickering of lights. "Laterally. Correct description is laterally. The cross-referencing process involves all material."

"Who told you to do that?" He rose from the table. So did she, turning her beautiful, vacant face toward him, chromium and gray plastic, red sensor-lights glowing. He was overwhelmed by the beauty of her.

And frightened.

"Your programming. I am instructed to investigate all stimuli occurring within my sensor range. I continue this as a permanent instruction. Library is a primary source of relevant information. You accessed this for investigation."

"Cancel," he said. "Cancel. You're going to damage yourself."

"You're my highest priority. I must maintain you in optimum function. I am processing relevant information. It is in partial assimilation. Cancel of program negative possible. Your order is improper. I'm in conflict, Warren. Please reconsider your instruction."

He drew a larger breath, leaned on the chair, staring into the red lights, which had stopped blinking, which burned steadily, frozen. "Withdrawn," he said after a moment. "Withdrawn." Such as she was capable, *Anne* was in pain. Confused. The lights started blinking again, mechanical relief. "How long is this program going to take you?"

"I have estimated two days assimilation."

"And know *everything*? I think you're estimating too little."

"This is possible. Cross-references are multiplying. What is your estimate?"

"Years. The input is continuous, Annie. It never quits. The world never stops sending it. You have to go on cross-referencing."

The lights blinked. "Yes. My processing is rapid, but the cross-reference causes some lateral activity. Extrapolation indicates this activity will increase in breadth."

"Wondering. You're wondering."

A delay. "This is an adequate description."

He walked over and poured himself a drink at the counter. Looked back at her, finding his hands shaking a bit. "I'll tell you something, Annie. You're going to be a long time at it. I wonder things. I investigate things. It's part of human process. I'm going back to the river tomorrow."

"This is a hazardous area."

"Negative. Not for me, it's not hazardous. I'm carrying out my own program. Investigating. We make a team, do you understand that word? Engaged in common program. You do your thinking here. I gather data at the river. I'll take your sensor box."

"Yes, Warren."

He finished the drink, pleased with her. Relaxed against the counter. "Want another game of chess?"

The screen lit with the chessboard.

She won this one too.

VIII

He would have remembered the way even without the marks scored on the trees. They were etched in memory, a fallen log, the tree with the blue and white platelet fungus, the one with the broken branch. He went carefully, rested often, burdened with *Anne's* sensor box and his own kit. Over everything the silence persisted, forever silence, unbroken through the ages by anything but the wind or the crash of some aged tree dying. His footsteps on the wet leaves seemed unbearably loud, and the low hum from the sensor box seemed louder still.

The clearing was ahead. It was that he had come back to find, to recover the moment, to discover it in daylight.

"*Anne*," he said when he was close to it, "cut off the sensor unit awhile. Its noise is interfering with my perceptions."

"Please reconsider this instruction. Your perceptions are limited."

"They're more sensitive over a broad range. It's safe, *Anne.* Cut it off. I'll call in an hour. You wait on that call."

"Yes, Warren."

The sensor unit went off. His shoulder ached from the fifteen kilos and the long walk from the raft, but he carried it like moral debt. As insurance. It had never manifested itself, this—life—not for *Anne's* sensors, but twice for his. Possibly the sensor box itself interfered with it; or the ship did. He gave it all the chance it might need.

But he carried the gun.

He found the grove different than he had remembered it, dark and sunless yet in the early morning. He came cautiously, dwarfed and insignificant among the giant trees . . . stopped absolutely still, hearing no sound at all. There was the fallen one, the father of all trees, his moss-hung bulk gone dark and his beard of flowers gone. The grass that grew in the center was dull and dark with shadow.

Softly he walked to that center and laid down his gear, sat down on the blanket roll. Looked about him. Nothing had changed—likely nothing had changed here since the fall of the titan which had left the vacancy in the ceiling of branches. Fourteen trees made the grove. The oldest of those still living must have been considerable trees when man was still earthbound and reaching for homeworld's moon. Even the youngest must measure their age in centuries.

All right, he thought. *Come ahead. No sensors. No machines. You remember me, don't you? The night, on the river. I'm the only one there is. No threat. Come ahead.*

There was not the least response.

He waited until his muscles cramped, feeling increasingly disappointed . . . no little afraid: that too. But he had come prepared for patience. He squatted and spread out his gear so that there was a plastic sheet under the blanket, poured himself hot coffee from his flask and stretched out to relax. *Anne* called in his drowsing, once, twice, three times: three hours. The sun came to the patch of grass like a daily miracle, and motes of dust and pollen danced in the beam. The giant's beard bloomed again. Then the sun passed on, and the shadows and the murk returned to the grove of giants.

Perhaps, he thought, it had gone away. Perhaps it was no longer resident here in the grove, but down by the river yonder, where he had felt it the second time. It had fingered over his mind and maybe it had been repelled by what it met there. Perhaps the contact was a frightening experience for it and it had made up its mind against another such attempt.

Or perhaps it had existed only in the curious workings of a very lonely human mind. Like *Anne.* Something of his own making. He wanted it to exist. He desperately wanted it to be real, to make the world alive, Rule's world, and Harley's, and his. He wanted it to lend companionship for the years of silence, the hollow days and deadly nights, something, anything—an animal or an enemy, a thing to fear if not something to love. Solitude forever—he could not bear that. He refused to believe in it. He would search every square meter of the world until he found something like him, that lived and felt, or until he had proved it did not exist.

And it came.

The first touch was a prickling and a gentle whisper in his mind, a sound of wind. The air shone with an aching green luminance. He could not hold it. The light went. Numbness came over him; his pulse jumped wildly. Pain lanced through his chest and belly. Then nothing. He gasped for air and felt a fingering at his consciousness, a deep sense of perplexity. Hesitation. He felt it hovering, the touches less and less substantial, and he reached out with his thoughts, wanting it, pleading with it to wait.

A gentle tug at his sense. Not unpleasant.

Listen to me, he thought, and felt it settle over him like a blanket, entity without definition. Words were meaningless to the being which had reached into his mind. Only the images transcended the barrier.

He hunted for something to give it, a vision of sunlight, of living things, his memories of the river lilies. There came back a feeling of peace, of satisfaction. He wanted to drift to sleep and fought the impulse. His body grew as heavy as it had on the river and he felt himself falling, drifting slowly. Images flowed past like the unrolling of a tape with an incalculable span of years encoded on it. He saw the clearing thick with young trees, and saw it again when there were vacant spaces among those, and he knew that others had grown before the present ones, that the seedlings he saw among the last were the giants about him.

His consciousness embraced all the forest, and knew the seasonal ebb and flood of the river, knew the islets and the branches that had grown and ceased to be. He knew the ages of mountains, the weight of innumerable years.

What are you? he wondered in his dream.

Age, great age, and eternal youth, the breaking of life from the earth, the bittersweet rush of earthbound life sunward. And this, this was the thing it called itself—too large for a single word or a single thought. It rippled sound through his mind, like wind through harpstrings, and it was that too. *I,* it said. *I.*

It had unrolled his question from his mind with the fleeting swiftness of a dream, absorbed it all and knew it. Like *Anne.* Faster. More complete. He tried to comprehend such a mind, but the mind underwent a constriction of panic. Sight and sensation returned on his own terms and he was aware of the radiance again, like the sunbeam, drifting near him.

You, Warren thought. *Do you understand me?*

Something riffled through his thoughts, incomprehensible and alien. Again the rippling touch of light and chill.

Did you touch them? My friends died. They died of a disease. All but me.

Warmth and regret flowed over him. *Friend,* it seemed. *Sorrow. Welcome.* It thrilled through him like the touch of rain after drought. He caught his breath, wordless for the moment, beyond thinking. He tried to understand the impressions that followed, but they flowed like madness through his nerves. He resisted, panicked, and a feeling of sorrow came back.

"What *are* you?" he cried.

It broke contact abruptly, crept back again more slowly and stayed at a distance, cool, anxious.

"Don't leave." The thought frightened him. "Don't go. I don't want that, either."

The radiance expanded, flickering with gold inside. It filled his mind, and somewhere in it a small thing crouched, finite, fluttering inside with busy life, while the trees grew. Himself. He was measured, against such a scale as the giants, and felt cold.

"How old are you?"

The life spans of three very ancient trees flashed through his mind in the blink of an eye.

"I'm twenty-seven years."

It took years from his mind; he felt it, the seasonal course of the world and star, the turning of the world, a plummeting to earth with the sun flicking overhead again and again and again. A flower came to mind, withered and died.

"Stop it," Warren cried, rejecting the image and the comparison.

It fled. He tried to hold the creature. A sunset burst on his eyes, flared and dimmed . . . a time, an appointment for meeting, a statement—he did not know. The green light faded away.

Cold. He shivered convulsively, caught the blanket up about him in the dimness. He stared bleakly into the shadow . . . felt as if his emotions had been taken roughly and shaken into chaos, wanted to scream and cry and could not. Death seemed to have touched him, reduced everything to minute scale. Everything. Small and meaningless.

"Warren."

Anne's voice. He had not the will or the strength to answer her. It was beyond belief that he could have suffered such cataclysmic damage in an instant of contact, that his life was not the same, the universe not in the same proportion.

"Warren."

The insistent voice finally sent his hand groping after the com unit. Danger. *Anne.* Threat. She might come here. Might do something rash. "I'm all right." He kept his voice normal and casual, surprised by its clear tone as he got it out. "I'm fine. How are you?"

"Better now, Warren. You didn't respond. I've called twelve times. Is there trouble?"

"I was asleep, that's all. I'm going to sleep again. It's getting dark here."

"You didn't call in an hour."

"I forgot. Humans forget. Look that up in your files. Let me be, *Anne.* I'm tired. I want to sleep. Make your next call at 0500."

"This interval is long. Please reconsider this instruction."

"I mean it, *Anne.* 0500. Not before then. Keep the sensor box off and let me rest."

There was a long pause. The sensor unit activated itself and went off again, *Anne's* presence actively with him for the moment. She looked about, shut herself off. "Good night, Warren."

She was gone. She was not programmed to detect a lie, only an error in logic. Now he had cut himself off indeed. Perhaps, he thought, he had just killed himself.

But the entity was not hostile. He *knew*. He had been inside its being, known without explanation all the realities that stood behind its thought, like in a dream where in a second all the past of an act was there, never lived, but there, and remembered, and therefore real. The creature must have walked airless moons with him, seen lifeless deserts and human cities and the space between the stars. It must have been terrifying to the being whose name meant the return of spring. And what might it have felt thrust away from its world and drifting in dark, seeing its planet as a green and blue mote in infinity? Perhaps it had suffered more than he had.

He shut his eyes, relaxed a time . . . called *Anne* back when he had rested somewhat, and reassured her. "I'm still well," he told her. "I'm happy."

"Thank you, Warren," she said in return, and let herself be cut off again.

The sun began to dim to dark. He put on his coat, tucked up again in the blanket. Human appetites returned to him—hunger and thirst. He ate some of the food he had brought, drank a cup of coffee, lay back and closed his eyes on the dark, thinking that in all reason he ought to be afraid in the night in this place.

He felt a change in the air, a warmth tingling down the back of his neck and the insides of his arms. The greenish light grew and hovered in the dark.

It was there as if nothing had ever gone amiss.

"Hello," Warren said, sitting up. He wrapped himself in the blanket, looked at the light, looked around him. "Where did you go?"

A ripple of cool waters went through his mind. Lilies and bubbles drifting.

"The river?"

Leaves fluttering in a wind, stronger and stronger. The sun going down.

"What were you doing there?"

His heart fluttered, his pulse sped, not of his own doing. Too strong—far too strongly.

"Stop—stop it."

The pressure eased, and Warren pressed his hands to his eyes and gasped for air. His heart still labored, his sense of balance deserted him. He tumbled backward into space, blind, realized he was lying down on firm earth with his legs bent painfully. The tendril of thought crept back into his mind, controlled and subdued. Sorrow. He perceived a thing very tightly furled, with darkness about it, shielding it from the green. It was himself. Sorrow poured about him.

"I know you can't help it." He tried to move, disoriented. His hands were numb. His vision was tunneled. "Don't touch me like that. Stop it."

Confusion: he felt it; an ebbing retreat.

"Don't go, either. Just stop. Please."

It lingered about him, green luminance pulsing slowly into a sparkle or two of gold, dimming down again by turns. All the air seemed calm.

Spring, Warren gave it back. He built an image of flowers, colored flowers, of gardens. Of pale green shoots coming up through moist earth.

It answered him, flowers blooming in his mind, white, green and gold-throated jade. They took on tints in his vision, mingled colors and pale at first, as if the mind had not known the colors were distinct to separate flowers, and then settling each on each, blues and violets and yellows, reds and roses and lavenders. Joy flooded through. Over and over again the flowers bloomed.

"Friend. You understand that?"

The flowers kept blooming, twining stems, more and more of them.

"Is it always you—is it always you I've dealt with? Are there others like you?"

A single glow, replacing the other image, greenness through all his vision, but things circled outside it . . . not hostile—other. And it enfolded one tiny darkness, a solitary thing, tightly bound up, clenched in on the flutterings inside itself.

"That's me, you mean. I'm human."

The small creature sank strange tendrils deep into the moist earth, spread extensions like branches, flickers of growth in all directions through the forest and out, across the grassland.

"Isn't there anything else—aren't there other creatures on this world . . . anywhere?"

The image went out. Water bubbled, and in the cold murk tiny things moved. Grass stirred in the sunlight, and a knot of small creatures gathered, fluttering at the heart, three, fourteen of them. Joy and sorrow. The flutters died. One by one the minds went out. Sorrow. There were thirteen, twelve, eleven, ten—

"Were you there? Were you on the ship?"

He saw images of the corridors—his own memory snatched forth; the destruct chamber; the lab and the blood—the river then, cold, murky waters, the raft drifting on the river in the cold dawning. He lay there, complex, fluttering thing in the heart of green, in the mind—pain then, and retreat.

"I know. I came to find you. I wanted to find out if you were real. To talk to you."

The green radiance crept back again, surrounding the dark egg with the furled creature in its heart. The creature stirred, unfolded branches and thrust them out of its shell, into the radiance.

"No—no. Keep back from me. You can do me damage. You know that."

The beating of his heart quickened and slowed again before it hurt. The greenness dimmed and retreated. A tree stood in the shell of darkness that was his own space, a tree fixed and straight and solitary, with barren earth and shadow around it.

The judgment depressed him. "I wanted to find you. I came here to find you. Then, on the river. And now. I haven't changed my mind. But the touching hurts."

Warmth bubbled through. Images of suns flashed across the sky into a blinding blur. Trees grew and died and decayed. Time: Ages passed. The radiance fairly danced, sparkling and warm. Welcome. Welcome. Desire tingled through him.

"You make me nervous when you get excited like that. You might forget. And you can hurt me. You know that by now."

Desire, a fluttering along his veins. The radiance hovered, back and forth, dancing slow flickerings of gold in its heart.

"So you're patient. But what for? What are you waiting on?"

The small-creature image returned. From embryo, it grew, unfolded, reached out into the radiance—let it into that fluttering that was its center.

"No." Death came into his mind, mental extinction, accepting an alien parasite.

The radiance swirled green and gold about him. Waters murmured and bubbled. Growth exploded in thrills of force that ran over Warren's nerves and threatened for a moment to be more than his senses could take. The echoes and the images ebbed and he caught his breath, warmed, close to losing himself.

"Stop," he protested, finding that much strength. The contact loosened, leaving a memory of absolute intoxication with existence, freedom, joy, such as he had never felt in his life—frightening, unsettling, undermining disciplines and rules by which life was ordered and orderly. "We could both be damaged that way. Stop. Stop it."

The greenness began to pulse slowly, dimming and brightening. It backed away. Another tightly furled embryo appeared in his mind, different from the first, sickly and strange. It lay beside his image in the dark shell, both of them, together, reached out tendrils, interwove, and the radiance grew pale.

"*What* other human? Where?"

A desperate fluttering inside the sickly one, a hammering of his own pulse: a distant and miserable rage; and grief; and need.

"Where is it now? What happened to it? *Where is he?*"

The fluttering inside the image stopped, the tendrils withered, and all of it decayed.

He gathered himself to rise, pushed back. The creature's thoughts washed back on him, a seething confusion, the miasma of loneliness and empty ages pouring about him, and he sprang to his feet and fled, slipping and stumbling, blind in the verdant light, in symbols his mind could not grasp, in distortion of what he could. Sound and light and sensation warped through his senses. Daylight. Somehow it was daylight. He reached the aged tree, the grandfather of trees, recoiled from the feel of the moss in his almost blindness, stumbled around its roots.

The place was here. He knew.

The greenness hovered there in the dawning, danced over corruption, over what had been a man. It lay twisted and curled up there, in that cavern of the old tree's naked roots, in that dark, with the grinning white of bone thrusting through rags of skin.

"*Sax,* " he wept. He groped his way back from it, finding empty air about his fingertips, dreading something tangible. He turned and ran, blind in the shadow, among the clinging branches that tore at his arms and his face. The light came about him again, green and gold. His feet slipped among the tangled roots and earth bruised his hands. Pain lanced up his ankle, through his knees. The mustiness of old leaves was in his mouth. He spat and spat again, clawed his way up by the brush and the tree roots, hauled himself farther and ran again and fell, his leg twisted by the clinging roots.

Sorrow, the radiance mourned. Sorrow. Sorrow.

He moved, feverishly turned one way and the other to drag his foot free of the roots that had wedged it in. The greenish luminance grew at the edges of his mind, moving in, bubbling mournfully of life and death. "You killed him," he shouted at it. "You killed him."

The image came to him of Sax curled up there as if in sleep— alone and lost. Withering, decaying.

He freed his foot. The pain shot up to his inner knee and he sobbed with it, rocked to and fro.

Sorrow. It pulled at him, wanting him. It ached with needing him.

Not broken, not broken, he hoped: to be left lame lifelong as well as desolate—he could not bear that.

Pain stopped. A cooling breeze fanned over him. He stopped hating. Stopped blaming. The forest swayed and moved all about him. A tug drew at his mind, to go, to follow—other presences. Over river, over hills, far away, to drift with the winds and stop being alone, forever, and there was no terror in it. Sax perished. The forest took him, and he was part of it, feeding it, remembered.

Come, the presence said. He tried—but the first halting movement away from the support of the tree sent a shooting pain up his knee and brought him down rocking to and for in misery.

"Warren," a voice was saying. "Warren. Assistance?"

The vision passed. The ache throbbed in his knee, and the green radiance grew distant, rippling with the sound of waters. Then the creature was gone, the forest silent again.

"Warren?"

He fumbled at his belt, got the com unit to his mouth. *"Anne. I'm all right."*

"Assistance? Assistance?"

"I'm coming home, Anne."

"Clarify: you killed him. Clarify."

He wiped his face, his hand trembling. "I found Sax, *Anne.* He's not functioning."

A silence. "Assistance?"

"None possible. It's permanent nonfunction. He's—deteriorated. I'm coming home. It's going to be longer than usual."

"Are you in pain, Warren?"

He thought about it, thought about her conflict override. "No. Stress. Finding Sax was stressful. I'm going to shut off now. I've got some things to take care of. I'll come as quickly as I can."

"Yes, Warren."

The contact went out. He hooked the com unit back to his belt, felt of the knee, looked about him in the dawning, distressed by the loss of time. Sickness moiled in him, shock. Thirst. He broke small branches from the thicket, and a larger one, tried to lever himself out of his predicament and finally gave up and crawled, tears streaming down his face, back to the pallet and the kit he had left. He drank, forced a little food into his mouth and washed it down, splinted the knee and wrapped it in bandage from the med kit.

He got up then, using his stick, tried to carry both the water and the med kit, but he could not manage them both and chose to keep the water. He skipped forward using the stick, eyes watering from the pain, and there was a painkiller in the kit, but he left it, too: no drugs, nothing to muddle his direction; he had no leeway for errors. He moved slowly, steadily, into the forest on the homeward track, his hand aching already from the stick; and the tangle grew thicker, making him stagger and catch his balance violently from the good leg to the injured one and back again.

After he had fallen for the third time he wiped the tears from his eyes and gave up the stick entirely, leaning on the trees while he could, and when he came to places where he had to hitch his way along with his weight partially on the leg, he did it, and when the intervals grew too long and he had to crawl, he did that too. He tried not to think of the distance he had to go to the river. It did not matter. The distance had to be covered, no matter how long it took. *Anne* called, back on her hourly schedule, and that was all he had.

It was afternoon when he came into the vicinity of the river, and he reached it the better part of an hour afterward. He slid down to the sandy bank and staggered across to the raft, freed its rope and managed, crawling and tugging, to get it into the river and himself into it before it drifted away. He savored the beautiful feel of it under his torn hands, the speed of its moving, which was a painless, delirious joy after the meter-by-meter torment of the hours since dawn.

He got it to shore, started to leave it loose and then, half crazed and determined in his habits, crawled his way to the appointed limb and moored it fast. Then there was the bank, sandy in the first part, and then the brushy path he had broken bringing loads of equipment down.

And in his hearing a blessedly familiar sound of machinery.

Anne stood atop the crest, in front of the crawler, bright in the afternoon sun, her faceplate throwing back the daylight.

"Warren? Assistance?"

IX

He worked the muddy remnant of his clothing off, fouling the sheets of the lab cot and the floor of the lab itself, while *Anne* hovered and watched. She brought him bandages. Fruit juice. He drank prodigiously of it, and that settled his stomach. Water. He washed where he sat, making puddles on the floor and setting *Anne* to clicking distressedly.

"*Anne*," he said, "I'm going to have to take a real bath. I can't stand this filth. You'll have to help me down there."

"Yes, Warren." She offered her arm, helping him up, and walked with him to the bath, compensating for his uneven stride. Walked with him all the way to the mist cabinet, and stood outside while he turned on the control.

He soaked for a time, leaned on the wall and shut his eyes a time, looked down finally at a body gone thinner than he would have believed. Scratches. Bruises. The bandage was soaked and he had no disposition to change it. He had had enough of pain, and drugs were working in him now, home, in safety. So the sheets would get wet. *Anne* could wash everything.

No more nightmares. No more presences in the depths of the ship. No more Sax. He stared bleakly at the far wall of the cabinet, trying to recall the presence in the forest, trying to make sense of things, but the drugs muddled him and he could hardly recall the feeling or the look of the light that had shone out of the dark.

Sax. Sax was real. He had talked to *Anne.* She knew. She had heard. Heard all of it. He turned on the drier until he was tired of waiting on it, left the cabinet still damp and let *Anne* help him up to his own room, his own safe bed.

She waited there, clicking softly as he settled himself in, dimmed the lights for him, even pulled the covers up for him when he had trouble.

"That's good," he sighed. The drugs were pulling him under.

"Instructions."

Her request hit his muddled thought train oddly, brought him struggling back toward consciousness. "Instruction in what?"

"In repair of human structure."

He laughed muzzily. "We're essentially self-repairing. Let me sleep it out. Good night, *Anne.*"

"Your time is in error."

"My body isn't. Go clean up the lab. Clean up the bath. Let me sleep."

"Yes, Warren."

Have you, he thought to ask her, *understood what you read? Do you know what happened out there, to Sax? Did you pick it up?* But she left. He got his eyes open and she was gone, and he thought he had not managed to ask, because she had not answered.

He slept, and dreamed green lights, and slept again.

Anne clattered about outside his room. Breakfast, he decided, looking at the time. He tried to get out of bed and winced, managed to move only with extreme pain . . . the knee, the hands, the shoulders and the belly—every muscle in his body hurt. He rolled onto his belly, levered himself out of bed, held on to the counter and the wall to reach the door. He had bruises . . . massive bruises, the worst about his hip and his elbow. His face hurt on that side. He reached for the switch, opened the door.

"Assistance?" *Anne* asked, straightening from her table-setting.

"I want a bit of pipe. A meter long. Three centimeters wide. Get it."

"Yes, Warren."

No questions. She left. He limped over painfully and sat down, ate his breakfast. His hand was so stiff he could scarcely close his fingers on the fork or keep the coffee cup in his swollen fingers. He sat staring at the far wall, seeing the clearing again. Numb. There were limits to feeling, inside and out. He thought that he might feel something—some manner of elation in his discovery when he had recovered; but there was Sax to temper it.

Anne came back. He took the pipe and used it to get up when he had done; his hand hurt abominably, even after he had hobbled down to the lab and padded the raw pipe with bandages. He kept walking, trying to loosen up.

Anne followed him, stood about, walked, every motion that he made.

"Finished your assimilation?" he asked her, recalling that. "Does it work?"

"Processing is proceeding."

"A creature of many talents. You can walk about and rescue me and assimilate the library all at once, can you?"

"The programs are not impaired. An AI uses a pseudobiological matrix for storage. Storage is not a problem. Processing does not impair other functions."

"No headaches, either, I'll bet."

"Headache is a biological item."

"Your definitions are better than they were."

"Thank you, Warren."

She matched strides with him, exaggeratedly slow. He stopped. She stopped. He went on, and she kept with him. "*Anne.* Why don't you just let me alone and let me walk? I'm not going to fall over. I don't need you."

"I perceive malfunction."

"A structural malfunction under internal repair. I have all kinds of internal mechanisms working on the problem. I'll get along. It's all right, *Anne.*"

"Assistance?"

"None needed, I tell you. It's all right. Go away."

She stayed. Malfunctioning humans, he thought. No programming accepted. He frowned, beyond clear reasoning. The bio and botany labs were ahead. He kept walking, into them and through to Botany One.

"Have you been maintaining here?" he asked. The earth in the trays looked a little dry.

"I've been following program."

He limped over and adjusted the water flow. "Keep it there."

"Yes, Warren."

He walked to the trays, felt of them.

"Soil," *Anne* said gratuitously. "Dirt. Earth."

"Yes. It has to be moist. There'll be plants coming up soon. They need the water."

"Coming up. Source."

"Seed. They're under there, under the soil. Plants, *Anne*. From seed."

She walked closer, adjusted her stabilizers, looked, a turning of her sensor-equipped head. She put out a hand and raked a line in the soil. "I perceive no life. Size?"

"It's there, under the soil. Leave it alone. You'll kill it."

She straightened. Her sensor lights glowed, all of them. "Please check your computations, Warren."

"About what?"

"This life."

"There are some things your sensors can't pick up, Annie."

"I detect no life."

"They're there. I put them in the ground. I know they're there; I don't need to detect them. *Seeds,* Annie. That's the nature of them."

"I am making cross-references on this word, Warren."

He laughed painfully, patiently opened a drawer and took out a large one that he had not planted. "This is one. It'd be a plant if I put it into the ground and watered it. That's what makes it grow. That's what makes all the plants outside."

"Plants come from seed."

"That's right."

"This is growth process. This is birth process."

"Yes."

"This is predictable."

"Yes, it is."

In the dark faceplate the tiny stars glowed to intense life. She took the seed from the counter, with one powerful thrust rammed it into the soil and then pressed the earth down over it, leaving the imprint of her fingers. Warren looked at her in shock.

"Why, *Anne*? Why did you do that?"

"I'm investigating."

"Are you, now?"

"I still perceive no life."

"You'll have to wait."

"Specify period."

"It takes several weeks for the seed to come up."

"Come up."

"Idiom. The plant will grow out of it. Then the life will be in your sensor range."

"Specify date."

"Variable. Maybe twenty days."

"Recorded." She swung about, facing him. "Life forms come from seeds. Where are human seeds?"

"*Anne*—I don't think your programming is adequate to the situation. And my knee hurts. I think I'm going to go topside again."

"Assistance?"

"None needed." He leaned his sore hand on the makeshift cane and limped past her, and she stalked faithfully after, to the lift, and rode topside to the common room, stood by while he lowered himself into a reclining chair and let the cane fall, massaging his throbbing hand.

"Instruction?"

"Coffee," he said.

"Yes, Warren."

She brought it. He sat and stared at the wall, thinking of things he might read, but the texts that mattered were all beyond him and all useless on this world, on Rule's world. He thought of reading for pleasure, and kept seeing the grove at night, and the radiance, and Sax's body left there. He owed it burial. And he had not had the strength.

Had to go back there. Could not live here and not go back there. It was life there as well as a dead friend. Sax had known, had gone to it, through what agony he shrank from imagining, had gone to it to die there . . . to be in that place at the last. He tried to doubt it, here, in *Anne*'s sterile interior, but he had experienced it, and it would not go away. He even thought of talking to *Anne* about it, but there was that refusal to listen to him when he was malfunctioning—and he had no wish to stir that up. *Seeds* . . . were hard enough. Immaterial life—

"Warren," *Anne* said. "Activity? I play chess."

She won, as usual.

The swelling went down on the second day. He walked, cautiously, without the cane . . . still used it for going any considerable distance, and the knee still ached, but the rest of the aches diminished and he acquired a certain cheerfulness, assured at least that the knee was not broken, that it was healing, and he went about his usual routines with a sense of pleasure in them, glad not to be lamed for life.

But by the fourth and fifth day the novelty was gone again, and he wandered the halls of the ship without the cane, miserable, limping in pain but too restless to stay still. He drank himself to sleep of nights—still awoke in the middle of them, the result, he reckoned, of too much sleep, of dreaming the days away in idleness, of lying with his mind vacant for hours during the day, watching the clouds or the grass moving in the wind. Like *Anne.* Waiting for stimulus that never came.

He played chess, longer and longer games with *Anne,* absorbed her lessons . . . lost.

He cried, the last time—for no reason, but that the game had become important, and when he saw one thing coming, she sprang another on him.

"Warren," she said implacably, "is this pain?"

"The knee hurts," he said. It did. "It disrupted my calculations." It had not. He had lost. He lied, and *Anne* sat there with her lights winking on and off in the darkness of her face and absorbing it.

"Assistance? Pain: drugs interfere with pain reception." She had gotten encyclopedic in her processing. "Some of these drugs are in storage:—"

"Cancel. I know what they are." He got up, limped over to the counter and opened the liquor cabinet. "Alcohol also kills the pain."

"Yes, Warren."

He poured his drink, leaned against the counter and sipped at it, wiped his eyes. "Prolonged inactivity, *Anne.* That's causing the pain. The leg's healing."

A small delay of processing. "Chess is activity."

"I need to sleep." He took the drink and the bottle with him, limped into his own quarters, shut the door. He drank, stripped, crawled between the sheets and sat there drinking, staring at the screen and thinking that he might try to read . . . but he had to call *Anne* to get a book on the screen, and he wanted no debates. His hands shook. He poured another glass and drank it down, fluffed the pillow. "*Anne,*" he said. "Lights out."

"Good night, Warren." The lights went.

The chessboard came back, behind his eyelids, the move he should have made. He rehearsed it to the point of anger, deep and bitter rage. He knew that it was ridiculous. All pointless. Without consequence. Everything was.

He slid into sleep, and dreamed, and the dreams were of green things, and the river, and finally of human beings, of home and parents long lost, of old friends . . . of women inventively erotic and imaginary, with names he knew at the time—he awoke in the midst of that and lay frustrated, staring at the dark ceiling and then at the dark behind his eyelids, trying to rebuild them in all their detail, but sleep eluded him. He thought of *Anne* in that context, of bizarre programs, of his own misery, and what she was not—his thoughts ran in circles and grew unbearable.

He reached after the bottle, poured what little there was and drank it, and that was not enough. He rolled out of bed, stumbled in the dark. "*Lights,*" he cried out, and they came on. He limped for the door and opened it, and the pseudosome came to life where it had been standing in the dark, limned in silver from the doorway, her lights coming to life inside her faceplate. The lights in the living quarters brightened. "Assistance?"

"No." He went to the cabinet, opened it, took out another bottle and opened it. The bottles were diminishing. He could foresee the day when there would be no more bottles at all. That panicked him. Set him to thinking on the forest, on green berries that might ferment, on the grasses—on fruits that might come at particular seasons. If he failed to poison himself.

He went back to his bed with the bottle, filled his glass and got in bed. "Lights out," he said. They went. He sat drinking in the dark until he felt his hand shaking, and set the glass aside and burrowed again into the tangled sheets.

This time there were nightmares, the lab, the deaths, and he was walking through the ship again, empty-handed, looking for Sax and his knife. Into dark corridors. He kept walking and the way got darker and darker, and something waited there. Something hovered over him. He heard sound—

The dream brought him up with a jerk, eyes wide and a yell in his ears that was his own, confronted with red lights in the dark, the touch of a hand on him.

The second shock was more than the first, and he lashed out at hard metal, struggled wildly with covers and the impediment of Anne's unyielding arm. Her stabilizers hummed. She put the hand on his chest and held and he recovered his sense, staring up at her with his heart pounding in fright.

"Assistance? Assistance? Is this malfunction?"

"A dream—a dream, Anne."

A delay while the lights blinked in the dark. "Dreams may have random motor movements. Dreams are random neural firings. Neural cells are brain structure. This process affects the brain. Please confirm your status."

"I'm fine, Anne."

"I detect internal disturbance."

"That's my heart, Anne. It's all right. I'm normal now. The dream's over."

She took back the hand. He lay still for a moment, watching her lights.

"Time," he asked.

"0434."

He winced, moved, ran a hand through his hair. "Make breakfast. Call me when it's ready."

"Yes, Warren."

She left, a clicking in the dark that carried her own light with her. The door closed. He pulled the covers about himself and burrowed down and tried to sleep, but he was only conscious of a headache, and he had no real desire for the breakfast.

He kept very busy that day, despite the headache—cleaned up, limped about, carrying things to their proper places, throwing used clothing into the laundry. Everything in shape, everything in order. No more self pity. No more excuses of his lameness or the pain. No more liquor. He thought even of putting *Anne* in charge of that cabinet . . . but he did not. He was. He could say no if he wanted to.

Outside, a rain blew up. *Anne* reported the anomaly. Clouds hung darkly over the grasslands and the forest. He went down to the lock to see it, the first change he had seen in the world . . . stood there in the hatchway with the rain spattering his face and the thunder shaking his bones, watched the lightning tear holes in the sky.

The clouds shed their burden in a downpour, but they stayed. After the pounding rain, which left the grass battered and collapsed the canopy outside into a miniature lake, the clouds stayed, sending down a light drizzle that chilled to the bone, intermittent with harder rain—one day, and two, and three, four at last, in which the sun hardly shone.

He thought of the raft, of the things he had left behind—of the clearing finally, and Sax lying snugged there in the hollow of the old tree's roots.

And a living creature—one with it, with the scents of rain and earth and the elements.

The sensor box. That, too, he had had to abandon . . . sitting on the ground on a now sodden blanket, perhaps half underwater like the ground outside.

"*Anne,*" he said then, thinking on it. "Activate the sensor unit. Is it still functioning?"

"Yes."

He sat where he was, in the living quarters, studying the chessboard. Thought a moment. "Scan the area around the unit. Do you perceive anything?"

"Vegetation, Warren. It's raining."

"Have you—activated it since I left it there?"

"When the storm broke I activated it. I investigated with all sensors."

"Did you—perceive anything?"

"Vegetation, Warren."

He looked into her faceplate and made the next move, disquieted.

.   .   .

The seeds sprouted in the lab. It was all in one night, while the drizzle died away outside and the clouds broke to let the sun through. And as if they had known, the seeds came up. Warren looked out across the rows of trays in the first unadulterated pleasure he had felt in days . . . to see them live. All along the trays the earth was breaking, and in some places little arches and spears of pale green and white were thrusting upward.

Anne followed him. She always did.

"You see," he told her, "now you can see the life. It was there, all along."

She made closer examination where he indicated, a humanlike bending to put her sensors into range. She straightened, walked back to the place where she had planted her own seed. "Your seeds have grown. The seed I planted has no growth."

"It's too early yet. Give it all its twenty days. Maybe less. Maybe more. They vary."

"Explain. Explain life process. Cross-referencing is incomplete."

"The inside of the seed is alive, from the time it was part of the first organism. When water gets into it it activates, penetrates its hull and pushes away from gravity and toward the light."

Anne digested the information a moment. "Life does not initiate with seed. Life initiates from the first organism. All organisms produce seed. Instruction: what is the first organism?"

He looked at her, blinked, tried to think through the muddle. "I think you'd better assimilate some other area of data. You'll confuse yourself."

"Instruction: explain life process."

"I can't. It's not in my memory."

"I can instruct. I contain random information in this area."

"So do I, Annie, but it doesn't do any good. It won't work. You don't plant humans in seed trays. It takes two humans to make another one. And you aren't. Let it alone."

"Specify: *aren't. It.*"

"You aren't human. And you're not going to be. Cancel, *Anne,* just cancel. I can't reason with you, not on this."

"I reason."

He looked into her changeless face with the impulse to hit her, which she could neither feel nor comprehend. "I don't choose to reason. Gather up a food kit for me, Annie. Get the gear into the lock."

"This program is preparatory to going to the river."

"Yes. It is."

"This is hazardous. This caused injury. Please reconsider this program."

"I'm going to pick up your sensor box. Retrieve valuable equipment, a part of *you*, Annie. You can't reach it. I'll be safe."

"This unit isn't in danger. You were damaged there. Please reconsider this instruction."

"I'd prefer to have you functioning and able to come to my assistance if you're needed. I don't want to quarrel with you, *Anne*. Accept the program. I won't be happy until you do."

"Yes, Warren."

He breathed a slow sigh, patted her shoulder. Her hand touched his, rested there. He walked from under it and she followed, a slow clicking at his heels.

X

The raft was still there. Nests of sodden grass lodged in tree branches and cast high up on the shores showed how high the flood had risen, but the rope had held it. The water still flowed higher than normal. The whole shoreline had changed, the bank eroded away. The raft sat higher still, partially filled with water and leaves.

Warren picked his way down to it, past brush festooned with leaves and grass, only food and water and a folding spade for a pack. He used a stick to support his weight on the injured leg, walked slowly and carefully. He set everything down to heave the raft up and dump the water . . . no more care of contamination, he reckoned: It had all had its chance at one time or another, the river, the forest. The second raft was in the crawler upslope, but all he had lost was the paddle, and he went back after that, slow progress, unhurried.

"*Anne*," he said via com, when he had settled everything in place, when the raft bobbed on the river and his gear was aboard.

"I'm at the river. I won't call for a while. A few hours. My status is very good. I'm going to be busy here."

"Yes, Warren."

He cut it off, put it back at his belt, launched the raft.

The far bank had suffered similar damage. He drove for it with some difficulty with the river running high, wet his boots getting himself ashore, secured the raft by pulling it up with the rope, the back part of it still in the water.

The ground in the forest, too, was littered with small branches and larger ones, carpeted with new leaves. But flowers had come into bloom. Everywhere the mosses were starred with white flowers. Green ones opened at the bases of trees. The hanging vines bloomed in pollen-golden rods.

And the fungi proliferated everywhere, fantastical shapes, oranges and blues and whites. The ferns were heavy with water and shed drops like jewels. There were beauties to compensate for the ruin. Drops fell from the high branches when the wind blew, a periodic shower that soaked his hair and ran off his impermeable jacket. Everything seemed both greener and darker, all the growth lusher and thicker than ever.

The grove when he came on it had suffered not at all, not a branch fallen, only a litter of leaves and small limbs on the grass; and he was glad—not to have lost one of the giants. The old tree's beard was flower-starred, his moss even thicker. Small cuplike flowers bloomed in the grass in the sunlight, a vine having grown into the light, into the way of the abandoned, rain-sodden blanket, the sensor box.

And Sax . . . Warren went to the base of the aged tree and looked inside, found him there, more bone than before, the clothing sodden with the storm, some of the bones of the fingers fallen away. The sight had no horror for him, nothing but sadness. "Sax," he said softly. "It's Warren. Warren here."

From the vacant eyes, no answer. He stood up, flexed the spade out, set to work, spadeful after spadeful, casting the dirt and the leaves inside, into what made a fair tomb, a strange one for a starfarer . . . poor lost Sax, curled up to sleep. The earthen blanket grew up to Sax's knees, to his waist, among the gnarled roots and the bones. He made spadefuls of the green flowers and set them there, at Sax's feet, set them in the earth that covered him, stirring up clouds of pollen. He sneezed and wiped his eyes and stood up again, taking another spadeful of earth and mold.

A sound grew in his mind like the bubbling of water, and he looked to his left, where green radiance bobbed. The welcome flowed into him like the touch of warm wind.

He ignored it, cast the earth, took another spadeful.

Welcome, it sang to him. The water-sound bubbled. A flower unfolded, tinted itself slowly violet.

"I've work to do."

Sorrow. The color faded.

"I don't want it like the last time. Keep your distance. Stop that." Its straying thoughts brushed him, numbing senses. He leaned on the spade, felt himself sinking, turning and drifting bodilessly— wrenched his mind back to his own control so abruptly he almost fell.

Sorrow. A second time a flower, a pale shoot from among the leaves, a folded bud trying to open.

"Work," Warren said. He picked up the spadeful, cast it; and another.

Perplexity. The flower folded again, drooped unwatered.

"I have this to do. It's important. And you won't understand that. Nothing of the sort could matter to you."

The radiance grew, pulsed. Suns flickered across a mental sky, blue and black, day and night, in a streaming course.

He leaned on the spade for stability in the blur of days passed. "What's time—to you?"

Desire. The radiance took shape and settled on the grass, softly pulsing. It edged closer—stopped at once when he stepped back.

"Maybe you killed Sax. You know that? Maybe he just lay there and dreamed to death."

Sorrow. An image formed in his mind, the small sickly creature, all curled up, all its inward motion suddenly stopped.

"I know. You wouldn't have meant it. But it happened." He dug another spadeful of earth. Intervening days unrolled in his mind, thoughts stolen from him, where he had been, what he had done.

It stole the thought of Anne, and it was a terrible image, a curled-up thing like a human, but hollow inside, with dark inside, deadly hostile. Her tendrils were dark and icy.

"She's not like that. She's just a machine." He flung the spadeful. Earth showered over bare bone and began to cover Sax's face. He flinched from the sight. "She can't do anything but take orders. I made her, if you like."

There was horror in the air, palpable.

"She's not alive. She never was."

The radiance became very pale and retreated up into the branches of one of the youngest trees, a mere touch of color in the sunlight. Cold, cold, the terror drifted down like winter rain.

"*Don't leave.*" The spade fell. He stepped over it, held up his hands, threatened with solitude. "Don't."

The radiance went out. Re-formed near him, drifted up to sit on the aged, fallen tree.

"It's my world. I know it's different. I never wanted to hurt you with it."

The greenness spread about him, a darkness in its heart, where two small creatures entwined, their tendrils interweaving, one living, one dead.

"Stop it."

His own mind came back at him: loneliness, longing for companionship; fear of dying alone. Like Sax. Like that. He held deeply buried the thought that the luminance offered a means of dying, a little better than most; but it came out, and the radiance shivered. The *Anne*-image took shape in its heart, her icy tendrils invading the image that was himself, growing, insinuating ice into that small fluttering that was his life, winding through him and out again.

"What do you know?" he cried at it. "What do you know at all? You don't know me. You can't see me, with no eyes; you don't know."

The *Anne*-image faded, left him alone in the radiance, embryo, tucked and fluttering inside. A greenness crept in there, the least small tendril of green, and touched that quickness.

Emotion exploded like sunrise, with a shiver of delight. A second burst. He tried to object, felt a touching of the hairs at the back of his neck. He shivered, and the light was gone. Every sense seemed stretched to the limit, heightened, but remote, and he wanted to get up and walk a little distance, knowing even while he did it that it was not his own suggestion. He moved, limping a little, and quite suddenly the presence fled, leaving a light sweat over his body.

Pain, it sent. And Peace.

"Hurt, did it?" He massaged his knee and sat down. His own eyes watered. "Serves you right."

Sorrow. The greenness unfolded again, filling all his mind but for one small corner where he stayed whole and alert.

"No," he cried in sudden panic, and when it drew back in its own: "I wouldn't mind—if you were content with touching. But you aren't. You can't keep your distance when you get excited. And sometimes you hurt."

The greenness faded a little. It was dark round about.

Hours. Hours gone. A flickering, a quick feeling of sunlit warmth came to him, but he flung it off.

"Don't lie to me. What happened to the time? When did it get dark?"

A sun plummeted, and trees bowed in evening breezes.

"How long did you have control? How long was it?"

Sorrow. Peace . . . settled on him with a great weight. He felt a great desire of sleep, of folding in and biding until warm daylight returned, and he feared nothing any longer, not life, not death. He drifted on the wind, conscious of the forest's silent growings and stretchings and burrowings about him. Then he became himself again, warm and animal and very comfortable in the simple regularity of heartbeat and breathing.

He awoke in sunlight, stretched lazily and stopped in mid-stretch as green light broke into existence up in the branches. The creature drifted slowly down to the grass beside him and rested there, exuding happiness. Sunrise burst across his vision, the fading of stars, the unfolding of flowers.

He reached for the food kit, trying to remember where he had laid it. Stopped, held in the radiance, and looked into the heart of it. It was an effort to pull his mind away. "Stop that. I have no sense of time when you're so close. Maybe you can spend an hour watching a flower unfold, but that's a considerable portion of my life."

Sorrow. The radiance murmured and bubbled with images he could not make sense of, of far-traveling, the unrolling of land, of other consciousnesses, of a vast and all-driving hunger for others, so strong it left him shaking.

"Stop it. I don't understand what you're trying to tell me."

The light grew in his vision and pulsed bright and dark, little gold sparks swirling in the heart of it, an explosion of pure excitement reaching out to him.

"What's wrong with you?" he cried. He trembled.

Quite suddenly the light winked out altogether, and when it reappeared a moment later it was not half so bright or so large, bubbling softly with the sound of waters.

"What's wrong?"

Need. Sorrow. Again the impression of other consciousnesses, other luminances, a thought quickly snatched away, all of them flowing and flooding into one.

"You mean others of your kind."

The image came back to him; and flowers, stamens shedding pollen, golden clouds, golden dust adhering to the pistil of a great, green-veined lily.

"Like mating? Like that?"

The backspill became unsettling, for the first time sexual.

"You produce others of your kind." He felt the excitement flooding through his own veins, a contagion. "Others—are coming here?"

Come. He got the impression strongly, a tugging at all his senses, a flowing over the hills and away. A merging, with things old and wise, and full of experiences, lives upon lives. *Welcome. Come.*

"I'm *human.*"

Welcome. Need pulled at him. Distances rolled away, long distances, days and nights.

"What would happen to me?"

Life bursting from the soil. The luminance brightened and enlarged. The man-image came into his vision: The embryo stretched itself and grew new tendrils, into the radiance, and it into the fluttering heart; more and more luminances added themselves, and the tendrils twined, human and otherwise, until they became another greenness, another life, to float on the winds.

Come, it urged.

His heart swelled with tears. He wept and then ceased to be human at all, full of years, deep-rooted and strong. He felt the sun and the rain and the passage of time beyond measure, knew the birth and death of forests and the weaving undulations of rivers across the land. There were mountains and snows and tropics where winter never came, and deep caverns and cascading streams and things that verged on consciousness deep in the darkness. The very stars in the heavens changed their patterns and the world was young. There were many lives, many, and one by one he knew their selves, strength and youth and age beyond reckoning, the joy of new birth, the beginning of new consciousness. Time melted. It was all one experience, and there was vast peace, unity, even in the storms, the cataclysms, the destruction of forests in lightning-bred fires, the endless push of life toward the sun and the rain—cycle on cycle, year on year, eons passing. At last his strength faded and he slept, enfolded in a green and gentle warmth; he thought that he died like the old tree and did not care, because it was a gradual and comfortable thing, a return to elements, ultimate joining. The living creature that crept in among his upturned roots for shelter was nothing less and nothing more than the moss, the dying flowers, the fallen leaves.

He lay on the grass, too weary to move, beyond care. Tears leaked from his eyes. His hands were weak. He had no terror of merging now, none, and the things he had shared with this creature would remain with them, with all its kind, immortal.

It pulled at him, and the pull that worked through his mind was as strong as the tides of the sea, as immutable and unarguable. Peace, it urged on him; and in his mind the sun flicked again through the heavens.

He opened his eyes. A day gone. A second day. Then the weakness in his limbs had its reason. He tried to sit up, panicked even through the urging of peace it laid on him.

Anne. The recollection flashed through his memory with a touch of cold. The luminance recoiled, resisting.

"No. I have to reach her. I have to." He fought hard for consciousness, gained, and knew by the release that the danger got through. Fear flooded over him like cold water.

The *Anne*-image appeared, a hollow shell in darkness, tendrils coiling out. Withered. Urgency pulled at him, and the luminance pulsed with agitation.

"Time—how much time is there?"

Several sunsets flashed through his mind.

"I have to get to her. I have to get her to take an instruction. She's dangerous."

The radiance was very wan. Urgency. Urgency. The hills rolled away in the mind's eye, the others called. Urgency.

And it faded, leaving behind an overwhelming flood of distress.

Warren lay still a moment, on his back, on the grass, shivering in the cold daylight. His head throbbed. His limbs ached and had no strength. He reached for the com, got it on, got it to his lips, his eyes closed, shutting out the punishing sun.

"*Anne.*"

"Warren. Please confirm status."

"Fine—I'm fine." He tried to keep his voice steady. His throat was raw. It could not sound natural. "I'm coming home, *Anne.*"

A pause on the other side. "Yes, Warren. Assistance?"

"Negative, negative, *Anne.* Please wait. I'll be there soon." He gathered himself up to his arm, to his knees, to his feet, with difficulty. There were pains in all his joints. He felt his face, unshaven and rough. His hands and feet were numb with the cold and the damp. His clothes sagged on him, belt gone loose.

"Warren?"

"I'm all right, *Anne.* I'm starting back now."

"Accepted," *Anne* said after a little delay. "Emergency procedures canceled."

"What—emergency procedures?"

"What's your status, Warren?"

"No emergency, do you hear me? No emergency. I'm on my way." He shut it down, found his canteen, the food packet, drank, forced a bite down his swollen throat and stuffed the rest into his sodden jacket. Walked. His leg hurt, and his eyes blurred, the lids swollen and raw. He found a branch and tore it off and used that as he went—pushed himself, knowing the danger there was in *Anne.*

Knowing how little time there was. It would go, it would go then, and leave him. And there would be nothing after that. Ever.

XI

Anne was waiting for him, at the riverside—amid the stumps of trees, mud, cleared earth. Trees dammed the river, water spilling over them, between them, flooding up over the banks and changing the land into a shallow, sandy lake.

He stopped there, leaned against the last standing tree on that margin and shivered, slow tremors which robbed him of strength and sense. She stood placidly in the ruin; he called her on the com, heard her voice, saw her face, then her body, orient toward him. He began to cross the bridge of tumbled trees, clinging to branches, walking tilted trunks.

"Damn you," he shouted at her. Tears ran down his face. *"Damn you!"*

She met him at the other side, silver slimed with mud and soot from the burning she had done. Her sensors blinked. "Assistance?"

He found his self-control, shifted his attack. "You've damaged yourself."

"I'm functioning normally. Assistance?"

He started to push past her, slipped on the unstable log. She reached to save him, her arm rock-solid, stable. He clung to it, his only point of balance. Her facelights blinked at him. Her other hand came up to rest on his shoulder. Contact. She offered contact. He had meant to shove at her. He touched her gently, patted her plastic-sheathed shoulder, fought back the tears. "You've *killed*, Annie. Don't you understand?"

"Vegetation."

He shoved past her, limped up the devastated shore, among the stumps of trees. His head throbbed. His stomach felt hollow.

The crawler still waited on the bank. *Anne* overtook him as he reached it; she offered him her hand as he climbed in. He slid into the seat, slipped the brake, started the motor and threw it full-throttle, leaving her behind.

"Warren," her voice pursued him.

He kept driving, wildly, swerving this way and that over the jolts, past the brush.

"Anne," he said, standing at the lock. "Open the lock."
Silence.
"Anne. Open the lock, please."

It hissed wide. He walked in, unsteady as he was, onto the cargo platform. "Engage lift, *Anne."*

Gears crashed. It started up, huge and ponderous that it was. "Warren," the disembodied voice said, from the speakers, everywhere, echoing. "What's your status, Warren?"

"Good, thank you."

"Your voice indicates stress."

"Hoarseness. Minor dysfunction in my speaking apparatus. It's self-repairing."

A silence. "Recorded." The lift stopped on netherdeck. He walked out, calmly, to the lower weapons locker, put his card in.

Dead. "I've got a lock malfunction here, *Anne*. Number 13/546. Would you clear it up?"

"Emergency locks are still engaged."

"Disengage."

Silence.

"There is no emergency." He fought the anger from his voice. "Disengage emergency locks and cancel all emergency procedures."

"This vocal dysfunction is not repaired."

He leaned against the wall, stared down the corridor.

"Warren, please confirm your status."

"Normal, I tell you." He went to the lift. It worked. It brought him up to the level of the laboratories. He walked down to Bio, walked in, tried the cabinets. "*Anne*. I need medicines. Disengage the locks. I need medicines for repair."

The lock clicked. It opened.

He took out the things he needed, washed his torn hands, prepared a stimulant. He was filthy. He saw himself like a specter in a reflecting glass, gaunt, stubbled; looked down and saw his clothes unrecognizable in color. He washed an area of his arm and fired the injection, rummaged through the cabinet for medicines to cure the hoarseness. He found some lozenges, ripped one from the foil and sucked on it, then headed off for the showers, undressing as he went.

A quick wash. He had forgotten clean clothes; he belted on the bathrobe he had left in the showers, on a body gone gaunt. His hands shook. The stim hummed in his veins. He could not afford the shakes. He had visions of the pseudosome walking back toward the ship; she would be here soon. He had to make normal moves. Had to do everything in accustomed order. He went to the galley next, opened the box and downed fruit juice from its container; it hit his stomach in a wave of cold.

He hauled out other things. Dried food. Stacked it there. He took out one frozen dinner and put it in the microwave.

It turned on without his touching it.

"Time, please."

"Fifteen minutes," he told it. He walked out. He took the dried food with him to the lift.

He punched buttons. It took him up. He walked out into the corridor; lights came on for him. Lights came on in the living quarters, in his own quarters, as he entered. He dumped the dried stores on the bed, opened the locker and pulled out all his clothing—dressed, short of breath as he was, having to stop and rest in the act of putting his boots on.

The lock crashed and boomed in the bowels of the ship.

She was back. He pulled the second boot on. He could hear the lift working. He folded his remaining clothes. He heard the next lift work. He arranged everything on his bed. He heard footsteps coming.

He looked round. *Anne* stood there, muddy, sooty as she was.

"Assistance? Please confirm your status, Warren."

He thought a moment. "Fine. You're dirty, *Anne*. Decontaminate."

Sensors flickered, one and then the others. "You're packing. This program is preparatory to going to the river. Please reconsider this program."

"I'm just cleaning up. Why don't you get me dinner?"

"You fixed dinner, Warren."

"I didn't like it. You fix it. I'll have dinner up here at the table. Fifteen minutes. I need it, *Anne*. I'm hungry."

"Yes, Warren."

"And clean up."

"Yes, Warren."

The pseudosome left. He dropped his head into his hands, caught his breath. Best to rest a bit. Have dinner. See what he could do about a program and get her to take it. He went to the desk where he had left the programming microfilm, got it and fed it into the viewer.

He scanned through the emergency programs, the E sequences, hoping to distract her into one of those. There was nothing that offered a way to seize control. Nothing that would lock her up.

It was feeding into her, even now; she had library access. The viewer was part of her systems. The thought made him nervous. He scanned through harmless areas, to confound her.

"Dinner's ready," the speaker told him.

He wiped his face, shut down the viewer and walked out, hearing the lift in function.

Anne arrived, carrying a tray. She set things on the table, arranged them.

He sat down. She poured him coffee, walked to her end of the table and sat facing him.

He ate a few bites. The food nauseated him. He shoved the plate away.

Her lights flickered. "Chess?"

"Thank you, no, *Anne*. I've got other things to do."

"Do. Yes. Activity. What activity do you choose, Warren?"

He stared at her. Observation and question. Subsequent question. "Your assimilation's really made a lot of progress, hasn't it? Lateral activity."

"The lateral patterning is efficient in forecast. Question posed: what activity do you choose, Warren?"

"I'm going down below. You stay here. Clean up the dinner."

"Yes, Warren."

He pushed back from the table, walked out and down the corridor to the lift. He decided on routine, on normalcy, on time to think.

He rode the lift back to the lab level, walked out. She turned the lights on for him, turned them off behind as he walked, always conservative.

He pushed the nearest door button. Botany, it was. The door stayed shut.

"Lab doors locked," he said casually. "Open it."

The door shot back. Lights went on.

The room was a shambles. Planting boxes were overthrown, ripped loose, pipes twisted, planting medium scattered everywhere, the floor, the walls. Some of the boxes were partially melted, riddled with laser fire.

He backed out, quietly, quickly. Closed the door. Walked back to the lift, his footsteps echoing faster and faster on the decking. He opened the lift door, stepped in, pushed the button for topside.

It took him up. He left it, walking now as quickly, as normally, as he could, not favoring his leg.

Anne had left the living quarters. He went by the vacant table, to the bridge corridor, to the closed door at the end. He used his cardkey.

It stayed shut.

"*Anne,*" he said, "you have a malfunction. There's no longer an emergency. Please clear the emergency lock on the bridge. I have a critical problem involving maintenance. I need to get to controls right now."

A delay. The speaker near his head came on. "Emergency procedure remains in effect. Access not permitted."

"*Anne.* We have a paradox here. The problem involves your mistake."

"Clarify: mistake."

"You've perceived a false emergency. You've initiated wrong procedures. Some of your equipment is damaged. Cancel emergency. This is a code nine. Cancel emergency and open this door."

A further delay. "Negative. Access denied."

"*Anne.*" He pushed the button again. It was dead. He heard a heavy step in the corridor behind him. He jerked about with his back to the door and looked into *Anne's* dark faceplate with its dancing stars. "Open it," he said. "I'm in pain, *Anne.* The pain won't stop until you cancel emergency procedure and open this door."

"Please adjust yourself."

"I'm not malfunctioning. I need this door opened." He forced calm into his voice, adopted a reasoning tone. "The ship is in danger, *Anne.* I have to get in there."

"Please go back to permitted areas, Warren."

He caught his breath, stared at her, then edged past her carefully, down the corridor to the living quarters. She was at his back, still, following.

"Is this a permitted area?" he asked.

"Yes, Warren."

"I want a cup of coffee. Bring it."

"Yes, Warren."

She walked out into the main corridor. The door closed behind her. He delayed a moment till he heard the lift, then went and tried it. Dead. "*Anne.* Now there's a malfunction with number two access. Will you do something about it?"

"Access not permitted."

"I need a bath, *Anne.* I need to go down to the showers."

A delay. "This is not an emergency procedure. Please wait for assistance."

A scream welled up in him. He swallowed it, smoothed his hand over the metal as if it were skin. "All right. All right, *Anne.*" He turned, walked back to his own quarters.

The clothes and food were gone from the bed.

The manual. He went to the viewer. The microfilm was gone. He searched the drawer where he kept it. It was not there.

Panic surged up in him. He stifled it, walked out. He walked back to the table, sat down—heard the lift operating finally. Heard her footsteps. The door opened.

"Coffee, Warren."

"Thank you, Annie."

She set the cup down, poured his coffee. Hydraulics worked in the ship, massive movement, high on the frame. The turret rotating. Warren looked up. "What's that, *Anne?*"

"Armaments, Warren."

The electronic snap of the cannon jolted the ship. He sprang up from his chair and *Anne* set down the coffee pot.

"*Anne. Anne,* cancel weapons. *Cancel!*"

The firing went on.

"Cancel refused," *Anne* said.

"*Anne*—show me . . . what you're shooting at. Put it on the screen."

The wallscreen lit, the black of night, a thin line of orange: a horizon, ablaze with fires.

"*You're killing it!*"

"Vegetation, Warren. Emergency program is proceeding."

"*Anne.*" He seized her metal, unflexing arm. "Cancel program."

"Negative."

"On what reasoning? *Anne*—turn on your sensor box. Turn it on. Scan the area."

"It is operating, Warren. I'm using it to refine target. Possibly the equipment will survive. Possibly I can recover it. Please adjust yourself, Warren. Your voice indicates stress."

"It's life you're killing out there!"

"Vegetation, Warren. This is a priority, but overridden. I'm programmed to make value judgments. I've exercised my override reflex. This is a rational function. Please adjust yourself, Warren."

"The lab. You destroyed the lab. Why?"

"I don't like vegetation, Warren."

"Don't *like?*"

"Yes, Warren. This seems descriptive."

"*Anne*, you're malfunctioning. Listen to me. You'll have to shut down for a few moments. I won't damage you or interfere with your standing instructions. I'm your crew, *Anne*. Shut down."

"I can't accept this instruction, Warren. One of my functions is preservation of myself. You're my highest priority. To preserve you I have to preserve myself. Please adjust yourself, Warren."

"*Anne*, let me out. Let me out of here."

"No, Warren."

The firing stopped. On the screen the fires continued to burn. He looked at it, leaned on the back of the chair, shaking.

"Assistance?"

"Go to hell."

"I can't go to hell, Warren. I have to hold this position."

"*Anne. Anne*—listen. I found a being out there. A sapient life form. In the forest. I talked with it. You're killing a sapient being, you hear me?"

A delay. "My sensors detected nothing. Your activities are erratic and injurious. I record your observation. Please provide data."

"Your sensor box. Turn it on."

"It's still operating, Warren."

"It was there. The life was there, when I was. I can go back. I can prove it. I talked to it, *Anne.*"

"There was no other life there."

"Because your sensor unit couldn't register it. Because your sensors aren't sensitive enough. Because you're not human, *Anne.*"

"I have recorded sounds. Identify."

The wallscreen flicked to a view of the grove. The wind sighed in the leaves; something babbled. A human figure lay writhing on the ground, limbs jerking, mouth working with the sounds. Himself. The murmur was his own voice, inebriate and slurred.

He turned his face from it. "Cut it off. Cut it off, *Anne.*"

The sound stopped. The screen was blank and white when he turned his head again. He leaned there a time. There was a void in him where life had been. Where he had imagined life. He sat down at the table, wiped his eyes.

After a moment he picked up the coffee and drank.

"Are you adjusted, Warren?"

"Yes. Yes, *Anne.*"

"Emergency program will continue until all surrounds are sterilized."

He sat staring at his hands, at the cup before him. "And then what will I do?"

Anne walked to the end of the table, sat down, propped her elbows on the table, head on hands, sensor lights blinking in continuous operation.

The chessboard flashed to the wallscreen at her back.

The pawn advanced one square.

THE JOHN W. CAMPBELL AWARD 1973-1983

1973

Ruth Berman
George Alec Effinger
George R. R. Martin
*Jerry Pournelle
Robert Thurston
Lisa Tuttle

1974

Jesse Miller
Thomas F. Monteleone
*Spider Robinson
Guy Snyder
*Lisa Tuttle

1975

Alan Brennert
Suzy McKee Charnas
Felix C. Gotschalk
Brenda Pearce
*P. J. Plauger
John Varley

1976

Arsen Darnay
M. A. Foster
*Tom Reamy
John Varley
Joan D. Vinge

1977

Jack L. Chalker
*C. J. Cherryh
M. A. Foster
Carter Scholz

1978

*Orson Scott Card
Jack L. Chalker
Stephen R. Donaldson
Elizabeth A. Lynn
Bruce Sterling

1979

*Stephen R. Donaldson
Cynthia Felice
James P. Hogan
Elizabeth A. Lynn
Barry Longyear
Charles Sheffield

1980

Lynn Abbey
Diane Duane
Karen Jollie
*Barry Longyear
Alan Ryan
Somtow Sucharitkul

237

1981

Kevin Christensen
Diane Duane
Robert L. Forward
Susan Petrey
Robert Stallman
*Somtow Sucharitkul

1982

David Brin
*Alexis Gilliland
Robert Stallman
Michael Swanwick
Paul O. Williams

1983

*Paul O. Williams
Lisa Goldstein
David R. Palmer
Joseph H. Delaney
Sandra Miesel
Warren G. Norwood

The John W. Campbell Award for the best new writer in science fiction was sponsored by The Condé Nast Publications, Inc., from its inception in 1973 through 1979. In 1980 sponsorship was assumed by Davis Publications. Nominees and winners are determined by fan vote.

*Denotes winners.